Copyright © [04/06/2014] by [A.E.Murphy]

Title [Connected]

ALL RIGHTS RESERVED.

This book contains material protected under International and Federal Copyright Laws and Treaties. Any unauthorized reprint or use of this material is prohibited. No part of this book may be reproduced or transmitted in any form or by any means, electronic or mechanical, including photocopying, recording, or by any information storage and retrieval system without express written permission from the author / publisher.

To my cats.

we are Connected

a.e. murphy

Chapter One

Dear Guinevere,

I'll be sending Jeanine to collect Dillan for me on Thursday the eighth. Please have him ready with enough supplies for the weekend. I'll send him back the following Monday. If this date is an issue for you, please contact Jeanine; I know you both still talk.
Regards
Nathan.

A torrent of emotions flit through me as I grip the perfectly written, letter sized note in my hands, ready to screw it into a ball and throw it at something.

How dare he?

After everything he put me through, after the way he just left us without a second glance, suddenly he wants to see Dillan? He's so infuriating.

Does he honestly think I'll just let him take Dillan without speaking to me first? Without explaining anything first? He's crazy.

I immediately type out a text to Jeanine, feeling a little better when I send it.

Guinevere: Please tell Nathan I respectfully decline his request to take Dillan for four nights. If he wants to see his nephew he can come and collect him personally. This is nothing against you; I just don't feel comfortable using you as a go between, especially when it concerns my son's welfare.

My anger dissipates for a few seconds when a thought comes to mind that shocks me. I instantly push it away, cursing myself for thinking something so vile about a man who, even though he's been mean as of late, has always been there for Dillan and I, even when it was clear that he didn't want to be.

Nathan will never be his Grandfather. Not all abuse victims end up as abusers themselves. I can't believe I even entertained the idea.

That's not the issue here; the issue is that I'm finally getting on with my life. I've got an amazing job at a bakery around the corner called 'Valentine's' where I'm working for a lovely elderly lady called Valentine. Best cakes in town. My mum and I are finally in a good place and I'm enjoying being a mum myself. Dillan is happy and is thriving as much as a baby can. I love him so much.

Nathan let go of me! Not the other way around. He doesn't get to decide anything. It's not my fault that I saw what I saw. I didn't deserve his treatment then and I definitely don't deserve it now.

Pain slices through my chest when I think back to the DVDs I discovered, showing me the vile things that will forever plague my mind.

The sound of my phone snaps me from the horrendous images that I wish I could forget. I pick it up with a trembling hand and sigh with relief at her response. I was worried she'd find my text offensive.

<u>Jeanine</u>: I told him this but he wouldn't listen. I'll pass the message along.

I wonder how he'll react. I can already imagine his lips thinning to a white line as his hands fist by his sides.

Good. I hope he gets angry.

<u>Guinevere</u>: Thank you :)

Is it wrong that I still miss him?

My mum comes upstairs and pokes her head into the room. "Everything okay?"

I shrug. "Yeah."

"Was it from Nathan?" It's obvious because I never get mail, especially not handwritten mail.

I nod and sigh. "Yeah." He hates me.

"We'll talk about it soon; I'm going to be late for work." She ducks back out of my room and moments later I hear the shower running.

Dillan starts to stir and I take a moment to feed him and change him. Whenever I'm tending to him, my thoughts stay on him. I know I should stop using him as a distraction and face my jumbled thoughts, but I don't want to.

My mum suggested I keep a journal but I'd fill the book in less than a day. I worry too much.

When Dillan is settled on my bed, on his back between my open legs, I read the letter again and curse Nathan in my mind. I don't fully understand why he refuses to acknowledge me. I get that I saw something I shouldn't have, but does he not want to see me because of embarrassment or shame?

If so, doesn't he realize he has nothing to be ashamed of? Nothing that happened to him was his fault.

My phone alerts me to another text.

<u>Jeanine</u>: He says to stop being ridiculous, he wants to see his nephew. (His words, not mine. I'm with you on this.)

<u>Guinevere</u>: Is he kidding? Please tell me he's kidding. Tell him, from me, to go and bleep himself. If he wants to see Dillan he can come to me personally. Otherwise he's not having him. Tell him it's that way or no way.

Dillan gurgles and I smile, "Yep, all of this fuss is because so many people love you." Even though I'm shocked that Nathan got in touch at all, I'm also relieved that he still wants to see Dillan. They had a strong bond. Nathan really stepped up and acted like a Daddy to Dillan. I don't want to stop their contact but, after the way we parted, I need to know that Nathan is mentally stable enough to look after him.

I feel guilty for feeling this way but it's a rational thought I suppose. Nobody can blame me for wanting to protect my son, even if it is from family.

Especially considering what happened with Nathan, I trust Nathan, truly I do, but I need to be sure. His family does not have the best track record and I can't risk Dillan suffering the same fate.

Nobody knows what transpired back at Nathan's, not even Sasha. I just tell them we had a very bad argument. They all know I'm withholding from them, but it's not my business to tell. Besides, I wouldn't know where to begin.

<u>Jeanine</u>: He's agreed and will pick him up on the eighth. I'm glad that's sorted. How are you?

I should ask her about Nathan but I don't want her to be stuck in the middle. It's not fair on her, considering she has to work with him. As much as I'm tempted, I don't want to make this awkward for her so I tell her my news instead.

<u>Guinevere</u>: I got the job!! So I'm great. Dillan is trying to eat my knee and my mum is a lot better than I expected.

<u>Jeanine</u>: Oh my darling, I'm so happy for you. Maybe this move was the best thing for you after all.

Falling back onto my pillow, I pick up Dillan and cuddle him to my chest. His little head bobs up and down, a trail of drool dribbling from his lip to the curve of my breast. Nice. "Gross little monkey!" I giggle, causing him to smile again.
He looks so much like Caleb when he smiles, but it doesn't break my heart; it warms it and fills my mind with beautiful memories.
My mum leaves without more than a goodbye; she's really late. I wave to her using Dillan's baby fist before closing the door and sitting down in the living room. After placing him in his bouncer I slump on the couch and let out a long and tired sigh. I can't wait until Sasha arrives. Maybe she'll let me sleep for a while.
Doubtful.
"He just puked on me, which would be okay if it was normal baby milk out of a carton, but it's not. It's breast milk, from your boobies obviously, which is really grossing me out!" This is Tommy, who has decided to tag along with Sasha.
"Stop being such an idiot," Sasha laughs and begins wiping at the small spot of drool and dribble on Tommy's black polo shirt with a bib.

I smile at their close proximity. I've never noticed before just how good they both look together. I don't think Caleb did either, or at least he never mentioned it.

Neither of them have been able to hold a partner down for long and now I'm wondering if all of these dates they go on are nothing more than a way to get at each other's jealous sides. Nah, I'm reading into things to distract myself from my own mess of a life.

"Nathan got in touch today," I chew on the inside of my cheek as I assess their reactions. They look as shocked as I felt at the time of receiving the letter. "He wants to take Dillan for a few days on the eighth."

"A few days?" Sasha questions and then shrugs a little. "He probably misses him." Well duh. "Reckon he'll speak to you too?"

I hope so. "He'll have to if he wants to take Dillan."

"In other news," Tommy announces, noticing my discomfort over speaking about Nathan. "I'm graduating early."

"What?" I breathe, smiling broadly. "Oh my god, Tommy that's amazing!" I rush to him and hug his head, mainly so I don't crush Dillan between us.

"I start an internship at a firm in Doncaster in a few weeks."

Wow. "Are you moving there? It's a long commute."

"It's only a two hour drive. I'll be home most weekends." Realising I'm still hugging him, I release his head and slap him when he pouts at being separated from my boobs. "But they're so big and bouncy."

"They might leak on you." Sasha chips in, making us both giggle when he cringes.

"Take the baby. I need to piss." Tommy hands Dillan to Sasha before exiting the room.

"I need to get him settled." I hold out my hands and she reluctantly passes him to me.

My friends leave not too long after I settle Dillan and I'm starting to wonder if they actually come to see me or him. Not that I'm complaining. It's good to see them, whatever the reason.

Sleep comes quickly, but then I have had a busy day.

Valentine is a character. She doesn't have any rules. As long as I make shit she can sell (her words, not mine) then she's happy. Obviously she has to have certain customer favourites up front, but mostly she tries to do something different every day.

It's fun and it helps me to stop worrying about Dillan every two seconds.

Her counter staff seem to be nice women; they know how to work a till and clean up after the customers and mostly they keep to themselves, which I'm grateful for. It might sound awful but I'm not looking to make friends. I just need to focus on making money and dealing with my life right now. Distractions aren't something I can afford.

"They're loving your cookies," Elle, one of the two women who work in the front, smiles, showing slightly crooked teeth as she brings me an empty tray. My face reflects my joy. This is great news. "I kind of ate two though."

"No problem, I'll make some more." Taking the tray from her arms, I place it by the sink and begin prepping my ingredients. I think I'm really going to like it here.

"You're doing great. I think you may be a better baker than me," Valentine chuckles and flicks at me with the tea towel.

"I doubt that, but thank you," I respond kindly and look down at my flour covered hands. Yep. I'm definitely going to like it here.

Chapter Two

"He's just his uncle." My mum says calmly. "You don't have to let him take Dillan."

But I feel like I kind of do. "He's been like a father to him." My voice is soft and quiet as I admit the words I should feel guilty about but don't. "He loves Dillan a lot. I don't want him to lose that." Because Nathan is as broken, if not more so, than me, and Dillan is my anchor. Maybe he can be Nathan's too.

"It's your choice." She grasps my hand and gives it a gentle, yet reassuring squeeze. "But if you feel that the time away from Dillan is too long for you, tell him he can have him until tomorrow night. Don't force yourself into doing something you don't want to do. Dillan is only eleven weeks old."

"I haven't expressed and frozen enough breast milk for more than two days anyway," I sigh. I genuinely tried, but failed. My exhaustion has known no bounds recently, what with my new job and such. "He'll be here in a minute."

My mum nods and grabs her bag from the side, "I'll be back later." She kisses my forehead on her way past and gives me another squeeze, this time with both arms around my shoulders. "Good luck."

I'm going to need it.

I pace the kitchen, nervously twisting my fingers together. He'll be here soon.

What am I going to say to him? Should I hug him?

"You're dead to me."

I shudder. His words echo through my brain and I suddenly feel nauseous.

I fluff up my black hair with my fingers and stare at myself in the mirror for a moment. Tired grey eyes stare back at me. Only a hint of light green eye shadow rests upon the lids and my lashes are tinted with mascara. I look okay, I think.

Why do I care how I look? It's not like I'm dressing up for him so he notices me, is it?

There's a knock at the door. I dart to it, quickly checking my breath by cupping my hand over my mouth, and then I pull it open.

There he is, dark trousers, his hair teasing the collar of his shirt. I can see he's had a trim, but I'm glad he hasn't removed too much of the length. Piercing, almost chocolate coloured brown eyes linger on my face. His scent assaults me, always so clean. It's fresh linen and soap and Nathan.

It takes a lot for me to resist the urge to throw my arms around him, bury my face in his neck and cry for our lost friendship.

"Hi," I breathe. Christ, I've missed him.

He gives me a nod, his lips pressed together in a thin line. I move to the side and motion for him to enter.

"Is he ready?" He clips, glancing around my hallway.

Wow, straight to the point. "He's in his car seat. He fell asleep."

"So I'm allowed to take him then," he seems slightly relieved, his body relaxing a fraction.

Nathan, always so tense. Not that I'm surprised. "Yes, but not until Monday as we planned."

And there go his muscles; he didn't stay relaxed for long, "I've driven all of this way."

"I only managed to express enough milk for two days," I explain, walking into the room where Dillan is sleeping soundly in his car seat.

"I've given you plenty of time," he bites out, his frustration clear.

I sit on the couch, hating the glare aimed my way as he stands in the doorway. "I know. I've just been so tired, I really haven't had the time." I'm not a cow that squirts out milk by the gallon.

His frown deepens, "Tired?"

"Yes, I got a job two weeks ago," I smile excitedly. "I now work at Valentine's; it's a bakery around the corner. Best in town."

"A job?" His eyes darken and his fists open and close as if fighting the urge to clench them.

Eye roll. "I have to pay for my son's nappies somehow."

"And the money I've been sending you?" He hisses angrily. "And where, may I ask, is Dillan whilst you work?"

Money? "What money?" I glare back at him. "And Dillan stays with my mum whilst I work weekends and goes to nursery when I work in the week."

"Nursery?" I barely hear him, his voice is that low and dangerous. He closes his eyes for a moment, his calm composure failing. "He's not even three months old."

"I can't not work, Nathan." I snap, standing again. "What do you even care? I'm dead to you, remember?" I walk over to my son and pick up his bag that sits on the ground beside his seat. Turning, I thrust it into Nathan's arms, ignoring the guilty look on his face. "Bring him back Saturday afternoon."

He looks furious. I don't care. I'm not his business anymore. "Dillan needs his mother around."

"What Dillan needs is a roof over his head and clothes on his back," I argue tiredly. "How can I provide them if I don't work?"

"I'll send more money." Nathan places the bag on the arm of the couch and walks towards his nephew.

"What money?" I snap and then let out a long sigh to calm myself. "Forget it. I don't want nor need your money. My life is none of your business."

Nathan remains silent as he drops to his knees and runs his gloved fingers over Dillan's cheek. "I'll bring him back Saturday afternoon."

"Can I ask?" Should I? Nathan looks at me over his shoulder expectantly. "Why do you want to take him?"

"Why not?" He stands once more and turns to face me. "He's my nephew. I miss him."

"Is he the only thing you miss?" Oh god, why did I say that?

Nathan looks as shocked as I do but it doesn't stop him from responding. "Yes."

"I see." The carpet is suddenly very interesting. Lifting my eyes slowly to his, tears pooling on the lower lids, I whisper a confession that I probably shouldn't. "I miss you. A lot more than I should."

He shows no reaction; he doesn't care. His words confirm my thoughts. "I'm sorry; I don't feel the same." Way to stab me in the chest. I look away quickly but feel a tear fall from my left eye. "I'll bring him back on Saturday afternoon." He lifts the car seat.

I quickly rush to my sleeping son and plant kiss after kiss on his face and hands. "Love you baby." Ignoring my aching heart, I look up at Nathan. "Call me if anything happens."

"I will."

I grab his arm, stopping him from walking away from me, "I mean it, Nathan. Please."

He tugs his arm free. "I said I will."

Blowing out a breath, I give my son another kiss and follow Nathan to his car. He places Dillan in the back and straps him in. I kiss my son yet again.

"Nathan," I say, following him around to the driver's side.

He stops with his hand on top of the open door. "Yes Guinevere?" Exasperation is his only tone. "What now?"

"Why do you still stay in that house?" I ask and wince when I see the pain in his features. "It seems like a torturous way to live."

He gapes at me for a moment, seeming to be in shock that I addressed something so secret, so disturbing. Instead of responding, he climbs into his car and slams the door. Seconds later he reverses out of my driveway without even looking my way.

Shit.

I miss my boy already.

Which one? My conscience asks me.

Both, my heart answers, with an ache that brings more tears to my eyes; tears for what and whom, I don't know.

"I don't like it," I say to Valentine as I beat the hell out of a ball of dough that I should be kneading gently. She steps in, removing the dough from my fists of fury. "I miss him. I didn't sleep a wink last night."

"The first night away from your child is always the hardest." She says with a slight smile. "He'll be fine. You need time to yourself."

CHAPTER TWO

"I don't like time to myself." Time to myself means dwelling on things that could have been but never will be.

"You're so strange; I can't wait to get rid of my kids sometimes," Tiffany, the woman who works behind the counter, states. "You should go out for a few drinks."

"I'm breastfeeding," I mumble, resisting the urge to rub my swollen and aching breasts. Because I haven't had Dillan, I have been able to express a lot more milk than usual.

"We have a problem. There's a guy here wanting to speak to the person who made the fudge birthday cake, the one shaped like a bottle of Jack Daniels." Elle says quietly, stepping into the kitchen.

Oh shit. "Was there a problem with it?"

"I don't know, but the guy is smoking hot." She fans her face dramatically.

"Okay." I ignore her 'smoking hot' comment and quickly wash my hands. I'm covered from head to toe in flour and other ingredients. I look ridiculous, but I don't care. I'm here to work, not play.

Valentine doesn't offer me any input on how I should handle this. Great.

I inhale a deep breath and let it out before stepping out of the kitchen with a nervous smile on my face. Elle points to a man sat at a table in the far corner. He has a hot drink in one hand and his phone in the other. His hair is blonde, almost like golden silk, cut only a couple of inches from his scalp and mussed, like he's just rolled out of bed. It really suits him. I make my way over to him, anxiously biting my lip. "Umm... hi." I give him a small wave to get his attention and he blinks up at me with shining hazel eyes.

"Hi." He grins and stands. He holds out his hand and I check my hands once more for flour before shaking it. "You're the person who made the Jack Daniels cake?"

I nod and gulp all at once. "Yes. Was there a problem?"

"Yes." He seems reluctant to admit as his eyes sweep me up and down. "We found this baked into the bottom layer." He pulls something from his pocket.

Oh my god. "Oh my god!" I squeal and snatch it from him, my eyes burning. I'm going to lose my job. I almost lost my ring. Somebody could have choked! But my ring...

I look at my left hand and back to the simple diamond ring that I hold in the palm of my right hand. How could I not have noticed that it was missing?

"Are you okay?"

"I... was anybody hurt?" I hope nobody bit down on it and broke a tooth.

"Fortunately not. Perhaps you should take jewellery off before you bake." He suggests, his eyes twinkling with humour. "It's not a big deal; I just figured you'd want it returned." He tilts his head, his eyes questioning my distraught state. "And considering the way you've reacted, I'm glad to have made that judgement."

"I'm sorry." I wipe at my eyes and close my fist around the ring. "I'm sorry for losing this in your cake. I appreciate you returning it. I'll go and get my boss."

"Hey, you don't have to do that. It's honestly not a big deal." He watches as I slide the ring back onto my finger. It doesn't fit; I've lost too much weight since Caleb died. Even during pregnancy I didn't put on much.

I shake my head. "I'm so sorry." How could I not notice? "I'll make you something special, on the house."

He frowns slightly. "Now I feel terrible. I hate it when girls cry. It breaks my heart." His smile is endearing, but his words completely rupture my heavy heart. More tears fall, along with a few unattractive sobs. Caleb used to say that about crying, but about me specifically rather than girls in general. Oh my god. I'm completely humiliating myself. "Should I hug you? I feel like I should hug you."

I start giggling through my tears, trying to push away the awkwardness of this situation, "I swear, I'm not usually this emotional. This ring means a lot to me."

"Ah, I'm guessing you've been looking for it."

That's the problem; I didn't even realize it was missing. I've been so focused on Nathan and Dillan that my mind has hardly been on Caleb as of late. "Yeah." I lie and chew on the inside of my cheek. "Do you have time? I'll make you something and I swear this time it won't have anything other than the proper ingredients in it."

He glances at his watch and shakes his head. "Unfortunately I don't." A smile lights up his face. "Rain check?"

"Sure, just come on in and ask for me," I tap my name tag. "I'm Guinevere, but call me Gwen. And thank you, for not making me lose my job."

"Great, I'm Eric. Just call me Eric. Or bastard." He jokes. "You know, for making you cry."

"Trust me, they were happy guilt tears." I wince. Why am I such an idiot? Why do I say stupid things?

His smile widens; it's charming and handsome. Good lord, he has dimples. I'm a sucker for dimples. "I should be going. It was nice to meet you, Gwen. I'll pop by soon for that something special."

"Sure, I'll look forward to it." I lower my face, my cheeks heating as he stares at me for a moment longer.

"See you around, Gwen."

"Oh... thanks for not getting me into trouble and for being so kind about it. If it makes you feel any better I wash my hands like a crazy person." Shut up, Guinevere! Just shut up! "Bye." I dart under the counter and hide in the kitchen before I can say anything else to humiliate myself.

"You do realise he just asked you out on a date, right?" Elle pops a bubble from between her lips and chews on the bubble gum for a moment after sucking it back into her mouth.

"No he didn't." That's absurd. I'd know if he asked me on a date.

"He so did, or he implied that your next meeting wouldn't be just a meeting." She wags her eyebrows and pops her bubble gum once more.

"Shut up." I moan and bury my face in my hands. "I don't want to date anyone. Plus, he probably assumes I'm engaged."

She eyes me suspiciously. "You're not engaged?"

Oh right. I've kept myself to myself; nobody knows about Caleb. "Not anymore." I twist the ring around my finger and exhale a long breath. "Don't look at me like that. It's complicated."

Her quirked brow flies higher. "I'm not looking at you like anything."

"You're wondering why I'm still wearing the ring." That I should take off before I lose it again.

She shrugs. "It's a normal thing to wonder about when a person states they're not engaged anymore but still wears the ring. Either you're still in love with the guy and refuse to let him go, even though he's gone, or you just really like the ring and don't want to wear it on the other hand, or..."

I raise my ring free hand and laugh. "Stop, stop. I'll tell you… sometime. Just not right now." I need to lick my wounds in peace.

"Sure. If he comes back within the next few days for that 'something special'," she uses her hands to imitate air quotes, a wry grin on her face, "then you know he's not just looking for his reward for returning that."

"Whatever." I wave her off and go to my bag. Removing the ring from my finger, I place it in the inside pocket and zip it tight. Now that I know it's not there, my finger feels naked.

How could I not have noticed? Am I losing my mind?

Probably.

My phone rings as I'm entering the bar with Sasha, the same one I used to frequent with Caleb, Sasha and Tommy, back in the day.

I can't believe how long ago that seems.

I look at the screen and frown at the fact the number has been withheld. I normally don't answer but I figure it can't be a company at this time. "Hello?"

No one responds.

"What drink do you want?" Sasha asks after waving the bar tender down.

"Just a coke," I step to the side and place my finger in my free ear so I can hear my phone better. "Hello?"

"You're in a bar?" Nathan asks; he does not sound pleased.

"Yeah, it took a while but my friends managed to convince me. Is Dillan okay?" I miss him so damn much.

Nathan clears his throat, "He's fine."

"Oh, well, good." Part of me wishes Dillan could talk already, so I can ask him what he's been doing and not get baby babble back in response. "So, what's the problem?"

"You're in a bar."

I frown; now I'm confused and slightly irritated. "And that's a problem because?"

More silence…

"Nathan, are you still there?"

"Yes."

"Can I help you with something?" What's he playing at? I don't understand him at all.

CHAPTER TWO

"No." He clips and suddenly the line goes dead.

What just happened? If I didn't know any better, I'd say he sounded jealous. And if he's jealous then that means he still cares. I think. Why does this make me feel happy to a certain extent? I'm secretly mean, that's why. I don't want Nathan jealous. Why would he be jealous?

If I could call him back, I would, but I still don't have his number. Maybe I should have gotten it from him before he left; that seems like a responsible thing for a parent to do. I should kick myself but I don't like pain.

"Here," Sasha thrusts a drink into my hand, causing the dark liquid to slosh over the top of its glass confinement and trickle over my fingers. Great, now I'm going to have to wash my hand. "Sorry."

"No you're not." I laugh and sip my drink, almost spluttering as the strong taste of rum burns my throat.

"I got you a double." She shrugs and bounces on the spot to the beat of the music.

"Thanks." I gasp and clear my throat before taking a more tentative sip this time. It has been over a year since I last tasted alcohol. I was a lightweight then. I dread to think of how badly I'll be a lightweight now. I shouldn't even be drinking. "How's work?"

"Far too boring to talk about on what should be an awesome night out." She states and wiggles her hips a little. "Cheer up."

I'm not being cheery? Oh. "Sorry."

She throws my words back at me with a mischievous smile. "No you're not." Nope, she's right. I'm so not. "Who was on the phone?"

"Wrong number." I lie. Why am I lying? It's not like I have anything to hide.

She instantly becomes distracted by the sound of her name being called from somewhere to our left. I look up but don't recognise the girl who has yelled her name. With a shrug and the thought that I have nothing better to do, I follow Sasha and receive brief introductions, forgetting their names only moments later.

This really isn't for me anymore. I miss my son. I miss my bed. For Sasha I will try though. She's done a lot for me; I owe her a good night.

But first I need to wash this stickiness from my hand.

Leaving Sasha with her friends, I head into the toilets and cringe at their lack of soap. Hot water will have to do.

Oh... great, no hot water either.

I pour my drink down the sink and watch as it swirls down the drain. I'll replace it with a coke when I go back out there. I don't feel comfortable drinking when I'll need to start feeding Dillan the day after tomorrow. Having him away from the breast for too long worries me. I'm worried he'll get used to bottles and won't be able to latch onto my nipple. That's something I can't risk; baby milk isn't an expense I can afford right now.

Leaving the toilet I head straight to the bar and order myself and Sasha another drink. She drinks fast; she'll definitely need another. My phone rings as I'm waiting to be served, withheld number again.

"Yes?"

"Dillan just vomited." Nathan says, sounding slightly concerned. "Is he sick?"

"He's eleven weeks old; it's probably just trapped wind." The barman decides to serve me now, just great. "Coke and a vodka lemonade."

"You're not drinking?" Nathan enquires. Although he doesn't sound interested, I have a feeling he is forcing this neutral tone to his voice to sound indifferent. The fact he's asked kind of cancels that out though.

"No."

"Why not?"

"How's Dillan?" I thought I was dead to him? Meaning that he wouldn't be interested in me anymore. I shouldn't exist to him, not that I'm complaining about his calls. I'm actually happy to hear from him. "You said he was sick."

"We'll be fine. I just wanted to make sure you were aware. Should I do anything?"

"Give him cool boiled water between feeds." I respond automatically as I pay for my drinks. "Are you going to be okay?"

"Of course." he sounds offended that I asked.

"Can you please text me your number?" Before I forget. "It doesn't feel right knowing you have Dillan and not being able to contact you."

He blows out a long breath. "Fine."

"Okay." pause. "How have you been?"

He remains silent for what seems like minutes but it has in fact only been seconds. "Don't get drunk, Guinevere."

"I'm not drinking, Nathan." My tone is soft and laced with amusement.

"Good night."

CHAPTER TWO

"Come on!" Sasha shouts and waves me over. Do I have to? Apparently so...

Yay... not.

Sasha manages to get me to drink two vodka and cranberries, which help me loosen up a tad. Not much, but enough for me to let go of my reservations. After an hour I'm feeling a little woozy from those two glasses alone, so I stop drinking and instead enjoy the animated conversation that flows between Sasha and her friends. I even join in from time to time when I manage to keep up with their drunken ramblings.

This isn't actually so bad.

When the clock strikes twelve I pull a Cinderella and escape Sasha and her friends. Fortunately I don't lose my shoe on the way home, although I do pick up a follower.

My mind reels as I hear the light footsteps behind me. I glance over my shoulder at the male who seems to be walking in the same direction as me. It makes me nervous when people I don't know walk behind me. Maybe I should stop and wait for him to pass, make it look like I can't text and walk at the same time.

No, because that will give him time to grab me.

Have I listened to myself recently? I sound ridiculously paranoid.

It's just... after seeing those recordings of Nathan as a young boy, I now know what the world is truly capable of, and crap you think isn't going to happen to you does actually happen. Caleb died. That never should have happened, but it did, and Nathan was molested by somebody he clearly loved and someone who should have loved and cherished him.

Knowing my luck I'll pick up a murderer on my way home.

Damn it.

I pick up the pace. My street is only five minutes away, so I know I'll be okay as long as I'm quick. The footsteps behind me seem to pick up speed too. Maybe it's my imagination.

No. I'm not going to write this off as some random happening. That's how people lose their guard and end up in ditches. Right now I'm going to assume he wants me dead and I'm going to push on.

My hand goes inside my pocket. I grasp my phone tightly and pray that, whatever happens, I have enough time to call the police.

Just as I turn the corner of my street, the male who was following me passes. I hear the muffled sound of a heavy bass beat and realise he has earphones in. He's probably just on his way home from work.

I race home and lock the door behind me, my heart beating a heavy rhythm in my chest. I'm so paranoid. There is something seriously wrong with me!

It's probably from being so secluded for so long. I'm not used to being out and about, especially at night. Nathan lives in the middle of nowhere and doesn't have any friends, not including Lorna, a girl who used to come round for what I can only assume was sex. I'm not sure what exactly their relationship was, but something told me that Lorna wanted more than Nathan would offer.

I don't think I'd be able to be somebody's sex piece with no strings. Then again, I did give myself to a man I loved, so the thought of tainting that is abhorrent.

My mum isn't back from work yet. She works in a bar in town, not a very nice one but a popular one. This means she probably won't be back for a few more hours.

After a quick shower I climb into bed and pray that my little boy is okay. I miss him, a lot. I hope Nathan is coping. After twirling my ring between my thumb and forefinger, I carefully place it on the photo frame that holds Caleb's smiling face on my bedside table. The sparkling diamond points at his face as the circular band rests in the corner. I don't feel like it's time to take it off, but keeping it on is clearly hazardous. I'd rather have it somewhere that I know it's safe. I'd put it on a necklace but... it wouldn't feel right after having Nathan's jewellery around my neck for so long. Even though I don't have it anymore, it still wouldn't be right.

Besides, at least if it's on here I can't lose it.

This thought doesn't comfort me. Why do I feel like a chapter of my life is closing? Why do I feel like I'm betraying him? It's not that I don't love him, because I do, but I need to get myself back together before I lose it, and I don't mean my ring.

A few silent tears fall as I shut my eyes. Tomorrow will be a better day; it has to be.

Chapter Three

Work begins and I have to admit, even though I miss Dillan it was nice not having to get up an hour earlier just to sort him out as well as myself. It's busy, but then I expect it to be. It is Saturday after all.

We've created a lot of treats to place in the fridge up front, but clearly not enough, as people swarm in for coffee and snacks. By one we've run out and my feet are killing me. I have yet to have a break. I don't know how Valentine does it; she's a lot older, yet doesn't seem fazed at all.

The bell chimes, signifying the entrance of another customer. I'm shocked when I hear a familiar baby squawk.

"That's Dillan." I say to Valentine, who is covered in flour from head to toe. I'm very much the same, but I also have strawberry jam splatter marks across my midriff.

"There's a man up front asking for you." Tiffany calls through the kitchen doorway.

I hastily wash my hands and rip off my apron before darting into the front. Nathan stands by the counter, looking at the cakes on display, a car seat in one hand and his phone in the other. Yep, he's wearing his gloves.

"Hi." I blink, shocked to see him. "I thought you were coming back tonight."

"Ran out of milk." He responds, placing Dillan's car seat on a nearby table. "He's hungry."

Well that doesn't make sense. "How did you run out? I made enough to last you until tomorrow morning."

"I had an accident with the last three bottles." Nathan pulls a new box of glass bottles from the changing bag, which is hanging from one shoulder. "I replaced them."

"Oh." Ducking under the counter, I make my way towards them, wishing I could pick up my son but refraining due to my current state. "I…" I motion to my clothes, trying to avoid eye contact. "Can't really pick him up right now."

Nathan frowns, clearly not happy at the current predicament. "Well what do you expect me to do?"

"I have some milk at home in the freezer. I've been expressing the past few days."

He checks his watch. "I have to leave soon."

"And I have to work." I hiss, my eyes narrowing on him. "Mum has gone out thinking she wouldn't be having Dillan today. Besides, you weren't supposed to bring him back until later. It's not fair that you're messing us around like this." He opens his mouth to argue but I cut him off. "No, you wanted this responsibility. You can't just drop everything because you feel like it."

He runs his tongue over his lower lip and I'm shocked at how much I've missed this small quirk of his. "Fine. Give me your keys."

"Everything okay?" Valentine asks as I enter the kitchen and walk over to where my bag rests in the closet.

"Fine. Just a Dillan issue. It's sorted." Got them! "I'll be back in a moment." Nathan looks around impatiently, one hand rocking the car seat whilst the other taps his hip. "Here."

"When will you be finished?"

"Not until six." I respond, but Valentine quickly calls out.

"Seven!"

"Right, we have an order to do for a private party." Darn. "I'll call my mum."

Nathan lets out a long sigh, picks up Dillan after pocketing my keys and heads to the door.

"It's nice to see you." I blurt, causing him to stop for a second. "Thank you for having him."

He dips his head, only a small noncommittal acknowledgement of my words. I watch him walk away, wishing things were different; I hate this gap between us.

CHAPTER THREE

"Well he seemed nice," Valentine remarks sarcastically.

"He is, he's just... he's just Nathan." Now... where was I?

Arriving home is nerve wrecking. I'm wondering whether Nathan will be here or if Mum is back and has taken over Dillan duty. When I see his car in the driveway I don't know whether to be relieved or not.

"Hey." I call as I walk inside and peel my coat from my torso.

"I have to go." Nathan states, immediately brushing past me. What the hell?

I grab his arm and tug him back to me, a frown of confusion showing the reality of my feelings. "What's wrong?"

"I've put Dillan to bed." He says, without looking at me. With a sharp tug, his arm is free of my grasp.

"Seriously?" I scoff and chase after him, stopping as he pulls open his car door. I push against it, placing my body between him and the vehicle. "Is this how it's going to be?" His eyes stare at a spot over my shoulder and I want to huff in frustration. "Please Nathan. Stop shutting me out."

I notice his eyes soften for a brief second, but it's gone as quick as it came. "Move, Guinevere."

"Umm... no, I don't think I will." My look is defiant as I cross my arms over my chest and raise my chin a little. "Not until we've... hey!" His hands grip my arms and quickly pull me away. I'm backed into the window beside the open, front door of my house and memories of the night he raised his fist in anger flood through me, causing me to shy away. He either doesn't notice my sudden flash of fear or he doesn't care.

The heat from his body seeps into my chilled bones. I shiver a little as he steps closer, only an inch separating us. "I'm pretty sure I told you a few things before you left."

I nod, remembering his words clearly, not to mention the way he said them. So sincerely, so cruelly, so angrily.

"You're dead to me."

"Then why do you insist on still conversing with me when I clearly don't want your attention?" He sounds so formal, so well-spoken and above me, a lot like he sounded when we first met. "I'll be there for Dillan, but just..."

A brief flash of pain swims in his almost chocolate coloured eyes. "Stay away from me."

I should stop, but I don't. "I don't understand. I won't mention what I saw." Please, just give me a chance to show you how sorry I am for all that happened to you and for not being able to squelch my curiosity. "I don't feel any different about you because of what I saw. Please, Nathan."

"I'm leaving. I'll call you again in a few weeks." He snaps, running a hand through his longish hair.

"Maybe I'll refuse to answer." I say this petulantly. I'd never stop him from seeing Dillan but if I have to insinuate that I would, to get our friendship back, then that's what I'll do.

His entire body tenses, his face freezing as if zapped by an electric current. "Then I'll knock on your door and insist that you allow me access to my... nephew." What was that pause all about? Was he going to say something else?

"And if I refuse? I don't think it's nice for him to be around you when you so clearly hate me." This is only slightly true. Nathan loves Dillan; I know he'd never do anything to hurt him, emotionally or physically. "How's that?"

"How's that?" He laughs in disbelief. "How's this?" Suddenly his face is inches from mine. "Dillan is the only decent family I have left. He's the only link I have to Caleb. If you even think about taking him from me, I will take you to court and trust me when I say..." The tip of his nose brushes the side of mine; his hands lie flat against the wall causing his arms to cage me in. Gulp. "I'll make it impossible for you to win."

My mouth drops open, shock freezing my mind. I wasn't expecting that. "But... you're... I."

"Have a good evening, Guinevere," he hisses and leans back slightly so his eyes can glare into mine. "I'll see you in two weeks."

"But you said three." I breathe, not trusting my voice to hold my emotions in check.

A sneer curves his lips and he narrows his eyes. I lean further back away from him so my head is against the wall. "Yes, well, clearly I've changed my mind." He spins away from me and storms to his car. I clutch my chest with one hand, willing this pain to stop but knowing that it won't.

I should never have used Dillan as a weapon and that's exactly what I just did. I'm just... desperate. Now I'm not so sure what I am. After all that he just said, I'm not entirely sure I want to fix our relationship. Why do I feel like my heart is breaking? Do I...? No. I won't even entertain the thought, especially when it comes to a four letter word that begins with L and ends with E.

With trembling hands I shut the door behind me. On legs of jelly, I make my way to the shower whilst Dillan still sleeps. I'm disgusting, and I'm not just talking about my flour covered body, I'm talking about my ability to threaten a man with taking away the only decent person he has in this world: my son.

"You look sad." My mum states as I cradle Dillan to my chest and rock backwards and forwards in his nursery on the rocking chair.

"I'm fine." I lie and kiss Dillan's sweet head, making him grumble and mewl slightly before settling once more. "Sasha can't come tonight; she's got a project due."

"Tommy?"

I shrug. "I haven't heard from him since he visited last."

"Nathan?"

Ah, well, therein lies the problem. "Nathan's being... difficult."

"That's not fair on you."

"Yep," I agree, but don't delve further into the reasons behind my agreement. Nathan is an arsehole. The end. "I should go; I'm going to be late."

She takes my son and strokes the back of my neck lovingly. "I'm sure he'll come around."

Somehow I don't think he will. "Thanks Mum."

"Go on, get to work."

But I'm so tired. I spent all night tossing and turning, trying to figure out what to do next. Should I give up on Nathan or keep trying? Maybe I should just give him time. He obviously doesn't want to see me right now. Maybe he'll come around, or maybe I don't want him to.

Do I need to speak to a solicitor?

I'm not sure what I'm doing.

Gah! This is why I couldn't sleep. I need to stop obsessing over this. I'm in a good place right now. Nathan can wallow for the moment; I need to focus on my own life. "Kay."

Work is slow, not because of a lack of customers, oh no, there are plenty of those. It's just slow because I'm exhausted and troubled.

I miss Caleb so much. What would he do after I'd had a bad day at work? I can hardly remember. Maybe he'd cuddle me and kiss me, making it all better. Or maybe he'd rub my shoulders and kiss my neck before making love to me in an attempt to make me forget.

It seems like a life time has passed since he died. In reality it has only been seven months. I can barely recall the way he smelled, or the sound of his laugh, or the feel of his soft lips on mine.

The entire situation still angers me. I feel like I have nowhere safe to sit and weep any longer. Not because of a lack of a home, I have one of those, but because I'm scared that if I shed even the smallest tear, the floodgates will open and I'll spiral into that darkness once more. Nothing, nowhere and nobody can stop my descent into that pit of despair. I just need to keep moving forward.

I wonder what life would be like if I didn't have Dillan, if Caleb hadn't left me pregnant. Would I be happier, or would I be a mess due to having no anchor in my life? Dillan is my anchor and he makes me happier than I think I've ever felt, but I still can't help but wonder.

Although Nathan never would have taken me in if I hadn't been pregnant. I'm not sure how I feel about that.

"I think that dough is done." Valentine comments, pulling me from my thoughts.

She's right; it was probably done about five minutes ago. I may have rolled it a little too much; it looks like a thin sheet of dough coloured paper, albeit a wonky one. Oops.

Tiffany pops her small head around the door. "Hot guy, up front. He's back for his something special."

Gulp. "Did he specifically ask for me?"

"Yes." And she's gone.

Oh crap. Well, at least I'm not covered in flour and other ingredients now, not like the last time.

CHAPTER THREE

"I'll be back." I say to Valentine and hastily hang my apron on the back of the door with the others.

Oh god. There he is. "Hi." I go for chirpy, but it sounds awkward and a little bit pained. "Eric, right?"

"Guinevere, right?" He gives me a wink and leans over the counter slightly. His crooked smile is very handsome, very charming. I bet the ladies love him.

Elle sighs beside me and my thoughts are confirmed. Yep. The ladies love him.

"I'm back for that something special." He states mischievously, his eyes twinkling. How old is he anyway? He can't be older than twenty-six.

"Sure." I chew on my lip, staring directly into his eyes, trying to implore him to order baked goods only. Why do I get the feeling that I'm also on that menu? "What is it you..." Don't say fancy! "Fancy?" God damn my stupid mouth!

His smile widens, ugh, those dimples... need I say more? "Well, seeing as somebody could have choked to death and died," my mouth drops open in horror at his words, "or broken a tooth, I figure you owe me big. Real big. Too big."

Oh crap. "That's a lot of 'ifs'."

"It is." His hazel eyes flick to my hand. "Where's your ring?"

"At home." I rub my naked finger absentmindedly, willing the conversation to move on.

"With your... fiancé?"

My eyes widen. What do I say? "I'm... umm... not engaged."

Now he looks perplexed. "Oh. Family heirloom?"

"Something like that." Nervously tucking my hair behind my ears, I glance around at the empty tables, praying for something really funny to happen to distract him so I can scuttle away. Or something really bad. Maybe I can make somebody start a fight.

"So, your ring is at home with..."

I frown. "Why do you want to know who I live with?"

He lets out a laugh. "Actually I was trying to find out if you're single."

"She is!" Elle shouts from the kitchen. I just got very lightheaded.

"Brilliant." Eric grins and laces his fingers together on the counter before him. "So, I'll pick you up at eight?"

"I..."

"Eight it is." He responds. I open my mouth to speak, but he cuts me off. "Or seven, is seven better for you?"

"No..."

"She finishes at six!" Elle shouts and I make a mental note to kick her bony arse later.

"You have customers Elle!" I shout back through gritted teeth and turn back to Eric. "I can't, I have to..." Where's he gone? What the hell? I see him climbing into a silver car that's parked outside the store window.

"He ran when you turned." Elle explains unnecessarily when I stare dumbfounded at the doorway.

Grumbling profanities to myself, I stomp into the kitchen, my face flamed red and my irritation in the danger zone.

"You'll thank me later." Elle calls, not caring that the three customers who were waiting to be served no doubt know that I'm going on a date later.

Oh my god! I'm going on a date later!

"Are you okay?" Valentine asks, clearly sensing my mood.

No I'm not. "Fine."

For somebody who doesn't want to go on a date, I certainly took extra care keeping myself ingredient free. It's now five fifty-three and I'm as nervous as Santa in a whorehouse.

Stop fidgeting. Stop shaking. Stop... just stop everything.

I can handle that.

The bell above the door chimes and in walks Eric, looking gorgeous in dark blue jeans and a white shirt. "Hi." He looks slightly nervous, almost as nervous as me. I kind of feel bad for the guy now. "Are you ready?"

"You insisted on picking me up from work." I look down at my almost ingredient free clothing. "So nope, I'm not ready."

Ducking under the counter, I gulp when he steps towards me and offers his hand. I don't know why but I take it and allow him to pull me closer. He bends forward and plants his soft lips against my cheek, inhaling at the same time. "You smell like cookies."

"You sniffed me?" I remark, not sure whether to freak out or swoon.

"You work in a bakery. My first though was 'I bet she smells just like one'."

Blink. "What an odd first thought to have." Or is it? I'm uncertain how the male mind works.

He laughs silently and pulls me out of the store. "So, my full name is Eric Smith. I'll be your date for the evening."

Huh, he doesn't open my car door for me. I'm not sure if I like that. Or maybe I'm used to a custom that only exists in the Weston males. That's okay though, because I'm not getting in the car or going on a date.

"Problem?" He asks, still smiling.

I nod and decide to blurt it out. "I have to get home to my son."

"Your son?" At first I can see that he thinks I'm joking, but when he takes in my serious expression he looks mostly shocked. "Oh."

"Yeah, he's eleven weeks old and my mum is looking after him while I work. I'm living with her until I can afford my own place."

He just gawps at me, rather rudely I might add. "Eleven weeks old? Where's his dad?"

I should just tell him. I probably won't see him again. It's for the best. "His dad died when I was four months pregnant, in bed beside me." Now he looks even more stumped. I point back to the store. "They don't know that. I tried to tell you earlier but... well you kind of ran off."

He remains silent for a moment, "Ah. So I'm guessing that's who the ring is from?" Don't cry, don't speak, only nod. "I'm really sorry for your loss." He says softly, resting his arms on the roof of the car that still separates us. "Can I give you a ride home?"

Shaking my head, I take a step back. "No, that's okay. I only live around the corner. I'm really sorry for messing you around."

"You didn't." His smile is reassuring. "It's my fault for getting ahead of myself. I knew you'd say no; I just never put much thought into why."

"Sorry Eric, and thanks again for bringing my ring back."

"Please let me give you a lift? My guilt is gnawing at my insides." He tilts his head and smiles again. This time it's a real one, an easy one.

Should I? "Maybe next time." I duck my head and turn away.

"Good night, Guinevere." He calls. I wave at him without looking back and pick up the pace.

The first thing I do when I get home is pick up Dillan and lie in bed with him on my chest. I need my anchor right now. I need him bad.

His wrinkly forehead bobs up and down as he raises his head off my chest and looks at me with familiar eyes. I smile at his open mouthed smile and kiss his tiny nose, speckled in little white milk spots. "I love you baby Weston. Never forget."

The week goes by and I don't hear from Nathan, nor do I hear from Eric. This is good. It allows my mind a break from endless unnecessary thoughts.

Dillan is such a smiley baby. I love it, especially when I wake up in the morning and he's looking at me through the gaps of his cot, smiling at the fact I'm awake and ready to feed him.

I wonder vaguely if Nathan was as happy as Caleb and Dillan before his grandfather destroyed him. Unwillingly, my memory conjures the images that I was exposed to when watching the home movie. I remember Nathan before his grandfather did what he did. He was happy, excited even.

That poor boy.

Poor Nathan. I just want to hold him and cry for him, but I know he won't appreciate that.

"You still haven't told us how your date went. I've been waiting and waiting." Elle smirks and pops a chocolate ball into her mouth. "Oh my god. Heaven in ball form."

Rolling my eyes good naturedly, I help her place the fancy trays full of treats into the display fridge. "I didn't go on a date."

"But I thought…"

I wave her off. "Don't think about it. It's not a big deal. I'm just not in that 'dating mood' right now." Whatever the hell that is.

"There is something seriously wrong with you if you can't get in the dating mood for a guy like that." If only she knew. "That boy is tastier than your Sunday cookies."

"Liar." I snigger and close the display. "If you like him so much, why don't you date him?"

"Babe, I'm almost thirty five and I have a partner who I love dearly." She winks at me with a smile. "This is why I need to live vicariously through you." Clasping her hands under her chin, she pouts dramatically. "Please, oh please, please, please date him and tell me all of the details."

"You're shameless." I laugh and smack her on the arm. "Move it. I have cookies that are going to burn if you don't."

"Can't let her burn our precious cookies." Tiffany interjects, as if the thought is worse than the world ending, and pulls a still begging Elle out of the way.

I brush past them, still smiling, and get back on with my work. Things are starting to look up.

When I get home I'm in the mood to clean and organise, even though I'm exhausted. Dillan is happy on my bed nearby. I've placed padding around him to stop him rolling off the large mattress, but I have one eye on him at all times anyway. I'm never more than a foot away. My room isn't big enough to allow me much distance.

He kicks obliviously at the toy by his feet. Every time his foot connects, the part that hangs above his torso lights up. I don't think he realises he is the cause of the flashing lights and jingling music, but it certainly gets him excited.

"I have to leave soon." Mum calls as she barrels up the stairs and into my room. "Christ." she lets out a pant and clutches her side. "I'm getting too old for that."

"You're like forty; get a grip." I remark and pull out a pile of junk that has been kicked under my bed. Mostly it has been kicked there on purpose. Ever since I started this new job I've been too exhausted to clean and my mum has been dealing with the rest of the house.

"Sasha stopped by an hour before you got home. She said she's sorry she hasn't called and dropped off your jacket. It's downstairs in the hall. You left it in her car when she picked you up from Nathan's."

"Thanks." I glance at my son again, ensuring his safety, before returning to the task at hand. "Have a good night at work."

"Kisses." She crawls onto my bed and kisses Dillan's open mouth. "I love you, my sweet boy." With a pat on my head, she leaves me to my chores.

Dillan coos and gurgles. "Shut it you." I say in a soft, gentle and happy tone; it only causes him to make more noises.

Once my room is done, I hold my son in one arm and descend the stairs. I'm definitely exhausted now, even though the night is young. It can't be later than six.

I text Sasha and thank her for bringing my jacket. I'd completely forgotten about that.

<u>Sasha</u>: No problem girly xxx I'll call you tomorrow. Xxx

She doesn't call and Tommy rarely responds to my texts. Another week goes by and I'm finally wondering whether I had real friends at all. I get that I have a kid now but, after everything we've been through, you'd think they'd at least invite me places. This isn't the case. I took Dillan for a walk the other day and decided to stop in at the old café where I worked. Sasha entered not long after me with a group of university friends that I don't recognize. She came over and said hello, with promises to call.

More promises broken.

I leaned down to my son and made him one promise that I would definitely keep. "Me and you against the world. I promise to never abandon you."

Chapter Four

My phone rings. It's not even seven in the morning. Nathan. Ugh, what does he want? It's too early to argue. "Hello?"

"Get Dillan ready. I'll be there in two hours." And the line goes dead.

Are you fucking kidding me? No. Dillan had me up half of the night. I'm sleeping and I'm going to remain this way until he wakes me up again. Screw you and your orders.

Besides, my eyes won't stay open long enough for me to get out of bed.

I let out a startled choke when the blanket is pulled from my body, disturbing me from my pleasant dreams that I no longer remember. "What the hell?" I blink away my blurred vision and glare at a scowling Nathan. He's looming over me in a way that tells me he probably wants to throttle me right now. "I could have been naked." I practically am, in only a top and knickers.

"I called you two hours ago, only to find you still sleeping?" He scoffs and walks over to the cot where Dillan is now awake and crying, probably from my sudden screech of fear.

"I don't remember a call." I lie and sit up. My hands immediately begin rubbing my eyes. Wait... "How did you get in?"

"I knocked; your mum answered."

"And she just let you in?" I frown, not believing that for a second.

"When I explained to her it was my weekend to have Dillan, yes, she did. I saved her the trouble of waking you yourself."

"Oh. It's nine in the morning. Why are you wearing a suit?" Not that he doesn't look good. He really does.

"Could you get up and pack his things? I'll bring him back on Monday."

"I never agreed to the length of time, or you even picking him up." I stand, not feeling modest in the slightest. "I'm going to have a shower."

"I have places I need to be." He snaps and my anger at his tone peaks.

"Then you shouldn't be taking Dillan!"

"I'll get him ready myself."

"You do that." I say around a yawn and pull open the door. "I'll be about fifteen minutes. I want to say goodbye before he leaves."

His jaw clenches but he remains silent, which I'm eternally grateful for.

I take my time showering, just to be awkward. I also take my time getting dressed and drying my hair, again… just to be awkward.

"Today would be nice, Guinevere!" Nathan calls up the stairs, making me snigger. Why am I pushing him?

After making him wait another ten minutes, I finally make my way downstairs. He's sitting on the couch with Dillan on his chest, looking casual and content. Well, as casual as one can look in an expensive suit. "Sorry it took me so long." No I'm not. Not in the slightest.

Nathan lifts Dillan up and over his face, making him smile and gurgle. "She's not is she? Not at all. She's silently laughing at me." His voice is high and happy. I love it when he speaks to Dillan like this. "Mummy is mean, yes she is." Uh-oh.

"Puke face." I say with a wince, but it's too late. A splat of white, lumpy baby vomit leaves my son's mouth and lands directly beneath Nathan's chin. I get ready for the dramatics and grab baby wipes from the side. "Here." I hastily make work of removing the vomit from his neck. Fortunately he doesn't seem too fussed, but lets me clean him anyway. I use this moment of peace between us to bring up our last meeting. It didn't end so well and I behaved appallingly. "I'm sorry for what I said." What a ridiculous way to apologise. His eyes meet mine. It fuels my courage and calms me slightly, enabling me to continue. "I should never have used him as a weapon like that. I'm ashamed of myself."

"You reacted to a… difficult situation." He responds, his eyes softening on me.

"That's not an excuse."

"No." He disagrees, smiling once more at Dillan. "It is an excuse, not a great one, but a forgivable one." I sag slightly with relief. He forgives me and that actually feels pretty good. "He urinated all over my front the last time I had him." Nathan shudders slightly at the memory. Typical Nathan to want to move on from our emotional moment, although I'm glad he doesn't linger or hold grudges for too long. "He thought it was funny."

Good boy. I mean... "Sorry."

Nathan waves me off and tilts his head to the side as I pull his collar open and wipe at the spillage that has seeped beneath. "Here, take him. I need to change my shirt."

Okay, so maybe he is freaking out a little. Or maybe he just doesn't want to have a stain near his collar for his drive home.

"Kay." I grab Dillan, making sure to keep him at an angle just in case he needs to puke again.

"Did you have any plans for the evening?" Nathan asks as he walks back in, his white shirt gone. In its place is a baby blue one that looks amazing against his skin tone.

"No." I say with a shake of my head, willing myself to look away. He takes Dillan back and sits down. I'm shocked, as I can see the nappy bag is fully packed to its limit so he really has no reason to linger. Nathan doesn't like lingering. I'm glad he is.

"You went out." He prompts, his brows raised.

"Yeah, it wasn't as fun as I'd hoped it would be."

"Why?"

Sigh. "It just wasn't. I'm not used to being in crowds, supermarket not included."

He licks his lower lip, his eyes scanning my face. "Are you dating?"

What? "Come again?"

"Are you dating?" He frowns like I'm the stupid one here.

"Is that a serious question?" I laugh in disbelief. "It's been seven months." Nearly eight, but let's not split hairs.

"That's plenty of time for you to start getting your life back." I'll never get my life back. Caleb died, remember? "You're a stunning girl." Girl? "I find it shocking that you haven't been asked...although you're hardly warm towards people that aren't already your friends or family." What a hypocrite!

"I have." I blurt, feeling slightly defensive. "Someone has asked me actually."

His face falls. "Who?"

"A very nice man named Eric." Why am I telling him this? "Very good looking too."

His eyes burn with an intensity I can't place. What is he thinking? "Are you going on a date with him?"

My shoulders sag. "No. I said no."

"Huh." His hand runs through his hair and I notice his gloves are gone. Was he wearing them when he came in? I can't recall.

Well, this silence is awkward. "What about you? Are you dating?"

"I don't date, Guinevere." He sighs with a roll of his eyes.

"Why?" Ha, I certainly spun this back on you!

"I think you know." He lowers his eyes and my breath hitches at the amount of shame I saw in them before they looked to the ground. After placing Dillan in the car seat and buckling him in, he finally breaks the silence. "I should go."

I stand quicker than him and grab his hand without thinking. It was meant to be a consoling gesture. What the hell have I done? I wait for the explosion. I even shut my eyes and turn my face away. I try to pull my hand back, but his closes over it; very slowly I feel his fingers lace through mine and my breath hitches. We both stare at our entwined fingers and touching palms. Nathan slowly brings it up, gulping as he does, before placing the top of my hand to his lips and holding it there for a moment.

A bolt of electricity travels down my arms and crashes into my stomach. I feel weak. He's kissing my hand, but he may as well be kissing somewhere else for all of the feeling it gives me.

My mouth goes dry when his eyes come to mine and he slowly lowers my hand back to my side. "Have a good weekend, Guinevere." Picking up the car seat, he slings the bag over his other shoulder and gently cups my cheek with the hand that held mine not moments ago. "You should date; you're young. Don't let my brother or Dillan stop you from having the fun you need. You'll end up resenting the both of them."

As his words mull through my fogged brain, I watch them both leave and wonder vaguely if that's the reason he's started having Dillan. If so, why does he even care? Especially after his reaction the last time. He didn't sound happy when I told him I was out.

Maybe he feels guilty because his brother should be here and isn't. In my opinion, he feels way too much guilt over things that aren't his fault. Is it wrong that I want to relieve him of it? Is it wrong that I want to share his pain so he doesn't have to carry it all?

I wonder what Caleb thinks of me now, but then I shut that thought off because Caleb isn't here and Nathan is. He's my friend and he needs me, even if he doesn't realise it yet. I just hope my body recognises that and doesn't keep crossing lines that should be walls of titanium. Nathan is Caleb's brother. I have to stop my body responding the way it does to him. It's not right or fair, to Caleb or Dillan.

Maybe that's the whole point. Maybe it's because he looks like Caleb and is a part of Caleb. Could this be the reason I seem to react the way I do? Either way, it has to stop.

Part of me is hoping that Eric comes in for that something special, although a guy like him clearly doesn't need my baggage. It'd be a good idea to hang around with another male for a while. I'm probably just horny, though the thought of having sex with anyone else makes me feel slightly ill.

I can't do it, I just can't; but I'm going to do it eventually.

Only when I'm ready and right now I'm definitely not ready.

My phone beeps. I pick it up and frown at the unrecognised number on my screen. It's Nathan.

<u>Nathan</u>: Don't get drunk. N.

My mouth falls open. He just text ordered me. How dare he?

He always dares. I'm unsure why he thinks he has free reign to do as he pleases, especially when it comes to my life.

Well, at least I finally have his number.

<u>Gwen</u>: Not that it's any of your business, which it isn't in case you were wondering, but I don't plan on it. In fact I have no plans, seeing as my friends are too busy for me and my mum is working. Unless you plan on personally surprising me with a bottle of vodka and a night of dancing, which you probably aren't, then don't worry. No alcohol will be consumed during your time with Dillan.

Take that!

Nathan: Good.

"Oh!" I cry and throw my phone on the couch. God, he infuriates me like no other.

Good? What kind of a response is that?

Tiffany immediately assaults me at work, literally as soon as I step through the door. "Mine tonight - I'm making cocktails and we're stealing from the local bakery."

My brow quirks. "You mean the place we work?"

She giggles and clicks her fingers. "I knew you'd know it."

"Weirdo." I mutter, smirking at her as I pass. Hanging my coat up, I nod in agreement. "Alright, sounds fun. What time?"

"Duh." Elle chimes in. "When we finish, silly."

Right. "I'm not drinking though. I have to express this weekend."

"That reminds me of this thing I saw on TV about ice cream made with breast milk." Tiffany taps her chin in thought. "I'd try it."

My mouth falls open and my jaw hits the floor, right before I laugh and push her away. "I'm not making ice cream from my boob juice."

Elle shudders along with me. "Tiffany... I... need I say more?"

"What?" The innocent look on Tiffany's face makes me laugh even more. She genuinely doesn't see what we're so grossed out about. "We all drank it once."

"Here then." Elle grabs the top of my t-shirt and pulls it down, exposing the cups of my lace bra. I shriek and pull away from her. "Have a suck."

"You are vile." I choke out, trying to calm my laughter but failing miserably.

Tiffany cackles right along with me, her curly hair bouncing with each breath.

"If that's my something special, I so wish I'd come in sooner." Oh my god. I know that voice.

"What's all the fuss about?" Valentine hobbles through the kitchen door as I pull up my shirt and pretend I'm busy doing something where my back needs to be turned to Eric. After a few seconds of awkward silence I realise eyes are on me, my so called colleagues' curious eyes to be exact.

Letting my shoulders sag, I turn to face the handsome man that has plagued so many of my thoughts recently.

"I'll leave you young people to your fun," Valentine mutters when nobody tells her the joke. It's not like we can explain it; it was one of those 'you had to be there' moments. I'll tell her later.

"I've got shelves to clean and Elle has shelves to stock." Tiffany says, way too cheerfully, and pulls a nosy Elle away by the scruff of her neck.

"Hi." I finally look at him and instantly feel my cheeks heat. He's gazing at me, in that way that only really handsome men can gaze at you and make you feel like you're completely naked. "What can I get for you?"

His eyes flicker to the curves of my breasts and his smile widens. I throw a pen at him. Fortunately he finds it funny and doesn't sue me for assault. "Feisty. I like it."

"I'm going to spit in your cookies."

He lets out a chuckle and shrugs. "As long as you don't make them with breast milk." Did he hear all of that? Please say no. "Although…" I launch another pen at his suggestive tone. "I'm kidding. I'm actually here to collect doughnuts for a friend. He said he'd already called. Josh Rode."

"I've got it." Elle calls and gets to work on the dozen donuts.

Why do I feel slightly disappointed that he's not here to see me? "Okay, so maybe I volunteered to come because I wanted to see a certain somebody again." His eyes are soft now, and aimed at me.

"He's talking about me," Tiffany whispers loudly in my ear and leans on the counter. I know she's joking, but Eric looks slightly frightened. Elle pulls her away, both of them giggling like teenagers. Sigh.

"Sorry about them. They were quiet when I first met them. I don't know what happened." I joke and glare fondly at the two women. They quickly duck their heads and return to their duties. "I didn't think I'd see you again." It has been two weeks since I saw him, two weeks since Nathan had Dillan, and two weeks of sheer boredom.

"I wasn't sure if you wanted to see me again." He admits, tucking his hands into his jacket pockets. "I think this is the first time I've seen you flour free."

My cheeks heat. "Yes. I've only just arrived myself, not long before you came in."

"Both are stunning."

"Huh?"

"You covered in flour, you not covered in flour." He leans over the counter and smiles crookedly. "Stunning." Gulp. "I get that you don't want to date right now." You can say that again. "But I really don't like being told no. It's not good for my ego." I'll bet. "So I'm going to suggest something and you're not allowed to say no because it's completely innocent and totally platonic."

He's charming; I'll give him that. "And what's that?"

"I have this thing tomorrow and I need a date." I open my mouth to say no, but he quickly continues. "Well, not a date but a friend to join me."

"And what is this thing?"

"I can't tell you because you'll say no."

Is he serious? "But if you don't tell me, I'm going to say no."

"You'll enjoy yourself, I promise. You can also bring your baby if you want to." Not a chance, but what is it that would allow me to bring a four month old? "Please say yes."

Chewing on my lip for a moment, I contemplate my options. Stay at home, lonely and bored, or take a chance on a possibly good day out with a seemingly nice guy? "Sure. Dillan is with his uncle tomorrow so I'm free."

"Excellent." He grins and slides a folded note across the counter. "I'm giving you a chance to back out. If you haven't texted me by eleven in the morning, I'll leave you alone and never bother you again. Well...not including my frequent trips to the bakery where you happen to work." I pocket the note and tuck my hair nervously behind my ear. "No hard feelings at all."

Damn he's sweet. "Thank you."

He gives me another smile as Elle hands him the box of doughnuts. "Until tomorrow."

"You still haven't ordered anything." I comment. "I owe you."

"I'll collect it when the time's right." His cheeky smile is the last thing I see before he exits the store and climbs into his car.

The girls start cheering, almost deafening me in the process. I blush like a virgin and scarper into the safety of the kitchen where Valentine awaits eagerly to hear the story. Elle tells her about Eric before I even get the chance and soon Valentine is cheering with them. There's a pharmacy across the road; I'm definitely buying ear plugs during my break.

As it is, I don't need earplugs because the bakery gets way busier than normal. Apparently there's some kind of kite festival down on the beach and everyone is stopping off here for iced drinks and sweet snacks. By noon I've not stopped baking and already we've run out of the favourites. Valentine fortunately prepared for the festival, but she didn't make enough. Nobody expected it to be such a turn out, but with the weather being perfectly windy and not too cold, the town is swarmed like it never has been before.

When I look through the window I can see some of the larger kites in the air. One of them is shaped like Shrek and it makes me smile. I bet Dillan would love this if he were older. It's been a while since we had this festival in town. I think the last time was when I was five and I thought it was brilliant. I hope it comes around again when Dillan is that age.

"Okay, these old bones need a break." Valentine announces and flops onto a nearby chair, using a book to fan her face. "Can you handle the rest for a while?"

I nod. "No problem. Why don't you go and lie down for a bit?"

"I need to be here, just in case you get stuck."

This is obviously a possibility, but I refuse to admit defeat. "It's fine. I've got this. Everything is almost ready to come out anyway. You go, and I'll shout you if we need anything."

She mulls it over for a moment before nodding wearily and climbing back up from the chair. "I knew I'd be glad I hired you."

I smile at that and get back to work cleaning our used utensils. She pats me on the back as she walks past and soon disappears through the door that leads to her flat upstairs.

Okay, I can do this.

"I think I'm definitely going to be joining you for non-alcoholic cocktails and treats tonight." I say to Tiffany, flopping into the same chair that Valentine flopped into hours ago.

Tiffany grins and claps her hands. "Brilliant. I'll stock up a box of whatever is left."

"Yay." I say, but it comes out sounding tired and defeated. "I need to go home and have a shower first."

"Duly noted. You go on ahead; we'll handle the lock up. I'll pick you up in about forty minutes."

Well at least I don't have to walk to hers on my aching feet. I hang up my apron and head home. As soon as I fall through the door, I stumble to the shower and barely get my clothes off before climbing in. I even go as far as to sit on the tiled floor; my body just can't hold me up. I'm exhausted, but I don't want to sleep. I want to have fun.

It's a huge change. A few months ago the idea of fun was abhorrent to me. Now I feel like I want to start living again. Caleb... I'm sorry.

"One virgin Tiffany surprise, without the surprise because it's virgin." Tiffany grins and hands me a tall glass of purple, ugly looking liquid. I take a tentative sip, surprised when it actually tastes good. "It has grapes in it."

"It's great." I nod slowly with a smile and watch Elle switch to the music channels via the TV remote.

Tiffany takes a picture of me holding the glass, much to my annoyance. I hate pictures and I don't ever use the social networking sites that are available. She still uploads it. I'm grateful I'll never see it.

Am I dull? I sound really dull.

"How's the baba?" Elle asks, turning the TV down low after the neighbours bang on the wall a few times. Tiffany glares at the wall as if it's to blame. This makes me snigger.

"He's great." Although I have yet to hear from Nathan. I should text him.

Gwen: How are you both? Is he being good?

"He's gorgeous. I want baby cuddles but I never get to see him outside of work." Elle moans.

Tiffany nods in agreement. "Yeah, we should all go for lunch soon." Even though we either work at the same time or on different days. "We'll figure something out. Are you working tomorrow?"

I shake my head. "No, it's Sunday. I never work Sundays."

"I do, every freakin' Sunday." Tiffany grumbles and sits in between Elle and myself. "Which means I have to be really careful to avoid a hangover."

"Woe is me." Elle jests and places her hand to her forehead. I can't help but giggle.

"Shut up."

My phone vibrates in my pocket and I pull it out and read the text.

Nathan: All is well. He's sleeping. How is your evening?

Gwen: It's actually really good. I'm sat with two ladies from work, Elle and Tiffany. They're drinking cocktails, mine is virgin. I haven't laughed so much in a really long time :-)

"Who's on the other end of the texting line?" Tiffany leans into me, attempting to see my message. "Aww, Elle, she thinks we're ladies."
Another round of laughter begins.

Nathan: Virgin? Alcohol free I assume?

Gwen: Yes...

"Are you texting pretty boy from earlier? You're all smiley." Elle says and downs the rest of her drink. Tiffany refills it for her with the glass jug full of ugly purple fluid on the table.
"No, it's Nathan." I admit and place my phone back in my pocket.
"Dillan's uncle? Damn, he's hot."
"And brooding. Did you see that smouldering look he had on his face?" Tiffany adds and fans her face. "He single?"
I nod. "But he's complicated."
"You're taken." Elle snaps playfully at her friend.
"I can dream. So, what's the deal with Nathan? Why's he got Dillan and not his brother?"
I should tell them, but I feel like such a sob story when I do tell people. It'll just ruin the night.
Fortunately I'm saved from explanations when her phone starts ringing. They seem to forget when Tiffany trips over the coffee table on the way to answer it and ends up sprawled on the floor in an uncomfortable looking starfish position. My gut hurts from laughing so hard.

Chapter Five

"Mum?" I say as I lean against the doorframe to the kitchen. She stirs her coffee slowly, still half asleep.

"Yeah?" She looks at me through swollen bloodshot eyes. "You look nice."

"You're working too hard." I frown and wipe down the area around her cup after entering the kitchen. "Do you think it's too soon for me to start dating?"

She tenses, her hands gripping the cup tighter than before. I daren't look at her to gauge her reaction, just in case I see judgement in her eyes. Suddenly her hand wraps around mine and I gulp, waiting for her harsh words of wisdom.

"Baby," I'm shocked at the soft tone of her voice, "I don't think so. I think you're young and I think you need to have some fun." I look at her in horror, but she laughs and shakes her head. "Not kinky fun."

"I don't know. I'm just... I feel so guilty."

"Are you ready?"

"Will I ever be?" My eyes water. I lower my head onto my arms and tilt it towards her fingers, which begin running through my hair.

She lets out a long breath. "Don't push yourself into it and don't let anybody else push you into it. I think you're now at a place where you can entertain the idea. You're doing a lot better than you were."

"You think?" I sniff and peek up at her through my lashes, my eyes now probably as swollen as hers.

"Yes. When you first came home you were..." She shudders slightly at the memory. "A robot. But then again, you had just been through a lot with Nathan." Her eyes seek mine as she leans closer. "I know you care about him."

My teeth find the inside of my cheek and grip it tight.

"Maybe more than you should." She whispers this and I'm unsure why.

"No." I deny it. It's not true. "We never... nothing ever happened between us. Not like that." Well it did, but it was all him. Not me. I didn't reciprocate it. Did I?

Her lips tilt up at the corners. "I know. You don't need to have sex to love somebody."

My mouth opens, then closes, then opens again. "That... I don't love him that way." I love him, just not in a romantic way. Like a brother maybe? No, that's not right. I don't think I've ever seen Nathan as a brother. Love leads to sex when it's not in a familial sense. Could I have sex with Nathan? The thought isn't as appalling as it should be.

"Okay." She definitely doesn't agree, so why is she agreeing?

How can I be so ridiculous? Me and Nathan? No way. Not a chance. "This guy asked me out. He's picking me up in an hour." Now Eric, he should be the kind of guy I'm thinking of in those terms. I think...

"Oh." She nods slowly. "Is he hot?"

"Mum!" I laugh, my cheeks heating. "Yes, I suppose he is good to look at."

Fortunately she seems pleased with this. "Good. Where's he taking you?"

Shrug. "No idea."

"You be careful. Keep your phone tucked in your bra!"

"Yes mother." I sigh good-naturedly and step away. "Want to help me get ready?"

Her lips stretch into a wide smile. "Definitely. I never got a chance when you were with Caleb. He loved you the way you were."

Giggles overcome me. "Why do you look so upset about that? That's what all parents should want for their kids!" She joins in my laughter and gives me a small shrug.

"I wanted to do your hair and makeup and get excited over your dates. Instead I got a 'hi mum, bye mum' and then an 'I'm moving out mum'."

"I'm sorry. Things with Caleb, they were very..." What's the word? "Intense. Fast paced."

"Perfect." She adds and pats my hand. "He was pretty darn perfect. Until he got you pregnant that is, but even now, when I look at my grandson, I can't fault him for that oopsie. Come on. Let's go and get you ready."

Nathan texts as my mum is curling the ends of my hair, in a way that looks very natural and very pretty.

<u>Nathan</u>: Jeanine wants to have Dillan for an hour or so today. Are you okay with that?

Am I? Jeanine, I miss her.

<u>Gwen</u>: No problem :-) Have you got any plans?

<u>Nathan</u>: Yes.

<u>Gwen</u>: Care to elaborate?

"Stop moving." Mum chastises as she applies mascara to my long lashes. "Sorry."

<u>Nathan</u>: I'm going to visit a friend. That's if we can still be classed as friends.

<u>Gwen</u>: You have friends?!?!

<u>Nathan</u>: Ouch. That one hurt. I almost forgot how much of a bitch you can be.

<u>Gwen</u>: I guess it doesn't matter anymore. You have a new friend now.

<u>Nathan</u>: Nope. She's a bitch too. Though you're so much better at it.

<u>Gwen</u>: She? Lorna by any chance?

"Done." My mum beams and turns my face towards the mirror. "Beautiful."

I admire my natural looking waves and the slight shade of grey above my eyes, shadowed by super black lashes. "Thank you."

"Now for the clothes."

Oh god, I hate picking out outfits, especially when I don't know where I'm going. Fortunately my mum takes control. I just lie on my bed and wait for her to throw something at me.

<u>Nathan</u>: No, she was done with me a while ago. Besides, we were never friends.

<u>Gwen</u>: I'm sorry to hear that. I hope you have fun. I have to go. It was nice conversing with you again. I've missed it :-) xox

<u>Nathan</u>: Me too.

Does this mean we're okay now? What does this mean? This is good I think. We're talking again. I feel like dancing a little, but I won't; mostly because I'm still angry at his attitude towards me and the fact that he showed up without warning and took my son.

But maybe he'll start letting me in and he'll let me help him. I won't let him go through this alone anymore. I can only imagine what being in his mind is like with all of those memories, such terrible memories. He deserves to be understood. I want to try.

Poor Nathan. That poor, poor boy. That poor, poor man.

My mum finally decides on dark blue skinny jeans and a white vest with a long grey wool cardigan over it. I pull on my boots and wait nervously in the hall. I've been telling myself this isn't a date, but I'm not stupid; of course it is. It's just not a 'date-date'. It's less date like, if that makes sense, because it's not dinner by candlelight or whatever dates are supposed to be. I'm useless at all of this.

"I'm really nervous." I twist my hands together before me, my teeth worrying my lip.

"Too late, he's here. My, my. He is yummy."

"Get away from the window." I screech and pull her laughing form away. "Stop it."

"He saw me."

Can I shake her? I feel like shaking her.

There's a knock at the door. I shove my mother towards the living room and take a deep breath before opening it. "Hey." I sound breathless, probably because I am, but it's not from exertion or because he looks handsome. For some reason it's from the huge fist of guilt that just nailed me in the stomach. Seconds ago I was giddy and excited and now I just feel... meh. There's no explanation for how I feel now. Only pain.

I ignore it, push it way deep down, and smile brightly at the very handsome man before me. He looks great in a polo shirt and... shorts? Football trainers? What the hell am I being dragged to?

"Let's go."

"You have knee high socks on." I state, looking at the thick blue fabric.

"Aye." he chuckles, throwing his arm around my shoulders. "You look gorgeous."

Blush. I need a blood filter to my cheeks; I'm so tired of turning red. "So, I'm guessing the obvious here. You're going to force me to watch football aren't you?"

He grins wickedly, showing a slightly crooked smile that lifts higher on one side than the other. It's very pretty. "Get in the car and then I'll tell you."

"So I can't run? That hardly seems fair." I joke and do as I'm told.

Yet again he doesn't open the door, but I'm prepared for it this time. Clearly I've been spoilt by two men who were raised as gentlemen. It's funny because whenever Nathan didn't open the door for me, I knew he was angry. Sometimes, even when he was angry, he still opened it, almost as if his burned in the brain manners got the better of him. Caleb was the same, but we never fought; I can only remember two arguments in our entire relationship. Sure we had minor disagreements, but eventually I usually got him to see things my way.

My mum is right. He was perfect. Too perfect. Suddenly things in my mind seem to be slightly clearer. My rose tinted glasses have a tiny hole in them and certain things are coming back to mind.

"I want to marry you on Wednesday."

I don't remember this. I don't remember Caleb saying this. I remember him being ill, but the days before his death are just... a blur. So why am I hearing his voice now? The urgency in it... it's very surreal.

"Hey, are you alright?"

What? I blink back to reality. "Sorry. I lost myself for a moment there."

He lets out a laugh. "I said your name six times."

"Sorry." I give him an apologetic smile and look towards him. "So, what's with the footie gear?"

"I'm taking you to meet a few of my friends. There will be terrible food and lukewarm drinks and probably ants in the grass, but you get to watch two five-a-side teams laying into each other."

"Ah, well that makes it so worth it then."

"Exactly." He smiles, his eyes twinkling. "I thought you'd be more comfortable in a group setting."

It's a thoughtful gesture, but the wrong one. I'm shy, does he not realise this? I'll be sat there awkwardly with whoever is present, twiddling my thumbs and mumbling incoherent answers to whatever is asked of me.

"Sounds great." I lie. I'm nervous as hell.

"You do eat meat, right?"

"Yes."

He lets out a breath. "Good."

"I wish I'd known there would be food. I would have brought some cakes or something." I mumble, my finger twisting a lock of my wavy hair around the tip.

He shrugs. "Never thought of that. Maybe I should have prepared you. The guys would really go for cakes." He gives me a kind smile. "Next time, eh?"

"Sure." Did I just agree to another time before I've even managed to get through the first?

"You're bad luck." He jokes, wiping the sweat from his forehead with a damp towel that rests across his lap. "Oh my god, everything hurts."

I roll my eyes. "If you spent more time on your feet then you wouldn't have been trampled on."

"I slipped."

My left brow hits my hairline. "Six times?"

"It's called a sliding tackle."

"No." I laugh and open the door after we pull up in the driveway. "It's called falling and trying to make it look like a sliding tackle."

"Whatever, you're just jealous of my wicked moves." This makes me laugh even harder.

Overall he and his team were actually very good, they certainly didn't lack passion. I barely got to meet his four male friends as I was quickly scooted to the side and placed with their fan girls, who were actually very friendly and in no way overbearing; I even knew one of them from my college days. Not personally though, we never spoke but we took the same English class from what I can remember.

It was fun and I'm glad I went. The food was in fact a few of those portable barbecue trays and a hell of a lot of sausages and burgers. It was as terrible as expected, but it didn't matter. I felt included in something normal, something fun and exciting. After five minutes in I was cheering Eric and his team on along with the rest of the women.

"So, how was our fake date?" He asks, his eyes twinkling with amusement.

I nod slowly. "It was actually really good. Thank you for taking me."

He steps around his car and pops open the boot. I hear the rustling of a plastic bag before one finally comes into view. "Popcorn and a movie?"

"Umm…"

"Awesome, take these; I'll be back in an hour." He gives me a wink, climbs into his car and leaves my stupefied arse in the driveway.

Opening the bag I see the DVDs, all newer titles, and a bag of sweet popcorn. How do I feel about this?

"Did you have fun?" Mum asks as I walk through the door, bag in hand.

"It was pretty good to be honest."

"What's in the bag?"

"He wants to come back in about an hour." I throw my coat on the hanger and sigh when it drops to the ground, forcing me to pick it up again. "There are too many jackets on here." I grumble and grab my other dark jacket, slinging it over my shoulder before sorting through the rest. "I'll take these upstairs."

As I'm throwing my pile of coats and cardigans on the bed, I hear a clatter on the ground and blink in shock at the sight of the plain black DVD case. It's familiar and the mere sight of it makes me break out in a sweat. Grabbing it from the ground I look for a place to hide it. The implications of me holding onto such a vile recording could be dire, but I can't bring myself to get rid of it.

Using sticky tape, I stick it to the underside of my desk. I'll figure out what I'm going to do with it later.

The title glares at me and sticks in my mind. *'He Knows'*. Who knows? And what do they know?

After giving the house a quick clean and changing into comfier clothing, there's finally a knock at the door. I answer it with nervous jitters and my smile instantly falls.

"Nathan?" I blink in shock. "What are you doing here? Is Dillan okay?"

He shifts on the spot and licks his lower lip. His silence doesn't reassure me and my panic rises. He sees this and holds up his gloved hands. "He's fine, I was just..."

"Hey!" Oh god no, this isn't happening. "I've parked on the front. Don't worry man, I didn't block your car in." This really can't be happening. Gulp.

Nathan's eyes open as he looks from me to Eric and then back again.

"Eric." I say and Nathan's eyes narrow on the male. "This is my brother in law, Nathan. Nathan, this is Eric."

"Her not real date." Eric jokes, but it's lost on us. "It's nice to meet you. Gwen has mentioned you."

Nathan stares at Eric's outstretched hand. I step forward and grab it, pulling Eric closer to me in the process. He doesn't seem to mind. "Could you give us a minute? The movie is in the DVD player."

"Where?"

Oh crap. "My room, umm..." Nathan tenses. "My mum's home, so... upstairs first door on the right."

"Sure, popcorn?"

"Already up there." I say and shift to the side so he can pass. I turn back to Nathan, who is walking back to his car. "Hey, wait up. Where's Dillan?" I search for any sign of him in the car, but his seat isn't there.

"He's with Jeanine." Nathan states, his tone clipped with an undertone of anger. What did I do?

"So you're here because?" I prompt and manoeuvre my way between him and the driver's seat.

He shrugs. "I was in the area."

A laugh escapes me. "Three hours from home?"

He winces and tries to pull me out of the way, his eyes avoiding mine. "Have a good evening Guinevere."

Did he drive all of this way to see me? That makes no sense. Why would he do that? "Why are you here?" Oh my god. I was the person he was referring to in his texts. Grr, why does he have to be so confusing?

"I shouldn't be." This is hardly an answer. He looks up to my empty bedroom window, his lips a thin white line. "I should go."

I grab the wrist that is holding my own and click my free fingers in front of his face. "You can look at me, you know."

A muscle in his jaw ticks as he grits his teeth slightly. "No, I can't."

Blink. "Why?" I still try to meet his eyes, but he looks straight ahead. His stubbornness knows no bounds. "Hello?"

"Move out of the way."

"Are we really doing this?" I scoff. "What have I done now? Is this because of Eric? We're not dating..."

Nathan's eyes finally come to mine. "Don't lie Guinevere; it doesn't suit you."

"And finally he looks at me." I sigh and release my hold on him. He doesn't release me though and I'm unsure as to why. "Why are you angry with me?"

"I'm not angry with you." He snaps quite loudly. "I'm angry with myself."

"For?"

He takes a step back and runs his fingers through his hair. "For deluding myself."

"Deluding yourself?"

"Into thinking..." He lets out a breath and steps into my space, his body only an inch from mine. "Into thinking you felt even a fraction of what I hoped you did." My eyes widen of their own accord and my body goes slack, giving him the perfect opportunity to move me out of the way. He climbs into the car and shuts the door. After rolling the window down he grips the steering wheel with both hands and stares straight ahead. "That's my mistake."

I don't say anything. What can I say? I'm officially baffled.

"Nathan." I call softly as he starts the engine.

"Guys like me never win." Guys like him? He puts the car in gear. "It's high time I realised that." He finally reverses away.

Why do I feel guilty? Does... does Nathan... no. He's just... But... None of this makes sense.

I'm in denial. Everything Nathan did whilst I lived with him, everything all pointed to one conclusion. He even asked me to marry him! At first I thought it was out of some strange duty to the fiancée and child his brother left behind. He wants me. Or he did.

Does he still? His actions just now really point to the answer yes.

I head back inside, my mind no longer accepting of my date. I can lie to myself all I want, but that's what this is. It's a date. No longer do I even want to entertain the idea of seeing another man. What's worse is Caleb isn't the only reason behind my sudden change of heart. Nathan seems to be the most prominent one right now. I really don't want to hurt him. The thought of it is abhorrent to me.

So even as I sit beside Eric and laugh at the things he says as we share a bag of popcorn, I decide today is the last I'm going to see of him. Tomorrow I'm going to see Nathan and resolve this mess right away.

Eric leaves late with promises to call. I have to admit he's a lot of fun to be around and I'm glad he didn't try to kiss me at the end.

My mum just left for work, so I have the house to myself.

I'm about to call Nathan so I can talk to him about earlier when I hear the door open and close. My body tenses and my mind instantly goes on alert. Who could it be?

Feet pound up the stairs and I don't have time to reach for the lamp to defend myself before the door is swinging open. My heart hits my throat before falling out of my arse and jumping out of the nearest window. My brain follows it as I stare mindlessly at an infuriated looking Nathan.

"Umm... hi?" I say this questioningly and cross my legs on the bed. "Is there a reason you're barging in on me like this?"

His chest heaves as he takes in my room with watchful eyes. "No." Then it dawns on me and my cheeks heat at the same time as my anger rises.

"Were you checking to see if..." I let my words trail off as Nathan steps into the room and starts rummaging through my closet. What the fuck is wrong with him? "Umm... what are you doing?"

"Put this on." He barks and throws a thigh length black dress at me. "And these." A pair of kitten heel black pumps land at my feet.

"Why?"

He glares at me. I almost forgot how scary that was, "Because I'm bored. I want to use you as my personal Barbie doll." Did he just roll his eyes at me? "I want to take you somewhere."

"Why?"

"Because I'm bored." Oh, so that part was true at least.

"Fine." I don't argue; there's no point.

"Shower. Wash his stink off you." He snarls and slams the door behind him. I hear his footsteps pound on each stair as if punishing it for his bad mood. Gulp.

I think maybe I made him mad.

Chapter Six

"Y‍OU LOOK STUNNING." NATHAN says with admiring eyes that make me feel a tad uncomfortable and also slightly heated. "Let's go."

I shouldn't go with him after the way he's been talking to me and treating me, but I remind myself over and over that as angry as I want to be with him for being an arsehole towards me, I want to understand him more. For that to happen he needs to let me in. He deserves to have somebody at least try. So I take a calming breath.

"Where?" I ask and allow him to lead me to the car.

"You'll see." His cryptic response annoys my curiosity to no end.

I change the subject, knowing that asking him again will only result in a similar answer meaning the same thing. "I have to admit, I'm not happy about you giving up your Dillan time. It's not like you get much of it."

He nods. "Yes, well, needs must." What kind of a response is that? "Come, I'm certain you'll enjoy yourself."

"What's with the sudden one eighty? You hated me and now you don't?" I don't want to push him into doing another one eighty, but I need to know why he's suddenly changed his mind.

"I never hated you, Guinevere." He sighs and helps me into the car. Yep, he's definitely a gentleman. "Music? The radio is yours to enjoy."

"Seriously?" I grin a grin of disbelief. "I never get control of the radio."

"That's because your taste in music is appalling."

"There's nothing wrong with the top forty. I respond haughtily and turn on the beats.

"Just promise me something." His teasing tone piques my interest and I nod for him to continue. "Don't sing; my ears can't handle the pain."

My mouth falls open. I slap his arm and turn away from him, feigning offense. This only makes him laugh harder. I've missed the sound. "Meanie."

"You're good to look at and your voice is very... gentle and soothing. Until you sing that is."

"Caleb used to say I'd fit in perfectly with a group of very sick cats."

"I'm sure they'd accept you into their choir if they were to have one." He jests and places his leather clad hand on my knee.

"When have you ever heard me sing anyway?" It's not like I was in a sing song kind of mood during the time I lived with him.

He shrugs. "After Dillan was born you started humming and singing. It was wonderful for a while as it showed that you were happy again, to a certain extent at least."

"Oh." I shift my knee to the side so his hand slides onto the seat and stare out of the window. "I miss my little man."

Nathan moves his hand away and rubs it against his own thigh for a moment.

We're driving for twenty minutes before we pull up outside of a large building I don't recognize. It looks to be like some kind of Chinese restaurant, very fancy and it definitely holds the typical Chinese restaurant theme.

He helps me out of the car and leads me through the doors, where we're instantly led to a private table in a room that's absolutely beautiful. There's a fountain in the corner and the room is filled with plants and tiny trees I don't know the name of. The table we're seated at is only a foot off the ground. I guess we're sitting on the padded floor then.

"This is great." I smile and take in the scenery and sounds. "I didn't even know this place existed."

"Really? I'm surprised Caleb didn't bring you. Before he met you, this was one of the first places we dined when we came to this area with our father. They do authentic Chinese food, none of the stuff you get at a regular takeout. It's delicious."

"Caleb didn't like Chinese food as far as I'm aware." I shrug a little. "We had it sometimes but all he'd eat was the chow mein. Although, if you say this isn't that kind of food, it makes no sense that he wouldn't bring me here."

Nathan looks at me, his teeth worrying his lip. "He made friends with the staff a few years back. Maybe they had a fall out and he didn't fancy a confrontation."

Maybe. It's just a restaurant; it's not a big deal.

Still...

"I'll let you order for me." I give him control over my food for once, mostly because I don't have a clue what's on the menu. It's all stuff I've never heard of.

He nods and presses a button on the corner of the table. Seconds later the door opens and in walks a very friendly woman with a notepad. Nathan orders quickly before waving her away. It's barely a minute before she returns with our drinks. I'm glad to see they're just glasses of water and fresh juice. If he'd ordered alcohol I wouldn't be pleased. Now that I think of it, I've never seen Nathan drink. I don't remember there being any alcohol in his house either.

"So," I curl my legs beneath me and stare across at Nathan, who is sat with one leg beneath him and the other knee pointing at the ceiling. His arm is resting on the ground, keeping his torso lifted. I've never seen him so casual. Well, as casual as one can be in a suit. "What's the occasion?" I motion to the room and give him a questioning look.

His words come instantly after mine finish. "I'm sorry."

"What?"

"I'm sorry for... everything that happened before. You didn't deserve the treatment I gave you."

Okay, that's shocking. I'm not entirely sure what to say. "I forgive you?"

"Are you asking me if you should forgive me?" He smiles; it's mischievous and slightly alluring.

"No, I just wasn't sure what to say." My admission makes his smile falter. I look away and thumb at the mat beneath my legs, making the straw-like material fray slightly. "Do we talk about it?"

Out of the corner of my eye I see him tense. "I'd rather we didn't."

"Of course. But maybe we should."

He tenses further. "If it's about what you... what you saw, then don't. I really..." He exhales a shuddering breath and closes his eyes for a moment.

I can only imagine what he sees in the darkness of his mind. "So, this thing with you and Eric. I thought you said you weren't dating anyone."

Smooth change Nathan, I'm impressed. "Yes, I did say that."

He quirks a brow at me, "And?"

"And he persuaded me to change my mind." We both look away once more, almost as if saving each other from the emotions in our eyes. Mine are confusion and sorrow, two emotions I've felt quite regularly as of late.

"Persuaded you how?" His voice is barely a breath, his eyes watch the falling water not too far behind me.

"How do you think?" I snap, running my fingers through the roots of my hair.

The door opens, stopping him from responding. Trays of food in small dishes are placed before us. I'm relieved to see forks next to the chop sticks. I can't figure out chopsticks at all.

"You were right, this is delicious." I say around my first bite and groan a little. Nathan, who is now sat comfortably in front of his food, tucks in and nods his agreement. "It's not as good as your food though. I've missed that. I guess I became used to having dinner waiting for me when I arrived home."

I'm startled by his admission but I don't say anything. It's his fault he's missed out on that. As much as I'd like to pardon the way he behaved, I still lay a little of the blame on him. He reacted out of fear and anger. I understand that, but he still behaved like a dickhead and I can't so easily forget that. So I remain silent and continue eating.

"That's not the only thing I've missed." He adds a few minutes later. His voice is quiet, almost as if he doesn't want me to hear him but can't stop himself from telling me. "I've never liked living with another, not even my family as I was growing up. As you can imagine, I wasn't much of a people person after…" He trails off, but I know what he's referring to. The abuse that no doubt twisted him into the man he is now. He's not a bad man, just a… what's the word? Different maybe? Well, he's definitely different. "You forced me to take another look at my life, Guinevere." Our eyes meet, a silent connection forming between us. My eyes burn slightly as I think back to the pain he's been through and the pain he's forced on me due to his own sufferings. "You made me happy."

My breath catches and a choked sob escapes me. I don't know why I'm crying. Relief that he's here maybe, or memories of the hurt and the ache

I felt on his behalf. Memories of that small boy being hurt so badly, the same small boy I see in the shadow of vulnerability that comes across his gorgeous, almost chocolate brown eyes.

"Gwen." His voice is pained. He moves around the table in an instant and pulls me into his arms. I cling to his chest and let it out, my hands fisting in his shirt, no doubt creasing it. I don't care.

In one swift move he's cradling me on his lap as I cry into his neck. One hand combs through my hair as the other grips my ribs. "Don't cry." His hoarse voice only makes me cry harder.

"I want to resurrect him and kill him, Nathan." I sob and pull away slightly so I can see his face. "I would honestly commit murder if he were alive. I hate him so much." My anger pierces through my sorrow for him. Questions fill my mind; questions I know he won't appreciate but I have to ask. "How did your parents not know?" He looks away as I pull back in an attempt to make eye contact.

"Don't." He begs, pulling me back to him whilst rocking slightly.

Using my hands on his chest, I break free of his firm hold. "No, it just... why didn't you say anything? Why didn't anyone protect you?" Deep breath. "I don't mean this in a horrible way but it's not like it isn't obvious that you're hurting. Especially with the..." I motion to his hands and he winces. "Issues you have. If Dillan suddenly hated being touched or hated using his hands, I'd wonder why." He doesn't answer. I search his face but read nothing. "They didn't know... did they?"

"Not that I'm aware of." He clears his throat and shifts on the spot. "Can we please not talk about this; it's making me mildly uncomfortable."

I shake my head. "I know and I'm sorry. It just doesn't make sense to me." God, I hate his parents. "Why didn't you tell anybody?" Placing my hand on his cheek, I smooth my thumb over the soft skin beneath his eye. "Did Caleb know?"

"Caleb rarely stayed at our grandfather's. Now... can we please stop this?" Seeing the shattered look on his face forces my conscience to pull my lips back together.

I sigh and press my face into his neck. If he won't talk about it then I'm going to make one thing clear. "I don't want you in that house anymore. Not on your own. How can you stand it?"

"Hush." He soothes and brushes my tears from my cheeks with the back of his bare knuckles after removing his gloves. "No more. We're supposed to be having fun."

I let out a half laugh half sob and sniff unattractively. "Sorry. I've got it. I'll hold it together."

"You don't ever have to keep anything inside, not from me. I just don't want your tears to be because of something that happened so long ago. He doesn't deserve them." He whispers and presses his lips to my head. "Stand. I want to dance with you."

Blinking in shock, I pull back and look at him. "Dance?"

"Yes."

"There's no music." I point out and wipe my face on a napkin, cringing when the white comes back tinged with black from my running mascara.

He shrugs off his jacket and places his phone on the table. Music instantly starts humming from the speakers and laughter escapes me. I don't know what the song is, but it sounds beautiful. It's not in English and is very soft and slow. Perfect to dance to with a romantic partner. Which is why this has suddenly become awkward.

Nathan guides me closer with his hand holding mine. My chest touches his and his jaw rests at my temple. His hand clasps mine between us, so I can feel the frantic beat of his heart against the back of my fingers.

At first I felt awkward but now I feel relaxed, almost as if I could fall asleep resting against him as he moves us back and forth. I close my eyes and allow myself this moment of peace. I allow myself this moment of emotion and feeling.

"You're a good dancer." I say softly, still moving with him in perfect synchrony.

He smiles slightly, almost as if wanting to withhold the glee he feels at my words. "I've never danced."

What? "Never?" I almost choke. He can't be serious.

"I've never done much of anything. I've watched a lot of TV and movies though." He gives a small shrug, looking almost embarrassed by this admission.

"Huh, I can't even tell. So... what made you decide to try it now?"

He pales and I can almost see the cogs working in his head. Letting out a long breath, he looks up to the ceiling for a moment. "When I was a young boy, I never had the desire to do much of anything." I can imagine. I keep the pity from shining through my eyes for fear of destroying this moment. "It was the same when I was growing. I felt better secluding myself from people, for fear of them looking through me and seeing the truth."

"The truth?"

"The truth of what I was allowing my grandfather to do to me." He clears his throat and runs his tongue over his lower lip for a moment. I remain silent, waiting for him to continue even though his words make no sense. He wasn't allowing his grandfather to do anything. Does he truly believe his own words? He continues. "I thought I was happy, wallowing in my own pity and loathing. The loathing was so fierce that I began to hate the world, not only myself and my grandfather."

"Go on." I prompt kindly, letting him know I'm listening and not judging in any way.

"It turns out, I'd never even felt happiness, never let myself feel it. Until recently."

I can't stop the smile that comes forth, nor can I stop the assumption. "Dillan?"

"No." He whispers and my heart drops. "You."

My heart soars. I press my forehead to his neck again and inhale deeply. I fit so perfectly here. He always smells so fresh and clean; it's soothing. "When?"

He doesn't answer, only pulls my hand back to his chest and holds it there, still rocking me to the gentle tune. "Thank you for forgiving me. Everything I've done..."

"Hey." I cut him off, my brows pushing together. "I get it. Please don't apologise. I should never have given up on you. I never should have walked away, even when you forced me to."

"I'm glad you did."

"What?"

"If you hadn't, I might not have realised just how much I now crave human contact. Your contact." Gulp. "Physical and emotional. You bring out a part in me that never existed."

Eye roll. "It always existed; it just needed a little coaxing to the surface."

"You never gave up on me, not fully. I know that now, but at the time it felt like you were. Even though I was the one to push you away, part of me died when you left and didn't return." He runs the back of his knuckles over my cheek. Our bodies have stopped moving to the rhythm, but my heart only seems to beat to a faster tempo. "You have no idea how much you mean to me."

My breath catches. I remain silent, allowing him this moment and gentle touch.

"I don't even have an idea of how much you mean to me." He laughs lightly, his frustration over something I'm unsure of abundantly clear. "I'll never hurt you again. Not intentionally. It's just that... I was so ashamed of how I behaved and ashamed of my past, I thought you'd hate me and I got used to that. So I kept trying to push you away, out of protectiveness or out of embarrassment, I'm not sure, but I don't want to anymore."

Turning my face into his soothing caress, I close my eyes and absorb this moment, willing it to stay put in my memory forever. "I know. And... umm... ditto."

He chuckles, his lips lightly skimming my temple. "Come. You need your rest. I'll escort you to your mum's."

Oh... right, the other thing I noticed. "Why do you always say 'to my mum's'? It's my place too."

"No it isn't." I'm pretty certain it is. "Your home is with me."

"Are you...?"

"I'm not getting ahead of myself; I'm merely stating a fact. Or maybe I'm stating it the wrong way around." He dips his head, his nose running along the side of mine. "My home is with you and Dillan."

Why does most of me agree? I shouldn't be agreeing. "We do make a rather good team."

"That we do. I want you to come back." That sweet vulnerability shines through. I love seeing this side of Nathan, but I also hate it because he's no longer guarded and I get a glimpse of the sweet child inside that never got to be.

And I'm about to crush whatever hope he has. "I can't."

"You can." He starts moving us again. "We will collect your things and bring you back to my home."

Shaking my head, I say it again. "I can't."

"You can."

"No, Nathan." I go to pull away, but he holds me tighter.

"Please."

"And what happens the next time I do something to upset you? That's not fair on me or Dillan."

"I won't behave that way again. I swear to you." His unguarded eyes search mine. His hand comes up to brush the hair from my face as I tilt it back to look up at him through my lashes. My hands fist in his shirt; I'm not sure whether I want to push him away or hold him closer. "Please, Guinevere."

"No. I'm sorry but I have a life here." This time he does release me, his arms dropping to his sides. My fingers keep hold of his shirt. He's going to walk away again, proving my fears to be true. He's going to break his promise before it even had a chance to begin. "I can't go back with you."

"Then what if I come here?"

Snort. "Don't be..."

"I'm serious. I can't... lose you again. My life is meaningless without you."

"No it isn't." Why does he think these things about himself?

"It is." He implores, his jaw set. "I want you home with me. I want Dillan home with me."

"Why?"

"Why?" He seems shocked that I can even ask that.

Huff. "Yes, why?"

"Because."

"Because of what?"

"You make me happy."

My brow quirks. "Until you're angry."

"I just swore I wouldn't..."

I cut him off, finally releasing his shirt. "I know, and I want to believe you. Part of me wants to go back but... I don't think I can live there, not now I know what you've been through."

He takes a step back, almost as if I've kicked him. "Then I'll buy a new house, a nicer one, and we'll live there."

"That's not healthy. We don't need to live together!"

"Why not?" Now he's affronted. Great. This isn't going well.

"Because of everything that's happened between us. I can't trust you not to lose it again."

"Can you blame me? I was... disgusted that I'd tainted..."

Turning away from him, I throw my hands in the air, wanting to curse to the sky. "Stop acting like any of this is your fault. It's driving me mad!"

"Gwen, please, come home with me."

My mind is set and when it's set, that's that. "No."

"Is this because of Eric?" He growls, his chest now against my back. "Do you want him?"

I gasp and spin to face him, my annoyance evident. "That's what you think?"

"It seems suspicious timing. Your relationship with him, what is it?" His eyes narrow before widening.

Oh crap. "So what if I do?" I respond haughtily and inwardly kick myself. I don't want Eric. I don't want anybody.

His hands run through his hair, his shock as clear as the sky above. "Do... do you want him?"

"That's the whole point of dating, isn't it? To find out whether or not you want somebody."

"I see I've made another error." he bites out, glaring openly at me now. "I'll leave you to your life, Guinevere."

Eye roll. "It's not like you haven't before."

"I think this excuse is a justifiable one. Have you forgotten Caleb already? My brother."

Oh, he didn't. But he did. "You... you..." My eyes burn, my anger now forgotten. "Christ, you really know how to make me hate you."

"Have you fucked him?" He demands, ignoring my sorrow and guilt. Strong hands grip my biceps, his face is now inches from mine. "Have you?"

"And if I have?"

He staggers away from me, seeming to be in pain. "You hardly know him."

"I know him enough."

"I'll call you a taxi." He spits after a moment of staring at me like he's never seen me before.

"Good." I snap and walk towards the exit.

Something smashes. I don't get to look and see as I'm being grabbed from behind. I hate being pulled along like a dog on a lead.

"Will you stop dragging me places? It's irritating!" I stomp my foot to emphasise my point.

Nathan looks at me, almost as if looking at me for the first time and not liking what he sees. "How could you sleep with him, Gwen?"

"Well, there wasn't much sleeping involved. There was plenty of..."

CHAPTER SIX

His hand clamps over my mouth. I don't tell him I'm lying. I don't want to. If he's going to assume then I'll let him. "Don't say it."

"Say what? I don't see how it's any of your business what I do and don't do."

"Why him? Why now?" He snarls, his face an inch from my own, his hands now gripping my arms. Why him? Why now? What's he talking about?

"Let go of me." I shout and shove him with as much strength as I can muster. He only moves back a step. "Are you insane?"

"Are you?" He bellows back, his face turning red from the strain.

We both stand and stare at each other. Nothing can be heard but the heavy breaths escaping us and the tinkling of the fountain only a few feet away. I shake my head with a sigh. "And you honestly expected me to move back with you?"

"What?" His face softens, his eyes widening slightly with realisation. "If there were ever a good time to curse, now would be that time."

"Yeah." I laugh humourlessly and scoop my bag off the ground. "Agreed. And no, I haven't even kissed Eric, let alone anything else. I'm sorry for making you believe otherwise."

"Good." He blurts and reaches for me, but I step out of reach. "I'd like to go home now, Nathan."

He blinks as if shocked. "Home?"

"I have a headache." It's the truth too; my head is pounding. "You should get back to Dillan."

He runs his tongue over his lips and looks up at the ceiling for a few moments. Brown eyes meet mine. "I'm sorry. I overreacted again. I'm not used to not getting my own way."

"Don't worry. I'm fortunately used to your mood swings."

"You shouldn't have to be." He mumbles, his fingers rubbing at his eyes. "I'm sorry, Gwen. Truly. I'm not good at this."

"Good at what?"

"This, whatever this is."

"Right now," I wave a hand between us, "this is nothing. I promised myself I'd hold my tongue, I'd try to reason with you gently when you get like this, but I'm going back on that. You can't keep doing this. I want to empathise, I really do. I genuinely want to understand you, but don't think for one minute that I'll take your crap anymore. You don't get to talk to me like that just because I've annoyed you."

He gapes at me, shocked by my outburst.

I continue, "You need to decide whether or not we're friends and what it is you want."

We stare at each other for a long moment. It feels like minutes pass before I finally turn away and move towards the door.

"I want you to come home with me." He says calmly, almost pleadingly.

"You've said that; I've declined."

"I want you both back in my life permanently."

Sigh. "And I want you back in ours. Trust me, you have no idea how much I've missed you. You have no idea the pain I've felt on your behalf from knowing what I now know about you." Wincing slightly, he looks away. I really need to stop bringing it up; it's all just so fresh to me. It's hard not to bring it up because I'm constantly being tortured by it. "I'm here if you need me, for anything. I care about you, but keep this up and I won't bother. Honestly, missing you hurts a lot less than hearing your cold tone and witnessing your anger towards me over nothing." I'm bluffing. I'm not sure there's anything he can do that would make me never want to see him again. I shouldn't threaten him like this. I feel guilty. Although, he's done it to me…maybe it's time to turn the tables to knock some sense through his thick skull.

"I'll do better." He says quickly, taking a step towards me. "I swear it."

His words put me at ease. My stresses seep away as I stare into his sincere eyes. "Me too." I smile and walk over to him. He drops his hands to his sides. They quickly come back up again when I wrap my arms around his back and press my face into his chest. "Are we done fighting now? Are we in agreement?"

I swear I hear him grit his teeth, although his body doesn't tense like it usually does so maybe I'm imagining things. "For the moment."

He throws money onto the table before we leave. We move through the restaurant in silence, him never more than two steps behind. When I stop suddenly, he collides into my back, his hands coming up to grip my arms in an attempt to steady us both.

"Oh my god." I gasp and stare at the couple kissing in the corner like teenagers in the back of a car.

"Isn't that your mum?" Nathan enquires. I hear the smile in his voice.

"Who the hell is that guy?" I hiss and dart towards the exit before she looks up and sees. "And why has she never brought me here before?" I thought she was working.

Nathan starts chuckling as I cup my hands around my face and look through the window. His arm rests along my shoulders before he slowly guides me away. "Stop it."

"What are the chances? Caleb always did say I always seemed to be in the right place at the right time."

Nathan leads me to the car, my shock at the disgusting scene I just witnessed clouding my judgement. I'm pretty sure I was angry with him a moment ago. Now I'm fighting the urge to vomit. "What do you want to do? We'll do anything."

"Really?" I'm sceptical. I've never heard those words from Nathan's mouth. Plus, wasn't he just telling me I need my rest? Confusing male. "Anything?"

He gives me a pointed look, "Within reason."

"Yay."

He glances at me out of the corner of his eye. "Did you just say... yay?"

"What of it?" Chin up. "A lot of people say yay."

"I'm certain they don't." He's teasing me.

"Shut up."

His finger and thumb pinch my hip, making me yelp and rub the sore spot dramatically. "So, where to?"

"There's one place I haven't been for a long time." I admit and stare across the car park as memories surface. "I'd like to go. I haven't dared since..."

He suddenly looks very nervous, I notice as he guides me to his car. "Where?"

"The beach." I say with a shrug and wait for him to climb into the driver's side. "Want to?"

"No." He immediately responds, making me frown.

"Why not?"

"I don't... enjoy sand." Oh, the weird phobia he seems to have I assume.

"You won't be touching it."

"It'll be touching me; sand gets everywhere." He has a point.

With my lower lip sticking out, I give him the largest, cutest, puppy dog eyes I can manage. If I can just get him to try, maybe I can help him beat it. Or is that naïve of me to think so? "Please?"

His eyes suddenly become fearful. "Oh not that. Anything but that." I pout even more, even going as far as to rub my temple on his shoulder like a cat. "Stop!" He laughs, nudging at my head. "You're being very childish."

"Please, please, please."

"No."

"You're smiling." I lean back and point at his face, burning his glittering brown eyes and smiling lips to my memory. He has very nice teeth and even though I've noted this before, I note it again. "That means it's not a definite no."

"No means a definite no." He snorts and flicks my cheek. Ouch. "Let's do something else."

I grin eagerly and blurt. "Ice-skating!"

"Honestly, Gwen, you have such terrible taste in fun."

"And you have no taste." I bite back, pouting once more. "You said anything; it's either the beach or the ice. Pick one, pretty boy."

"Pretty boy?" His brow quirks almost adorably. He looks horrified.

"Yes, you're very pretty."

"Now you're just being insulting."

"And you're being difficult."

"I'm far from pretty; that's not being difficult."

This is fun. "What would you prefer to be called?"

He looks at me like I'm stupid. "Nathan wouldn't go amiss, or maybe even the devilishly handsome, master in …"

"Don't even finish that sentence. It'll make everything awkward and weird and I'll suddenly start imagining you in ways I shouldn't, against my will." I see his body shake before I hear his laughter. His head falls forward onto his arms as he roars with it. I'm startled. Do I laugh with him or stare in amazement? Both, according to my body. "I don't even know why I'm laughing."

"And here's me always thinking of you as the shy, polite and slightly virginal Gwen." He manages to get out after breathing deeply for a moment. "I was going to say Master in getting his own way, but your thoughts sound much more interesting."

"You can't be a master in *that* area. I almost forgot… you don't give oral." I remark boldly and pinch my lips together to stop myself from smiling.

His laughter gets loud again. "Yes and after seeing what comes out of that area, I don't think my mouth would appreciate the company."

Oh my god, he didn't just say that. "Stop it. I'm going to get crow's feet by the morning."

"You have a beautiful laugh." Aww, swoon. "It's a shame your singing is so bad."

"So first you insult my vagina and now my singing? You have a strange way of asking for forgiveness." I snap playfully and ruffle his hair so his longish locks go from neat to messy.

He grins at me, his eyes twinkling, looking boyish with his messy hair and easy smile. "Do we really have to ice skate?" His face is now very serious and his tone is almost whiney. I've never heard this tone from him. I like discovering new things about him.

"Yes."

"I'm never asking you what you want to do again."

"I'm female."

He quirks a brow, finally starting the car at the same time. "What does that have to do with anything?"

"You'll always ask me what I want to do, because I'm female and it's your job to keep me happy."

"Is that so?" He runs his tongue over his lower lip and places his hand over mine.

"Yep." I give a firm nod and look down at his hand over mine that's resting on my thigh. "You need to get back to Dillan though and I doubt anywhere is open for ice skating at this time."

After a moment he sighs and nods his agreement. "I'll take you home."

"To my whore of a mother." I add, making him chuckle as I shudder in disgust at the public display of way too much affection I saw back there.

"She's just enjoying her life."

"It's sickening to see. Why would she hide that though?"

He shrugs, thinking on it for a moment before saying something that makes way too much sense. "Maybe she's worried, with everything that's happened to you these past twelve months, that seeing her happy will make you feel like your life isn't." He cringes. "I didn't explain that right."

"I know what you mean. You're right I think. I thought she'd been working way too many hours recently. I feel bad that she's had to tiptoe around me. Am I really that depressive?"

"No, but she is your mum and she obviously cares about how you feel."

"Maybe." I say around a yawn and snuggle into my seat. "Thanks for driving all of this way to see me, Nathan. I've had fun, despite the arguing."

He smiles softly, his hand tightening on mine for a second. "Good."

"What's going on with your store? I thought it was ready to go?"

He tenses and shifts, quickly removing his hand from mine to change gear. "It is. I've just not been as enthusiastic about it as of late."

"Why?" I know my tone is snippy, but I don't care. I remember how happy he was organising the store for opening. I'd never seen him so invested in anything before.

"I'd say the answer to that is obvious." He snaps right back. "You were one of the main reasons I was opening it in the first place."

Blink. "That's just stupid. It made you happy."

"You made me happy."

"And you're emotionally incapable of receiving joy from anything else?"

"When your heart is broken because you've lost the only thing you've ever loved, then yes. It's actually extremely difficult to find joy in anything other than the bottom of a bottle of bourbon." He bites out and we both fall silent, both of us holding our breath.

"Nathan..."

"Don't." He pleads, his tone not angry or snappy but pleading.

I quickly close my mouth and stare ahead, my heart pounding at this revelation. He's never said he loves me, never. Now what do I do?

When we arrive home, Nathan climbs out and walks around to my side. I wait for him to open my door for me; it's a habit. He holds out his hand. I take it and slide from my seat, before facing him, trying to understand him by the way he's holding his body. He's very tense but is giving nothing away.

"I'll be back with Dillan the day after tomorrow." He says after a few very long seconds and closes the door. "Sleep well."

I rush to the front door before I say something stupid, although I'm not entirely sure what words are sitting on the end of my tongue. I just know I shouldn't say them. Pulling it open, I race inside and lean against it when it closes behind me. My body refuses to move from this spot until I hear his car disappear into the distance.

My phone vibrates in my pocket and I pull it out expecting it to be Nathan. It's not, it's Eric.

Eric: Breakfast tomorrow?

Should I? No I shouldn't.

Gwen: Sure :)
But I say yes and I have no idea why.

Chapter Seven

"Good morning," I say to my mum, avoiding her eyes so she doesn't see my discomfort over knowing she still makes out with guys like a teen in public places.

"You're up early." She remarks with a smile as her eyes scan me up and down. "You look nice too."

"I'm going out for breakfast with Eric." I tell her as I pour a glass of water and sip it slowly. "Was work okay last night?"

"Same old." Vague answer.

"Cool." We both stare at each other, nodding our heads slightly.

The knock at the door breaks our awkward silence. "That'll be Eric."

"Yep." I dart into the hall and pull open the door. There he stands, looking handsome and happy. "Hi."

"Well hello there." He grins and swoops in for a hug. The contact shocks me. I'm not sure what to do with it, so I place my hands on his shoulders as my feet dangle a few inches from the ground. "You look gorgeous."

"Thanks." I mutter, my stupid cheeks heating again. Stupid body responses. "Where are we going?"

"McDonald's." He says with a straight face only inches from mine. "I'm kidding. There's a breakfast café on the high street that I love. I thought we could go there."

"I need my feet on the ground if I'm to go anywhere," I laugh and he immediately drops me with an embarrassed smile. "You're so light, I forgot I had you."

"Dork." I jest as he leads me to his car. I climb in myself and wait for him to start the engine and back out of the driveway before starting conversation. "So, how have you been since I saw you yesterday?"

"I had a dream last night."

"Do I want to know about it?"

"It involved a dragon and cakes."

"I don't want to know about it." I giggle when his face drops in shock.

"You're mean."

"I'm female."

He looks me up and down. "I don't know, maybe I should check." With a squeal I slap his groping hand away, slapping him on the arm twice for good measure when he laughs loudly and proudly.

"Nice boobs."

"Pig."

"Are they real?" I know he's joking, but I still scowl at him and look the other way. "Maybe I should check again."

"Stop!" I order on a laugh and push his hand away. "You're going to make us crash. Pay attention."

"Aww." He whines, his lower lip sticking out. "What about if I stop the car?"

"You're not touching my boobs."

"Boring."

Eye roll. "Typical man."

"But I'm cute so it's fine." He gives me a cheek showing me those dimples I seem to enjoy seeing. "You didn't agree with me."

Shrug. "I mustn't tell lies."

"Just for that I'm not taking you to breakfast." He says as he parks between two cars behind the small shopping centre. "You can stay here and starve."

We climb out of the car and make our way through the precinct. It only takes a few minutes as it really isn't that big. He wraps his arm around my shoulders to keep me close and leads me onto the high street. I put my shades on to block out the glaring sun and walk comfortably beside him. This is what I should want; this is what is right.

So why does it feel so wrong?

And why does the thought of seeing Nathan again feel so right?

We order the full breakfast. It's far too much food for me, but it looks amazing. "So, have you always been into baking?" Eric asks, making polite small talk.

"Yes, I took a culinary course in University." I respond, swallowing my mouthful first. "What about you? I don't think I've ever asked you what you do."

He smiles. "I'm just a car salesman, nothing fancy. Only took a few weeks of training. Unfortunately I couldn't even make it through college." I notice how he seems ashamed to admit this.

"I had to quit university." I say to make him feel better.

His smile returns. "Rebel."

"Without a clue." I nod, flicking my shades back down and posing with my thumb and forefinger along my jaw.

He laughs loudly, startling the other customers around us. "You're so weird." His eyebrows wag. "I like it."

"I need to be at work in thirty minutes." I say after checking my watch.

"I'll drop you off. I fancy one of those cinnamon swirls." He states and pats his stomach. "I can just tell that being acquainted with you is going to make me fat."

"You could never be fat. You're one of those lucky people that can eat and eat and never put on weight."

He scoffs. "Says you. How old is your son?"

"Four months."

"My mum would hate you. She's still trying to remove her pregnancy weight and my sister is nine now." He chuckles and drains the rest of his coffee.

"You have a nine year old sister?"

"Yep; she's bloody annoying but also remarkably cute and smart when she wants to be. Gullible too, she believed me when I told her that mum found her in the monkey exhibit at the London zoo. It made for an awkward meeting with her teacher at school when my sister got stuck up a tree."

"You're kidding?"

"Nope. She wanted to be one with nature, like her primate ancestors."

"Oh my god!" I gasp, trying not to laugh but failing miserably. "How old was she?"

He quirks a brow and cocks his head to the side. "This was only last month."

I almost spit my tea on him. "That's so funny. You meanie."

"It was totally worth it, until my mum beat me over the head with my cap. I don't wear hats around her anymore because of this reason."

"That's hilarious. I wonder if Dillan will ever be like that."

"Kids are awesome, unless that child is me. My mum said I was the worst child she's ever met. I was always in trouble, or dirty, or falling off things. I broke my collar bone twice before I turned ten and my wrist once when I was eleven."

My mouth falls open. "Seriously? That sounds painful."

"Yep, it wasn't pleasant. I was climbing the tree outside my house trying to look in my neighbour's window. She had..." he cups his hands to his chest. "Amazing boobs. I never thought I'd see better until..." He leans forward, his eyes on my cleavage.

"You're such a pig!" I choke out around another laugh and throw my teaspoon at him. "Was that your initial thought?"

"No, my initial thought was 'who's the idiot that left a ring in my cake?'."

"I don't think I like you anymore."

"And then I saw you and the first thing I noticed was the fact you looked like a female version of Casper. I wondered if maybe you'd rolled yourself in flour. Then I noticed how pretty your eyes are and then..." He holds his finger up and grins wickedly. "I noticed your..." His hands go back to his chest. "Lovely boobs."

"I noticed your dimples."

"That's it?" He feigns offence. "Just my dimples? What about my arse as I was walking away?"

"You have an arse?"

"I've decided I'm not taking you to dinner tomorrow." He responds haughtily, but his dimples remain in place so I know he's joking. "In fact, I'm never taking you anywhere again."

"That's okay. I prefer men with an arse."

He throws his head back and laughs. "You're cold."

"And you're a pervert."

"Yes." His eyes zero in on my chest once more. "Yes I am."

"Going to work." My mum calls and I hear the door close. She only just got home. Does she honestly think I'm that stupid?

I will be talking to her about this male tomorrow after I get Dillan back. It's not fair on her that she has to tiptoe around me to be happy. I want her to be happy; she deserves it.

Nathan: I'll bring Dillan back in a few hours. Setting off shortly, just having lunch first.

Oh crap, I'm supposed to be meeting Eric in a few hours. What do I do?

Gwen: I thought you were having him until tomorrow?

Nathan: I've got to speak with a friend in the morning. He's leaving for Spain in the afternoon. I can't postpone it.

Gwen: Does this mean you'll actually be opening the store? :-D

Nathan: I haven't decided yet. It's not about that. I'll speak to you when I arrive.

Gwen: Would you like me to cook dinner?

It was originally for me and Eric, but I'm going to have to cancel that now. Not that I mind. I should, but I don't.

Nathan: I should say no, but I can't resist. What are you making?

Gwen: French style carbonara and then chocolate shots for dessert.

Nathan: Leaving now.

I laugh and throw my phone on the table, cursing when I realise I have to call Eric and let him know. Unfortunately he doesn't answer. He's probably at work, so I leave him a message and send him a text to tell him how sorry I am. I know I won't get a response until he finishes at three, as he told me yesterday, so I begin preparing dinner for later.

I'm shocked that Sasha still hasn't called, a little annoyed too. I've texted her a few times and never had a response. It's true what they say, you do seem to lose people when you have a baby. I just never thought Sasha and Tommy would vanish off the face of the earth. It's crap.

As expected Eric understands and reschedules for tomorrow night instead. Why do I feel so guilty about this, like I'm cheating on him in some way?

"Hey baby." I squeal and snatch Dillan from Nathan's arms. "I've missed you, yes I have!"

"Hello to you too." Nathan says, but I know he's smiling.

"Yeah, hi." I don't look at him. I continue munching on my baby boy's chubby cheeks. "You feel like you've put on at least a pound." Dillan gurgles at me, his mouth open with a smile. I kiss his open mouth and hold him in one arm. "Mummy has to cook, so you be a good boy and play in your bouncer."

I lay him in his swinging, bouncing and vibrating chair in the living room before turning to Nathan and frowning at him. "He's wearing new clothes."

"I took him shopping." I hate it when he blinks at me like that, his face expressionless.

"He has clothes."

"Well now he has more clothes. Besides, you should have told me you'd opened a new account. I've been putting money into your old one since you left and not a penny of it has been used."

I wave him off. "I lost my card."

"Normal people order a new card."

"I was embarrassed; that's the fifth card I've lost since I met your brother, so I opened a new account at a new bank. I did it when I was living with you. Which reminds me, I really need to change the address." I look him up and down, admiring his dark jeans and white turtleneck. "You look very nice. New clothes for you too?"

"I know you get irritated by my suits at times."

"It's hard to relax in a suit." I point out and lead him into the kitchen.

He rolls his eyes. "How would you know? Have you ever worn one?"

Good point. "That's not the point. You don't look relaxed in a suit."

"Well... I don't like it when you wear those horrid wool cardigans you seem to favour so much."

Gasp. "Those cardigans are lovely!"

"For a hippie." He retorts playfully and leans forward to kiss me on the cheek. "You smell like a bakery."

I shy away. "So I've been told."

"What?"

"Huh?"

"What did you say?" His smiling face is no more, a frown now in its place.

"Nothing, it's just something I get told a lot." I play it off with a happy façade and skip to the prepared food that has been sat in the oven keeping warm for the past few minutes. "Sit. Food is ready."

This seems to distract him. Thankfully. "How has your free time been?"

"Good, nothing to report." I place the plates on the set table and take the seat across from him.

"Is there something you want to tell me?" He asks, his eyes narrowing slightly.

Yes! I'm dating still! And you need to know, so you don't continue to get the wrong idea about us. The wrong idea that you shouldn't get because you are the brother of the love of my life. Which makes it so, so, so wrong.

"No." I look directly into his eyes, my palms flat on the table so my hands don't shake. "Like what?"

Suspicious eyes scan my face for a few more seconds. Why can't I tell him? What's the big deal? Don't I want him to look at me like a friend?

It's because I know that he'll probably never talk to me again and it's not like Eric and I are serious. We haven't even kissed.

I'll tell him if or when that happens. "So, this guy you're meeting tomorrow, that's assuming he's a guy, I'm pretty sure you said he's a guy... right? Anyway, what's that all about? It sounds important. Is it important?"

"You're rambling." He points out, placing his fork on the plate before him. "What's wrong?"

"Nothing." I lie.

"You're lying."

"I don't like the fact you're sending me money." This is another lie but it shocks him enough to not see my quirks that scream 'LIE!'

"Why not?"

"Because… we're not yours to look after and I make enough to provide for us both. You already have Dillan; that's enough."

"It's not much; it's only a hundred a week." This makes me splutter on my water. "I'm responsible for you both."

"No you're not."

"I feel like I am." He doesn't say this with disdain or hate, it's merely a statement.

"But…"

"Stop." He raises his hand and pinches the bridge of his nose with his free hand. "You're giving me a headache. I forgot how frustrating you can be."

Gasp. "You are such an arsehole sometimes."

He smiles, totally unaffected by my tone and insult, which is shocking because he usually goes a tad over the top when I swear. "Yes… well. You bring that out in me."

"Oh no, you don't get to blame me for your mean ways. I'm not frustrating. I'm adorable and funny and fun and…"

"Infuriating."

"Am not."

"Are too."

"Oh, be quiet." I run my fingers through my hair and stare down at my barely touched plate of food. "I'm done."

"You've hardly eaten."

"I'm genuinely not that hungry." I pick up my plate and move it onto the side by the sink. Nathan finishes his in record time, before placing his empty plate by mine and following me into the room where Dillan is now asleep in his swinging chair. "Did you have fun with Dillan? What did you both do?"

"Not much. He had a rough night last night. We both ended up sleeping in until eleven this morning. It was refreshing."

"Great. So, what's going on with this meeting tomorrow?"

He shrugs. "I'm looking to move."

Blink. "Move?"

"Yes."

"To...?" I prompt, hoping for more than that.

"Here, or close to here."

Blink. "Why?"

"Don't look so horrified." He scoffs and lowers himself onto the seat by the door. "I want to be closer to Dillan."

"And me?"

"Well, Dillan does live with you." He rolls his eyes and stares blankly at the powerless TV. "Is that a problem?"

Yes. "No." Screw my polite ways. "I guess I just don't understand."

"What's to understand? I miss you. If you won't come to me, then I'll come to you."

"What about your home?"

He gives me a pointed look. "Did you not listen to a single word I said the last time we spoke about this?"

"I did, I swear, I just... find it hard to believe."

"Why?"

"Because right now you're looking at me like you can't stand the sight of me." His eyes soften immediately at my words. He exhales a long breath, his body sagging with the motion. "Gwen, I never have and never will think that about you."

"Your eyes say different." I stand and make my way to the window. It's just started raining. Not a small amount either, but large heavy droplets falling in millions from the sky. "Are we friends?"

He's silent for a moment. "What kind of a question is that?"

"I'm sure you know what I mean. Are we friends or... do you want more?"

I hear his sharp intake of air. "Gwen... I..." His feet almost silently pad towards me, stopping when I feel his heat against my back. Hands slide up my biceps, causing me to shiver as my skin breaks out in goose bumps. "Do you?"

"Do I what?" I ask, my body stiff and tense as he moves the hair from my neck and runs his nose from the curve to my ear.

"Want more... from me?" His whisper tickles the shell of my ear, sending a burning tingle straight to my core. "Or do you just want to be friends?"

"Friends." I respond automatically and listen to him sigh softly. "Just friends."

"Why?" He asks and rubs my shoulders gently with his fingers and thumbs.

"Because..."

A banging at the door breaks the moment. I pull away and dart from the room, hoping he doesn't see my flushed cheeks and, if he does, I hope he thinks they're from embarrassment and not from arousal.

"Oh my god." I laugh as my mum stumbles inside. "You look like a drowned rat."

"Towel." she shivers.

Still laughing, I race to the cupboard under the stairs and pull out a large bath towel. She pulls her coat off and kicks off her soaking jeans before wrapping it around herself and vanishing up the stairs.

I go back into the living room, still laughing. "Mum's home."

"Okay." He relaxes back into the chair and switches on the TV.

I look at him curiously. "Don't you have to leave? It's getting late."

"Did I not tell you?" He cocks his head, a sneaky smile on his face. "My appointment is in town tomorrow. I thought I'd stay the night."

Blink. "What?"

"Yes, well, it makes sense. You have room."

"I have a couch." I snap, my hands on my hips. "A ten-year-old couch that I know you won't want to sleep on."

He shrugs. "I guess I'll just have to sleep with you."

"What!" I shriek, stumbling backwards into the couch before falling onto it on my arse. "No... no way." My libido can't handle it and it's... well it's not fair on Eric. Right?

"We've slept in a bed together before."

"What?" Great, mum's here.

"Hello." Nathan says to her, his face blank. "I hope you don't mind; Guinevere has invited me to stay for the night. I have a meeting in town tomorrow."

My mum looks at me, as shocked as I feel inside. "No, that's fine of course."

"Thank you, you won't even know I'm here." Nathan winks at me. It's so unlike him.

"I will..."

"What's that?" Nathan asks as my mum tightens her robe around herself and asks. "Tea anyone?"

"Please." Nathan responds before looking at me again. Mum waits for my answer.

"No thank you, Mum." She nods and leaves the room. I glare at Nathan. "Are you crazy?"

He thinks about it for a moment. "Yes."

"You can't stay here."

"Are you going to make me leave?"

Am I? I growl and bring my legs up to my chest. "No."

"Good." He grins and changes the channel on the TV. "It's been a long time since I watched TV, although I usually put the kids' channels on for Dillan. He likes the colours."

I look over at my sleeping son and smile. "Yes, he does. I'll go and get the blankets."

"What for?" Nathan frowns. I can't help but notice how adorably confused he looks.

"So I can sleep on the couch." I respond, standing and stretching my entire body. His eyes go to the bare skin of my midriff as my top rises with my tall stretch. When I relax back to my normal posture, his eyes come to mine. He looks annoyed. "You don't honestly think my mum will let us share a bed, do you?"

"I think she will. I think it's you who has the problem." He waves his hand in the air, as if dismissing me. "Do as you please."

"I shall." A gentleman would never normally allow a female to sleep on a couch, but Nathan won't be able to sleep on here. I understand that. The couch isn't exactly sparkling clean. It's as clean as a couch can be, but it holds stains from long ago that can't be shifted. I should know; I've tried everything.

Mum enters with a silver tray full of snacks and drinks. She places them on the coffee table and passes them out, leaving the biscuits and cakes on the platters. "Thank you." Nathan smiles politely at her and sips his drink. I snigger when he cringes. We share a look, mine of mischief from knowing my mum's tea making abilities are not great, his of scorn when he realises I knew what he'd be accepting.

"Be right back." I sing song and skip from the room.

Dillan starts crying as I'm gathering blankets, but I don't worry. I know my mum or Nathan will deal with him until I return. As expected, Nathan has Dillan on his chest when I return to the room. I place the blankets on the arm of the couch and go to take my son from his uncle, who waves me off.

"Do you want dessert now?" I almost forgot about the chocolate shots I made.

"Yes!" Mum announces and looks at Nathan. "I've been wanting to try these since she started making them yesterday." Fortunately she doesn't mention Eric. My mum can be quite intuitive.

"Yesterday?" Unfortunately, so can Nathan. "Seems a stretch to make dessert."

"I just had them ready yesterday." I shrug, playing it off as nothing.

He eyes me suspiciously. "Expecting company?"

My mum looks at me with a smirk. Yeah, yeah, I know, I mustn't tell lies. "No." Yet I still am. "I just wanted to try my hand at something new."

Nathan stares at me a moment longer before shrugging and turning back to the TV. "I'd love some."

"Great." I rush from the room again and bash my head against the fridge a few times.

It's when I've served pudding and I'm sat down that my phone starts going off. Won't life ever give me a break?

Eric: Hey sweet, are you okay?

Gwen: I'm fine, are you okay?

"This is gorgeous." My mum comments, dipping her spoon into the small chocolate filled glass.

"Definitely." Nathan adds with a smile. "Your phone is flashing."

"Oh." I pick it up off my thigh and read his message.

Eric: I'm good :-) Are you sure we can't do something?

Most definitely not.

Gwen: Sorry :-(

"Who's that?" Mum asks; she's where I got my curiosity from.

"Umm... it's Sasha." Why am I lying?

"Huh." She shrugs and looks back at the TV. My eyes zoom in on Nathan, who is cringing over another sip of his tea.

"You don't have to drink it." I laugh and stand, taking the cup from him. "Mum, next time don't offer to make tea when you know the person who's accepting is too polite to decline and has never tasted your version of tea."

She harrumphs in response and sticks her tongue out at me.

"It's fine." Nathan blanches. I've made him feel uncomfortable now. "I was enjoying that."

"Nobody enjoys Mum's tea. It's okay. I'll make you another." I give him a wink and saunter from the room, cup in hand.

"Well, I like my tea." I hear Mum mutter and smile in the dark.

Eric: That's okay, I understand. Your boy comes first. Speaking of which... when do I get to meet him?

Good question.

Gwen: Soon. What are you doing?

Eric: Crying over a lack of carbonara whilst eating a microwaveable spaghetti ready meal that I'm certain has more plastic than edible ingredients.

Giggle.

Gwen: Cook something then!

Eric: No...

Gwen: Why not?

Eric: Because...

Sigh. Yet I'm smiling.

Gwen: Because...?

Eric: I want carbonara and chocolate shots.

Gwen: I'll make it again for next time.

Eric: But I want it now.

Gwen: Stop being petulant. :-P Text you later xx

Eric: K :-(

"Here." I hand Nathan his tea and sit beside my mum on the couch. He winks at me and rests his lips against the dark fuzz on Dillan's head, his eyes on the TV.

"Well, I'm going to retire to my room." Mum announces around a yawn and stands abruptly. She grabs the tray and her empty cup and leaves the room, only calling goodnight before her footsteps can be heard on the stairs.

Nathan looks at me, almost expectantly.

My eyebrows rise of their own accord. If I had fur, it would be sticking up defensively. "What?"

He grins, a mischievous smile that really suits him, before looking away at the TV. "Nothing."

I take this moment to make my bed on the couch as he carefully places Dillan back in his swinging chair. He joins me, smoothing the sheet over the seat cushions at the bottom end whilst I handle the top.

"Movies and blankets." He nods thoughtfully. Sounds like a good night.

"I'm going to get ready for bed." If we're watching a movie downstairs, I want to be comfortable.

After pulling on my favourite peach coloured, satin nightgown and pulling my hair from the bun atop my head, I pad downstairs and snuggle under the blanket on the couch. Nathan joins me, sitting only a few inches away. Curling my legs beneath me, I rest my elbow on the arm of the couch and my cheek on my fist.

"What are we watching?" I ask, glancing at my son who's sleeping in his swinging chair, his mouth suckling at nothing but air every few seconds.

"I'm not sure. How do I get to movie channels on this TV?" He frowns in concentration, pressing numerous buttons on the remote control but coming up with nothing but menu options.

I laugh and snatch it from him. "We don't have movie channels. Dork. We have Freeview."

"Oh." He licks his lower lip. "Shall I go to the shop and rent something?"

"No." I shake my head, still smiling, and search through my mum's recorded shows and movies. "We'll watch this."

Nathan settles back into the couch and looks at me. "Really?"

"Nothing wrong with 'What to Expect When You're Expecting'."

"I can think of many things wrong with this movie."

"Oh stop moaning." I giggle and nudge his thigh with my foot. He rolls his eyes and shifts closer to me. After another moment he does it again. I eye him curiously through my lashes. Another few minutes pass and he moves again, his thigh now against my foot and rear. "Are you going to yawn, stretch and put your arm around me too?"

"Huh?" He looks genuinely perplexed. Does he think I'm stupid and wouldn't notice him shuffling closer? Or does he genuinely not realise what he's done?

Anyway... the movie has started.

"So, tell me what I've missed. We haven't really had a chance to speak properly." Nathan interjects, destroying the peaceful silence between us. Not that I mind.

"Not much to tell. I got a job, which is tiring but I love it; I made new friends in my co-workers and seem to have lost my old friends."

"I'm sorry to hear that."

"Don't be." I wave him off, ignoring the sour taste in my mouth that lingers after thinking about Sasha and Tommy. "Are you hungry?"

"Not really. I'll be surprised if you're not. You hardly touched your food."

I give him a pointed look, "I lose my appetite when stressed."

"I'm assuming you'd like me to apologise?"

"Only if you mean it."

He gives a nod, his lower lip pouting slightly as he thinks. "Okay then."

After he looks back to the TV, I wait for his apology. Then I wait some more. And more. "Ahem."

"Yeah?" Blinking, he turns back to me, his face wearing a secret smile.

"My apology?"

"What for?"

Grr. "For…" Good point, why was I angry again? "For stressing me out."

"My reasons were legitimate. Your arguments were nothing more than defensive and completely ridiculous."

He didn't. Oh… but he did. "You arse."

"See? Defensive and ridiculous." Oh, he looks so proud of himself right now.

"I'm not biting. I'm going to sit here and watch this movie in silence. If you need me, I'm not interested." I sit up straight, my feet now on the ground. This movement forces us to separate a few inches. He instantly shuffles closer, a smirk on his face. I move into the corner, but he follows. Now I'm squished.

Letting out a loud sigh, I slap my hands on top of the blanket before folding my arms over my chest and glaring at the TV. Stupid male jerk.

"Problem?" He moves even closer. Any more and he'll be on my lap, or I will be on his. "You seem uncomfortable."

I blank him, keeping my eyes pointed ahead, pretending I'm watching the movie when I'm not. I'm too busy trying to ignore his hand, which is now on my thigh beneath the blanket, his fingers trailing lazy circles along the bare skin. My breath hitches when his hand moves up a few inches, only a short distance from my core. No doubt he can feel the heat on the side of his pinkie finger and palm. It remains there, still trailing lazy circles.

Like the whore that I am, a shiver runs through me and my legs twitch, eager to separate further, hoping to feel his hands on me there. I clamp them shut, my heart hammering and my breaths shortening with each intake.

"Problem?" He whispers directly into my ear. I shudder at the feel of his breath touching the shell. A riot of blissful cells attack my spine as they fight their way to my entrance. When they settle in my stomach, I bite my lip and close my eyes.

Forcing my eyes open, they widen instantly when I see how close Nathan actually is. His face is an inch from mine. Leaning closer, he runs his nose along the side of mine and brushes his bottom lip ever so lightly against my top one.

This is wrong. What's he doing? What am I doing?

His hand slides up and up finally his pinkie finger rests against the soft fabric of my lady boxers. "Oh god." I breathe when he puts pressure there, almost cupping me but not quite. My head falls back and my legs part. Nathan's free hand cups my cheek; my hand grabs it at the wrist and my eyes come to his. He waits for a moment, scanning my face for my reaction.

Stop it! Get away! This isn't right!

But my head moves forward until our lips only gently skim each other. His breathing quickens and he shifts in his seat, getting a better angle. He swaps his hands, the one between my legs now gripping the back of my neck and the one that was holding my cheek is now holding my heated mound, which is almost unbearably wet.

I'm such a slut.

Heated eyes hold mine as we both go to kiss each other but never quite make it, our mouths teasing the other with skims and light touches. I sit up straighter, my hand gripping the top of his shirt. He smiles slightly, triumph clear in his eyes. I don't care. I feel warm. Too warm. And desperate. So very desperate to be filled, to be held, to be touched.

"Forgot my charger." And the moment's lost.

Nathan shoots to the other end of the couch, his stance casual as my mum enters the room. I blink out of my daze, sitting ramrod straight and looking anything but casual. Mum quickly grabs her charger. She gives me a look and I know she's seen a lot. Too much in fact.

I look away, feeling like a teenager again. "Goodnight." she calls and vanishes into the dark hallway.

Letting out a breath, I look at Nathan when I feel his eyes on me. He holds out a hand, the top side flat on his lap, inviting me to go to him once more.

I shake my head and stand. "I should get Dillan to bed. It's late."

Nathan sighs, his disappointment clear, "Okay Guinevere."

Taking my son, I do just that, going slow with every single step that getting Dillan ready for bed requires, from his nappy to his pyjamas.

When I go back downstairs, Nathan is in flannel pyjama bottoms and a white vest. He's also fast asleep on his front on the couch. I pull the quilt to his shoulders and run my fingers through his longish hair. When he sighs in his sleep, I leave him alone and retire to my bedroom.

What the hell did I just do? If my mum hadn't come in… I dread to think.

It takes me a while to fall asleep as is expected. Once my brain has finished over analysing every small detail regarding Nathan, without getting any answers as per usual, it finally allows me the rest I need.

An hour later Dillan wakes up. I feed him and fall instantly back to sleep but, when I do, warmth hits my back. I'm too far gone into the land of slumber to question who, why, how and what is behind me.

Chapter Eight

"We need to talk." Mum snaps after I see Nathan to the door.

Did he?

"Not now." I grumble and place my coffee in the microwave. This morning hasn't been a good one. It didn't help that I woke up sprawled all over Nathan, who seemed to be watching me whilst I slept, his fingers combing through my hair.

Yep, that didn't go down too well. Not with me, but with my mum, who caught Nathan in bed with me and has obviously assumed the worst.

I got up, got dressed and fed Dillan as Nathan got dressed and apologised to my mum without explanation. He had to leave for his meeting. I didn't utter a word to him before he left, even though he tried talking to me. Instead he followed me to the door, kissed my forehead and muttered goodbye, to which I grunted in response.

My mum, after slamming my bedroom door without saying a word, stomped downstairs and into the kitchen. Now I've got to deal with her and I don't want to.

"Have you stopped seeing Eric?" She snaps, her hands on her hips and her eyes angry. "Because last I checked you were both still dating?"

Oh god. "I know, Mum."

"What are you thinking?" She sighs, clearly exasperated. "You need to choose and you need to choose today, before things get serious!"

"Choose? There's no choice! I don't want Nathan like that!" I hear the words leave my mouth, but I don't feel them. Oh god. "It's wrong; he's Caleb's brother."

"I know that, but I don't think it's wrong. I think you both…"

"Mum!" I squeal, jumping back a step in shock. "It's even worse than if Caleb and I had broken up and I jumped into bed with his brother. It's sick and it's wrong."

"Then you need to make that clear to Nathan."

"I will."

"When?"

When? Damn. "I don't know. Today?"

"Good. Because if he asks, I won't lie for you and Nathan isn't stupid. He'll figure it out eventually." She walks over to me and places Dillan in my arms. "I love you very much, you're my little girl, but you're being very, very stupid. Eric is nice, but I think your heart lies somewhere else."

"Yes, with my 'should be' husband's ashes." I mutter, taking my coffee from the microwave. Great, it's cold again.

"Now you're lying to yourself."

"Eric is fun, he's handsome and he's not related to Dillan's father. He's easy and uncomplicated. That's what I need."

"No, that's what you think you need." Are my mum's parting words before she grabs her bag off the breakfast bar and leaves the room. I hear the front door close, but not before she calls, "Choose. Before it's too late and one of them chooses for you."

"I don't want your uncle." I say to Dillan, who looks up at me with smiling eyes. "Seriously. I don't."

Do I?

"Let's get you dressed chubby bubby. I've got things to do and you're coming with me." I kiss his open mouth, laughing when he wobbles his head in an attempt to suckle at my lips.

I glare at him, my anger apparent. "I can't believe you snuck into my bed in the middle of the night!"

"The couch wasn't comfortable. I couldn't sleep. Besides, it isn't like we haven't shared a bed before." He looks around the room and shakes his head. "This isn't it."

Nathan and I are currently looking at a few houses in town. This is house number one and he hates it. Not that I blame him; it stinks of damp and needs a lot of work. Although it has potential, Nathan wants somewhere he can just move into and soon.

He called me as I was strolling through the supermarket, Dillan strapped to my chest, filling my trolley with a week's worth of shopping, and asked me to attend these viewings. I agreed, mostly because I need to speak with him about last night, but also because I need to put a stop on our relationship, whatever that may be. The lines are very blurred.

"Whatever, look." I rub my eyes and follow him and the estate agent out of the door. My voice is low so the nosy arsehole who seems to glance at my breasts every few seconds doesn't hear what we're saying. "I don't want to address that right now."

"Hmm."

"Are you listening?"

"Are you going to tell me something I want to hear?"

Blink. "I'm going to speak what's on my mind."

"Not what I want to hear then." He mutters, his lips twitching at the corners.

"No, but it needs to be said."

"Later."

"But..."

He gives me a stern look and nods in the direction of the nosy estate agent. "Later."

"Kay." I grumble and allow him to take my hand.

We climb into the car after strapping a snoozing Dillan in and follow the agent to the next location. It's not too far from my mum's, only a ten minute walk. No doubt the garden leads onto the beach. The houses down here are quite large, all three storeys, and all have fairly long driveways, shrouded by huge fern trees.

"Can you afford one of these?" I ask as we follow the red car down a driveway on the right.

Nathan doesn't answer. He does, however, stop the car and climb out, grab Dillan's car seat from the back, walk to my side and help me out, before literally dragging me into the house. I wish he'd stop dragging me places; it's extremely irritating.

For good measure, I kick his calf. Only gently, though, as I don't want him to fall with Dillan in his hand.

He only looks at me over his shoulder and smiles wickedly, his teeth showing through the slight gap in his lips.

"I don't know why you're so proud of yourself." I mutter, still allowing him to drag me.

We enter the huge kitchen, large windows light the space, reflecting brilliantly off the light surfaces.

"Because even though you act annoyed at my dragging you around, you never protest much."

Cocky shit.

He's also correct. Damn him.

"What do you think?" He asks, the agent giving us space to look around. We head through to the dining room, which is big enough to fit a six seated table and not much else, or a four seated table and maybe a glass cabinet if you're into that sort of thing. The living room is as large as the kitchen and has a huge bay window that's padded on the base, obviously a good place to sit and read.

"It's very big." I comment as we wander up the stairs, and yes, I'm still being dragged.

"Four bedrooms and a study, which could be a fifth bedroom." The agent points out, smiling broadly, obviously thinking he's got a sale. He's also looking at my boobs again.

Nathan's body tenses when he notices. The agent fortunately turns and leads us into the master bedroom, which is at the back of the house. "If he looks at your chest one more time I'm..."

"Stop it." I chastise, yet inside I feel kind of nice that he's defending my honour.

Pouting slightly, he takes my arm and leads me into the room after him. "I like it. It has everything I need. The neutral colours are good also."

I hum my agreement before walking over to the closet and checking the inside. "Better closet space than your house in the middle of nowhere."

CHAPTER EIGHT

"Do you like it?" Nathan asks, watching me pace around the room with a blank expression.

"It's not up to me."

"Do. You. Like. It?"

"No need to get stroppy."

He sighs and says with a snappy tone, "Gwen. Don't make me ask you again."

"What's not to like?" I throw my arms up and let them fall back down. "Look at this place. It's gorgeous."

"And right on the beach." The agent says to my chest.

Seeing Nathan take a step towards him, I grab his hand and it's my turn to drag him from the room.

"Just one little punch?" He pleads quietly, making me giggle.

After seeing the next two houses, Nathan tells the agent we were going to go for coffee to talk about it. Dillan is awake and hungry and I need to feed him. The agent leaves us with his card, even though we have three already, and we head for my place of work.

"Well, I didn't expect to see you here today." Valentine smiles brightly at me as Nathan places Dillan's car seat on the table between us and carefully lifts him out.

"I didn't have a choice." I comment under my breath so she doesn't hear. It's not that I don't love her or this place. I do, I just can't talk freely with Nathan here and there's also the chance he'll find out I'm still seeing Eric. What a mess! I add, so she can hear, "I love your coffee."

Valentine snorts and waves me off. "Such love from such a valued employee. Don't know why I bother."

"But I love you more." I call after her as she vanishes into the kitchen.

Tiffany waves at me over the counter; she's busy serving customers. Elle isn't working today, which is a relief. One less person to blab about anything to do with me that Nathan doesn't need to know about.

"Which one did you like?" Nathan asks, sitting diagonally to me and using his jacket to shield me as I get Dillan to latch on. Smiling gratefully at him, I wave at Tiffany and call out our order.

"You could just queue like a regular person." She snaps playfully.

"I'll deal with it." Nathan leans forward and presses his lips to my forehead as his hand strokes the side of Dillan's head. I don't need to look at Tiffany to know that she caught that intimate moment.

Nathan and I really need to talk.

Although I can't deny the fact that I liked it.

No... I can deny it. I'm so denying it right now. I didn't like it, not at all.

"Cinnamon?" Nathan asks from across the way. I nod, staring at him for a moment. He's so handsome. I hate to admit it, but he really is. And so complicated and broody. His body is tall, fit and strong, but not overly so. He's almost painful to look at, knowing he wants me, knowing he's so many good things rolled into one and knowing I can't have him. Painful.

Why does he want me? Is it an accidental thing?

I belonged to Caleb. It's messed up.

Why can't he want someone that's not half of his brother?

Sigh. I'm so sick of this, these stupid thoughts that never stop twisting in my head. I'm going to resolve it and I'm going to resolve it today.

"Here." Nathan places my cup in front of me. I thank him and sip the delicious drink. "So, which one?"

"It's your choice." I shrug, not meeting his eyes.

"Well, you are going to be living with me, so it's your choice too."

Oh dear god. "Nathan..." He looks down at his cup, his tongue worrying his lower lip. I continue. "What is it that you want from me?"

His eyes shoot up, his brows raised in question. "Want from you?"

"Yes. I don't understand this feeling you have where you seem to think you need me to move in with you. It makes me assume things, which keeps me up at night whilst I try to figure out the ifs and buts and reasoning behind it all."

He glances over at the window, his eyes holding a faraway look that tells me he's wondering what to say next. Silence is all I receive.

"It doesn't make sense. All you've said is that you want us living with you and that we're your home, but we don't need looking after anymore. I'm doing pretty well for myself."

"I'd say my intentions were pretty obvious." He leans back, folding his arms over his chest as his eyes narrow on me. "But now I'm not so sure that they are."

"Intentions?" Gulp.

"Do I have to spell it out for you?" He smiles and brings his cup to his lips. I watch his throat bob as he takes a healthy swig. And again... gulp... literally... but from him this time. "I think Dillan has finished eating. You're more or less smothering him with your breast, although he doesn't seem displeased about it."

"Oh!" I cry and pull my flailing boy away from my bosom. He wasn't literally being smothered, he'd just spat my nipple from his mouth and started wriggling. Poor boy.

I rest him on my knee and pat his back a few times. He looks around with an unsteady head and wide eyes, his mouth wide open.

"Anyway..." Nathan continues, but is interrupted by Tiffany who demands, "Give me the baby!"

And Dillan has left my arms.

Nathan looks at me expectantly, although I'm not sure what he wants.

"Could we get some service over here?" A customer demands irately, after two minutes of awkward silence and Tiffany cooing at Dillan.

"I'm coming!" Tiffany snaps, sighing as she hands Dillan to Nathan. "Speak to you soon."

"Have fun."

She only scoffs in response and saunters away.

"So, back to business." Nathan smiles now that we're alone again. "I think, after last night, two things were proven." Two things? "One being that you are definitely attracted to me." Oh heck. "Two being that you like me... a lot. Hopefully as much as I like you." Double heck. "At this point, it's safe to say, we should move forward. You, me and Dillan, we can be together again. There's nothing stopping us."

"Nathan..." I try, but he raises his hand and adds, "Nothing apart from you and your morals."

"Which are legitimate morals; you're Caleb's brother."

"Look, I don't want to talk about this here. You will change your mind, Gwen. Be sure of that." He glares at me for a moment and I look away. I hate it when people stare, even people I know well. "So, am I to stay in your bed again tonight?"

Bastard. I throw my napkin at him, giving him the same glare he gave me only seconds ago. "Sometimes murder seems like the only option when it comes to you."

Looking at his cup he smiles, his gloved fingers tapping on the table, the other hand cradling Dillan to his chest. "When you first moved in with me I thought the same thing." He looks up at me, his eyes sparkling with mischief.

"Trust me, you weren't the only one."

He chuckles, still smiling. "You're adorable when you're being stroppy."

"Let's add insults, because that'll make Gwen less likely to kill you." Sarcasm laces my tone.

"How was that an insult?" Yep, that smile is still there.

"I'm not stroppy, nor am I ever stroppy."

"You're full of it." He laughs and I'm shocked at his words.

"Somebody is starting to sound like me." I point out, my lips tipping up at the ends.

He shrugs. "I like the way you sound."

"Your mum called me common."

"My mum would call the Queen common; she's genuinely that far up herself."

This starts another round of laughter, mostly at the shock of the way he's talking more than anything else. "Why can't you be like this all of the time?" I say carelessly through my laughter. "You're so much easier to be around."

His face falls and I instantly curse at myself. Why did I have to say something stupid? "You don't think I'm easy to be around?" The vulnerability in his voice tears through the outer layer of my heart.

Darn. "I do, genuinely I do. You're amazing when your guard is lowered." He smiles softy at me, but it doesn't reach his eyes. "I'll never purposely hurt you. You know that right?"

He brings my hand to his lips and holds it there for a moment. "You're the only person I trust to make that statement." Our hands go to the table, but he doesn't let go.

But aren't I purposely hurting him right now? By denying him something he clearly wants? I need to tell him. I need to make it clear.

Unfortunately, at the same moment I open my mouth, my phone starts ringing. "It's Sasha." I blink in shock at her name on the screen. "Excuse me for a moment."

"Of course." Nathan nods and rests his smooth chin against the dark fuzz on Dillan's head.

I give Tiffany a wave as I leave the bakery and answer the phone. "Hello?"

"Why do I feel guilty? Oh yeah, I'll tell you why, because I've hardly said more than two words to my best friend in the past month. I miss you and I'm sorry." Sasha rambles. "I miss Dillan. I've just been so busy and I was worried you wouldn't want to talk to me anymore. The longer it got, the harder it got to call and the easier it got to not call."

I don't say anything; I'm not sure what to say.

She continues. "I feel so bad. So does Tommy. I didn't realise he hadn't called and trust me when I say I tore him a new arsehole." Classy. "Can I come and see you tomorrow?"

I look back through the window at Nathan and Dillan. "I can't tomorrow. Nathan is moving to town and staying with me for... I don't know how long. Sunday maybe?"

"Yes! I'll call you. Forgive me?"

"I'll tell you Sunday." I smile slightly and look at the flat greying shapes on the ground that were once chewing gum now smashed into the pavement.

"Brilliant! I've got to go; I have to meet my mum at Home Bargains."

"Okay, have fun."

"You too."

Déjà vu. I remember the last time somebody called to make amends, my mum to be exact. Nathan and I were eating at a restaurant in London. Crazy.

"Everything okay?" Nathan asks as I retake my seat and reach out for my son.

"Yes, hopefully it will be. Sasha just called to make amends."

He nods thoughtfully. "That's good."

"Yeah."

"Shall we leave? I'd like to have that conversation now."

I frown. "What about the house?"

"That conversation can come after we decide our fate."

Our fate? "Nathan..."

He places his finger over my mouth, his eyes narrowed in annoyance. "You can give me an hour of your time. I deserve that at least."

Ugh, guilt trip. What do I do now? Well... I agree of course. "Sure."

We arrive home and I'm not relieved in the slightest to see that my mum isn't here. If she were here, this talk might not happen just yet, which would be a relief.

"I'll just change him real quick." I mutter, following Nathan into the room. Nathan nods as I take Dillan from his seat and he follows me up the stairs, much to my dismay. I need a moment to clear my head. Just a moment. "Can I have a moment?"

"So you can think of ways out of this?" Nathan grins. It's very attractive and it throws me a little, mainly because of my strong reaction to it. What with him in my bedroom, now sitting on my bed, smiling casually like he's never done before. "Not a chance."

"Right." I turn, my throat clenching as I swallow. "I'll be just a minute." Dillan starts wailing, not happy to be disturbed as I take my time changing his nappy and clothes. "Can you settle him for me? I need to wash my hands."

"Sure." Before the word is out of his mouth, I'm out of the room and the bathroom door is shutting behind me. I lean against it for a moment, gathering my thoughts and catching my breath. After knocking the back of my head against the wooden door a few times in the hope that it'll knock some sense into me, I finally step away from the door and do what I came to do. I wash my hands, but also splash water on my face.

Staring at myself in the mirror, I question my looks. I'm not one who'll sit there picking at herself; I've never had the patience for that. I don't think I'm hideous, but I'm not model material either. Why does he want me? Why did Caleb want me? Why does Eric want me? They all must see something in me that I don't.

Or maybe that's why, maybe it's because I'm not arrogant or self-assured. I just am what I am and that's that.

But still... all of this angst and emotional ache. All of this yearning.

From whom? Why do I assume he's yearning? Nathan I mean.

Oh god. It's not him who's yearning, or if he is, then he isn't the only one.

When I re-enter my bedroom, Nathan is lying on my bed with his arms behind his head. He looks at me and winks. It's subtle and sweet and makes me sway on the spot a little. "I want to move here. If you won't come back with me, that is."

He waits for my answer, his brown irises peeking through hooded lids. I respond "I can't. I'm happy here."

"Okay." He holds out his hand for me to take. Stepping forward, I do just that. "Then it's settled. I'll move here and have Dillan for you while you work."

"I can't move in with you."

He lets out a breath, but I see him relent before he confirms my thoughts. "I know. Maybe not right now, but soon."

"And what about when we start dating? Living together will be weird and you know it."

His brow furrows, but then his lips twitch as his mind switches from one thought to another. "You wouldn't like it if I dated?"

"That's not what I meant." I grumble, but that's exactly what I meant. I just didn't know it until I said it.

"How would you feel about dating me?" He asks, catching me completely off guard.

I blink, my mouth opening as if trying to catch the right words to say from the air around me. "Umm..."

"That wasn't a no." He leans up on his elbows after releasing my hand, his longish hair falling in his eyes. I reach forward and push it back slowly, so silky, so soft. "I still don't hear a no."

"It's weird." I whisper, sitting on the side of the bed and looking at his collar in an attempt to avoid his eyes. "I don't think I can."

"You could try."

I shake my head. "It wouldn't be fair."

He uses his finger under my chin to tip my face up. "Caleb's dead. He'd want you to be happy."

"I wasn't talking about Caleb." I admit, feeling shamed. Now he looks confused. I don't blame him. "It wouldn't be fair on you."

"How so?" He leans forward even more, his eyes searching mine. They flicker down to my lips as his hand moves from beneath my chin to cup my cheek.

"You deserve better." I say, trying to deter him. It doesn't. If anything, he smiles even more and I'm wondering what's so funny. "I'm serious."

He chuckles, sliding his hand around my neck to pull me closer. My hands immediately go to his chest as one of his legs go behind me and the other goes over the side of the bed. I'm now effectively sitting in between his legs. The heat from his crotch is hitting me right in the hip. Oh god. "You don't know your own worth. Don't pull away. I can see it in your eyes, just like the other night. You want me."

"I can't be what you need me to be. I can't give you what you deserve." I try to explain, but still he moves closer.

"You already do." He moves closer still and I make no attempt to move away. The thought of his clearly soft and inviting lips on mine makes me want to inch closer, but it's not fair on him right now. He needs total honesty.

I moan about him not talking to me, him not being honest with me, yet I'm not doing the same. "Stop. We need to talk."

"It can wait." he pushes, his nose now only an inch from mine.

"No, really it can't."

"It can." He says breathily. I feel it on my lips; my nose picks up mint, Nathan and coffee. I bet he's delicious.

Using what small amount of willpower I have left, I stand and back away from him. My lips are tingling with the need to feel his. "This can't happen. Ever."

"Why?" He follows. I knew he would, but I prayed that he wouldn't. Caging me in with his arms, he leans forward once more. Dear god. He's relentless.

"I'm still seeing, Eric." I blurt and my chest aches with a sharp pain when he immediately takes a step back, pain evident in his eyes.

"Then stop seeing Eric." He bites out, running his hand through his hair. "Tell him you don't want to see him anymore." He waits for my agreement, his eyes narrowed in anger. After a moment of silence, his eyes widen in realisation. "You like him."

Do I? I should like him. He's a nice guy and he's charming, funny and very sweet. He's handsome and, sure, I'm attracted to him. Also, he's not Caleb's brother. "I'm just seeing where it goes."

"Seeing where it goes." He repeats in a quiet voice. Seconds later, his eyes come back to mine. "And the reason you're choosing him?"

"Choosing?" Now I'm confused.

"Yes. You barely know him, whereas you know me very well. I'm offering you the same as he is, but with the guarantee of trust and respect. You already get both from me. You have done for a long time now." All very valid points. His voice lowers and his eyes darken. "I won't chase you, Guinevere. If this is a game you're playing, don't. Choose wisely."

A game? "This isn't a game." I scoff, scowling at him. "How could you think that of me?"

"Because you still deny yourself the chance to be with the person you love, on the grounds of me being Caleb's brother. Caleb, who is unfortunately deceased. Caleb, who would want you to be happy with the person you choose and you know it."

"Love?" I blink in astonishment. "You think I love you?" I do, of course I do, but not in that way. Doesn't he know that?

He looks at me, his eyes wary. "You don't?"

"No." Oh shit, why'd I have to say it like that? "I mean... not in that way."

"In what way?"

Good question, "I don't know."

"Tell me, because you love Tommy right? And you don't let him touch you the way you let me touch you." He smiles smugly, but it falls at his own words. "Do you?"

Ewww. "No! Of course not."

"Then explain what kind of love it is you have for me. It's definitely not brotherly, not the kind of love you'd have for me if Caleb were alive." This is also true. "So what is it?"

"It's not enough!" I shout, my hands fisting by my sides. "It's not enough." I say softer this time.

"I'm not?"

"No, you are, but you're just... it won't work."

He laughs coldly. "You haven't tried."

"I can't look at you and not think of him!" I yell, my hand pointing to the picture on my nightstand. "And what you're proposing is just too weird for me to fathom."

"You'll get used to it." He grabs me, one hand on my cheek and the other on my shoulder. "We'll get used to it together. Just try."

"I can't." I snap. Why won't he stop pushing?

"Tell me why!" He's looking as angry and as irritated as I feel.

"Because I will never love you as much as I loved him!"

He rolls his eyes. "You'll love me a different way. It'll take time, but I'm willing to wait." His hands go to my hips and pull me into him. "You're already halfway there. Let me help you the rest of the way."

"Stop it." I try to shove against his chest, but he doesn't let me. "Let me go."

"Stop trying to pull away. Your excuses are feeble and you know it. Why won't you let yourself be happy? Who cares that I'm his brother? You can't help who you fall in love with."

I want to kick him. Why won't he stop? "I'm not in love with you."

"That's rubbish." He grits out, pressing me into the door. "I don't believe you. You're running out of excuses."

"I don't want to be with you. It's weird."

"Another lie. Keep going. I want to keep ticking them off of the mental list in my head." He presses his forehead to mine, his eyes shining with determination. "You want me; I know you do. You crave me almost as much as I crave you."

"Shut up." I plead, still pushing at him.

"Just admit it. We can date, take it at your speed. I'll be patient; I won't push you. You've got no excuse, just..."

"I promised him." I shout, slamming my hands against his chest, my chest heaving and my body sagging. "I promised him I'd stay away from you."

This time he does let me go. He takes two staggering steps backwards. "What?"

"He made me swear." I explain, my eyes burning as they look into Nathan's. "And I swore that I wouldn't."

Nathan nods, his tongue and teeth worrying his lower lip. "He made you swear?"

"Yes."

"And what did he say exactly?" His voice is a growl, one that tells me if Caleb were alive, he wouldn't be for much longer.

Does he really need to know the specifics? "I don't remember exactly what was said. Just that I made him a promise and I'm not going to break it."

"Fine." His voice is no longer a growl, but deceptively calm. "I should go."

"Nathan." I reach for him, his blank face hitting me deeper than it would if it weren't blank. When it is blank, it tells me he's hiding his feelings, and when he's hiding them, he's dealing with them alone. He's done enough of that in his life. "We can be friends."

He laughs coldly like he did earlier and moves away from my reaching hand. "Friends? Gwen, I have no interest in having friends. Nor did I ever have an interest in having a girlfriend until you came along."

"Nathan..."

"Do you honestly wish to torment me in such a way? Knowing how I feel? Knowing that I know how you feel? Yet you'll allow me, as your *friend,* to see you with another man. I never knew you to be so cruel."

Great, the formal talk is back out. "I'm sorry."

"It's fine." He spits. "I lost you once already. I can deal with it again."

"And what about Dillan?" I shouldn't ask, but I need to know.

"I..." He closes his mouth and looks over at the cot where Dillan lies peacefully sleeping. "I don't know. I'll be in touch."

He nods his head, telling me to move out of the way. I do so and watch as he pulls open the door. He stops in the frame, his shoulders tense. I wait for him to speak. "If only you knew what kind of man my brother was, you wouldn't be so quick to turn me away."

"What?" I charge after him. "What is that supposed to mean?"

He continues forward, opening the front door without speaking a word before slamming it shut behind him. My hair whips across my face with the draft formed by the power of the slam. I stare at the door for a long while. What did he mean? Caleb was perfect. He never did anything wrong, not to me.

Chapter Nine

"Hey, are you listening?" Eric throws a cheesy puff at me and it bounces off my forehead. "You're proper spacing out on me this morning."

I blink myself from my thoughts and give him a weak smile. "Sorry, I've just got a lot on my mind."

He slides closer to me and puts his arm around my shoulders. "It's cool. You space out; I'll just stare at you."

Giggle.

"So, what has you spacing out?"

Wince. "It's a long story."

"I have time." He checks his watch. "So do you."

This is true. "My mum will be back with Dillan soon."

"Good, I want to meet him." I open my mouth to argue, but he cuts me off. "I think it's time."

"What?" I laugh incredulously. "We're not serious or anything. We haven't even kissed yet."

He grins wickedly. "I could change that, right now."

Using my hand flat on his face, my palm over his comically puckered lips, I push him away. "You've been eating cheesy puffs for breakfast. I think I'll pass."

He throws his head back and laughs, then his eyes come to me. "Now I have to kiss you."

"You really don't." I scoot away but he moves closer. "Stop."

"You're laughing, which means you're not serious."

My phone rings, effectively cutting off my laughter and his shoving. "Hello?"

"Did you pay off my credit card this morning? I forgot to ask and you were in a foul mood when I woke up." My mum asks.

"Hello to you too." I joke.

"Well, after the grunts I got from you when I woke at noon, I wasn't sure whether or not I should get straight to the point or try for nice."

"Yes Mum, I paid your card off for you. Are you bringing Dillan back soon?"

"Is Eric still there?"

I glance at him and respond. "Yes, he's still here. He wants to meet him."

"Okay, we'll be home in about half an hour." She pauses for a moment. "You made your decision then?"

"Mum..."

"I'll take that as a no."

"I made it; it's settled. I'm hanging up now."

I hear her sigh before the line goes dead and turn to Eric, who immediately asks. "Settled?"

"It's nothing." I smile and stretch my arms above my head. "Do you need something to wash that crap down with?"

"Something sugary. Preferably coke." He smiles and shows me his white teeth. "Reckon I'll still have these when I'm thirty?"

"You're not thirty?" I jest, earning me a slap on my arse as I walk by. I ignore the fact that his hand lingers and squeezes for a moment and scurry to the kitchen to make drinks.

As soon as my mum walks in, she hands Dillan to me and goes upstairs, no doubt giving us our privacy. I feel slightly nervous as I step into the room, cooing at my little man. What will Eric think? Will he run for the hills? Will he be all weird and distant?

There's only one way to find out. "Eric, meet Dillan. Dillan, meet Eric." Then I pray that he doesn't puke on the shiny man on the sofa.

"Well he's very handsome." Eric grins as I sit beside him with Dillan balancing on my knees. Dillan smiles at Eric, followed by a few gurgling noises and a slight giggle. "He also finds me funny. This is good. If he'd screamed at me I may have cried and hid behind the sofa."

I laugh. "What?"

"That's what I did when my little sister was brought home. She screamed at me. I cried and hid behind the sofa."

"You really aren't normal, are you?"

He scratches his head and grins. "I was afraid you'd figure that out."

"Want to hold him?"

He thinks about it for a moment before nervously holding out his hands. I slide Dillan from my knee to his, where Eric tentatively reaches for him and holds him under his arms with his fingers splayed across his back. "This isn't so bad. I was worried." Dillan smiles as he usually does. "He doesn't look like you much."

"I know." I run my fingers over the fuzz on my little boy's head. "He looks like his dad. Same easy smile, same eyes."

"I've seen his picture in your room. I definitely see the resemblance." He winks at me and nudges me with his elbow. "What do I do now?"

Dillan answers for him, grabbing the bottom of his top with his tiny fist and pulling it to his mouth. I sigh and tug it away. He only goes for the sleeve of his top this time, bending his body forward so his mouth can reach. "He'll be teething soon. Keep hold of him for a second; I need to grab his teething ring before he chews a hole through whatever part of you he can reach."

"We don't mind, do we buddy?" Eric coos in a baby voice, causing me to lift a brow. He looks at me defensively. "What? I like babies."

Eric left ten minutes ago, after staying for lunch and dinner. It's kind of lucky that Nathan did leave yesterday, seeing as Eric showed up on my doorstep this afternoon without warning. Mum was out with Dillan by this point; she likes going for a walk when she wakes up and usually takes him with her.

At least now I can wallow in peace. I don't think I handled yesterday very well. Not at all. My emotions are all over the place.

Nathan isn't right for me, but what he said was right.

I do love him. I know that.

I just don't love him like he loves me, or like he thinks he loves me.

No, he definitely loves me; that much is obvious. I've been a fool. A complete and total idiot.

I can't believe after he told me he loved me, straight out, no pretences, I asked him to be my friend. What the hell is wrong with me? Am I really that selfish?

Apparently so.

I want to say that I'm sorry. I want to take it back, but I can't, because it won't change. Nothing will. It's not fair on him if I do that.

It's not right.

Eric is right. He's new, he's uncomplicated and he respects me... so far anyway. Gah.

But Nathan... well... he's Nathan.

Caleb begged me to stay away from him. I already broke that, but I didn't have a choice. Why would he ask that of me? It makes no sense.

Is that really the reason I'm not with Nathan right now? I heard the words come out of my mouth and I felt them as I said them, but before now it's never been an issue.

Or maybe it has.

"I'm coming." I say to my crying little boy, who is no longer happy in his swinging chair.

He doesn't stop when I pick him up. He's grumpy and tired and no doubt a little bit hungry.

I have a feeling this is going to be a long night.

"You look dead on your feet." Valentine clucks at me, her face a mask of concern.

"Rough night." I reply, placing the large tray of cinnamon bagels in the oven.

"Dillan?" I nod in response. "Sip a bit of brandy before you feed him at night. It'll wipe him out."

"It's not the nineteen twenties anymore, or whatever year it was that drinking alcohol whilst breastfeeding was acceptable." Elle calls on a laugh.

"How does she hear us?" I whisper, eyeing the open doorway to the kitchen suspiciously.

Valentine just shrugs and moves away. "She's a special girl."

"You've got a visitor." Elle calls and Valentine grins and rushes to the door. "Not you. I'm talking to Gwen."

The old woman huffs and stomps past me, throwing a dishrag on the side as she goes. Giggling, I step into the main area and smile at Eric, "Is it lunch time already?"

"Holy crap!" He blinks, looking me up and down. "I was expecting Casper, not the Jammerwocky."

"The what?" I laugh, looking myself up and down.

"You know, the Jabberwocky? But with jam, because you're covered in the stuff."

"Hello to you too." I grin, ducking under the counter after throwing my apron onto the side.

He cups my cheeks with his hands and gently butts his forehead against mine. I start laughing. What the hell was that? "Hey."

"What was that?"

"A butt greet."

"I don't get it." Elle shouts, though her shouting isn't necessary. We're no more than ten feet away from her.

"We haven't kissed yet." Eric says by way of explanation. It goes straight over our heads. He sighs and continues. "How else am I supposed to greet her? If I hug her, I'm covered in jam, because we all know that apron is useless when it comes to Gwen."

"You could have just shaken her hand." Valentine shouts from the kitchen.

Elle looks at me with wide eyes. "How the hell does she hear us?"

They really don't know how funny they are.

I pull Eric to the nearest table and sit. My aching feet appreciate it. A loud and unattractive yawn escapes me.

"Tired?"

"Hmm." I rest my head on my folded arms. "Exhausted. It happens when you only sleep for two hours."

"Dillan? He was getting cranky before I left. Maybe he missed me."

Or he sensed my mood. "Yeah, possibly."

Eric plays with the side of my hair. It feels good until I realise he's actually picking out sesame seeds. "Do you swim in baking ingredients back there?"

"Shut it." I stick my tongue out at him and close my eyes for a moment. "What do you want for lunch? Tell Elle, she'll grab it for you."

"There goes my something special." Eric jokes, still picking sesame seeds from my hair. "They just keep appearing!"

Peeking open one eye, I stare up at the handsome man who looks like a monkey picking bugs from its partner. Normally I'd shy away from such a ridiculous display, but right now I'm too tired. My eyes close again and unfortunately I don't realise I've fallen asleep until I feel Elle stab me up the nose with a drinking straw and almost punch Eric in the face.

"Take her home, I can manage today." Valentine says, waving her hand at Eric. "Go on, before I change my mind."

"Thank you."

"Go on, be in tomorrow an hour early. You can help me prep."

"Okay." I can sleep! Sweet happy times.

Eric leads me to his car. I laugh when he places a towel over the seat and helps me in. guarding his car from my messy clothes.

"That's the first time you've helped me into a car and it wasn't for me, it was for your car." I point out, making his cheeks pink slightly.

"You have arms; you can open the car door yourself." He puts the car in gear and pulls out into the street. "We're going to my place, if that's okay? You can shower there."

Blink. Shower there? "I don't really..."

"Please? You've never seen my place before." When he asks so nicely, how can I say no?

It's only a fifteen minute drive and five minutes of that was down to traffic congestion. His house is small, I can see that already, but it's very cute - a terraced house in between two houses that don't look to be in great condition. The painted bricks are flaking very unattractively. Eric's house is lovely though. Either he or his landlord keep up with the work.

The inside is as expected, plain apart from the few pictures on the walls of friends and family. "Welcome to my humble abode. Follow me."

I follow him up the steep, narrow staircase and onto the landing. We enter a bathroom and he immediately hands two large, fluffy, white bath towels to me. "I'll fetch you something to wear. Take your time."

"I really do need to sleep." I say, not liking how pushy he's being. "Maybe I should just..."

"Babe." He cups my cheeks with his hands. "You're fine. Have a shower. I'll make you something to eat, give you a quick tour and then you can sleep."

"Where?"

"I do have a bed." His smile is full of mischief. I don't like it much. He rolls his eyes on a sigh. "I don't mean it like that. Go on, let me look after you this once."

Sigh.

He leaves the room and I lock the door.

The shower takes me a while as it took me forever to figure out how to work it. It's linked to the taps, so you have to adjust both of them to get the desired temperature; shift one a fraction too far and the water is too hot or too cold.

Once I'm done, I wrap up in a large towel, running a comb through my wet hair, and grab the boxers and T-shirt that are neatly folded on the ground outside the door.

When I exit the bathroom I tread quietly down the stairs, my messy clothes shoved into my bag which is hanging from my shoulder. I really like Eric, I do, but I don't feel comfortable in his house. Especially not whilst I'm wearing nothing but a tight pair of his boxers and a long T-shirt.

I follow the sounds of clattering into the kitchen. "Hey." Eric beams, looking me up and down. He doesn't bother to hide the heat in his eyes. "How are you feeling now?"

"Clean." I smile sheepishly, pulling on the bottom of his shirt to make sure it's covering my arse and lady parts. I'm wearing boxers but they're tight and don't leave much to the imagination. "What's this?"

He shrugs, looking sheepish himself. "Lunch."

"Looks good." I stare at the sandwich that has to be fatter than my mouth is wide.

"It's my mum's homemade bread, although it probably pales in comparison to yours. Here, sit." I follow him to the tiny round table with two seats and do as he says. "What time do you have to be home for Dillan?"

"He's at nursery today until six." I respond, rubbing my stinging eyes. He slides my sandwich in front of me. I look at it for a moment, assessing the best way to hold and bite. Following his lead, I crush it down with my hand before picking it up. It's really good. "I should go home after this. I really do need to sleep."

He chews and swallows the food in his mouth before answering, "Sleep here. What's the big deal?"

"I don't know you, or your house. It's weird." I respond, trying to sound as polite as possible so he doesn't take offence. "I'm not dressed either."

"Yeah, I'm still finding it hard to believe I managed to get you naked and in my clothes before I've even kissed you." Reaching over the table, he flicks my nose and tugs on the loose braid that hangs over my shoulder. "Honestly, I brought you here because we have more privacy. I know your mum is probably home and whenever we do anything, there always seems to be someone else there."

Narrowing my eyes, I point out. "But I'm going to be sleeping."

"Exactly, I'll get to learn a few things."

"Like?"

"If you snore, if you fidget and if you drool." He shields himself from my pinching fingers and takes away our plates, smiling the entire time. "Come on. I'll show you to my room."

Well, at least it's tidy. His bed is huge; it looks clean and very comfortable. He pulls back the red cover and pats the mattress. With a sigh I climb in. It is as comfortable as it looks.

Eric sits on the side of the bed, making a show of tucking me in and tugging on my braid again. "I'm tempted to join you."

"My bed." I comment petulantly and burrow into the blankets. "Go do whatever it is you do at this time of the day."

He chuckles and gives me a salute before standing. "Aye, aye, Captain."

"Mummy! There's a girl in Eric's bed!" I hear a sweet young voice call, rousing me from my deep sleep.

Ugh, does Mum have friends over?

Wait... I'm at Eric's.

I peek open an eye when I hear footsteps bounding up the stairs and see a cute little dark haired girl staring at me. She can't be older than ten and, if memory serves me right, Eric said she was nine, although I don't think he shared her name with me.

"Get out of my room, Kara!" Eric shouts, after almost falling through the door. I scoot up the bed, blinking the sleep from my eyes.

"A girl?" I hear a woman's voice call, followed by more footsteps on the stairs. "What girl?"

"She's pretty." Kara states, smiling and showing two deep dimples on her cheeks. "You're pretty."

"Umm…" I stammer, not knowing what to say as Eric grabs his sister, tosses her over his shoulder, gives me an apologetic smile and heads to the door. His mum beats him to it and now, standing in the doorway, is a round woman who Eric definitely gets his facial features from.

"Oh my." She beams at me, then slaps her son on the arm.

"What was that for?" Eric whines, still holding his squealing sister.

"Put your sister down and introduce me to your girlfriend." She looks way too excited.

"Mum, she's just woken up. Please leave the room." He hisses, giving her gentle nudges with his free hand.

"I'll see you downstairs." She grins, placing her hand on the doorframe so Eric can't throw her out. "Coffee?"

I nod, still not saying anything as my heart beats a rapid beat in my chest. Girlfriend? That's what she said.

Eric comes back inside moments later and winces. "I'm sorry, I didn't know they were coming."

"That's okay. I'll just hide in here until they're gone."

He frowns. "Don't be daft. Get out of bed and come and say hello or I'll never hear the end of it."

Is he serious? "I have no clothes."

He blinks in realisation. "Right. Shit. Umm… here." And his dressing gown lands on my head. He laughs, pulls it off and brushes my fringe from my eyes. "Sorry."

"I look like a whore." I snap, pulling the gown on.

"Don't be ridiculous. I'll explain the situation. My mum is really cool; she won't judge you." I don't believe him but I have no other choice than to suck it up and go downstairs. He wraps his arms around me from behind as I pass him in the doorway and presses his lips to my ear. "I promise. She'll love you."

"Hmm." I try to hide my nerves. I'm not great at meeting new people, especially parents. Never was and probably never will be. Caleb's parents hated me, but even before then I rarely went to friends' houses because I was scared of their parents. I'm strange, I know.

He spins me in his arms and presses me against the wall. His hands find their way inside my dressing gown and rest on my hips. "If you want to stay in my room you can. If you're not ready for this, my mum will understand. Although Kara will definitely put up a fight. She's far too nosy for her own good."

"It's fine." I lie. It's totally not. "Let's just go."

He frowns slightly, clearly concerned. "Are you mad at me?"

Sigh. "No, of course not, I'm just... I don't know."

"Shy?" He steps closer, his body against the length of mine.

"Yeah, something like that."

"I'll hold your hand." He says this like it will help me at all. I can't hold his hand in front of his mum! Is he insane? "But first, something I've been wanting to do for a while."

I'm about to ask what, but it's cut off by his lips gently pressing against mine. It takes me a few seconds to figure out what's going on before I melt into it. He's a good kisser; he tastes nice, his lips aren't too moist and he's soft. There's no force behind it, only gentle coaxing.

Well, that is until his tongue pushes past my lips. He changes then, completely. Not in a bad way either.

Overall he's a good kisser, but there are no fireworks or sparks, nothing like there was with... I'm not going to mention him whilst I'm kissing another man, that's not fair on Eric or Caleb.

His hand slides around to the small of my back, pulling my hips away from the wall and into him.

He groans into my mouth, clearly excited. I can't say that I'm completely unaffected. I wish I were.

But I'm not affected in the way I should be affected. It's not lust I'm feeling, it's guilt. All I can see is his face. Not Caleb's... Nathan's.

I can't do this. This feels wrong.

I'm about to push him away, but he moves back first, a smile lighting up his face.

"Okay, you stay here." Eric pants, his breath fanning against my lips. "I'll go and get rid of them."

Clearing my throat nervously, I scrape my teeth over my tingling lower lip and look down. I really hope he doesn't mean what I think he means.

"Mum, they're kissing!"

"For crying out loud!" Eric hisses, his body shaking with laughter. "Come on." Taking my hand, he leads me down the stairs as I pull the gown closed.

Eric's mum is very sweet; so is his little sister. They constantly smile, laugh and joke with each other. Eric was right too, she didn't judge me at all. We all sat in the living room for half an hour. She asked me about my life, but not in the way that she was prying, trying to see what kind of woman her son is dating. She was just genuinely interested, even more so when she heard about Dillan and announced that she loved babies.

Eric sat to my right, his arm behind me over the couch. He didn't say much, only spoke when he was spoken to. I love his little sister; she's adorable, not to mention extremely well mannered. Well...not including when in somebody else's bedroom in front of a sleeping person.

Overall I was glad to have met them. Eric made me feel at ease, which was nice, and I'm grateful for that.

Now we're on our way to mine. I'm wearing nothing but his boxers, top and my shoes and jacket. I still have to pick up Dillan from Nursery. I miss my little man.

I was relieved when Eric didn't pick up where we left off on the landing when his mum and sister were at his. Now I'm wondering why that makes me happy. I should want to kiss him all of the time. Shouldn't I?

He's about to pull up in my driveway, but stops when we both notice the car already parked there.

"Oh shit." I whisper, my hands starting to tremble and my stomach suddenly churning.

"Isn't that Dillan's uncle's car?" Eric asks, seemingly oblivious to my sudden change in mood.

This isn't happening. This really isn't happening.

I want to tell Eric to drive away, but I know Nathan has probably seen the car already. What's he going to think when he sees how I'm dressed? Well, it's pretty obvious what he'll think, but how will he react?

What's worse is that Eric gets out of the car, obviously wanting to walk me to my door or something.

Taking a deep breath and calming my quivering body, I open the car door and climb out.

"I was about to ask you where the hell you have been for the past three hours, but I can see that question is already answered." Nathan spits as he climbs from his car, Dillan in his arms. He doesn't look happy with me at all.

"Why do you have Dillan?" He's supposed to be at nursery.

"If you'd pick up your phone, you'd know exactly why I have Dillan." Nathan glares at me, his body tense and his lips a thin line.

Shit. My phone! "I must have left it at work."

He turns his glare onto Eric, looking him up and down before looking back at me. His eyes widen as he takes note of my bare legs and the bottom of the tight grey boxers that cling to the top of my thighs. I pull my coat tighter around myself, praying it gives me the shelter I need from his pained stare.

"The nursery couldn't contact you. They called your mum but she's at work. Luckily I was still in the area. I was planning on leaving only twenty minutes after they called." Nathan's voice is a lot calmer now, but it's deceptive. I know he's trying to put that blank mask back on.

"Give her a break man, she's been sleeping all afternoon." Eric frowns, placing his arm around my shoulder in an attempt to comfort me.

I stay stiff, waiting for Nathan to say something else. He doesn't. He only walks towards me, hands the nappy bag to Eric and hands Dillan to me.

Dillan doesn't have a temperature. I'm relieved.

"Get inside; you're barely dressed." Nathan hisses, giving me a lingering look that screams of disappointment. "I'm leaving. I'm not coming back."

My lips part with a gasp. "What about Dillan?"

"What about Dillan?" He states, laughing cruelly. "He's not..."

"Don't." I snap, holding up my hand. "You're about to do it again." He closes his mouth, his jaw tensing. "Don't say something I can't forgive you for. Go inside and we'll talk."

"Forgive me?" He breathes the words, his disbelief apparent.

"Why do I feel like I'm missing something?" Eric asks, pulling me tighter to his side.

"Because you are." Nathan snaps, looking directly at him.

"Nathan." I warn, but it falls on deaf ears.

"Don't you have somewhere to be?" He snarls at Eric, who instantly puffs out his chest in challenge.

I look to Eric, pleading him with my eyes. "Please, I really need to talk to him."

"I don't feel comfortable leaving you on your own with him." He eyes Nathan still, but his body is turned towards me.

Nathan takes a step towards him. I shoot him a look and he instantly stops. "He'd never hurt me."

Eric sighs, but I see him relent. "Fine. Call me later." Then he does something that shocks the hell out of me. Being careful of the sleeping baby in my arms, he hooks his hand around my neck and pulls me into him until my lips are touching his. I'm mortified but I don't have a chance to say so, because as soon as I gasp in shock, his tongue pushes into my mouth briefly. He pulls away just as abruptly, his eyes staring into mine. On another sigh and a slight shake of his head, he gives me a weak smile and walks away.

I don't have time to assess that reaction as I hear the front door slam. Nathan has gone inside.

Chapter Ten

I'M NERVOUS WHEN I walk in and place Dillan in the chair in his room. I'm not sure what to expect. This needs dealing with and it needs dealing with now.

I follow the sound of movement up the stairs and into my room. Finding Nathan pacing should be a comical sight. Nathan doesn't pace, but he is.

Opening my mouth to speak, I don't get the chance as he talks first. "It's the same as before, exactly the same. I'm beginning to wonder if this would have happened last time, even if I had been first. You won't choose me. I was right when I said it. Guys like me don't win. Why would they?"

Nathan doesn't ramble either, but he is. "Slow down. I don't know what you're saying."

"He's fun, right?" He stops, stares at me and runs his fingers through his hair. "He's everything you want and everything you need, all wrapped up in one male bundle with stupid dimples and the body of an athlete."

Well... what the hell do I say to that?

"It doesn't matter that I saw you first." He laughs incredulously and I have to repeat his words a few times in my mind to understand them. I still don't understand them, so I ask. "Saw me first?"

"I didn't show up in town a year ago to take you in out of obligation to my brother." He says the word *brother* with such venom it scares me a little.

"Why did you then?"

He runs his tongue over his lip, his eyes scanning me up and down. I see the flash of pain in them before the shutters come down. "It doesn't matter anymore."

"It matters to me." I say softly, placing my hand on his arm. He pulls away from my touch, turning alarmingly pale in the face. "Sorry." All of that progress, completely gone. "Tell me."

"If I tell you, you might never forgive Caleb." He says, going to sit on my bed, but after looking at my attire once more, he thinks better of it and stands at the window instead.

"Tell me." I insist, standing beside him with my hands on the windowsill.

"I was going to, but I don't need to anymore." He motions to my current attire. "It's already too late."

Oh, right, he thinks I've done the deed with Eric. I can't blame him for thinking that. "I haven't slept with Eric, Nathan. I was tired. He took me to his, I had a shower and I slept. My clothes were covered in flour, sugar and jam to the point where they were more like cake than they were fabric."

"You've kissed him."

"You saw me." I clear my throat and look away.

"Just kissing? Is that it?"

"Only twice, once at his, once in front of you." Why am I explaining this?

He smiles slightly, his brows still furrowed. "Choose me."

Whoa... what? A one eighty flip just happened.

"I'm serious." He says, backing me up into the door. "Choose me."

Is this happening? "What?"

"Choose me." He dips his head and looks directly in my eyes. "You don't want him."

"You don't know that."

"I do." He places his hand on my cheek and traces his thumb over my lower lip. "I know that when he kissed you, your thoughts were on me, worrying how I felt, worrying about how I'd react." Well... "Stop being stubborn and choose me. It's simple. Just say yes."

"But..."

"Don't think about Caleb." He implores, his other hand gripping my bicep. "Please, he doesn't deserve your loyalty."

Blink. "What the hell is that supposed to mean?" It's not like Caleb is here to defend himself, so I don't appreciate his cryptic sentences about him.

"You don't know him like I do. You think you do, but you don't. He wasn't always a good person, Gwen."

Eye roll. "He changed. He was very good to me."

"Yes, so it would seem." He mutters conspiratorially.

Shaking my head, I frown at the scowling man before me. "Like what? Tell me damn it!"

"I saw you first!" He shouts, his fingers biting into the skin of my arm. "He would have never have met you if I hadn't sent him down to that beach to get you!"

My breath leaves me in a whoosh. I feel like I've been punched in the gut. "What?"

"I saw you, every single day, from the window of my hotel room. You would walk down the beach. I'd watch you every day, wishing I wasn't the way I was, just so I could talk to you."

"I don't understand."

He growls and gives me a small shake. "I hate sand. Hate it. But you enchanted me. I had to meet you." This is insane, completely insane. "I even took pictures of you and wrote about you in my damn journal. I had to meet you. I once waited at the end of the beach near that kids play area on the pavement. You'd always walk up to there and back, looking over your shoulder every so often whilst smiling at nothing. Sometimes you'd walk backwards with your arms out to the sides. You were mesmerising."

"W... what does that have to do with Caleb?"

"I asked him to fetch you. Begged him in fact." His eyes darkened. "I paid him ten grand to do it for me." Ten thousand? That's insane. "I didn't realise how sore he was that our Grandfather left me the majority of his money and properties in his will."

"Get to the point." I demand, my breath quickening. I can't breathe.

"Caleb agreed to meet with you and bring you off the beach to meet me. He said he'd become your friend and lead you to me."

"Can I walk with you?"

Caleb's first ever words to me ring through my head. I feel dizzy. "Maybe... maybe he just liked me too."

"Oh, he definitely liked you." Nathan spits, the vehemence in his tone only showing a fraction of how he really feels about the situation. "He led you right by me. I thought maybe you were shy and he was finding the right moment to introduce us."

"What happened next?" I need to know. I need to hear it.

"He promised me that you were meeting him the next day, he'd introduce us. Then you were shy and timid and that day wasn't good timing." He says this in a mocking tone, using his fingers to accentuate the words 'good timing'. "He told me where to wait, so I waited by the hotel. I had the perfect view of you both. He'd lied about the time. It looked like you'd been spending time together for a while before I got there. I trusted him."

What do I say to that? Nothing. There's nothing to say right now. I should just listen.

"I saw you both kiss." He brushes my hair from my temple, his eyes sad. "You were the first girl I've ever liked." Yeah right. "I'm serious, Gwen. I wouldn't lie to you about that. You know me better than anyone." He shrugs. "I thought he would get bored like he usually did. Instead..."

"Go on." I need to hear this.

"He took you in the back of his car, no doubt down a dirt road outside of town." Cringe. "I saw the car because I didn't believe him. I saw the stain." My cheeks heat at the memory. "I wanted to kill him. He'd already told me he was staying behind. I had told our parents, anything to get him away from you."

"Why would you do that?" I whisper.

"I... can't get into that right now." I want to push him, but I need to process the information I already have. "But then... I was mad at you too. In my head you were on this pedestal. You were this perfect woman to me, beautiful, graceful, carefree and innocent. It came off you in waves. Why would you...?"

"I didn't." I blurt, holding my hand up to silence him. "We didn't have sex in the car."

"I saw..."

"You saw a stain and yes, we fooled around, but in actuality, I didn't lose my virginity to him until after we'd moved in together." Why would Caleb lie about that? "Caleb...whatever he did to you, he never hurt me, never pushed me. He waited until I was ready and then he... I hate that he did that to you. I'm sorry that he did that to you. If he were alive, I'd..."

"You'd what?" He asks, his voice low and his eyes wide with wonder. "Shout at him? Break up with him and go with me? Don't say things you don't mean."

"I don't know what I'd do." I admit, reaching up to trail my fingers along the side of his neck. "All I know is that the only silver lining of Caleb's death is that I got the chance to know you."

He pushes forward, his chest against mine. "So choose me."

"If I don't?" I ask quietly, resting my forehead against his neck. "What happens if I don't?"

I feel his chest deflate. His hand tips my head back and he looks into my eyes. "I'll leave with no hard feelings. I'll never bother you again, I swear." He pauses for a moment. "But please, choose me."

"And what will happen if I do?"

"I'll never let you go. Never."

I believe him, truly I do, but this is a difficult choice to make. If I choose him, will people judge me? Do I care if they judge me? Not really. If I don't choose him, will I regret it?

How do I feel about him?

I think back to our time together, living with him, how I felt when I left, how I felt when he touched me and held me in his sleep. So many things to consider.

He makes me happy. He's never let me down, but I can't just forget everything he's put me through. What if I step out of line and he tells me to leave again? Can I handle that? Probably not.

And then there are the secrets he clings to, not just his grandfather but everything else. Those envelopes that kept getting sent to me, what was in them? Why does he hate Caleb? Surely it can't be all because of me? And if it is because of me, there has to be more to it than what he's told me. He's hiding something, I know it.

But all of that will come in time, I know it will, otherwise we won't work. So what do I do? How do I feel?

Gah... have mercy, this is too much to consider.

Can I do this? Eric is everything I should want. He's different.

Eric is Caleb.

I don't want another Caleb. I want complicated and broody, because when Nathan finally gives part of himself to me, it feels like the greatest reward. I want to figure him out, unlock his secrets and help him through them.

But what if I'm wrong?

"Gwen?"

"Okay." I whisper, ignoring my morals and rapidly firing thoughts. Switching off my mind, I decide with nothing but the muscle beating in my chest. "Okay."

"Okay?"

"I'm not choosing you." His hands go to release me. I grip his hair with one hand and the front of his shirt with the other. "There's no choice to make."

He scrunches up his nose, "Well I feel rather moronic right now."

"That's not what I mean." Eye roll. "You were never second best; you were never a choice. I'm sorry I didn't realise it sooner."

"You're not making any sense."

"I mean," how do I say this? "I love you. I think I have for a really long time." I know I have. I've just been too ashamed of the circumstances to admit it, or try to rationalise it.

"Don't say that if you don't mean it. If you're saying it because of what I've told you…"

"I'm not," I promise and let my body relax. "I've been an idiot. I've been awful to you, I know I have, and I'm sorry. I'm ready now, if you'll forgive me. I'd like to try."

He blinks, seemingly astonished. "You're choosing me?"

"But if we're going to do this properly, we need to be completely honest with each other. No more secrets."

He gulps, looking away nervously. "I don't want to talk about what happened."

"That's fine, but you need to talk about what happened before I found out about your grandfather. You're not being let off the hook that easy." I chastise him, though I still have a smile on my face. "There are things we need to deal with."

He sighs. "I was hoping we could just kiss now, but you've ruined the moment."

I grin. "We were having a moment?"

"*Were,* being the key word here." He steps into me again. "Now, be quiet. I've waited for this for a very long time."

"Kay." I lean back, closing my eyes as I wait for him to press his lips to mine. He moves slowly, sending tingles of anticipation straight down my spine. I feel his breath on my lips, but then it's gone.

I decide to open my eyes when a few seconds pass and I notice that my slightly puckered lips are going to waste. Nathan's eyes twinkle with amusement at my confusion, but then he sobers and a look of contentment overcomes him.

A gloved hand touches my arm, the fingertips barely grazing the skin as it moves upwards and rests on my shoulder. My breath hitches when those same fingers brush a gentle path up my neck, to my jaw and to my ear. I whimper, tiny bumps prickling along the surface of my arms and the swell of my breasts.

Nathan looks at his hand and frowns. My eyes follow his movements. I watch closely as he slowly removes the glove and places it into his pocket. His bare fingers make the same journey they made a moment ago, starting at my wrist before finishing at the corner of my mouth. I shudder and close my eyes when he scrapes his fingers upwards and brushes the side of my hair over my ear.

This is it, I think over and over as his eyes hold mine and his face moves slowly closer. My heartbeat quickens, my chest tingles and my mouth goes dry. I wet my lips quickly in preparation, waiting for him to finally kiss me.

His nose touches mine and strokes the bridge with a barely there touch. Gulp.

A small smile lights up his face, making his eyes become hooded.

Watching his pupils dilate as his top lip touches mine is definitely a sight I'll never forget. I wonder if that's what he's doing, burning this exact moment to memory.

A gasp escapes me when I feel his free hand trail along the edge of the boxers I'm wearing, before dipping under my top and sliding around to my back. He pulls me to him, his hips against mine. I feel how much he wants me and the thrill it sends through my body is almost unbearable.

I'm about ready to grab him and devour his mouth in a wicked way, when I feel his bottom lip finally skim mine.

My eyes close, my body heats and I'm sure my cheeks turn pink.

The anticipation is killing me. I've never felt so alive, so on fire.

"Nathan." I whisper so quietly, I barely even hear it myself.

A moan leaves my throat when his tongue lightly touches the centre of my top lip. I'm startled by the force of feeling such a gentle touch creates.

Yes. Finally.

A wail from downstairs forces my eyes open.

Damn it all!

Nathan scrunches up his nose and sighs. "Dillan. I'll get him."

Shit, my son. He's poorly. What kind of a mother am I?

Nathan bumps my nose with his. "They said it's just colic and possibly a cold, don't worry. I'll deal with him."

"Okay, I'm going to get changed."

"Have a shower too, wash him from your skin." He kisses the curve of my neck and pulls me out of the way of the door.

Scowling at him, I stomp past and enter the bathroom, ignoring his chuckle as I go.

Nathan taps on the door as I'm pulling Eric's top over my head. "Hey, Gwen?"

"Yes?"

"Actually, it doesn't matter. I'll tell you later."

"Okay." I throw the top on the ground and step out of the boxers. I don't need a shower but I know how fussy Nathan can be.

Staring at myself in the mirror before I climb under the hot spray, I look at my reflection and ask her one thing. "Are you sure this is what you want?" Then I nod with a smile and climb under the spray. It is what I want.

It's what I need.

Wiping the mist from the mirror, I run a comb through my wet hair to get rid of the tangles. I look flushed from the hot water. I've also never felt so clean. After brushing my teeth, I double check the towel that's wrapped around my body is tight enough and pad into my bedroom.

I have to admit, now that a decision has been made, I feel like a weight has been lifted. My shoulders suddenly feel a lot lighter.

I just wish I knew how Caleb felt about this.

Christ... have I gone insane? He's dead! He's not coming back and I'm still alive. I need to remember that.

"It's definitely colic. He's not drinking the milk and he keeps bringing his legs up to his chest." Nathan says as he walks into my room with a squawking Dillan in his arms. "He doesn't have a temperature so I'm not too wo..." He stops in his tracks, his mouth hanging open. "...rried."

"Yeah, I need to get dressed."

Nathan blinks and sits. "Feel free to do so."

My brow lifts. "Out."

"Oh come on, I have permission now."

I snort. "Says who?"

"Says you, when you just agreed to be my girlfriend." Playful Nathan equals a Nathan I enjoy greatly, although I'm not sure I like the title girlfriend. It seems so juvenile. He looks at Dillan, who is still squawking. "Quiet. Mummy, aka my girlfriend," there's that label again, "is busy entertaining me." He looks up at me, his face straight and showing no sign of humour. "He says get your tits out."

I choke on my surprised laughter. That was so not what I expected to hear from him. Not at all.

"What?" He asks innocently. "He said it."

My body leans forward as laughter forces its way upwards. It's almost painful. Make it stop.

"You never cease to amaze me, Nathan Weston," I giggle, pulling the towel tighter around me. "Out. Give him some cool boiled water for me."

"You've been my girlfriend for twenty minutes and already you're ordering me around."

"What's with the label?"

He smiles mischievously. "Well you are my girlfriend." His smile widens. "I have a girlfriend."

"You're going to keep saying it, aren't you?"

He nods once. "Yes, yes I am."

Sigh. "Whatever. Out please."

"But..."

"Out."

He grumbles under his breath as he leaves the room. It's then that Dillan finally starts smiling.

Quickly pulling on some clothes, I braid my hair over one shoulder and add a little mascara to my long lashes. I can hear Dillan crying again, so I quickly dart down the stairs and take him from Nathan, who looks perplexed about what to do.

"Maybe we should take him to the doctor?" Nathan suggests, but I shake my head and reply,

"We'll give him some gripe water and he'll be okay. Can you make him a bottle up; there's some gripe water in the cupboard next to the fridge, top shelf. It's a grey bottle. Just a couple of drops."

He gets to work immediately as I put Dillan over my shoulder and pat his back. It does little to soothe him. My poor baby.

Two hours go by before he finally sleeps. I'm starting to wonder if it's my breast milk that's upsetting him. I've been eating the right foods as far as I'm aware. Maybe I should put him onto formula.

No, all babies get colic at some point. I'll speak to Dillan's doctor tomorrow and see what she says.

"Relax." Nathan murmurs, running his gloved fingertips over my still damp braid. I feel it all the way to the base of my spine and let out a little shudder. Nathan, taking this response as permission, pushes it out of the way and shuffles closer. I feel his warm breath on my neck before I feel his lips.

Exquisite.

Carefully leaning forward, I place Dillan back in his chair and turn towards Nathan, tilting my head to the side so my neck is exposed to him. He strokes the delicate skin on the opposite side of my neck to where he's kissing, with his glove free hand.

This should feel weird, I mean… it's Nathan. But it doesn't, not in the slightest.

He pulls back an inch, his pupils dilated and his cheeks slightly flushed with a tinge of pink. I move my hand up to caress his face and marvel at the heat coming from him.

I stare at him for a few seconds, my breath coming out of me in pants. His is the same and it gives me a thrill knowing that I'm doing that to him.

"I brought pizza!" My mum shouts as the front door swings open.

"Bloody hell," Nathan sighs and we separate quickly.

Mum walks in and places two pizza boxes on the coffee table in the centre of the room. She smiles at me, but that soon fades when she sees Nathan. "Sorry, I didn't realise we'd have company."

"Yeah, I was going to call." I chew on my lower lip for a moment. "Dillan's poorly. Nathan picked him up from nursery for me."

My mum nods and shrugs a little. "There's plenty. How's Dillan now?"

I look at him resting in his vibrating chair and smile when his big, round eyes come to me. "I gave him some gripe water and his stomach has settled. He's a bit snotty though. I'll take him to the doctor tomorrow."

"How's Eric?" She pointedly asks, giving me one of those looks that only Mums can give you.

My mouth falls open. She just ratted me out! Of course Nathan already knows, but she doesn't know that. "I don't know. How's my new step daddy?" Two can play at that game.

Her mouth falls open and her eyes narrow in horror. "You know?"

"That you still make out in public like a hormonal teen saying goodbye to her boyfriend at a bus stop? Yeah, we know."

Her eyes go to Nathan, who quickly pretends to start looking for something in his jacket pockets.

Letting out a sigh, she runs her fingers through her hair and a dreamy smile touches her face, "He's lovely. You'll like him Gwen."

"Don't get pregnant," I order, earning me a scowl.

Nathan chuckles beside me but stops when my mum turns her scowl his way. He starts searching through his pockets again.

Sigh.

For some reason, this action from him reminds me of how young he is. He always holds himself so confidently, so proudly. I forget that he's only twenty-five. I think... hell, I don't even know when his birthday is.

We eat pizza in an uncomfortable silence. It would be comical if there wasn't so much tension in the air, although I do almost laugh when Nathan eats his slices with a knife and fork. After I stare at him for a few seconds, he gives me the most adorable look and says, "What?"

This makes me laugh.

I clean away the empty boxes as Mum and Nathan wash their hands.

Then I make us drinks and again, we drink them in an uncomfortable silence. All that can be heard is our slurping every few seconds.

I'm wondering what to tell my mum. I told her I'd chosen Eric and now I've got to tell her I've chosen Nathan, but haven't yet told Eric. I was actually hoping I wouldn't have to say anything to her and she'd just get the message after a while of seeing me with Nathan but not Eric. This won't be the case, I can tell by the looks she's giving me every so often. She wants me to explain and I don't blame her.

"You're staying here?" Mum breaks the silence as I'm rocking Dillan side to side on my knees.

I close my eyes briefly, keeping my head down. Maybe they won't see me.

"If I have your permission to do so," Nathan politely says. I don't look at him; I'm too busy clapping Dillan's hands together and making him smile.

"That's fine. Gwen will make up the couch?" Why's this worded as a question and not a statement?

Then Nathan says something that makes me squeeze my eyes shut and mentally start punching him in the back of the head. "No, I'll be staying with my girlfriend, Gwen." There's that damn label…

It falls eerily silent again.

"Anybody want dessert?" I jump up, startling Dillan who I immediately hand to Nathan. "I have jam roly-poly I can heat up." I look at Mum. "Do we have custard?"

"I feel like I'm missing something." My mum's words make me freeze on the spot.

"Nope, it's exactly like he said." I smile. It's forced and completely fake. "Pudding?"

"Maybe you should explain."

"Or not."

"Gwen." I hate that tone.

"Yes?" I try for sweet, but she only gives me that look again. Sigh. "Isn't it obvious?"

She shakes her head. "No, actually it's not."

I glare at Nathan. "This is your fault."

He smiles alluringly. "Are we having a tiff?"

Throwing my hands up in the air I let out a growl and walk out of the room, grumbling the entire way.

"Would you like to explain?" Mum says to Nathan.

"Certainly," he states. I wait for him to continue. He doesn't.

My mum loses her patience. "Well? Go on."

"Go on what?"

"Explain."

"Explain what?"

My mum lets out a growl similar to the one I just did only moments ago. "Explain what the hell is going on with you and Gwen."

"Oh, you could have said that." She's going to hit him, I just know it. I snigger slightly, wanting to see my mum's face but not daring to look around the doorway for fear of being pulled into the conversation. "I'll have pudding," Nathan calls. "If you're still offering."

"Why will nobody answer me?" Mum whines to herself because nobody answers her. "We'll talk tomorrow, Guinevere."

I hope not.

Chapter Eleven

Climbing into bed with Nathan after settling Dillan in his cot, I lie on my back beside him, our arms touching. He turns onto his side, propping his head up with his elbow. His hand traces my face, starting at my brow and brushing over it softly before moving down my nose.

I close my eyes and ask the question that's been gnawing at me ever since he confessed his secrets earlier today. "Why did you hit Caleb? Was that because of me?"

His fingers, that were moving over my cheekbone, go still. "That's a long story."

I peek at him through slightly parted lids. "We have time."

He sighs, flopping backwards onto his back. "I'm tired. Can we discuss it another day?"

I roll onto my side and prop myself up on my elbow, much like he did seconds ago. "You've already told me some of it. Surely you can…"

He gives me a look, the same look he used to give me when I was living with him and he found me irritating.

"Fine," I snap and roll over, putting my back to him. "You promised no secrets."

"If it's all the same to you, I'd rather not discuss the man who took your virginity whilst I lie in bed beside you." He says this softly, his tone not matching the look he gave me. "Why did you used to walk backwards on the beach? I used to sit and worry you'd fall. Not that you'd hurt yourself; apparently sand is soft to land on when you're not too high."

"Footprints." I gulp, thinking back on the days I was, as he said, carefree and innocent. "I used to be amazed by footprints."

He moves closer. I feel his chest against my back. Again, he props himself up using his elbow and starts stroking his fingers through the side of my hair. "Footprints?"

"Yes. Footprints."

"Why footprints?"

"Because on the sand you can see them, but only for a short while."

He runs his chin over the curve of my shoulder. "I'm still not following."

"It's silly. I used to be obsessed with wondering who had walked over that spot before me. Were they sad? Were they happy? What had they been doing?" I laugh a little at the thought. "I miss having such a clear mind, where those kinds of thoughts were the only ones I woke up with."

His lips press against my shoulder. I feel them smile against my skin before his arm comes around my waist and his face nuzzles into my neck. "Go to sleep."

My eyes close and my body relaxes, especially with his heat smothering me in the most delicious way.

Just when I think he's fallen asleep, he shifts and presses his cheek against my ear. In the quietest voice, he whispers, "Tell me you love me, Gwen."

My breath catches in my throat. I push back against him, snuggling my backside into his crotch as my hand finds his by my breast. I hold it tight and whisper in the quietest voice, "I love you, Nathan."

He kisses the side of my jaw, directly below my ear and holds me even tighter.

Moments later, we fall asleep.

When I wake up in the morning I'm shocked to find the bed empty beside me. I'm also shocked that the sun is shining and Dillan hasn't awoken yet. Upon further inspection, I see that Dillan is also missing.

Nathan.

Climbing out of bed, I rub my tired eyes and try to focus through the blurry coating of dryness that rests over my eyeballs. I don't prevail, so I stagger into the bathroom and splash water on my face.

"Morning."

"Jesus!" I yelp, spinning on the spot. My hands immediately clutch the sink behind me as I try to calm my beating heart. "What are you doing?"

"Bathing Dillan." He says this like I'm stupid. Which I am, because that's exactly what he's doing and it's clear to see. "He woke up four times last night. You didn't wake up once. You must have been tired."

Or I knew Nathan would deal with it, so my mind wouldn't switch on. "Sorry."

He shrugs. "He was easy to manage."

"Good." I chew on my lip for a moment, staring at a bare chested Nathan, kneeling on the ground next to Dillan's baby bath, who is kicking away happily in the warm suds.

"You need a bath." Nathan says, patting the shower door. At first I think he's telling me I'm unclean, but then I realise he's talking about our lack of a bath tub. "Hold out the towel."

I do as he says and wait as he carefully picks Dillan up and hands him to me. We wrap him together and I clutch him to my chest as Nathan dries his hands and pulls on his gloves.

"If you go and get ready, we can be at Jeanine's by one." Nathan lifts Dillan out of my arms and nuzzles his chubby cheek with his nose. "Quickly, you'll need to feed him before we go. I gave him some more gripe water with his morning bottle, but you're out of expressed milk."

"Jeanine's?" He follows me into the bedroom.

"Yes, she wants to see Dillan and I want to take you somewhere."

"Where?" I enquire, rummaging through my drawers to find the perfect outfit. "Outdoor or indoor?"

"Outdoors, it's not too cold out today." He nods when I hold up a long, loose, baby blue dress. "Wear a cardigan on top."

I do as I'm told, grabbing a black woollen one which hangs loosely over the shoulders.

Nathan takes Dillan's nappy bag and leaves the room, but not before telling me I only have five minutes to get ready.

It's a good thing I braided my hair yesterday or it'd be a frightful mess right now.

Before long we're in the car and on the road. I'm grateful my mum wasn't up whilst we were getting ready. It means I got to miss out on the interrogation.

"Do I still get free reign over the radio?"

Nathan waves his hand towards it.

Yay.

"I'm thirsty." I announce after a few more minutes of silence.

"Me too, but we don't have time to stop." He rubs his chin. It's the first time I've seen him with any stubble. It's only a light shadow, but I have to admit it makes him look very handsome.

"We'll just run in, grab a drink and run out again." I suggest.

He shakes his head. "No food or drink in the car."

"Are you serious? You've let me before."

He rolls his eyes. "That was one time; you were pregnant and grieving."

"Well now I'm breast feeding and wondering whether or not you want this journey to be relaxing or not," I threaten, smiling smugly.

He completely ignores me, his eyes staring at the road ahead.

"Nathan?"

"Yes?"

"Can I ask you something?"

He shifts in his seat, his tongue swiping at his lower lip. "What do you want to know?"

How do I say this? "Was... umm... was Caleb..."

His hands tense on the steering wheel; any tighter and I'd be worried about the strength of the wheel. "No."

This brings me relief. "I don't understand why it was just you that..."

"Caleb rarely went to our grandfather's. Maybe he didn't have the opportunity."

I don't believe him. "Don't get me wrong. I'm glad that he wasn't... I wish you hadn't had to... but..."

"Spit it out," he snaps, clearly getting annoyed with my lack of proper English at present. It's a difficult thing to talk about. I can't just say it outright. Can I?

"It makes no sense that he'd only target you."

He doesn't respond. His face holds that usual blank façade that I hate so much.

If he doesn't want to talk about it, I guess I can't blame him. There are other things we should discuss. I'll mention those instead.

"Are you going to tell me why you hit him now?"

"No."

"But..."

"It'll put me in a bad mood and spoil our day. Let it go." He's not already in a bad mood?

Huff. "Fine."

He lets out a long breath, his eyes narrowed in irritation. "Don't start being mardy. I don't want to talk about it."

"I don't see why, you promised no more secrets," I point out, glaring at his profile.

"And I said I wouldn't keep secrets from you, but I didn't say when I'd divulge said secrets. I will tell you... eventually."

I laugh in disbelief. "If we want to move forward then we should talk about these things."

"I agree." Finally! "But right now, at this point in our relationship - which, may I remind you, has only just begun - it isn't time to get into such things. They'll only upset you and I don't want that. Especially not today."

Crossing my arms over my chest, I continue to argue. "Or they'll upset me more when our relationship is further along because I'll wonder why you kept things from me for such a long time."

"Or you'll never talk to me again."

"That could happen now or in the future, depending on the severity of the secrets."

He looks at me, anger and pain evident in the hard set of his jaw and the widening of his eyes. "That's good to know."

"If you just..."

"Enough!" He shouts, suddenly pulling the car to the side of the road, forcing me to grip the handle above my head. "I told you; I'll tell you in my own time and on my own terms, not yours. Life isn't as simple as you think; there are a lot of things to consider. If you don't want that, then tell me now so I can at least leave with a small shred of dignity."

Blink. "But..."

"Gwen," he snaps, turning in his seat to face me. "This is me; this is how I'm always going to be." He holds out his hands for a moment as a way of showing me himself. "This is how I want to do it and I'm not going to change my mind. Decide right now if you want that. If you don't, then we've made a severe error where this relationship is concerned. If you do, then be quiet and just enjoy the day!"

He's almost panting by the time he's finished. He's also right.

"Don't talk to me like that," I say quietly, looking away from his glare. "I really hate it when you talk to me like that. You make me feel like a child."

He sighs and puts the car back in gear. "Why do you have the ability to make me so angry, yet so... annoyingly guilty all at the same time? I'm sorry for shouting."

"I'm not sorry for prying, but I am sorry for pushing."

He rolls his eyes heavenward as if praying for help with the issue that is me. "You're not going to let it go are you?"

I answer honestly. "No. Especially not if it concerns me, which I know it does."

Reaching over the console, he places his hand on my thigh. "Then do me one favour."

"What?"

"Don't bring it up again for just a few weeks. Let's just enjoy being us and get to know each other before we tackle the heavy subjects."

Gah. Can I do that? "I can do that."

He smiles and taps his cheek with his finger. Feigning reluctance, I lean into him and press my lips to his cheek for a few moments. When I pull back the first thing I notice is his closed mouth smile. "You spoil me," he jokes, giving my thigh a squeeze. "Let's go."

I wait for him to start driving before I announce, "In the time it took you to tell me off, we could have stopped and had a quick coffee."

"Please," he begs jokingly. "Somebody get me a gag."

Arsehole.

His face sobers as his hand leaves my thigh and comes to my hand. "I know I can be difficult, but always keep this in mind: any decisions I make regarding you will always be because of how I feel for you." He gives me a sharp look, one full of determination and concern. "I will always protect you, always. You might not agree with that but you will have to deal with it, because it's never going to change."

Something fills inside me, something that's felt hollow for a really long time. I smile softly at him and wonder how I ever thought he was a cold unfeeling person. "Good to know," I respond breathlessly and squeeze his hand back. "So... what are we doing today?"

"It's a surprise."

"I hate surprises." I lie; I love them. I'm just very impatient.

He grins and points out a sign to the next service station. "Ten more miles. My girlfriend's thirsty."

Sigh. "Are we starting with that again?"

"Yes." He gives a firm nod, making me giggle in response.

Jeanine holds me tight as soon as she sees me. And by tight I mean *tight*.

"Can't breathe," I choke out and she finally pulls back.

"Good god girl, I've missed you!" She beams, pinching my cheeks with both hands. "How are you?"

"I'm fine. I've missed you too." It's the truth; we bonded during my time here with Nathan. At times she was my only friend, not to mention the fact she delivered Dillan safely and I'll be forever in her debt. "How is everything?"

"Nothing to complain about," she says, still beaming. "Come on in. Bring that little boy with you."

"That's fine. Nathan can walk now, haven't you heard?" I comment dryly, squealing when Nathan squeezes the back of my neck and gives me a scowl for good measure.

"So, all I know is, I'm to watch this gorgeous little bundle for a few hours. May I ask as to why?" Jeanine cuts right to the chase the moment we step through the door.

"It's a surprise," Nathan says and gives me a look that tells me to 'wait for it'. "For my girlfriend." And there it is.

"Kill him," I tell her, too busy staring at Nathan to notice her reaction to his words. "I swear, that's all he's done for the entire journey. He actually let me eat in the car, because his girlfriend was hungry. We shared a coffee, because his girlfriend was thirsty. Oh…" I narrow my eyes. "And then there's the whole, 'how is my girlfriend?' every ten minutes and 'is this music okay for my girlfriend?'"

Nathan only looks proud. When I look at Jeanine, there are tears in her eyes. Oh good lord. She didn't know.

"I knew it would happen, I just knew it!" She slaps Nathan on the chest. "Didn't I say she was perfect for you? What took you so long?"

"My girlfriend is stubborn."

"Really?" I say, looking for a sharp object. "What are you... twelve?"

He chuckles and hands Dillan over to Jeanine. I kiss my little boy's fuzzy hair and step back so Nathan can run his hand over the place I just kissed. "Thank you Jeanine, for watching Dillan. We'll be back before dark."

"Go, have fun."

"I'll make sure my..." Nathan starts to say but I cut him off with a "Don't you dare."

Shoving him out of the house, I keep my arm around his waist as we walk to the car. Looking up at him through my lashes, I give him a sweet smile, hoping he'll tell me now. It's whilst I'm smiling sweetly that I notice how nervous he looks.

"This was a stupid idea," he says as he helps me into the car.

"Stupid?"

"You're going to think it's stupid." he shakes his head. "Well, too late to turn back now."

"What is it?"

He shrugs. "We're just going for a walk."

"With you, right?"

He looks confused and then wary. "Yes, why?"

"Then it's not stupid." I rest my hand on his leg and move my fingers in slow circles.

We're driving for twenty minutes before we make it to his grandfather's house. I glare up at the building that became my home whilst I was pregnant. Nathan, sensing my anger towards the place, guides me to the boot of his car and opens it.

"Here, put these on." He hands me a pair of dark brown walking boots.

Grinning from ear to ear, I slip off my pumps and grab the still packaged socks from the boot. After sliding them on, followed by the boots and tying the laces, I jump a few times to test their comfort and lean up to kiss Nathan's jaw. He turns his head at the wrong moment and I end up with my lips against the corner of his mouth.

His hand immediately goes to my elbow and his eyes close slowly.

The hand that I have flat against his chest tingles with the feel of his heartbeat picking up speed beneath it. I smile and pull back, using my thumb to wipe away the shimmering gloss that my lips left behind.

Clearing his throat, he grabs a bag and throws it over his shoulder. It looks almost empty.

"Let's go." He takes my hand and pulls me towards the woods. Considering it's only spring, the sun is really beating down on us today. Fortunately it's coupled with a nice, cool and gentle breeze.

We walk in silence for a while through the thick trees. Nathan, obviously knowing this place like the back of his hand, leads me easily around the bushes and through the trees. It's not until I see the huge clearing full of thigh-high length grass that I start freaking out.

He steps into it, not realising I've stopped until the hand holding mine pulls him backwards.

I stare at the grass and then look at him wide-eyed. "This is where the demon rats with red eyes almost got me and feasted on my flesh."

He blinks, shakes his head and laughs. "What?"

"I came out here for a walk when I was pregnant. Do you know how many critters are probably hiding in this long grass, just waiting for suckers like us to walk through?" I whisper, just in case they can hear me. The last thing I want is for them to know that I know their plan.

"Really?" He tries to keep a straight face but fails. "It's just grass."

"And sand is just sand," I retort, my brow quirking. "I'm not going in there. Let's go around."

He grabs me before I can walk away. "It'll take an extra hour to get around all of this."

"Well let's just stay here then." I stamp my foot on the ground, my nerves getting the better of me.

"Is it weird that I'm enjoying this? It's nice knowing I'm not the only weird one." He chuckles and drops the bag that was on his back to the ground. Then he crouches in front of me and holds his arms out behind him. "Up."

"What?" My body moves me back a step without permission, but I'm not entirely sure what he's doing.

"Come on, we haven't got all day."

"You want me to get on your back?" Why is this so hard to believe? I clearly remember Nathan carrying me around when I was pregnant, not on his back but in his arms. Usually when I fell asleep downstairs.

"Yes."

"But I'm heavy."

"Gwen..." His tone is warning. I sigh and place my hands on his shoulders.

I squeal and almost pull away when he slides his hands up my thighs, lifting my dress out of the way before picking me up with ease. My arms automatically wrap around his strong neck.

Swooping down, he grabs the bag and hands it to me. I grip it tight in front of his chest as my thighs grip tight to his hips.

"I was hoping the first time I'd get your legs around me, it'd be in a different position," Nathan comments crudely, his lips tipping up in a smirk.

What the hell do I say to that?

Nothing. I grab his nipple with my free hand and twist.

"Carrying you through demon grass here. If you hurt me, we're both going down."

Good point.

"Are you sure you can carry me all the way across there?" The distance looks daunting, like in a scary movie where the hallway just seems to get longer and longer. That's how I feel right now.

"Too late to go back now." He bunks me up a little and gives my legs a squeeze.

I am so glad I shaved my legs.

It takes a while and I can tell Nathan is getting tired by the time we pass the burned barn, which makes me feel sick and want to kill something.

"You burned the barn down didn't you?" I ask.

He blows out a breath and squeezes my legs tighter to me. "Yes."

I lean forward and press my lips to the shell of his ear for a long moment. My voice is a whisper when I tell him, "I would have done the same."

"Stop talking." He says it softly, kindly, almost pleadingly.

I kiss him again and press my forehead against the back of his head. "Okay."

When we reach the edge of the grass I immediately drop to my feet and rub his back as he stretches. He grins, remaining silent as he takes the bag from me and pulls me forward.

"So, what's going on with your jewellery?" I ask, stepping over a fallen log.

He shrugs. "I just haven't put much thought into it as of late."

"That's a shame. I was planning on raiding your store when it opened." I give him an honest smile and touch my bare neck. I miss my necklace.

"They aren't that good."

"The fact that I know you believe that to be true just goes to show what an idiot you can be some times." I roll my eyes with my words and he smiles.

"You're too sweet, Gwen."

"I'm not saying it to be sweet, Nathan. I'm saying it because it's true. You have serious talent and you're wasting it every moment you're not showing it off."

"Hmm," he murmurs, still walking.

Now I'm out of things to say.

"Are we nearly there yet?" I ask, although it's not because I'm not enjoying myself. I am. This place is beautiful in the spring, what with all of the blossoms scattered across the hard dirt ground after floating in a flurry from the trees around us. It's almost surreal.

"Nearly," he says absently.

I go quiet again. I see that he needs to concentrate.

"Finally, I forgot which side it was on for a moment," he says, scratching his head for a moment. Reaching forward, he pulls on something hidden by thick moss. "Look up."

I do and what I see makes me gasp. "A tree house?"

A boyish grin comes over his face. "I found it when I was small. It's well built. I'm assuming it belonged to my grandfather when he was a child; this land belonged to his father before him. My family apparently owned the entire village at one point, but back then it was nothing but trees and rocks. It should be safe. I came out here a few weeks back to check it out."

Should be?

There's a rattling noise when whatever he's pulled on releases a sturdy looking wooden ladder that drops to the ground. It's when he moves away that I notice the rope leading from the platform above to some strange wooden lever that is nailed into the thick tree.

"You go first," he says and guides me to the ladder. "Don't worry, it's clean."

"I thought I could smell bleach," I mumble but I don't think he hears me. Using my hands at head level, I test the strength of the ladder before taking that first step.

When I go up onto the third, Nathan follows directly behind, his head level with my shoulders and his hands either side of my ribs. I feel his chest against my back. It distracts me but I manage to not fall.

When I finally climb over the top, I look around in surprise. This is not what I expected. It looks like a very small living room that you'd imagine a troll would live in. There's no couch, but the far corner has pillows placed carefully on the polished wood floor. The walls are painted grey; the paint is peeling in places but that's to be expected.

I was expecting it to look like the inside of a shed. Instead it's like a little boys' dream. There are shelves with torches, matches, little tool kits and a few old toys. A trunk sits by the pillows and there's a radio on an upturned bin. Other than that it's clean and empty.

"Wow," I say as I stand to full height, moving out of the way so Nathan can climb up after me.

I have to duck under the rope attached to the ceiling and ladder as I make my way over to the trunk. My curiosity gets the better of me.

"Don't open that," Nathan says, placing his hand on the curved top. "Not yet."

"Why didn't you ever bring me here when I lived here?"

"Could you have climbed the ladder in your condition?" Point well made. He looks around, his lips pinched together. I wonder if he's embarrassed. I'm about to tell him he shouldn't be, but he starts talking and I'm not sure whether or not I like what I hear. "This was my safe place." He sits on the pillows, patting the spot beside him. It's then that I notice the window opposite is longer than the rest. I imagine at one point you'd have been able to see above the trees. This tree is a lot larger and a hell of a lot wider than all of the others, but they're quickly catching up in size. All I can see through the window is the green leaves and pink blossoms of the closest tree.

I'm amazed this place has survived for so long. Surely the tree it sits upon should have crushed it by now as it grew? It just seems to have grown around it more than anything.

"Safe place?"

"Yes, I learned to kind of..." he waves his hand in the air as if searching for the right word, "sense when my grandfather would be in one of *those* moods. I'd come here."

I gulp, keeping my eyes straight ahead and keeping my emotions bottled. He needs me to listen, not to interfere and start crying all over him.

He continues. "He'd leave me alone, but I'd have to go down eventually."

The thought of a small boy cowering in the corner with nothing but a torch and his gloves for comfort almost breaks me.

"My safe place." He raises his hands. "The only place in the world I could truly be myself."

Still silent, I place my hand over his between us and rest my head on his shoulder.

"I haven't been here since I was about twelve."

"Why?"

He shrugs, his cheek against the top of my head. "That's when it stopped."

Six years... for six years he went through that alone. "What made him stop?"

"I got too strong for him." Do I really want to hear this? No, I don't, but he needs to tell his story and I'll be damned if I'm going to give up on him. "For a while I didn't fight back. It became normal." He gives a little laugh. "And then I learned sex education in school. I knew what sex was, but for some reason I never put two and two together. Don't get me wrong, I knew what we were doing was bad and I hated it. I hated the pain, I hated... I just hated it." He lets out a breath and shudders. "But I never truly realised what it was we were doing. I'm not making any sense, am I?"

"You actually are." This is all I say as I want him to continue.

"I fought back. I probably could have fought back before then, but like I said, I didn't know that I should. He was shocked that I'd pushed him to the ground when I usually made it so easy for him. We never spoke about it, not until the day he died." His eyes narrow and his lips form a sneer. "He apologised. He actually had the gall to ask me for my forgiveness."

Holy crap. "Did you give it to him?"

"I told him to rot in hell."

"I hope that's exactly what he's doing," I sneer with him. "Why didn't you tell anybody? Your mum? Your dad?" He gives me a look that answers my question. I've met his parents, but do I really believe they'd have allowed something like this to go on? No matter how cruel they are I believe they would have done something. It'd ruin them if Nathan started telling people. None of it makes sense. "Caleb?"

"By the time Caleb was old enough to understand, the attacks had stopped."

"How is it that not one single person suspected a thing? Your mum must have known something was wrong. It's not like you're a ray of sunshine," I snap, but I'm not angry at him. I'm angry at the situation.

He snorts. "Thanks, I find you pleasant too."

"You know what I mean," I mumble, feeling ashamed at my tactless outburst. "I'm sorry, I'm just... it makes me so angry knowing you've been through that alone."

Almost chocolate brown eyes shimmer with a look I've never seen from him before. It holds so much love and possibly hope. "I have you now... right?"

This time when I press my lips to his jaw, I don't miss. "Yes."

His hand runs through my hair as I tip my head back to look at him. Giving me a soft smile, he says, "That's enough story time for today."

"Okay," I agree, not wanting to push him, especially so soon after promising him I wouldn't. "So, this is my surprise?"

He licks his lower lip and shrugs. "Half of it. I promised you you'd know all of my secrets." He grins and pats the cushions around him. "This is my biggest secret of all."

"The one that nobody knows but you."

"And now you."

"So." I move so I'm on my knees facing him. Bouncing excitedly I demand, "What's my other surprise?"

"Patience."

"I have none."

His smile is blinding. I was worried for a moment that our deep conversation would spoil his mood. It hasn't; nor has it affected mine. I'm sad about it, obviously, but I'm more grateful that he's trusting me with this. "One of the many things I love about you."

"You can list the rest, I won't mind listening to them," I jest, moving my aching legs from beneath me and sitting cross legged instead.

This new position gives Nathan the perfect opportunity to grab my legs by the ankles and pull them over his thighs. His strong hands grab my hips and a gasp escapes me when he pulls me towards him. My dress stays behind, pulling far up my thighs. Any further and my knickers will be on show.

Nathan notices and instantly his eyes heat.

"I think you have the best legs I've ever seen," he states, his hands resting on my bent knees. Thumbs touch the inside of my thighs as his fingers splay across the top and outside. He pushes forward slowly, his leather gloves making tingles shoot straight down to my core.

God, that feels good.

We both watch what he's doing, both mesmerised by the feeling.

My skin breaks out in tiny little goose bumps as he gets higher and higher, the tips of his fingers now only two inches away from the most sensitive area on my body; not just my core but the area around it, especially where my legs meet.

When his fingertips lightly touch there, sliding my dress up further and exposing me to his view, a shuddering moan escapes me. He pulls away in an instant, his hands roaming up my sides before cupping my cheeks and tilting my head back.

He smiles. "This is part of the surprise."

"Huh?" My brain can't register anything right now. Please leave a message.

"Perfect silence while we finally have that first kiss we've nearly had too many times to count, but never succeeded in getting."

Gulp.

"It's probably not the prettiest place, but it's different. Memorable."

Now I see what he's trying to do. He's competing with his brother in a weird backwards way.

I look at him, wanting him to just kiss me but needing to reassure him first. "If it had been in the car in the driveway, or at the house, it still would have been memorable." But I have to admit, I like this a lot.

He doesn't respond. Instead he moves forward and grips my neck with one hand while the other moves to my hip. I wet my lips in preparation, my body humming with excitement.

The first thing I feel, that sends sharp spasms of pleasure down my spine, is his breath fanning over my lips. My eyes want to close but I refuse to let them, mostly because his eyes are locked on mine and I swear, his pupils get larger and larger the closer he comes.

Pulling me in tighter, my knees against his ribs, my chest against his, he lets out a sharp breath when my groin connects with him. I barely stifle a moan.

A gentle hand brushes my fringe from my eyes and tucks my hair behind my ear. His face dips and his nose slides across mine. Soft lips barely brush my own before finally descending.

I melt into him, my body sagging as his hand holds my head to his. He takes a deep breath through parted lips and then moves them against mine. His brow furrows and a guttural groan escapes him. I feel it vibrate through his chest and notice that it sounds desperate, painful even.

His tongue teases my lips, asking them to open rather than demanding. I part them and meet it with my own. This time it's my turn to moan in desperation.

His lips are so soft and he tastes so good. Like Nathan, mint and coffee. It's my new favourite flavour. I doubt I'll ever get enough of it.

I fist one hand in his shirt, keeping him close, and the other winds its way up the back of his neck and into his soft hair. He wraps his arm around my back and pushes his hips upwards as he pulls me tight to him. I've never felt anything like it. I ache all over, but mostly I feel empty and having him rub against me this way makes me want to sob at the emptiness below.

He twists himself, moving to his knees without breaking our kiss. Slowly and gently he coaxes my body back onto the pillows, his arm holding me tight around the small of my back.

A raspy breath leaves him when I part my legs and allow him to slide between. This time the entirety of his swelling length presses against me.

Even more of his heat seeps into my body; I'm delirious with it.

A jolt spikes through me, causing me to tense for a second in his hold when I feel his hand slide beneath the top of my dress and grasp my breast. My already tightening nipples solidify in a second. He brushes over it with the tip of his finger, before holding the full swell of my breast once more and massaging slowly with a strong hand.

My head falls back and my eyes close as he continues to grind against me and rub me in the most perfect way. Using this opportunity to get to my exposed neck, he immediately licks a trail from the dip and up to my jaw before claiming my mouth again.

All of my inhibitions vanish. My mind goes blank, my body now nothing but a mess of feelings. Too many to describe, but all of them twisting into one thing. Lust. Pure, never ending, forever burning lust.

I need to feel more of him. I want to feel his skin on mine. My hands frantically start pulling at his jacket and he shifts a few times until I manage to slide it from his arms. When it's on the pillows to the side of us, he grabs my thighs and bucks his body into mine, pressing my back into the pillows. His lips are again locked on mine.

I scrape my fingernails across his shoulders. His entire body shudders and I feel my back arch as his hardness presses against my swelling clit. He presses himself into me again and again and I press harder in response, as if trying to rub the fabric away, so all that's left is him and the knickers that separate us. I'm so glad I wore a dress.

I work at the buttons of his shirt, loving the feel of his toned, smooth chest. He's so defined, so beautiful. After popping the fourth button down, his hand wraps around both of mine. He pulls them up and over my head, pinning them at the wrists.

When his hand releases my wrists a few moments later and descends to my breasts, I reach for the buttons again, but he leans up and off me. Using his hands, he pries open my legs and pushes my dress up so it gathers at my waist. Settling in between my thighs, he claims my mouth again. His hands grab at every inch of flesh they can reach, as if he's scared I'll vanish.

I'm probably going to have a few finger sized bruises tomorrow but I really don't care. He's not hurting me. It feels too good to be classed as any kind of pain.

"Nathan," I mutter as he kisses a trail down my neck, his hand gripping the bottom of my dress.

He pulls it up and over my head, throwing it behind him without a thought. I lie on the bed of pillows on my back, my legs bent either side of him.

"I want to see you." His voice is as breathy as mine. His eyes linger on my breasts, which are hidden behind a lacy black nursing bra. It's not my favourite one, but at this point in time I don't care. "All of you." Fingertips touch the hollow at the base of my throat, then trail down over the swell of my right breast. He lightly circles the nipple through the fabric, watching as it pebbles from his touch, pressing through the fabric like it wants to break free. He moves to the left one and does the same. I throw my head back and groan, his featherlike touches doing more to me than they should.

Both hands grasp me, massaging my heavy globes softly. He watches them as he does this, almost mesmerised by what he's doing and seeing.

Once he's done playing with me through my bra, he trails the edges of his nails across my skin, over the band of my bra to the hook at the back. Seconds later it's unhooked and he's gently sliding it from my shoulders before letting it fall on the ground.

He leans back again, just staring, no words spoken. Only our breathing can be heard and both of us are breathing heavily.

I daren't reach for him. I want to, my fingers ache to touch him, but something tells me I need to let him do this at his pace. So I do. I wait, allowing him time to run his fingers over every inch of my torso as if burning it to memory.

Lips and a warm wet tongue trail down the centre of my chest before he sits back on his knees. His hands help me out of my shoes; they pull off my socks and finally slide my fabric skirt from my body. I lie before him in nothing but a pair of black lace knickers that cover less than they showed on the mannequin in the store. My arse is definitely not a small one.

Dragging his hands up my calves and thighs, I'm relieved when he finally grips my lace knickers and slides them off too. Now he starts moving back up, his lips and tongue leading the way, his body brushing against mine.

Just seeing him peruse me again, leaning back slightly so he can see all of me, his eyes heated and sharp, taking in every inch of me, makes me feel like I'm the only woman on Earth. I should feel vulnerable and exposed, but the way he's holding himself, the way he's breathing, the way his lips are parted and his eyes are devouring me, I feel nothing but beautiful, powerful and magnificent. I don't remember ever feeling this way before.

He cups my arse with both hands as his mouth moves over mine again. A squeal escapes me when I'm suddenly flipped onto my front and his mouth is on my neck. I lick my lips, wiping away the taste of him with my tongue.

"Nathan?" I question as one of his hands grasps at my aching breasts, his movements no longer slow and sweet, but rough and needy. I like the change, I'm just not sure if I like the direction I'm facing.

My ears pick up the sound of a zipper and his skilful hand continues teasing my skin, grabbing me, stroking me. Goose pimples break out over my flesh.

His hands are gone from my body and I hear the cause of this sudden abandonment - a foil wrapper being opened. I watch him over my shoulder. His eyes are looking down at his hands as he rolls the condom onto his substantial length. I can't see it and I really want to. I want to touch him, why are we doing it in this position? I want to look in his eyes.

"You're beautiful, Gwen," he says into my ear, his chest against my back, his body bending forward slightly, forcing mine to do the same. I grip the edges of the pillows under my hands, wondering why he won't let me turn and wrap my legs around him. A tremble flows through me when his hand comes up to circle my neck from the front, his forefinger curving over my jaw. I feel his hot length at my entrance, his free hand placing it directly over the opening. "You mean everything to me." He tells me to my eyes and my heart swells.

I nod, gulping at the same time, before wetting my drying lips with my tongue. "You mean everything to me too."

He pushes inside slowly. Far too slowly. Only the head is in and the ache is almost unbearable. It's a pleasurable ache mixed with a small amount of pain as he stretches me.

It's been too long. Far too long.

He pulls out, leaving only the tip inside. Shudder.

"Are you okay?" He asks, the concern in his voice turning my heart into a puddle.

Smiling slightly, I nod and reach over my shoulder to caress his face. He leans into it and places a gentle kiss on the palm of my hand. Seconds later I let out a groan, not one of pain either, as he slams inside. Only half way, but Christ it feels good.

"Still okay?" He asks, moving in and out, each thrust getting more powerful but never going in to the hilt.

His hands that were holding my hips leave me for a moment. They return seconds later and I instantly recognise the feel of leather covering his fingers. I'm about to comment when he places two fingers over my clit and rubs in fast circles, his hips speeding up but still never allowing his solid length to enter me fully.

Again, I'm in a state where I don't care about the gloves or the fact he's still dressed, or the fact we're doing this all wrong. It feels too good.

No.

He feels too good.

Nathan grips my breast, pulling me back against his chest so my arms are no longer holding me up. I twist my head so he can kiss me, allowing him to swallow the moans that escape me. He doesn't go back to kissing my neck when I lean forward, gripping the pillows once more. I wonder if this is because of the perspiration that is now covering my skin.

I try to push my hips back towards him, wanting to feel him deeper. It doesn't work. He places a hand on my lower back, stopping me from pushing into him anymore. Why won't he go inside? This burning is driving me crazy. I need more, just a little bit more.

"Please, Nathan, harder," I pant, my head falling forward, my shame gone.

"Can't," he bites out and my eyes fly open. I want to look at him, so I turn my head as far as possible and peer at him through the corner of my eye. His torso is straight, his eyes clenched shut and his teeth biting into his lower lip.

My swollen clit begins to throb. I feel it pulse as a strong familiar burning sensation spreads through my body. I feel it in my feet, in my calves, my thighs, my arms, and directly behind my eyes, where it pops over and over again. It's coming, I can feel it. If he'd just go deeper…

"Come on, baby," he whispers, his tone demanding and forceful in my ear. "Let go."

"Can't." I repeat what he said to me moments ago.

"I can't last much longer," he warns and slows his thrusting. "You feel too good."

"Go harder," I order, placing my hand over his on my clit.

"Christ," he breathes, his eyes widening a fraction. "So tight." His lips tilt up at the edges. I scowl. Why's he teasing me?

My forehead hits the mattress as a sharp tingle hits me in my core and pools in my lower stomach.

"Deeper," I beg.

He ignores me, so I muster what little strength I have to look at him again. Seeing his brows furrow in pleasure, listening to his quiet moans and heavy breaths, feeling him tense with each shallow thrust, it tips me over the edge. I press his fingers hard onto my swollen nub and try my hardest to push back onto him.

Something pops inside of me and warm, liquid ecstasy pours into every vein, traveling around my entire body. The noises I make are indecipherable. The pleasure I feel indescribable. My legs buckle beneath me. Nathan catches me around the waist with ease as I continue to ride the wave.

My walls clench around him as if trying to hold him inside, even as my orgasm slowly begins to subside. I don't want him to leave me. He's still hard, he still hasn't reached his climax yet.

"Don't slow down," I gasp, my hand reaching out to grab his hip. He pushes it away, but I wrap my fingers around the belt loop and hold it tight. "Go deeper."

"Let go," he says, grasping at my fingers, trying to pry them off.

"Don't make me."

"Let go."

"Nathan," I plead, moving my hips back, my appetite for him not satisfied yet.

"Guinevere! Let GO!" He almost bellows, his eyes panicked and furious. I immediately release him and he pulls out and away instantly. My shock is apparent on my face as I roll onto my back, grabbing my dress and pulling it around me as I go.

"What's wrong?"

He turns. I watch as he rips the condom off and throws it into a small bin by the trap door. By the time he's turned around, he's zipped himself up and is already working at doing up the buttons on his shirt.

What just happened?

He lets out a breath and looks at me, his eyes scanning my body. I shouldn't be shy after that, though I can't help but pull the sheet tighter around me.

"Are you okay?" He asks, sitting on the pillow beside me, making it dip slightly and forcing me to lean into him.

I nod. "Are you?"

"Yes." He strokes my collarbone and the swell of my breast.

"Why am I naked and you aren't?" It didn't matter much when I was lost in the throes of ecstasy. Now that I have my mind back, I feel slightly awkward.

He doesn't respond. Instead he pulls his jacket on and makes his way to the trap door. Giving me a soft, lingering look, he says, "I'll just be a moment."

"Okay."

He leaves the tree house without looking back. Seriously... what just happened?

Did he orgasm? I'm sure he didn't. I look at the empty condom lying in the bin and scratch my head. This is confusing; he was definitely close. Did I not feel good to him?

Do I smell? Maybe I smell or something.

I hope not.

I don't feel so good right now. That glow most people get after having sex just vanished and I suddenly feel dirty.

I quickly get dressed, almost getting tangled in my long dress in my haste to look for Nathan. He still hasn't returned and it has been almost ten minutes.

Where is he?

"Nathan?" I shout, leaning over the hole in the ground. I can't see him. Damn it. "NATHAN!"

He steps into my line of sight. I notice him pulling the zipper of his trousers up. He must have gone to urinate.

Smiling nervously, he climbs up the ladder with ease. I marvel at the sight of his arm muscles tightening against the fabric of his shirt.

Holy crap. We just had sex.

I blush, avoiding his eyes as I stand and move out of his way, my hands twisting in front of me.

"Hey." He catches my wrist and places his finger under my chin to tilt my head back. "What's the matter?"

"Nothing." I shake my head, albeit a little frantically, and go to step into him. I need holding right now.

My heart aches when he steps back and crouches down by the bag he brought. He knew my intention then, I know he did.

Oh god. Is this all he wanted? To see if I was any good?

Was I not?

I did just kind of lie there, but in my defence I was trying to give him the space he seemed to need.

He pulls out two bottles of water and hands one to me. I carefully twist the lid off and take a few small sips.

Chapter Twelve

"Gwen?" Nathan says quietly as he sits back on the pillows.

"Hmm?"

He pats the cushions beside him. "Come here."

Still blushing slightly, I clear my throat and sink down onto the pillows beside him.

My body moves and suddenly I'm on my back with Nathan towering over me. I don't get the chance to yelp as it happens too fast. He grins mischievously; it's a look that is so different in contrast to how he was a few months ago. It suits him.

"What are you thinking?" I ask the typical question that most men hate.

He runs his nose along my jaw, his body sinking onto mine more. "I'm thinking," he moves up and kisses me gently before pulling away a fraction, "that I..." He dips down and runs his nose along the curve of my neck. "Am most likely..." I giggle when he nips at my over sensitised skin. "The luckiest man..." His mouth comes back to mine and his eyes stare deeply into my own. "Alive."

I feel his tongue press against my own and shudder before greeting it. Moan.

"You didn't orgasm," I say and instantly regret it. Ground, swallow me whole.

"I did," he lies, nibbling on my bottom lip.

"Didn't." Why would he lie?

"Yes I did." He smiles, moving from my lips to the lobe of my ear. His hand slides under my dress and grips my hip.

That's definitely not a gun I feel in his pocket.

"You didn't; I've seen the condom." I place my fingers in the back of his hair and gently pull his face up to meet mine.

"Hmm." This is all he says before he presses his lips to mine again. "Would you like to go again?" He grinds his hips into mine.

Definitely not a gun.

"Umm..." Shiver.

"Later," he responds for me, although my thoughts weren't saying later, that's for sure.

I watch as he stacks pillows against the wall and leans against them.

"Go to that trunk for me," he says politely. I do as I'm told and rest my hand on top of the curved lid. "Open it."

I do so, expecting to find toys, magazines and junk. Instead I find it to be full of neatly stacked books. In the right hand corner are a few bottles of disinfectant and packaged wipes. I smile and roll my eyes at these.

"Peter Pan should be on the top."

I see it immediately and run my hand over the tatty cover that has definitely seen better days. "Peter Pan?"

He shrugs, his tongue swiping over his bottom lip. "It used to be my favourite. I can't tell you how many times I read it growing up."

This breaks my heart. Shatters it. Destroys it.

The thought of Nathan, a young boy witnessing such torture finding a friend in a boy who doesn't have family and never wants to grow up, absolutely moves me yet shatters me all at once.

"Read it to me."

I immediately comply.

Being careful not to damage the book further in any way, I crawl over to Nathan and rest my head on his lap. Bending my legs at the knees, I use them as a resting place for the book as my fingers turn the pages.

I start reading and his hand starts stroking through my hair. "All children, except one, grow up..."

He rests his head back and closes his eyes, almost as if picturing the story in his mind. It's the most heart breaking yet lovely moment to be a part of.

Most couples are probably at work, or sat watching TV and arguing over the remote. I'm not. I'm in a fairy-tale.

CHAPTER TWELVE

I'm in a forest, in a tree house, reading Peter Pan to the man who loves me.

Will it be like this forever, minus the heartache that both of us feel over our pasts? Right now I don't feel heartache for anyone but him. Out here I'm no longer Guinevere, Mum to Dillan, widow to Caleb and heartbroken beyond repair.

Out here I'm just Gwen who loves Nathan.

I'm sorry, Caleb, I can't go back now. Plus, I don't want to.
Please, don't hate me. I can't help how I feel.

An hour passes by and even though my arse is starting to go numb, I continue reading. Nathan seems content to stroke the top of my cleavage or my hair whilst listening silently. I don't want to stop but I'm starting to get tired.

Nathan, sensing my need to take a break, pulls the book from my hands and moves to place it back in the trunk. I lie flat and stretch my body like a cat.

"Thank you." He smiles softly and lies beside me. "We should head back."

"Yeah," I reluctantly agree, not wanting to leave. I feel so disconnected from the world here. I can see why Nathan claimed this as his safe place.

He stands, pulling me with him, and stretches just like I did moments ago. Without another word, he grabs the bag and leads me to the ladder, climbing down a few steps. He waits for me to follow and holds my dress out of the way.

"I received a call after we had sex," Nathan says when I reach the ground. He takes my hand and leads me back the way we came.

Had sex? Well, I suppose that's true. We didn't make love and he didn't orgasm, so calling it sex sounds about right. "Go on."

"That house that we viewed on the seafront." Why does he keep trailing off?

"Go on."

"It's mine. I get the keys tomorrow." He looks nervously at me. "How do you feel about that?"

Good question. "I think it's nice that you're going to be closer." Then another thought enters my head. "What about your jewellery store? What's going to happen to that?"

"That's on hold indefinitely." He waves it away like it's nothing more than a bug. What the hell? I open my mouth to argue, but he speaks first. "I want you to move in with me. You and Dillan."

And we're back to this. "I don't need to live with you, Nathan."

He stops, turning me to face him, and bends slightly so his eyes are level with mine. "But I want you to. Both of you. That house is too big for just me."

"How are you paying for it exactly? You're not working right now."

"Gwen," he warns, as a way of telling me not to change the subject.

Sigh. "It's not the right time. I just... we're new."

"Hardly! We lived together for almost six months."

"Yes, I'm aware of that."

"Look..." He runs his hand through his hair. "I was thinking you could finish University. I'll have Dillan for you, or we'll pay for nursery."

Wow. "I... I'm not going to move in with you just because you're offering me something. It has to be the right time. Now isn't that time." I'm not doing a very good job of explaining my point.

"I'll let you decorate; we can have the kitchen redone or anything you want. Dillan will have his own room. It'll be better than before."

"I hardly saw you before and we weren't planning on becoming an item, so the comparison doesn't really count," I say, needing this conversation to end. "One day, but not now. Okay?"

"Fine," he relents, clearly not wanting to push the subject. "But promise me you'll think about it."

That I can do. "I promise."

He smiles, relieved, and starts walking again.

By the time we make it home it's dark and late. We get Dillan ready and go straight to bed, because I have work in the morning and Nathan has a house to prepare.

I burrow into Nathan's chest, loving the feel of his arms around me. I guess I didn't realise how much I'd missed this. I can't even remember Caleb's arms around me anymore. Why do I suddenly feel guilty?

I stare up at the handsome man who seems to be staring at the ceiling, holding me like he doesn't want to let me go.

CHAPTER TWELVE

"Tell me you love me," are the last words he whispers to me before we sleep.

"I love you, Nathan," are the last words I whisper to him. His arms tighten around me and his lips connect with my forehead.

"Hey, I'm home." A soft voice whispers into the darkness.

I smile and turn to the side, puckering my lips in acceptance of the kiss that I know is to come.

It doesn't.

Peeling my eyes open, I look at the figure looming over the bed. I can't see his face, but I know who it is.

"Caleb!" I grin, clambering from the bed and throwing my arms around him. I bury my face in his neck and inhale deeply; he smells so good. He always does. "I miss you."

His face finally comes into view. He's smiling. It tears at my heart but I can't quite put my finger on why. "You miss me? I'm right here." A warm hand cups my cheek. "You look so beautiful."

"Can you kiss me now? I feel like you haven't kissed me in so long," I whisper, pain flooding through me. Why do I feel grief?

"Certainly." He grins wickedly and his other hand comes to my other cheek. His lips descend. My entire body heats as I wait for our lips to touch. I feel like I've been waiting for this moment for a lifetime. Why am I so sad?

Our lips are about to touch. I shiver in anticipation.

They stop.

Caleb looks over my shoulder, his eyes narrowing and his head tilting. "You're not alone."

"What?" What's he talking about? Of course I'm alone.

I look over my shoulder and gasp at the sight before me. He's right. Somebody is in my bed.

"What the hell?" I whisper as Caleb moves me to the side, his arms trembling, and reaches for the blanket. He pulls it back in one swift movement and the room fills with a rage that's so thick I can taste it.

A red mist seems to swirl around him as he glares at the man in my bed.

"No!" Caleb roars, his angry eyes coming to me. "You promised."

"What?" Who is that? Why's he in my bed. "Who is it?"

"We're getting married tomorrow! How could you?"

"I don't understand. I don't know who this is."

"I told you to stay away from Nathan. You promised you would!" His tone is accusatory.

What? *"I don't know who Nathan is. I swear. I don't know this man."*

Caleb steps away from me. "How could you do this?"

"I... I didn't... Caleb, please." I hold out my hand. "Believe me."

He turns and walks over to my window. Wait... where's the cot? Don't I have a cot there?

Why would I have a cot? I'm still pregnant.

My hands find my flat stomach and I grasp at it desperately. "What's going on?"

Caleb doesn't answer. He only stares out of the window, his profile almost glowing in the moonlight. "I'll never forgive you for this, Gwenny."

"Wait," I plead, racing towards him.

The red mist flickers outwards, long smoky tendrils lashing out at the dark room, slowly swallowing it whole until I can see nothing but red. Caleb's hand reaches out and touches my cheek. He doesn't speak, or if he does I don't hear him. My heart starts beating a heavy rhythm as I'm overcome with fear and loss.

Caleb.

No. No. NO! I hit the floor with a thud, my body trembling and my front aching from my landing.

"Caleb," I gasp, pulling myself up and looking around the room. "Dillan!"

Confusion sets in as I pull myself out of my dream state and back to reality. I race to the cot and sigh with relief when I see Dillan sleeping soundly, his mouth suckling at nothing.

"Nathan," I whisper in realisation and turn towards the bed.

He's fast asleep on his back, one arm spread to the side as if it has been searching for me and is now waiting for me. I climb onto the mattress and stare at him for a moment, ignoring the heartbreak at losing Caleb all over again.

This isn't the first dream I've had of Caleb, but it's the first one with Nathan. It's all of this information I've received regarding him that's throwing me. It's too much to take.

I brush my fingers over Nathan's brow and sigh as guilt floods through me. How could Caleb do that to him? How could he hurt his brother like that, who so clearly needs love and trust?

If he were alive I don't think I'd be able to look at him for what he's done. I know that's easier said now that he's not here, but I know Nathan now. I know that, with a bit of patience and a sledge hammer combined, you can crack that outer shell and the sweetness that lies beneath is just... gah. It's amazing. He's amazing.

How could Caleb... my sweet Caleb, be so cruel to somebody so damaged and in need of affection?

As much as I want to be sad over Caleb's freak out in my dream, I can't be. I can only be sad that I didn't seem to know him at all. Or maybe he changed; I sure hope that's the case.

Leaning forward, I press my lips to Nathan's and run my nose along his. I know how much he loves that. It reminds me of a lion cub nuzzling the felines it knows and loves.

Nathan, stirring at my attention, peeks open one eye and smiles ever so slightly as he traps his body to mine with his strong arms. "Hi."

I laugh a little, feeling like I've been caught doing something naughty. "Hi."

"What are you doing?" He closes his eyes as I continue to nuzzle his nose with mine. I press my lips to his and run my hand up his chest until it rests over his steady heart. My lips take on a mind of their own and travel from his lips to his jaw, then down to his neck. My tongue tastes his skin as my nails scrape over the fabric of his vest. He lets out a breath and tickles my arms with his fingertips. "Why are you awake?"

"Bad dream," I murmur against his golden skin and continue kissing every inch of his neck.

He lets out a moan and slowly pulls me away. "What about?"

Do I tell him and ruin this moment? Or do I lie and keep trying to seduce him? "I don't remember." I go for the lie. He looks at me sceptically. "I swear, I don't remember." He loosens his grip and lies still as I get back to work on his neck.

"This is unexpected," Nathan murmurs, clearly still half asleep.

I slide his vest up to his neck and trail my fingers over his smooth chest. Shifting down, I press my lips to the spot directly above his nipple, which tightens instantly.

"Gwen," he chokes out, his chest dropping as his breath escapes him. Hands roughly grab my hair and pull my head up. "What are you doing?"

Umm... well, what does it look like? I give him a blank look and push his hands away. Shifting down again, I circle the tip of my tongue around his nipple. This time he groans, his skin rippling with the feeling.

I don't waste time and move down further, my tongue leaving a damp line as I go. I'm ready to taste him, ready to make him feel good. His fingers tangle in my hair, but this time they don't push me away. I slide down again, finally level with his belly button and that soft strip of dark hair that leads to where I want to be.

When he realises my intention, I'm roughly pushed away.

I land on my back on the bed, dazed for a second.

"What are you doing?" He snaps and sits up, his body tense and his gaze angry.

"Umm..." I slowly sit up and chew on my lip as my cheeks heat. "Did I hurt you?"

Running a hand through his hair, he pulls his vest down and folds his arms across his chest, almost as if protecting himself. "Go to sleep."

"What did I do?" That didn't go as well as I planned.

"Do you make a habit of touching people in their sleep?"

I jerk back, my entire body tensing as pain slices through me. "What?" I say breathlessly.

He rubs his face, his eyes softer when he looks at me. "I thought I was dreaming."

"I... I'm sorry. Your eyes were half open. I thought... I just..."

He turns over without letting me finish, his back now to me. Do I climb back into bed and hug him from behind?

I try, placing my hand on his back as a way to tell him I want him to turn over. He shrugs me off and rolls onto his front, leaving me tired, confused and sad.

"I'm sorry," I whisper, leaning into his ear. Although I'm not entirely sure what it is I'm apologising for. What man doesn't want a sneaky blowjob?

I just needed to forget everything for a while.

I just need him to let me know everything is okay, because when I'm with him, I forget everything else.

Chapter Thirteen

Dillan wakes me ten minutes before the sun is due to rise. I snatch him up and plant numerous kisses on his face and open mouth. Nathan remains sleeping as I leave the room and head down the stairs. He usually wakes. In fact, I can't remember a time he hasn't woken with myself and Dillan. This leads me to believe he's avoiding me and was most likely faking sleep.

My legs are moving before I even finish reading. Seconds later I'm throwing myself into his arms and all is right in the world.

Sigh.

Why can't things just be okay for longer than a day?

I sit on the couch and yawn quietly as Dillan suckles away, then turn on the TV so I'm not sat in silence with nothing but my thoughts to entertain me.

Dillan finishes after a few minutes and lets out a healthy burp. Playtime at last.

Hidey-boo only gets boring when your baby doesn't laugh at it anymore. My baby loves it, therefore I could continue for hours, or until he gets bored of it.

The couch sinks beside me but I don't look up. I'm having a conversation with my son in the form of giggles and babbles.

"Are you hungry?" Nathan asks, his fingers playing with the ends of my hair.

"No thank you," I snap. Even though I'm mad at him, I can't forget my manners.

"Thirsty?"

"No thank you. Hidey…" I hold the thin sheet an inch from Dillan's face before ripping it away. "Boo!"

He laughs, a long single sound from his open mouth. I see Nathan smile out of the corner of my eye. "I did this with him the last time I had him. He found it very enjoyable." He's nervous; I can hear it in his voice. "Here." He reaches for Dillan, so I quickly shuffle away. His hands fly back to his lap and he blinks, his mouth falling open in shock.

"Yeah, he loves this game. Hidey…"

"I'll make us coffee," he says quietly, scratching the slight shadow on his jaw. "Would you like anything else whilst I'm in the kitchen?"

"Boo!" And Dillan's magical laugh comes again. I glare at the man beside me and clip, "No thank you," before turning back to my smiling boy. He's so adorable. I just want to eat him.

Nathan stays seated for a short while, staring at me expectantly, possibly hoping for his morning hug and kiss. When he realises he's not going to get either, he stands, sighs and leaves the room.

"Not this time," I say to Dillan in a baby voice. "No way am I letting him get away with it this time." I lift him until he's eye level with me. "What do you think? Huh?" I nuzzle my face in his belly, eliciting another laugh and a high pitched squeal of excitement that I've never heard from him before. "Yes, I agree. We won't talk to him today." I nuzzle his belly, trying to get another squeal from him.

Squelch.

Dear Lord, I do believe my baby's bowels have become rotten during the night. Ugh.

"Nath…" Ah… damn it. That was close. I forgot I wasn't talking to him properly. "Looks like I'm going to have to deal with this one myself."

When we return to the room, Nathan is sitting on the couch slumped forward with his head in his hands. I look away when he looks up and sit in the seat across the room. Dillan has hold of a teething ring and is swinging it around. I doubt he even knows he's holding anything; he just likes moving his arms.

"Would you like me to take him?" Nathan asks, worrying his lower lip. "Gwen…" He stands and walks over to me. I turn sideways, trying to avoid his hands. They reach out and take Dillan. I can hardly play tug of war with my baby, so I release him pretty easily. "I'm sorry for the way I reacted. I'm sorry." Why does he sound angry?

"Great," I say flippantly and hold out my arms. "Can I have my son back now? I'm going to be at work soon. This is all I get with him before I get home at six."

His jaw clenches. "I said I was sorry."

"My son," I snap, holding out my hands.

"I'm not going to see him until later either, or have you forgotten I have to pick up the keys in an hour?" He bites back, turning to leave.

"Then wait until it's your turn!"

"Why do you get to decide when it's my turn?" He looks at me incredulously. "Because you're angry with me? I'm sorry, I should never have behaved the way I did, but there is nothing I can do about it now. Keeping Dillan from me is unfair to him."

"I'm not keeping Dillan from you; I'm having *my* morning time with him!"

"And I want *my* time with him!"

We stare at each other for a moment.

"Neither of you are getting time with him!" My mum shouts from the doorway, looking annoyed, tired and rather dishevelled. We've clearly woken her. She stomps to Nathan, snatches Dillan from his arms and gives us both the look. "This isn't healthy for him. Guinevere, stop being a bitch." She's kidding, right? "You're both acting like children and everything you do will affect him." She turns to Nathan. "Whatever you did to make her mad, your apology was terrible. Work on that." Then she turns to me. I feel like cowering. If I had a tail it would be between my legs right now. "Valentine called your mobile five minutes ago; you left it upstairs. I answered. She needs you to go in in twenty minutes. I said you'd be there."

Great.

She leaves the room with Dillan. I sigh and follow suit, needing to get ready and quick.

I feel terrible. I feel like a bad mum right now.

"Gwen." Nathan follows me until I slam my bedroom door in his face.

He only opens it again, as I knew he would, but at least I got my point across.

"I am sorry."

Gah. "You shoved me." I pull my pyjama top over my head and throw it on the bed, which, as per usual when Nathan stays, is made to perfection.

"What?" He takes a step back, a frown on his face.

"Last night, when I was kissing you, everything was fine and then suddenly..." I slice my hand through the air. "You shoved me and it wasn't gentle."

He visibly pales. "I..." His throat bobs as he swallows. "Did I hurt you?"

"No, but if I'd been any further to the right I would have fallen backwards off the bed."

Blinking a few times, he stands to his full height, nods and moves towards the door.

Now I'm confused. "I thought we were talking?"

"There's nothing to say." His face is a blank mask when he turns to face me.

"Don't you dare!" I snap and he freezes on the spot, his hand suspended in mid-air only a few inches from the door handle. "Don't you dare! That's my decision!"

"Sorry?"

"Do you know what? Forget it. Go. Run. I have to get ready for work." I snarl, pulling clothes from my drawers.

He opens the door, but stops again when it's wide enough for him to exit.

"If you're waiting for me to stop you, don't bother; you'll be waiting a long time."

He doesn't respond but I see the indecision on his face.

"I had a dream about Caleb last night," I tell him, not bothering to look at him this time. "He was angry, really angry. He told me he'd never forgive me."

He still doesn't speak. I'm starting to worry he's had a stroke.

"I didn't understand what was going on. It felt like the day before he died, except he wasn't sick." I tug my shirt over my head and do the buttons up the front. "And then I woke up; I remembered you and there you were, sleeping peacefully. I remembered I was angry at him for what he did to you. I just..." I turn to face him in nothing but my shirt and knickers. "I was sad; it hurt. I felt like I'd lost him all over again but then... then I remembered what you'd lost because of him. It made me angry." He looks regretful for a moment and opens his mouth to speak, but I don't allow him to. "For a while I just stared at you, trying to sort out my thoughts. Do you have any idea how hard this is already for me? Especially after yesterday, after what we did together..." Which had a rather uncomfortable ending, what with him not climaxing and then lying about it, but I don't add this part. "I just needed to forget for a while, which is funny because you're the cause of all of this angst. You're the reason for my guilt, yet you're the one person that makes me forget the world. How insane is that?"

"I assaulted you." He says, staring at me in disbelief.

"And I'm not making excuses for you. I'm also not forgiving you. But I'm warning you, if you leave now, or at any point in the future, I won't come after you. Not unless it's my fault." Which I really hope it's not. "Make your decision, because it will be your final one regarding us. But..." He tries to interrupt me, but I raise my hand. "If you decide to stay, then we'll start over. Properly. You opened up to me yesterday. I want to hear the rest of it. Not immediately, but soon. Only the things that regard me. For example," I tug on a pair of jeans and balance on one leg as I pull on a sock, "that envelope that somebody wanted me to see. I've literally scrambled my brain trying to figure out what it could be but I can't even..." I trail off, cursing when I see the time. Running a brush through my hair, I turn back to Nathan and give him a firm look. "Are you leaving or are you staying? You have thirty seconds to decide."

"I assaulted you," he repeats. I throw my arms up in the air and stomp past him. "I don't remember doing it and at the time I probably thought you were..."

"I know," I sigh, rubbing my tired eyes.

"Forgive me," he says so quietly I barely hear him.

The tortured look on his face breaks my heart. How many more breaks can my heart take before it shatters completely?

"I swear I didn't know it was you." He gently touches my hair and wraps a lock around his finger. "I can't bear the thought of hurting you." I know this too. "I promised you I'd protect you in any way. You accepted that." I nod in agreement because I did accept that. "I won't be staying with you for tonight."

"Will you be staying with me as my..." Not boyfriend, I hate that word. "Nathan?"

He tries to stifle a smile. "Your Nathan?"

"You know what I mean. I have to go."

"I'll escort you; I still have time."

"No." I lean up and kiss his jaw. "Stay with Dillan. We'll talk tomorrow."

He frowns. "I'll call you later, when you've finished work."

"I mean we'll talk properly tomorrow."

He gulps, his eyes widening. "You promised me a few weeks. Please… just give me two weeks."

I relent, kiss his lips softly and leave the house, but not before washing my face and brushing my teeth because that would be gross.

I'm halfway to work when I receive a text.

<u>Nathan</u>: Tell me you love me.

Normally I'd wonder why he demands this, but I realise that I don't care. I mean it, so if he wants to hear it, or read it, then I'll make sure he does.

<u>Gwen</u>: I love you. <3

He doesn't respond; he doesn't have to because I know he loves me too, probably a lot more than I love him. This sounds bad, but I don't mean it to be. It's just the truth. We both know that I'll never love anyone as much as I loved Caleb. I've accepted my circumstances and I'm making an effort to move on, but Nathan will never be Caleb. He's accepted that; he knows that and I appreciate that. And I do love him, a lot. More than I ever thought possible. I'm selfish; I should let him go and find someone who will love him as much as he loves in return, but I can't.

I can't lose him too.

Just seeing him making a move to leave, I've never felt so panicked in my life. Sure I stood my ground, but on the inside I was shaking worse than maracas on a whore's belt.

"Thank you," Valentine announces as I walk through the door. Two seconds later there's an apron on my head. Two minutes after that, Tiffany is here and an hour later, the three of us are covered in flour.

It's safe to say that by the time I'm finished, I've never been so exhausted in my life. I'm half tempted to call Nathan and demand he come to mine so I don't have to get up with Dillan through the night. I don't though; we need tonight apart.

Tiffany gives me a ride home and we moan the entire way about last minute bridal parties and their stupid orders. In reality we're very grateful for the custom, but we need something to moan about. We're tired and grumpy.

I'm halfway up the driveway when my mum comes rushing out of the house, drops Dillan in my arms and climbs into a car pulled up by the curb just across the street.

"Slut," I joke, smiling at my baby. I wonder when I'll get to meet this mystery man. I've been far too self-involved as of late.

Bed is the first place I go after having a shower and playing with Dillan for an hour.

It's almost nine when I feel my phone vibrate from under my pillow.

I look at it and smile.

<u>Nathan</u>: Look under your pillow.

I stare at the message for a while before finally moving my pillow out of the way. I immediately spot a small white velvet bag with a dark red ribbon tied into a bow around the top. Smiling, I loosen the bow and tip the contents into my hand. Two shimmering earrings rest on the palm of my hand, the diamond studs shaped like twin love hearts.

My heart warms as I lightly touch them with my fingers. They're beautiful.

My phone beeps, alerting me to another text.

<u>Nathan</u>: Go to your window.

I don't hesitate this time; I race towards it and throw open the curtains before scanning the driveway for the man I expect to find there. He's leaning on the hood of his car, which is parked at the end of the driveway. He looks up at me with a smile on his face. I smile back; I can't help it. He points at his phone, signalling that I should look at mine.

I do.

<u>Nathan</u>: I'm sorry.

Another one comes through.

<u>Nathan</u>: Really sorry.

Then another.

<u>Nathan</u>: Really, really sorry.

Followed immediately by another.

<u>Nathan</u>: Tell me you love me.

<u>Gwen</u>: Always.

I place my hand on the glass and wait for the next text. I can see him typing it on his phone.
I feel giddy when it finally comes through.

<u>Nathan</u>: Come down so I can kiss you.

Chapter Fourteen

I help Valentine load the numerous boxes into a white van. They're to be taken straight to the bridal party. As I'm climbing out of the back, backwards, only because I can't turn due to there being too many boxes and no room, I feel strong hands at my hips and shriek.

"Get off me!" I shout, spinning in my attacker's arms.

Eric raises his hands, taking a startled step back. "Whoa." He glances around, looking at the locals who have stopped to see what's going on.

"I'm sorry." I place my hands on my chest. "Honestly."

He grins and shrugs. "I was just helping you out, but I can see why you'd freak out."

I return his smile and grab the final box from the tray. He takes it from me and climbs into the van. "What are you doing here anyway?"

As he climbs out, I see his smile vanish. "You haven't called. I got worried."

Bugger. "Yeah." I nervously tuck my hair behind my ear. "I've been busy."

He lets out a breath, his eyes solemnly scanning me. "Do you want to hang out after you finish? I could come over?"

Well I can hardly break up with him in the middle of the street. Plus, I don't have any other plans. "Sure. I finish at four today."

"I'll pick you up." He grins, not looking so solemn anymore. "Food?"

"No, actually…"

"I have to go; we'll grab something on the way home," he calls, cursing at his watch. "Later."

"Great," I mutter, rubbing my eyes with my fists. What the hell am I going to tell Nathan?

"The truth?" Tiffany suggests from behind me. I startle and turn to face her. I didn't realise I'd spoken out loud. "What's the big deal? He already knows you're going to break up with him."

"Who?"

"Eric, it was all over his angelic face." She clasps her hands under her chin and sighs. "What a yummy male."

Nathan is definitely yummier. There's no question about that.

"You're right." I scratch my head. "Should I text him or call him?" Another thought flashes through my mind. "How did you know I was dating Nathan?"

She grins wickedly. "I didn't, but I do now."

"You're dating Nathan?" A voice I know to be Sasha's asks from behind me, her tone definitely one of shock.

Seriously? This is how my day is going to be?

Great.

"Since when did you start dating Nathan?"

I arch a brow and fold my arms over my chest. "Since when did you start taking an interest?"

"I deserve that," she mutters. "But give me a break, I've been busy and you've been busy, one week rolls into the next…"

Tiffany continues, "Which rolls into the next."

Sasha, seemingly grateful for the support from a woman she's never met, nods eagerly and holds out a bag for me. "I got Dillan a new outfit. I'm sorry. I know I've said this already, but truly I am."

Aww, look at the little denim jacket. "I'll have to think about it for a moment whilst I search through this bag." Once I've seen Dillan's new outfit, I look at my 'supposedly' closest friend and smile. "Okay, I forgive you."

Sasha beams and throws her arms around me. Tiffany, not wanting to be left out, squeals and throws her arms around both of us.

She's nuts.

Once Tiffany is out of earshot, I pull Sasha into the kitchen and sit her in the corner near my workspace.

"So... Nathan?"

I contemplate for a moment whether or not I should tell her. It's then I remember her encouragement of this exact situation, way before it even happened. So I tell her. I tell her everything, from the beginning to the middle, right up until today.

She stares at me unblinking, then she slowly slumps in her seat and says a simple, "Whoa."

"Yeah."

"If it makes you feel any better..." She clears her throat and looks at the lemon drop cakes cooking in the oven. "Tommy and his girlfriend split up." Another one? "I went to Doncaster to cheer him up and we... well... he... we almost slept together."

It's my turn to sag, lean back into the counter and say a simple, "Whoa."

"Yeah."

"I pay you to work you know?" Valentine says in a singsong voice from across the room.

"Sorry."

"That's okay." She turns and leans against her own counter. "I couldn't help overhearing... are you dating your son's uncle?"

"Yes."

"I used to have a huge crush on my husband's brother, but he got a receding hairline in his twenties and I realised I picked the right brother." She randomly tells us before going back to work. I'm not sure what the moral to that story is.

"So, you and Tommy...?" I stare at Sasha expectantly, trying to gauge how she feels about it all.

She shakes her head. "No, he freaked out. Said it was a mistake."

"Well, you have been friends for a long time."

"Yeah, but..." She looks at me expectantly this time. "I don't know what to say about any of it. I'm waiting for him to make the next move; I won't push him again."

In my opinion, I agree. Tommy is a complex male who loves a lot, almost too much. Maybe he's just not ready to settle down. He and Sasha together could be magical, but it could also be a disaster. They're too well matched; they like all of the same things. It's how they've stayed friends for so long.

"Whatever happens, I still love you," I assure her, flicking a cherry her way. She catches it and pops it into her mouth, smiling the entire time.

"Do you want to go for dinner later?"

I shake my head, sighing gravely. "I can't; I promised Eric I'd meet him after work. I need to break it off with him."

"Poor Eric." Sasha doesn't sound sympathetic at all. She also doesn't look it, if the smile on her face is anything to go by. "You and Nathan suit."

This shocks me. I wasn't expecting that. "You don't think it's weird?"

"Oh it's definitely weird, and so against the rules of relationships, but it works and he makes you happy. Right?"

It feels good hearing somebody else say that out loud. It slightly settles my nerves on the entire situation.

"Those cherry spirals aren't going to make themselves." There's Valentine's singsong voice again.

"I'll let you get on with work." Sasha squeezes my shoulder after she stands. "Text me later when Eric has gone and I'll call you."

Giving her a nod of agreement, I motion to Valentine that I'll be just a minute and hastily type out a text on my phone.

Gwen: I'm seeing Eric later. He's picking me up from work.

Only a few seconds pass.

Nathan: What time?

Gwen: I finish at four. We're just going to talk for a while.

Again, only a few seconds pass before I receive a reply.

Nathan: You're going to end it, correct?

Gwen: Yes.

Nathan: Good.

I'm really not looking forward to this. I should have listened to my gut in the first place and I should never have agreed to date. Things were too complicated and now they're even more complicated.

Why couldn't you have just lived, Caleb?

"What do you think Eric will say?" Tiffany hands me a cappuccino and holds her own to her chest.

We're on a break. Yet again the day has been busy, fortunately not as busy as yesterday or I think I'd cry.

"I think he'll be cool about it." Eric is a nice guy. It's not like we're serious about each other. We shared a kiss, well two if you count the second, which I don't want to do because I didn't actually kiss him back. "It's Nathan I'm worried about. I don't want him showing up and blowing everything out of proportion."

Tiffany frowns slightly. "What is his story? I get that he's Dillan's uncle, but what exactly is going on there? Where's Dillan's father?"

Sigh. I hate talking about this, but I don't think I can put it off any longer. "He died when I was pregnant."

Tiffany splutters on her drink, her face a mask of horror. "What?"

I nod, trying to detach myself from the story as much as possible so I don't feel it and break down. "I woke up one morning, before the sun had risen. He was dead. Some kind of heart condition that they thought had healed when he was a small boy."

Her frown deepens. "That makes no sense. Surely they would have noticed something?"

My eyes blur and sting as I try to keep the tears back.

"Babe," Tiffany breathes, her hand going to my shoulder. "I'm so sorry."

"He was sick." I sniff, taking a deep breath to try and calm the aching in my chest. "Before he died he was really ill. I wanted to take him to the hospital, but he begged me not to."

"No! I'll be fine in the morning, it's just the flu or something."

His words ring through my head; it's almost like he's saying them into my ear. "It kills me knowing that I could have saved him," I mutter, staring straight ahead. The first tear falls and trickles slowly down my cheek.

Tiffany reaches out with a napkin in hand and wipes it away. "Hey. You can't think like that, okay?"

"But it's my fault Tiff. If you'd seen how ill he was, you would have taken him in. He was really bad." Another tear falls and soon after they're spilling down my cheeks. It's just the memory of his frail and worn body lying in bed... I was always too mesmerised by his smile. He had one of those smiles that sucked you in and wrapped you in a warm blanket of love and joy. "I'm sorry, I just... it still kills me."

Tiffany's face crumples and she pulls me into her arms. "I'm so sorry, but don't blame yourself. He was a grown man. If he told you not to take him, then that's on him."

"I didn't have anywhere to go." I continue with the story once she releases me. "I had no money, nowhere to live; my mum abandoned me. And then," a smile teases my lips as tears still fall. I must look a mess. "Nathan came along."

"Your own knight in shining armour?"

I nod. "I guess so."

"And you fell in love?"

"No." I shake my head and gaze at the floor. "He fell in love."

"But you love him?"

"Yes, but..."

"Not as much as Caleb." She finishes for me.

I agree. "Exactly." And how guilty I feel for feeling that way. It eats at me.

She moves in front of me and gives me a shake by my shoulders. "You'll get there. You're still grieving. Just... don't tell Nathan that, not yet."

I let out a soft laugh. It's not one of humour; it's one of disbelief at my own situation. "He already knows. He loves me so much he'll take whatever it is he can get."

Her mouth drops open. "Wow."

"Yep." I pop the P. "I don't deserve him."

"But you have him, so you better try your best to give him what you think he deserves." And don't I know it. "Does Nathan know the guilt you feel over Caleb's death?"

"No, nobody does."

"You should tell him."

"It's not his burden," I mumble, wiping at my eyes. "I can deal with it."

"Can you?" The look she gives me is one of sympathy and concern.

Can I? That's a good question. One I don't have an answer for. "I've done okay so far."

CHAPTER FOURTEEN

Eric, forever beautiful and casual, kisses me on greeting. His face falls instantly when I don't kiss him back. He knows; I can tell by the silence as we climb in the car and pull away.

"We'll go to mine," he states.

"But..."

"I have something for you." An excited smile spreads across his face and my heart plummets further. I keep my face calm, hoping he won't notice. He doesn't seem to.

When we make it to his, I notice another car outside. I'm sure it's his mum's. My memory is terrible though, so I could be wrong.

"Come on," he urges, waiting for me by the gate that opens into his front garden.

He takes my hand and I follow him inside. I'm instantly greeted by the smell of garlic and beef. It smells divine. "Sorry." Well at least if his mum is here he probably won't try to kiss me.

I should have just told him in the car. Why didn't I tell him in the car?

I should have told him way before we got in the car... this is going to be awkward and uncomfortable.

"Guinevere!" Kara shouts, wrapping her arms around my ribs.

I look down at the beautiful nine-year-old. "Hey there sweetie."

"Kara," Eric warns and she immediately moves away. I throw him a chastising look and wait for him to lead me into the room.

His mum, whose name escapes me, shouts hello from the kitchen.

"I thought she'd be done by now," he mutters, scratching his head and wincing slightly. "I'm sorry. I was going to surprise you with dinner that she made and claim that I made it."

This makes me throw my head back and laugh. "Why would you do that?"

"Because you're an amazing cook and I'm crap." His cheeks pink slightly.

"Sorry sweetie, but you didn't have any salt or lemon juice in. I had to nip to the shop." She explains through the wall.

I start laughing again. "Don't be mean. My mum would never go to all of this trouble for me."

He leans in and whispers, "She probably wouldn't if she wasn't obsessed with the thought of me settling down and falling in love."

"I like your hair," Kara says randomly, saving me from responding, her wide eyes on me.

"Oh, thank you."

"Can I play with it?"

"Kara," Eric hisses.

"Sure." What harm could it do?

Eric mouths a "sorry" as Kara climbs onto the couch behind me and starts braiding my hair. Or at least that's what it feels like she's doing.

"Okay," Eric's mum calls and finally exits the kitchen, smiling at me broadly. "Come on Kara. Time to go."

"Aww, aren't we staying?" Kara whines, glaring at her brother. "You never let me stay."

Eric blinks and says flatly, "You always stay. It's freaking annoying."

His mum leans down and kisses his cheek. I stand and follow them to the door. "Thank you for making dinner."

"No problem dear." Her voice is warm and friendly. "I hope you enjoy it. If you don't, let's stick with the original plan and say that he made it."

Laughing, I step into the front yard and watch Kara open the gate.

A gasp escapes me as what happens next happens in slow motion. Kara's shoelace gets caught at the bottom of the metal gate; her foot snags, causing her to hop on the other foot. It's not enough, she starts to fall forward and pulls the gate with her. It tries to close on her leg making her cry out and attempt to protect the wrong part of her body.

Her face smashes on the ground and everybody stops breathing. The poor girl emits a shriek of pain and we all race forward. I quickly unhook the shoelace as Eric and his mum inspect the girl.

The first thing I see is blood, the next thing I see is her nose bent at an odd angle and damaged skin on her cheek. "Oh my god." After my few seconds of panic, I grab Eric's arm. "We need to take her to the hospital."

Nobody says anything. They don't know what to say. Eric picks up his baby sister and rushes her to his car as I race inside and grab clean towels and a bottle of water. I lock up and climb into the front as his mum sits in the back with the young girl.

"Here." I hand the towel and water to her.

Eric, his lips a thin line and his eyes tight, turns on the ignition and drives. I place my hand on his and give it a squeeze when he winces at the sound of Kara's screams of pain.

"It's okay, sweetie." Suddenly a bag is dropped onto my lap. "Can you dig in there and pull out my phone? I have blood on my hands. Her dad needs to know." Yet another family member I'm going to meet. I don't care about that right now though. "Just text him; he's under V for Vinnie."

I do as I'm told, keeping the phone on my lap just in case he responds. Oh crap. I left my phone at Eric's.

"How are you doing sis?" Eric asks, reaching behind him with one hand. He gives her knee a gentle squeeze as she sniffles and cries on her mum's shoulder.

"She's okay, aren't you? You're being very brave," I say to her, my heart clenching when I see tears fall from her eyes and spill over her cheeks. One of them is swelling at an alarming rate. The tears must sting the grazes on her beautiful porcelain skin.

She tries to give me a weak smile but fails when her lips tremble.

Eric, looking a little less worried, takes my hand in his and brings it to his lips. I'm completely screwed.

None of that matters though. Right now all that matters is Kara.

"Do you mind if I use your phone?" I ask Eric when we pull up outside of the hospital. "I need to call my mum and tell her to pick up Dillan."

He blanches and curses under his breath, "Shit, I'm sorry. I should have…"

"Hey," I cut him off and place my hand on his arm. "Kara is at the top of the list right now. I'm not leaving until I know she's okay. Okay?"

He nods and hands me his phone before lifting his little sister from the back seat of the car. His mum climbs out shortly after as I send a quick text to my mum. I try my hardest to pull Nathan's number from memory, but fail. I knew his old one, still do, but haven't bothered to memorise his new one. Darn. He's not going to be happy.

Although it's not like he can blame me for this. He would do the same… I think.

We're led straight through to accident and emergency. Nurses and doctors flock to us, so I remain in the waiting area whilst Eric and his mum deal with the private stuff, questions, allergies etc. I'll go in when that part's done.

The waiting room is near full, all but two of the seats taken. I don't take one; I can't relax right now.

Besides, the two seats available are in between four very sick looking people. I think I'll pass.

I'm pacing for about thirty minutes before Eric comes back out and folds his arms around me. "You should go."

"What?"

He looks down at my face. "You have Dillan."

"He's fine; Mum's sorting him. I'm not leaving until I know she's okay and until I know you're okay."

I notice his eyes flash with relief as he smiles gratefully. "Thank you. She's... her nose is broken. There's not much they can do other than push it back and set it with some tape. She's had painkillers and they've cleaned her face and stopped the bleeding."

"See? She'll be fine," I say, placing my cheek to his chest.

He rocks us slightly as we stand by the doors in the waiting area. It takes him a while, but he finally releases me and takes my hand. "Let's go and see her."

"Should we go to the gift shop first? She deserves a pink helium balloon."

"Good point. We'll go later. My mum is barely holding it together."

I nod and follow him through a set of double doors and into a long corridor, full of curtain covered sections. We make for the eighth on the right and slide ourselves between the edge of the curtain and the wall.

"They're realigning the nasal bones or something," their mum says, looking haggard and nervous. A mother's love always shows on her face. "She has to have an injection of anaesthetic to numb it first."

Kara, looking bruised, rough and tired, as is expected, gives me a weak smile before closing her eyes.

"Poor baby," I mutter. "I'm so sorry this happened to her."

Eric sits on the chair by the bed and reaches out to hold his sister's hand. Kara, whose eye is swelling shut by the minute, starts dozing off.

"You two go," Eric's mum says tiredly.

"Mum..."

"Go, she'll be fine and her dad will be here soon." The entire time she speaks, her eyes never leave her daughter.

Is this what I'll be like when Dillan has accidents? It looks awful. I can only imagine how it feels.

"I'll take Gwen home and then I'll be back," Eric states, standing once more.

His mum glances our way and gives me a small smile. "Thanks for being here, Guinevere."

I only nod and give her shoulder a squeeze. "I won't leave until Eric says so."

Eric laces his fingers with mine. "I say so now. Come on."

I don't want to leave them; I think I've been slightly traumatised by the accident and I was only a spectator. "I feel bad, leaving you."

He cups my face with one hand. "It's fine; I swear. I'll call you in the morning."

We leave quietly and drive home in silence. It's not until we pull up into my driveway that he finally speaks. "Thank you for coming today. I'm sorry we didn't get a chance to eat or talk."

"Me too." I unbuckle my belt and reach for the door.

"Wait." His tired, solemn eyes come to mine. Using his hand in the front of my shirt, he pulls me towards him and presses his lips to mine. I kiss him back for a moment. I don't have the willpower to say no to him right now. Unfortunately, my reciprocation only spurs him to kiss me deeper.

When he finally releases me, I lick my swollen lips and open the door.

"I'll call you tomorrow."

"Okay." I give him a wave and make my way to my front door. My eyes remain on the ground so when I look up, seeing Nathan stood in the doorway, a blank look on his face and his arms folded across his chest, it shocks the hell out of me. "Hey." I say this cautiously as he moves back and allows me entry into my home.

Did he see? Of course he saw. This is just great.

"Hi," he says back, no anger, no disappointment, just a normal Nathan kind of hi. This worries me.

"What are you doing here? Where's Dillan and my mum?"

"Dillan is happily playing on the mat in the room; your mum left about forty minutes ago after calling me." He places his hand on the small of my back and leads me into the room.

"I should make dinner," I tell him, still watching him warily. "Are you hungry?"

He nods. "Very."

"Let me just say hello to Dillan and I'll make us something."

"Great." He follows me into the room and sits as I pick up Dillan and attempt to make him smile. "How was work?"

"Tiring," I state, placing Dillan back on the play mat.

Nathan walks towards me and helps me up off the ground. He starts moving me backwards, his eyes locked on mine.

"I thought you were hungry?" I ask breathlessly as my back collides with the wall.

"I am." He grins wickedly and his mouth descends on mine.

As his tongue coaxes open my lips, I melt into him and my hands go straight to his thick hair.

"Remember that day in my house?" He suddenly says, breaking the kiss.

"I remember a lot of days."

He smiles, closing his eyes as he grinds into me. "The day you gave me the journal."

Memories resurface and I find myself blushing and stammering. "I... remember that day." Nervously tucking my hair behind my ear, I ignore the heating in my cheeks and press on. "What about it?"

"I want to do that again." He admits, his pupils fully dilating.

His eyes look black. I'm sure mine mirror them. "Okay."

"But without clothes this time."

Gulp. Nod. "Okay."

With that, he bends slightly, grabs my thighs and lifts me until my legs are around his waist. Shiver.

My fingertips smooth over his lips as I lean back on the wall in an attempt to get a better angle with my hips. I shamelessly move against him, trying to get his length to rub me on my core. Pushing me up his hips a fraction, he spins, making me squeal and grab his shoulders for balance. Moments later we start ascending the stairs.

"Dillan," I say, not wanting to leave him on his own.

Nathan nods and races down the stairs. He returns moments later with Dillan and places him in his cot. In this time I've already managed to strip down to my bra and knickers.

Nathan's eyes drink me in as I move towards him and reach for his shirt. He doesn't let me. Instead he folds his arms around me and works at the clasp of my bra.

"Let me," I say, shuddering as his lips tease and suckle on my neck. His hands cup my breasts and his thumbs roll over the nipples. I reach for his shirt again, but he pushes my hands away. "Please."

He ignores me and silences me with his lips on mine.

Oh god.

"Nathan," I pant against his lips, trying to reach for his shirt but failing miserably. Growl. "Will you just..." I'm spun and pushed face first onto the bed, my knees still on the ground.

Strong hands grip my sides, the thumbs moving in slow circles along my back. "You had really bad back ache that day."

"Yeah." I remember it well.

"I told you to relax," he says quietly. "I moved your top up your back." He moves his thumbs up the sides of my spine. "And I stroked your skin like this." His fingertips slide down my back, occasionally lifting and overlapping the invisible trails left behind. They dig into the base of my spine and I don't bother to bite back the moan. That feels good. "You told me not to stop." One of his hands leaves me, but the other continues working its magic. "I still remember the exact moment this." He smoothes his hand over the curve of my soft globes. "Connected with this." To make his point further, he pushes his hips into me. I move back, wanting to feel more. "Do you remember what happened next?"

I do. Oh god, I really do. "You told me I had flawless skin."

Soft and gentle fingers tease my ribs. "You do."

"You kept rubbing my lower back and dragging your fingers across my skin," I mutter in an almost trancelike state. "You asked me what I'd done in town. And we kept talking, even as you rubbed against me." He does it again. "I could feel you getting harder."

"Like now?" He whispers, pulling my knickers down to my knees after grinding himself into me once more.

"Yes."

His leather clad thumb presses over the swollen lips that hide my clit. He circles slowly and gently, driving me insane. Heat pools in my belly and a delicious tingling spreads through my limbs. I ache to be filled.

Fortunately I don't have to wait long. I hear a foil wrapper tear moments before he's at my entrance.

His hands continue to stroke my back as he sinks in slowly and gently, going in a fraction of a centimetre before pulling back and then doing the same again.

I've never felt such a sweet torture.

"Nathan." I moan his name and push back against him.

The head finally pops in; I feel the stretching and immediately clench down. The gasp he releases makes me do somersaults inside. There's nothing sexier than a man moaning during sex.

Another thought occurs; I'm having sex with Nathan... again. Wow.

Nathan seems to have the same thought about me because he reaches out and knocks the photo of Caleb off my bedside table. I should be angry, but right now I'm not anything but horny.

"Don't do this to me," I whimper as he continues only allowing the head entry. Whenever I push back, he moves backwards with me.

He chuckles, his hand going to my hip as the other slides up to my hair. I wince when he takes a large handful of my brown waves and pulls tight. "Ready?"

"Yes," I half shout in faux aggravation.

He slams home, his hand in my hair and the hand at my hip holding me steady. I'm expecting him to meet my cervix, he's definitely long enough. Hell, he could probably meet my cervix and still have a couple of inches outside. Abnormally large is the only way to describe his beautiful penis. No, not penis... cock. A crude word, but the only word that fits his manhood.

I reach down with my fingers as he slowly glides in and out, only allowing himself so much entry. My fingertips glide over my sensitive nub and reach for my entrance. I feel the underside of his cock and notice immediately that he's not pushing in further than the condom.

Why?

"Gwen, remove your hand," he bites out, grasping my arm and yanking it roughly from under me.

"I was just..."

"Don't."

"Nathan," I snap, feeling my lust go down a notch. We've both stopped moving, both stopped moaning and grunting.

He ignores me and after a quiet moment he reaches around my hips and slides his finger into my wetness, making sure to rub in the right spot. "Let me." He leans forward and I feel his clothed chest against my naked back. The buttons dig into me and the extra stimulation against my over sensitised skin sends tiny flames of pleasure that pop around my body. "Let me make you feel good."

I want to protest and tell him that I want to make him feel good too, but I don't. Something tells me that I should do this his way, no matter how irritating it may be. I love him, I respect him and I'm trying to understand him. The only way I can understand him is if I accept him and learn as we go along.

"You already are," I respond breathily, remaining still beneath him. This relaxes him; I can tell immediately by the way the muscles of his chest seem to soften against me. "Don't stop."

Smiling against my neck, he starts slowly thrusting in and out, his finger working me beautifully. I clench tightly around him, telling him with my core to go deeper but letting him decide. He moans loudly into my neck, his body shuddering.

Ten minutes pass of this, ten torturous minutes of every cell in me burning on the edge of a climax. I need release so badly and so does he, yet he continues at a slow grinding pace, never fully entering me and never leaving me entirely.

A gasp escapes me when he lurches upwards, his body going tight behind me. His cock swells almost double in thickness and a groan of pain leaves him. I stay perfectly still, my face buried in the soft bed sheets, my hands gripping them tight.

"Let go," I say, needing to feel him come inside me, needing to feel him pulse and buck with the pleasure that my body has given him.

A long rush of air leaves his lungs and I feel his cock begin to calm itself. It's disappointing but I can understand why he wants to last longer. It feels bloody brilliant.

"Please," I beg, desperately needing release now. "Deeper."

He pulls out. "I can't." I'm about to sob and beg for mercy, but it's stifled by the feel of two long, leather clad fingers entering me.

A choked scream climbs its way up my chest as he rubs against the spot on the inner wall that makes everything feel magnificent. Fingers on my clit and fingers inside me whilst in this position, this is new.

An orgasm tears through me within moments, his fingers doing what three inches of his cock couldn't do moments ago. My body shudders and shakes, my knees especially.

"Oh god," I pant, feeling the ripples of the end of my climax return to my stomach.

Nathan leans forward and kisses my shoulder. In one quick swoop, I'm in his arms and I'm being deposited on the bed, under the blankets, my body nothing but jelly. When I squeeze my thighs together I feel my wetness and the tingles that remain.

"I'll be right back," he says against my lips and hastily leaves the room.

Sigh. He didn't climax, yet again.

I rest back on the pillows, pulling the blanket over my breasts. There's no need to think about it this time; it's pointless. I promised him two weeks of silence before I start asking him everything I want to ask. I'll give him his two weeks.

He's certainly taking his time.

Padding out of the bedroom when he doesn't return after almost ten minutes, I knock on the bathroom door. The sound of the shower running probably covers up the knock. With a sigh I go back into my room and sit on the bed.

Nathan returns, wearing a dark vest and his dark boxers. Damn his body is amazing. He smiles kindly at me, his eyes full of adoration. It does little to soothe my unease over the situation.

"The shower is free." His voice is gentle. That was a hint if I've ever heard one.

"Right," I mutter, feeling extremely embarrassed right now. "I'll go and shower."

He blinks, realisation dawning. "It's me, not you. We both got a little bit sweaty." I really don't want to know that I smell bad, it's humiliating. "I don't like sweat."

"Whatever," I sigh, exhaustion settling in.

He watches me for a moment, his eyes holding an emotion I can't quite figure out. Or maybe I'm just too tired to try. "Gwen…"

"Don't, I'm just tired." Is it going to be like this every time we have sex? Are we just not compatible? Maybe that's it.

"I'm sorry." He sounds sincere but I just don't want to hear it right now.

"I know you are."

"Gwen." he reaches over and takes my hand in his. A flash of feeling and memory at where that hand has just been makes my cheeks heat slightly and my stomach clench in appreciation. "You're breaking my heart right now."

His words make my chest ache with a brutal pain that seems intent on slicing me open. I look towards his sad eyes and realise that he must feel just as embarrassed and as badly as I do, if not more. It's all well and good me sitting here moaning that he's not performing the way I expect him to, but how must he feel knowing he finally has the woman he loves and can't perform the way he knows he should?

Just like that, every single tinge of annoyance and anger leaves my body. I roll over, not caring if he hates my sweat right now. I need to hold him.

To my shock, he returns the embrace and pushes me onto my back. "I'm trying." He whispers so close to my mouth I can scent the mint on his breath and feel it on my lips.

My heart aches again. I lift my head and touch my lips to his.

He pulls back after a moment, looking deeply into my eyes as his fingers push my fringe from my face. "Tell me you love me."

"I love you."

"I know I haven't said it yet, but..." He licks his lower lip and presses his forehead against mine. "Thank you for choosing me."

What? "Choosing you?"

"Thank you for not choosing Eric."

Oh gosh, he thinks I broke up with Eric already... but he must have seen Eric kiss me. What do I do now?

"I got worried when your mum asked me to pick up Dillan, but when you came back..." He smiles slightly. "I didn't think you would."

I groan and place my arm over my eyes.

"What?" He chuckles nervously. "What is it?"

"Nathan," I begin, not daring to look at him. "I didn't tell Eric yet." I think back to all of the times I've seen on TV, or read in books, where the woman keeps something small from her partner, and in the end it blows up in her face. The entire time I've sat there and screamed at the woman to just tell him, it's not actually that big of a deal. I won't be that woman. Now I'm kind of wishing I could be that woman, but the one that gets away with it.

He pulls off me and rolls onto his back without saying a word.

"Nathan, let me explain." I sigh, holding out my hand so he'll take it. He doesn't, so I rest it on his chest. "I was going to tell him after work; we agreed to meet up." Nathan nods for the rest of the story. "When we got to his house, his mum was there with his nine-year-old sister. They stayed for about half an hour, if that. When we were seeing them out, his sister fell and hit her face really bad. We had to take her to the hospital. We were there for an hour before his mum kicked us out."

"But he dropped you off. You had time on the way home."

"Eric was devastated! I couldn't do that to him. It was very bad timing. I swear, I'll tell him soon. Just... let him have tomorrow at least."

"As you wish."

"As... as I wish?"

"Yes. We'll give him tomorrow."

Blink. "We?"

"If you don't break up with him by Friday, I will."

I baulk. "You'll break up with him?"

"Yes," he confirms, still staring at the ceiling. "And the way I do it won't be pleasant."

I should be annoyed by his possessiveness. Actually I am annoyed, but my lower parts are way more affected. "I'd rather do it myself."

"Then you have until Friday. After that..."

I hear the threat in his voice and can only nod. "Okay. Deal."

"Good." He rolls me back over onto my back and covers my lips with his.

After kissing me for a long moment, he leans back and looks at me curiously.

"What?" I laugh nervously at the way he's looking at me but not really seeing me.

"You still haven't had a shower and I find myself not caring in the slightest."

I snort and slap his arm. "Is that another hint?"

"No, I suppose I'll get used to it." He kisses me once more, slow and languid with a small amount of tongue. "Go to sleep."

"Yes, sir."

As my eyes close, he cups my face with one hand and runs his thumb over my lips. "Don't kiss him again, Gwen. I won't forgive you next time."

My breath catches in my lungs as I open my eyes to stare at him and a small wave of fear flashes through me at the thought of losing him. "Why forgive me this time?"

He frowns, thinking on it for a moment. "You're the first woman, the first person I've ever loved. I've waited for you for three years. I've watched you in the arms of my brother when you should have been in mine. I'll not lose you to another Caleb over a kiss. You're mine; I'm yours. I can forgive you once, but not twice." His body tenses and his head goes to my neck. "I won't share you and I won't chase you. You deserve better, but if you choose me, I'll not allow you to look for better."

"I've already chosen you." I frown, feeling the need to reassure him.

He shakes his head and leans over the side of the bed. He raises Caleb's picture and my heart starts thudding in my chest. "No, if given the chance, you'd choose him again in an instant. Eric and I would be forgotten." He places the frame back on the bedside table and stares at it for a moment. Tears burn the back of my eyes at the reality of this situation and his words. I don't let them fall. He turns back to me and taps my temple. "You've chosen me in here." His hand moves to my chest and rests over my heart, beating steadily against his palm. "But there's little space for me in here."

"Nathan, that's not..."

"True?" He cuts in, his brow arching and a smile teasing his lips. "Isn't it?"

I remain silent. There's nothing I can say. "I do love you."

His eyes slowly close and his forehead drops to my collarbone. "And I you, and for now that is enough."

"And in the future?"

"In the future," he says, looking back into my eyes as his hand plays with a lock of my hair that rests across my breast, "I will want more. I won't be second best to my brother forever, but my love for you at the moment will allow it. I'm not completely heartless and, as unbelievable as it may seem, I miss my brother too, so I understand your reservations."

I can only agree with him; he's right. He deserves the world and not just the love I can give him.

"I'm going to begin opening the store once my new furniture arrives," he whispers, resting on his back and pulling me onto his chest. He's not satisfied until I'm sprawled across his front almost entirely. "I'd like you to help me design the layout."

I snort. "Don't ask me, I have terrible taste in décor."

He chuckles and kisses the top of my head. "Yes, I saw the work you did in the house you lived in with my brother."

"Don't be mean; we loved it."

"No, you loved it and you have the amazing ability to make people love what you love in order to keep you happy." Fingers lift my chin and my eyes once again connect with his. "I've never seen a smile as radiant as yours. I do believe it was the first thing about you that I fell in love with." Gasp. "Again, I know it's unbelievable, but every morning I woke to your shattered spirit and solemn face, it tore at me."

"I was grieving."

"And I hope you never have to grieve again," he whispers, wrapping his arms tight around me. "Goodnight, Gwen."

"Hmm." Placing one last kiss on his peck, I snuggle into his warmth and close my eyes.

Chapter Fifteen

Sasha sits on the swing beside me, Dillan held carefully in her arms as she rocks slowly back and forth. I take a picture of the two of them on my phone and rest backwards into the metal safety bar that prevents idiots like myself from falling off onto the unforgiving tarmac below.

"Do you remember when we used to come here to drink coffee during our breaks?" Sasha asks, smiling at Dillan who seems to be enthralled by the scenery swaying backwards and forwards before his eyes. Every time the wind breezes across his face, he blinks rapidly and jerks his chunky arms and legs whilst his mouth hangs open in a near smile. "He's so cute."

"Yeah, I remember." I smile fondly at my friend, turned ex-friend, turned friend once more. "Nathan said if I moved in with him, he'd do everything in his power to get me back into university."

"Wow." She gives me a large smile. "Do it."

"I want to, but I don't want to move in for that reason."

"Why won't you move in with him?"

I shrug, not knowing the exact answer to that question. "Maybe because I don't need to live with him anymore. I like having my independence."

She nods, seemingly in agreement. "Tommy is visiting this weekend. We should go out."

I shake my head. "I can't, I'm in London this weekend. Nathan is finally setting up shop so to speak." He told me this morning and luckily Valentine agreed to give me the weekend off, but I have to work two extra days next week. He's adamant that I'm going to help him choose the layout and décor. I'm not going to argue with him; it sounds like fun.

"That's great."

It definitely is. "I have to break up with Eric tomorrow. I went to the hospital this morning to see Kara with him."

"How is she?"

"Her nose was set, but her face and eyes are so swollen." I shudder at the memory of the incident. "Eric is looking better now that she's better. Their mum looked positively dreadful."

"Not surprising," Sasha states and, yet again, I agree. She pulls Dillan tighter to her chest and lets out a small shiver. "It's getting cold, we should head back."

"How's your placement?" I ask as I stand and smooth down my clothing.

"Boring. It's always too busy to talk to each other and get to know anybody. By the time we have the time to talk, we're all way too tired. I'd rather work at Valentine's; there seems to be a good balance of busy, baking and making friends."

"Yeah." I nod and take Dillan from her arms. "It's nice. We're like a little family."

She follows me to the stroller and waits as I strap Dillan in and wrap him up tight. "Can I ask you something?"

"Well, seeing as you asked so nicely," I remark dryly, making her snort and give me a small shove.

"Okay, it's just... it's about Caleb."

I remain as passive as possible, not letting her see what just the sound of his name still does to me. "Okay."

"There's... well, I didn't want to mention it before because of how..." She waves her hand in the air, clearly trying to find the right word. "Raw everything was. Plus, I thought you didn't need crap in your head that may just be crap."

"Go on."

She lets out a long breath and stops me in the street, her eyes sympathetic. "Don't you think it's odd that he wanted to marry you before he died?"

"What?"

"I'm just going by what you've said. He was urgent, insistent to marry you, and then he died the day before the wedding."

My back stiffens. "I remember the day."

"I'm just saying." Her voice is calm and soft, the opposite of how I feel inside. "It just seems... odd."

"I'd rather not think about it." I start walking again, ignoring her shock at my words.

She catches up to me. "You really haven't put him to rest have you?"

"Of course I have!"

"No, you haven't."

"I don't want to talk about this anymore."

"Fine, but you need to think about it. It's odd..."

"It's over," I hiss, glaring at her, both of us stopping once more. "It's over and done with; there's no use thinking about it. It's not fair on anybody."

"You'll never be able to move on until you let him go, babe."

"I don't want to let him go," I whisper, staring at my happy son, drooling all over himself and his blanket. "Ever." She doesn't hear me, so I tell her that I'm going home and pick up the pace.

"Gwen, I didn't mean to upset you. It's just, none of it makes sense and if you really think about it, you'll see I'm..."

"Stop," I snap, facing her once more. "Please, don't. I can't... it's hard enough already."

"And yet you share a bed with his brother? That's hardly fair."

"It's none of your business. Just leave it." I walk away.

"Gwen," she calls, but I don't answer and she doesn't follow.

I'm too ashamed to face the truth of her words and I'm too scared to deal with them.

I don't want to think about it. It's done; it's over, so what's the point?

As I'm heading home, I think back to this morning. Nathan left early; he had to drive back to the countryside to pick up a few things. I won't see him until tonight. This morning was a good one though. He kissed me sweetly and made me melt when he kissed Dillan and told him he loved him. I've never heard him say it, not in the way he did, so full of emotion and love.

Eric was normal this morning when he picked me up. Luckily he didn't try to kiss me. He did bring my phone and my bag, though, which was a relief. Living without one's phone is almost like living without an arm. We went to the hospital but only visited for a short while as he had to work.

Now I just have to figure out the best time to break up with him. This is ridiculous. It's not fair on him that I'm doing this, but I can't just break up with him in the midst of a crisis. I mean… what kind of person would that make me?

I sit and wait on my doorstep for Nathan to come by. He's been hard at work all day and no doubt he's exhausted. When his car pulls into the driveway, I smile and race towards him. His eyes light up when he climbs from the car and opens his arms ready to catch me.

Leaping onto him, I wrap my legs around his hips and slant my lips over his.

"Somebody's in a good mood," he chuckles against my mouth, spinning us so my back is against the side of the car. His hands cup my arse to hold me up. He moans when I thread my fingers into his hair and climb up his body an inch. Giving a sharp yet painless tug, I pull his head back and kiss and nibble along his neck.

I vaguely feel us moving towards the house and I think the door shuts, but I can't be sure.

"Kitchen," I say when he moves towards the stairs. "I have a surprise for you."

Just as quickly as I jumped on him, I release him and take his hand in mine. He pouts like a child but follows me anyway.

When he enters the kitchen, his eyebrows hit his hairline and his eyes come to me. "What's all of this?" He waves to the candles spread out along the table and sides and the steaming hot food waiting on the table.

"You deserve a well cooked meal." I give a firm nod and pull him to the table. Pressing my hands on his shoulders, I force him to sit and wrap my arms around his neck from behind. He leans his head back against my shoulder and sighs in contentment. I kiss his cheek. "Tell me to tell you that I love you."

He inhales a sharp breath and his throat bobs against my arm as he swallows. "Tell me you love me," he whispers.

Grinning, I slide onto his lap, effectively straddling him and run my nose along his. Looking directly into his eyes, I say the words whilst my fingers run through his silky hair. "I love you."

His eyes soften as his lips breeze against my own in the gentlest kiss I've ever received.

CHAPTER FIFTEEN

"Okay, let's eat. I made lasagne." It's a sentimental thought. The first time I ever got to touch him was when we fought over lasagne and it spilled all down his front. The memory is one of my best. Weird I know. "All organic foods, all fresh."

I try to slide off his lap, but he doesn't let me. He holds me tight and buries his face in my neck. "Will it always feel like this with us?"

"What do you mean?"

"This." He looks at me and runs the back of his fingers down my cheek. "I never want this feeling to end."

I'm still confused. I let him know as much with my eyes only.

Taking my hand, he places it against his chest so I can feel the steady heartbeat against my palm. "This feeling, right here."

"I hope so," I answer, kissing the tip of his nose. He lets me climb off him and take my seat at the tiny table.

"Where's Dillan?"

I point to the baby monitor on the side. "He's sleeping. He only just went down so he'll be out for a while." I hope.

"Good. I'd like to have him tomorrow, while you work, if that's okay?"

Shrug. "Sure. Mum will probably enjoy the break. I'm not at work until eleven though." I cut into my lasagne and take the first bite as he does the same. "I'm such a cooking genius."

"I'm going to have to agree with you."

"So, tell me about your day. Did you get much done?"

He nods. "Quite a lot actually. I have all of my things in the car."

"I'll help you," I state, looking at his handsome face bathed in the glow of the candle. He's so handsome; sometimes I forget how much and then become mesmerised when I look at him. His hair needs a trim though, not too much, but just enough to keep it from falling into his eyes. "I'll come around after work."

"Thank you."

We fall into a comfortable silence, occasionally glancing at each other and smiling.

He finally breaks it after a few minutes, when his plate is clean and he's pushed it away. Stretching his long legs, he crosses them at the ankles and asks, "What's the occasion?"

"I just wanted to do something nice for you."

"You don't have to."

"I wanted to," I say, giving him a pointed look. "You deserve it. Also," I chew on my lip for a moment, feeling slightly uncomfortable by what I'm about to tell him. "I started taking my pill again."

"What?" He asks, looking adorably confused.

"I thought we could…" I let my words trail off, taking note of the slight fear in his eyes. "Go without the condoms this time."

"You went to the doctor?"

I shake my head. "No, they're left over from before Dillan, but they're still in date. I have a two month supply."

"Maybe you should go and get new ones, just in case," he says and I can't help but feel like he's keeping something from me. "They could be faulty now."

"Don't be daft. I asked my doctor. They still have another two years of life left in them."

He shakes his head. "We'd both need to be tested first." His eyes avoid mine, probably so he doesn't see the offence I've just taken by his statement.

"I haven't had sex with anyone but you."

"And Caleb," he mutters, standing abruptly. "We'll get tested first. If that's okay?"

I narrow my eyes as he picks up the plates and deposits them on the side. "I was tested whilst I was pregnant. And like I said, I've only had sex with you. I'm clean."

He braces himself on the counter. What did I do wrong now? "I've not been tested in a while."

"How long?"

"Six months."

"That makes no sense. You haven't done the deed with anyone else in the past six months. Have you?" He shakes his head, no. I step towards him and wrap my arms around him from behind. "There was Lorna, but that was way before then."

He gulps and it's audible. "Still, I should double check. Just to be sure."

"Fine." I kiss his shoulder and move away. "I made treacle sponge. Would you like some?"

"Sure." He relaxes completely. I can almost see the tension leave his body. It reminds me of the dream I had of Caleb, the red smoky tendrils licking at the air, pouring from around his body. I stifle a shudder at the thought and move back to Nathan. As soon as I sink into his warmth and his arms tightly hold me to him, all thoughts and memories fly from my mind. The power this man has over me is astonishing. He could make me forget the world. "Your hair smells divine."

"Honey and almond." I release him, giving him a quick kiss before moving to the oven where the bowls of treacle sponge and custard are keeping warm. "Sit. I'll serve."

He does as he's told, thankfully.

We enjoy our food in more silence. That's one thing I love about us: there are peaceful times where we can just enjoy each other's company without having to be in each other's faces all of the time. Neither of us craves attention from the other because we both get it when needed.

When we finish, I stack the dishes by the sink and stand in between Nathan's parted legs. My finger nails scrape his scalp and he leans his head forward and sighs. I move them down to his neck, determined to seduce him into not using a condom.

His hands, which rest on his parted legs, gently touch the sides of my thighs. I lift one leg over his and then the other and lower myself onto his lap.

"You are so beautiful," he mumbles almost to himself and presses his lips to mine. "I woke up this morning and couldn't believe that for once in my life I've finally gotten what I want."

I give him a soft smile, trying to hide the turmoil within me that wishes for the same. A brief flash of Caleb appears behind my eyelids after I close my eyes. I'll never get what I want because what I want is impossible to obtain. I hate myself for feeling this way.

He waits for a while, his eyes clearly expecting a response. I don't know what to give him, so I kiss him again, trying to torment him with my tongue. It works, or it seems to, as he moans long and low. I feel it vibrate through his chest and into mine, which is pressed up against him. Amazing.

The world fades out around me. Nothing matters but him.

I lie awake, my heart pounding and my body covered in a thin layer of sweat. Nathan is in the shower, no doubt washing me from his skin under a cold spray. He didn't orgasm, yet again. I'm starting to feel self-conscious. He also didn't undress again, or push all of the way inside... again.

And there's the fact he took me from behind... again.

I'm trying not to be offended or irritated, truly I am, I just can't. There's clearly something wrong and I want to know what it is, right now. Not in two weeks!

Turning over, I tuck the blanket between my legs and close my eyes, praying that I fall asleep before Nathan comes back into the room so he doesn't see how much he's tormenting me. It's not his fault. I just wish he'd help me understand. How am I supposed to get closer to him if he keeps me at arm's length?

Literally and figuratively.

That's the only part that's his fault, not explaining why he is the way he is.

It's so darn frustrating.

"Gwen?" He whispers moments after, entering the room and climbing into bed. "Gwen?" He says a little bit louder this time as his fingers drag my hair from my shoulder. He pulls it up so it's fanned out above my head. I remain perfectly relaxed and try to keep my breathing even.

Letting out a frustrated sigh, he wraps an arm around me and presses his face into the back of my neck.

When sleep finally claims me, it's not a peaceful one.

"You look tired," Mum comments warily, holding her cup of toxic tea close to her face.

I turn the page in the newspaper and shrug. "Didn't sleep well. How are things with you and the new guy?"

She smiles like a love sick teenager and even swoons a little. "His name is George and he is perfect."

My smile isn't fake when I respond. "That's great. When can I meet him?"

"Actually, I wanted to talk to you about that." She places her cup down and snatches the newspaper from me. I roll my eyes when she holds it over her shoulder, moments before Nathan enters the kitchen and takes it from her. "He'd like to take us out for dinner on Sunday night. I know you're in London until then, so if you're too tired we can..."

"Sunday's fine." I look to Nathan, who nods his consent.

"I'll watch Dillan then." Nathan, who takes the seat opposite, opens the newspaper and flattens it down on the table top with his leather clad hands.

"Speaking of Dillan..." I say, when his bawling travels from the living room. I pad through and pick him up carefully. He smiles at the sight of me and I return it with just as much enthusiasm. "Love you my lickle baba."

"Grab my phone, Gwen. I need to let George know." The way she says his name is almost sickening. Why she needs sugar in her tea I'll never know. She should just spit in it.

I laugh at my inner joke as I step into the kitchen, causing them to look at me like I'm crazy.

"What?" Mum's brow arches as I sit with Dillan on my knee.

"Nothing." I shake my head, still smiling. "Just a private joke between me and Dillan."

Nathan watches me, his eyes narrowed curiously. It's that look you get when there's something on your face.

"What?" I ask defensively, shifting Dillan to the side as he tries to chew my hair, which he's wrapped around his pudgy fist.

"Nothing." He looks away. It's too obvious and now I know for a fact there's something wrong with me.

"What?" I demand, my voice deeper this time.

He shrugs, glancing at my dark hair. "Did you do something different?"

"No?" I smooth my hand over the top of my hair and look at my mum who looks away also. What the hell? "What's wrong with my hair?"

My mum starts sniggering when she peeks around the back.

Taking Dillan with me, I dart to the mirror in the hall and see no immediate signs of hair distress. Turning my head from side to side, I still fail to see what they're sniggering about. I haven't combed my hair yet. It's only eight in the morning, but it looks no different to how it usually looks.

There's a knock on the door. I almost don't answer it for fear of my not apparent hair distress humiliating me.

"Eric," I breathe, blinking in surprise.

He grins, holding up a bag of food. "Breakfast?"

"I..." He pushes past before I can finish and enters the kitchen. "What are you doing here?"

My eyes immediately go to Nathan, who stiffens in a second and stares at Eric with his hands tightly gripping the edges of the newspaper.

"Morning Dawn," Eric says and his eyes fall on Nathan. "Hi, Nathan right?"

Nathan nods. "We've met."

"Yeah, briefly." Eric places the bag on the table and turns back to me. "I didn't think you'd have company; I apologise for intruding." He steps into me, not caring about our audience and pulls me into a hug.

"That's okay, Eric," my mum says around a yawn and brings her wide eyes to me. "Can I get you a drink?"

Eric shakes his head a little frantically. "No thanks, I'm still trying to get the hair off my chest from the last one I drank that you made."

I can't help it, I giggle and Nathan lets out a sound that resembles that of a growl. Removing myself from Eric's embrace, I step around him and retake my seat at the table. I know he needs to leave, but I can hardly say that to him while these two are here. It'll embarrass him.

"It's Friday, Gwen." Nathan points out, sitting back in his chair.

I give him a warning look.

"Oh dear," Mum adds, taking Dillan from my arms. Now I have nothing to keep me anchored.

"Nathan," I say when she leaves the room. "Don't you have something you need to be doing?"

Nathan's mouth drops open in shock and possibly hurt, before he quickly gets a grip of himself and puts on the blank mask that I know so well. "Nope."

"I'm sure there's something you could be doing," I push, glancing at Eric who is watching the exchange with suspicious eyes. "Sorry," I say to Eric and place my hand on his arm.

"No problem." He shrugs, but I can almost see the cogs in his head turning as he tries to figure out the one thing I don't want him to know right now. "Nathan, I'd appreciate it if I could just have five minutes with my girl before I go to work. I'm not going to see her until Monday."

Oh dear, now Nathan knows I told Eric of my plans. He inhales a sharp breath, his anger swimming in his now black eyes. "Why not until Monday?"

Please stop. Please. My mental begging does nothing.

"The London thing."

Nathan looks at me, his anger aimed my way and with good reason. I want to shrink into a hole in the ground. "The London *thing*?"

"Yeah, that's what I said." Eric straightens his back and puffs his chest out slightly. "Why?"

"Do you both have plans for Monday?" Nathan tries to smile but fails miserably. It looks more like a grimace.

"We're supposed to be seeing the new Godzilla movie."

'I swear I didn't make plans!' I want to scream, but I don't. Eric is completely twisting the truth of our 'plans'. He only asked what I was doing Monday, to which I responded that I wasn't doing anything. He said cinema at six to see Godzilla and I said that we'll see, but only because I knew I'd have to break up with him today and didn't want to make him... hell, I don't know. I've really messed this up.

"Really?" Nathan quirks a brow, folding his newspaper with precision. Oh hell, I'm in trouble.

"Nathan," I say softly and give him a pleading look. "Could you please give us ten minutes? If it's not too much trouble."

"I guess I could make your bed," he comments dryly. "I didn't get a chance to do that this morning seeing as you woke up after me." He stands and looks at Eric, who is staring at me expectantly, his jaw tight. "I'll leave you both alone."

I nod, my own anger apparent. "That would be nice."

As he's walking past, he plucks something from my hair and holds it in front of my face. I cock my head as I try to make out what is on the small square of paper. There's a damp stain and a written sentence that reads:

You drool in your sleep. Here's the proof.

I snatch it from his hand and screw it up into a ball, but the damage is already done. Eric glares at me and then at Nathan. "Wow, well, don't I look stupid."

"Yes," Nathan says smugly as I say, "No!"

I turn towards Nathan, my anger bubbling over. "You absolute arsehole. God... what in hell is wrong with you?"

He looks shocked for a moment and even takes a step back.

Eric shakes his head, his lips a thin white line. "Enjoy your breakfast." He storms past me and slams the door on his way out. I stand in the centre of the kitchen, my entire body shaking uncontrollably with anger, rage, sorrow, fright…I don't know.

This is all my fault.

"Finally," Nathan says, looking as casual and relaxed as he was before Eric arrived. He unfolds his newspaper and turns to the page he was at before he just completely ruined everything. "I thought he'd never leave."

His casual and happy façade irritates me so much, I barely even register what I've done until I see the water dripping down his face and soaking his shirt. He looks at me in shock, his mouth hanging open.

"Get out," I bite, closing my eyes to try and rid them of the red haze.

Nathan blinks, not seeming to understand what I've done any more than I can believe that I've done it. "Gwen…"

"No," I hiss, holding up my hand to stop him from making any move towards me. "He didn't deserve that at all. We could have parted ways as friends. He wouldn't have to know I left him for somebody else."

"You were hardly with him," he scoffs, wiping his face on his shirt.

"No, you're right, but he always treated me with respect. He didn't deserve that in the slightest!"

"You wouldn't have done it otherwise. You were making plans for Monday!"

"I told him I'd let him know and we had plans to see each other tonight, you idiot! I was going to do it then!"

"Well… it's done," he shrugs, clearly not seeing why I'm so angry, and tosses his damp newspaper in the bin. "You need to get ready for work. We're sorting out our new home before you go in, remember?"

Is he for real? "You really don't care do you?"

"About…"

"That you just stomped on him like he was nothing and totally disrespected my wishes."

He leans back, running his tongue over his lower lip before speaking. "He had his hands all over you."

"Because he thought I was his!" I shout and take a deep breath to calm myself.

"Yes, and whose fault is that?"

His snarky attitude makes me want to poke him in the eye.

"You had no right to interfere."

"I'm your boyfriend," he laughs in disbelief. "I had every right to interfere."

"You promised me you'd give me until Friday."

His smile is smug, much like it was earlier when he was speaking to Eric. "Yes and it's Friday. I didn't specify a time. Can you go and get ready now?"

"Not until you apologise." I watch him stand once more and look down at his shirt, which is almost see through with the amount of water that has soaked the cotton.

"Why should I apologise? You're the one who threw water at me!"

"You've ruined my reputation. He's going to tell everyone and I'm going to look like a harlot."

"Then maybe you shouldn't have dated two men at the same time." He says this with a tone so calm yet cold, I lose it and shout,

"Or maybe I shouldn't have fucked my fiancé's brother!"

He releases a choked gasp and looks at me like I'm an alien, like he doesn't know me at all. The pain in his eyes shoots into me and tears instantly blur my eyes. "I didn't mean that."

"Yes you did," he says, grabbing his suit jacket from the back of the chair.

Part of me wants to go after him when he walks away just like Eric did, but the rest of me is far too angry at what just happened.

"Well... that went well," my mum says, cringing openly. "Are you going after him?"

I shake my head.

"You should. That was mean and not like you at all."

"You always take his side," I snap bitterly, strolling past her with my chin raised. "I'm not wrong this time."

"And what he did was no better. I heard. I know it was mean and Eric didn't deserve that, but he's a man and he loves you. He doesn't want to lose you and he has been patient enough."

I growl and rest my forehead against the wall in the hallway. "Stop being right when I'm mad."

She laughs and places her hand on my shoulder. "You've been through a lot and you're still growing up. He'll understand."

"I'm not apologising."

She nods her head and thinks on it for a moment. "Sometimes apologies aren't necessary."

"Poor Eric."

"He's a handsome boy. He'll have moved on in a few days. Don't give yourself too much credit." I should be offended, but I can see she's joking. About the last part at least, the first part is most definitely true. "Go after Nathan before it gets out of hand."

I don't want to. I ignore her suggestion and make my way upstairs. No way in hell am I chasing him, especially not now. I need to calm down first.

Chapter Sixteen

Nathan hasn't contacted me all weekend and I don't blame him. Eric doesn't either and I have to admit, I'm kind of relieved that I don't have to face what I've done.

I've been an idiot.

I stare at myself in the mirror, mostly at the bags under my eyes from lack of sleep and indecision. This is all my fault. What the hell happened to that fun loving girl who'd laugh at everything?

She died with Caleb, my subconscious tells me and I can't help but agree.

I can't go on like this, I need to get her back. I'm making everyone around me miserable and it feels awful. I used to live to make people laugh, smile and feel at ease around me.

Damn you, Caleb. I could kill you if you were still alive.

Tiffany thinks I just need more time; she could be right.

Sasha thinks I need to drag myself out of this funk immediately or I'll be lost to the devil of despair forever. She could be right too.

My mum thinks I should go away for a while. Take a holiday, so to speak. She could be right too.

I think I should find Nathan, hold him tight and forget the world, but I've hidden behind him for long enough.

"Tell me what to do!" I shout to nobody, standing in the middle of my bedroom. "Tell me how to get past this," I whisper, feeling a tear slide down my nose.

I hear a thud and squeal in surprise. Scanning the room for wherever the noise came from, I see no suspects, not until I glance at the floor under my desk and see the DVD case that I hid a while ago.

My fingers tremble as I reach down and pick it up. Talk about timing. I should find a new hiding place for it.

For some reason I can't release it. I can't find a place good enough for it and something screams at me in my mind to watch it.

I don't want to watch it. Not again.

But the titles make no sense.

After a few torturous moments of indecision, I open the case and spin the DVD around its axis with one finger. Why am I doing this?

What will this prove?

Nothing. But it can't hurt anything either.

Blowing out a breath, I carefully remove the DVD from the case and, with nausea threatening to turn violent, I place it in the DVD slot of my laptop.

I fast forward to the place I was last time as soon as it opens on my desktop.

Why the hell am I doing this?

I press play and turn the volume down low. I can't bear to hear Nathan cry.

Tears automatically spring to my eyes at only the memories of the horrors I saw the last time I watched this.

I fast forward it past the part where Nathan's grandfather cleans him up, threatening and soothing him all at the same time. He seems to leave the camera hanging around his neck. A beep sounds and I realise that instead of stopping the camera from recording, he's taken a picture.

I skip it past the long walk home, trying not to let Nathan's sobs get to me, which is entirely impossible.

"Fuck," is the first word I hear, only ten more minutes into the movie. "Fuck." I recognise the gravel under his feet to be the driveway. "What the fuck are you doing here?" There's no fear in his voice, only anger.

"I came to pick up Nathan. His mother is back early from her trip to France and wishes to see him."

Is that...

Holy crap!

I return the DVD to its box ten minutes later with tears streaming down my face and a heart that beats so rapidly in my chest, I swear it's going to fail.

Taping it to the underside of a drawer this time, I curl up on my bed and cry silent tears. Does Nathan know? No... I don't think he does. Which makes this so much more sick and twisted.

Why did I watch? Why couldn't I have left myself oblivious?

"Now what do I do?" I whisper, my voice breaking with my sorrow.

You leave it and you help Nathan move on. You take care of him. Just like he's done for you. My conscience tells me and for once I agree with it.

But first, I need to calm down.

Gwen: Drinks later?

Sasha: On a Monday??? Hell yeah!

I feel bad for leaving Dillan. We had a good weekend, despite my constant sulk with the world. I really need to stop feeling sorry for myself. The situation isn't going to change. Caleb isn't coming back and that's that. I find myself thinking about our time together with a smile rather than tears. This is definitely an improvement.

Mum doesn't seem to mind. She's having a night in with George, who, I have to admit, is lovely and strikingly handsome. He's also a police officer. My mum met him when he apologised for knocking her out of the way while chasing a thief down the high street. He's charming, funny and he's completely different to the men she's brought home in the past.

I like him, but she doesn't need my approval, although she seems to want it.

Kissing my little boy's fuzzy head, I give my mum a wave and meet Sasha at the door.

"You look hot," she grins, scanning me from head to toe. I tug on the bottom of my cream netted dress and repeat the same to her. She does look hot, as usual. I wish I had her style and her wardrobe. "Just you and me tonight. You look like you need some girl on girl time."

I blink, laughing at her slip up.

"You know what I mean." She giggles with me, slapping my arm. "Shots first?"

"Hell yeah." The thought of alcohol makes me feel sick, but I need to start living again if I want to improve. Alcohol first, then I can move on to less self-destructive things that don't take me away from my son. Fingers crossed this works.

We squeeze our way to the bar and Sasha, not that it's a surprise, orders four shots. I stare at the pee coloured fluid in the shot glasses and cringe as I pick one up.

"Let's get this party started!" She grins, winking at the guy working behind the bar.

On three... one, two... three.

I tip my head back and swallow the sour fluid. Unfortunately it tries to escape and makes me gag. Sasha doesn't give me time to recover before she's forcing me to drink the next and is handing me a glass of coke to chase it down.

"That's my girl," she laughs, patting me on the back and ordering drinks that don't require immediate consumption.

"You're a bad influence."

"And you've become a hermit. Let's party."

I follow her onto the dance floor and stand awkwardly as she moves around me, trying to coax me into moving with her. This was a really bad idea.

"Hey, I never did say I was sorry for our last conversation," she shouts into my ear, forgetting that even though the beat of the music is extremely loud, I'm not drunk and therefore my hearing is not impaired.

"It's fine," I respond, shouting back so she knows how it feels. "I swear, it's over with."

She smiles gratefully and then smiles at someone over my shoulder. I look back and smile with her.

"Surprise," Tommy laughs, wrapping me in his big arms.

"Oh my god," I squeal and hold him as tight as possible.

My gang, back together.

"Can I get you ladies a drink?"

Need he ask?

"It won't stop," I cry, heaving again and cringing at the sound of the splatter on the pavement. "Why won't it stop?"

"UNDERNEATH YOUR CLOTHES, THERE'S A... what's next?" Sasha slurs, dancing around my puking form.

"Cock!" Tommy responds, going as far as to grab his package in the middle of the street.

My head spins and swims, my eyes trying to focus on anything, but they fail miserably and I stagger two steps to the side. "I need to go home."

"I need to dance!" Sasha giggles, still dancing around me.

"I need to fuck." Tommy laughs, grabbing hold of a very drunk Sasha around the waist.

"Awkward," I say in a sing song voice and take a few steps towards the nearest wall. My legs don't appreciate the demands my brain is making and I fall to the floor in a laughing heap. "Oh my god. Why did I drink so much? I'm going to be so hung over tomorrow."

"Can you understand what she's saying?" Tommy asks Sasha, who is grinding against him playfully.

"Something about not drinking enough." Her eyes light up. "More shots!"

I pull out my phone. I need to call a taxi. Oh dear, six missed calls.

My phone screen lights up as another call comes through and I answer. "Call me back, I need to get a taxi."

"Where are you?"

It's Nathan! "Guys, Nathan's on the phone!"

"Tell him to bring shots!"

"Gwen," he snaps. His voice hurts my ear. "Where are you?"

"I'll... oops."

Sasha starts cackling and grabs me by the arm, pulling me from the ground once more.

"Hello? Is anyone there?" I hear Nathan's voice travel through the speaker.

"Yes," I say, laughing when I realise the phone is upside down. "Sorry, I fell over."

"Again!" Sasha cackles, looping her arm through mine. "Are you coming out, Nathan?"

"Where are you?" He demands angrily.

"You're so cute when you're mad."

"Gwen, so help me god, if you don't tell me where you are right this minute..."

"I'm on the high street, I think." I look at the blurred street name, tilting my head from side to side, trying to see the words but not managing it in the slightest. "Yeah."

Oh dear. I drop my phone and my bag and lean over a wall.

Splat.

I don't feel well Mummy.

"We need to get her home." Sasha picks up my bag and clumsily rubs my back.

"Did you call a taxi?" Tommy asks, wrapping his arm around my waist as I finish vomiting.

"Shit, where's my phone?"

"In your bag."

Before I can grab it, we're stuck in bright headlights as a car clumsily pulls onto the pavement. We all scream like lunatics and I end up on my arse again, this time with Sasha on top of me. She starts laughing, Tommy tries pulling us up and I decide to lie down for a second.

A car door slams and I'm vaguely aware of Sasha's weight leaving me and warm hands cupping my face. "How much did she drink?"

"Hi." I smile at Nathan, giggling when I see his frown.

"No more than us." Tommy shrugs, taking hold of Sasha.

"Get in the car." Nathan orders the both of them.

"Nah, it's cool, we only live on the next street."

Nathan crouches beside me and expertly lifts me into his arms.

"I'm flying." Throwing my arms out, my hand connects with Nathan's cheek. "I'm sorry."

He doesn't talk, only carries me to his car and places me on the passenger seat.

Sasha and Tommy climb into the back when Nathan orders them to get in and sit sniggering under their breaths as I roll my head from side to side. Kicking my shoes off my aching feet, I turn my body to the side and place my feet over Nathan's lap.

CHAPTER SIXTEEN

"Guess what I did," I try to say, but it sounds like one jumbled word.

"Close your eyes." Nathan places his hand on my thigh and starts driving.

He looks so handsome.

He throws me a smile, his cheeks turning slightly pink and I realise I must have said that out loud.

"Gwen got called a bitch today," Sasha says, leaning between the two front seats. "Eric was out with his friends and they were not nice at all."

Yeah, that part of the night really wasn't much fun. I'd tried to smile at him and avoid him as best as I could, but his male friends kept making rude comments whenever they saw me. We left that club and went to another.

"And slut, don't forget slut," I add, closing my eyes tight to shut out the glare of the street lights.

"We're here," Nathan clips, climbing out of the car so he can open the door for Sasha.

After hugs goodbye, we wait by the curb until Sasha and Tommy enter his house. Or his parent's house. Whichever.

Nathan pulls my feet back onto his lap and silently drives us home. To whose home? I wonder.

His.

As soon as he opens the passenger side door, I immediately raise my arms and wrap them around his neck. He kisses my shoulder and holds me with one arm as he unlocks the front door.

I smell paint; it's making me feel ill.

He immediately begins to ascend the stairs and just as I expect to feel a soft bed beneath me, I feel a counter and blink my eyes open.

Nathan smiles softly at me, a sigh escaping him as he shakes his head. "You're a mess."

"Thanks." I snort.

"Arms up," he whispers and I do as I'm told.

He tugs my dress up and over my head, throwing it over his shoulder without a thought. One of his hands immediately goes to my neck as I begin to fall to the side. So tired.

"Open your mouth."

I taste mint and feel a toothbrush working its way over my teeth.

"Stand." He grabs me under the arms and pulls me to my feet. "Rinse and spit." His lips touch the curve of my neck. "Good girl."

"I think I drank too much."

"I think so too." His fingers wrap around me and my bra pings free, best feeling ever. He throws that over his shoulder too before peeling down my thong and sitting me back on the closed toilet.

My heavy eyelids begin to close as he swiftly disrobes himself. I want to watch, but I'm so tired.

"Don't fall asleep yet," he laughs, lifting me from the toilet and into his arms. I hear the sound of water running and cringe. Why do I have to shower? I just want to sleep.

"This is the first time I've had the chance to see you naked and I can't open my eyes."

Chuckling, he places me under the warm spray and holds me tight to his nude body. Well… almost nude. Why is he wearing boxers?

Soapy hands move over my body as I lean back onto the wall.

"You have the most amazing body I've ever seen in my life," Nathan says as his hands cup my breasts and squeeze gently. "I could worship you with my hands for hours."

He continues stroking me, his soapy hands gliding over every inch of my skin. When one of them parts my folds and a finger slides over my clit, I groan loudly and my back arches. "Make me come, Nathan."

His mouth meets mine as his middle finger pushes into me. "With pleasure."

I gasp and writhe as he rubs the heel of his palm against my sensitive nub, the hot water cascading down over both of us. His finger rubs the inner wall, pulling at the magic spot in my sex that sends waves of euphoria through my muscles.

"I've never done this before," he whispers in my ear, taking the lobe into his mouth and nipping it gently. A shudder wracks through me. "You're the first. You feel amazing. So warm and wet. I never understood the appeal until now."

He presses his arousal against my hip as I push my tongue into his mouth and smooth my hands over his chest.

Using his free hand, he lifts my leg and holds it around his waist so his hand has more room to move.

I've never felt anything like it. For a man that's never done this before, he really knows what he's doing.

"Tell me you love me," he murmurs in my ear as the pressure builds in my stomach, making me grind against his hand and beg for more.

"I love you," I cry, reaching for the waist band of his boxers. He gasps and pushes his hips into me to stop me from going further.

My body seems to implode, my drunken haze numbing everything but the intense pleasure that rips through me and settles in my womb. "Nathan," I moan breathily, my orgasm silent apart from his name passing my lips.

"Tell me you love me," he repeats, his hand leaving me and his solid length pressing against my mound.

"I love you."

"Again," he demands, his eyes closing tight before his face goes to my neck.

"I love you."

He grinds almost violently against me, his breath heavy and deep moans forcing their way out. "I can't stop."

"Then don't," I insist, wrapping my arms around him. "Let me feel you."

A choked sound escapes him. It's closer to a sob than a groan of pleasure.

"Please, Nathan, let me feel you."

"Tell me you love me," he orders, pressing me further into the wall and grabbing the back of my hair almost violently. His body tightens, every single muscle that he owns seem to bunch and quiver. He's going to orgasm. I need to see.

My eyes open and my hand pulls his face from my neck. I press my lips to his, smoothing my fingers over every inch of skin I can reach before finally trailing them down his back and cupping his amazing arse. "I love you."

"I can't stop," he bites out, his hips working against me furiously.

Another climax hits me. There was no build up, no warning. I cry out and it takes everything in me to remain standing.

"Tell me to stop," he begs. "Tell me…"

I don't, of course I don't. Instead, I push back against him with my own hips; circling them slowly and putting as much pressure on him as I possibly can.

"Let me feel you," I whisper against his mouth. "I want to feel you inside of me, all of you."

As if I've grabbed a bucket of ice and thrown it at him, he lunges back, making me tumble to the side and hit the adjacent wall of the shower. Ouch.

"I..." He says, his mouth hanging open in shock and disgust, but somehow I know that the disgust he feels is aimed at himself. Shaking his head, he steps out of the shower. Moments later I feel it turn off and I wait for his return. He doesn't.

I drunkenly stagger from room to room, wrapped in nothing but a towel. It's not until I check the driveway and see the lack of car that I realise he's gone.

Maybe he'll come back. I pull on one of his T-shirts and, after braiding my hair, I climb into his soft bed and close my eyes.

Damaged is the only word that comes to mind when I think of Nathan before I sleep.

I have no idea how to fix him.

Chapter Seventeen

I GO HOME AS soon as I wake, wearing nothing but Nathan's boxers and one of his shirts. It wouldn't be the first time I've gone home like this, except the last time it was in Eric's clothing. My neighbours must think I'm such a slut.

Fortunately my hangover isn't too bad and my mum isn't angry at me for staying out all night when I tell her where I was and explain why I was there. She doesn't ask questions, only hands me my son and makes me an instant cappuccino, which is the only hot drink she can make successfully. And that's only because it's in a sachet and all she has to do is add water.

Dillan chews on my collarbone as I charge my phone and power it up. He seems content to do that for a while, so I leave him to it.

Sasha: Hey, are you awake? I'm on my way over.

Gwen: I'm up and I'm shocked that you're up.

Sasha: I have so much to tell you!!!! :D

Gwen: I unfortunately have nothing to tell you.

Sasha: I'll be there in five. Hungry?

Gwen: I could eat.

Five minutes later she's still not here, which means she's picking up food from somewhere. My phone alerts me to another text. I have to blink a few times to make sure I haven't read his name and message wrong.

<u>Eric</u>: I'm sorry about last night, whatever happened with us, you didn't deserve that.

<u>Gwen</u>: I did. I'm sorry for messing you around.

He doesn't respond, but I don't expect him to. At least we're at some sort of impasse. Hopefully we can both put it behind us.
Now I need to contact Nathan. His phone is off. It's probably dead.

<u>Gwen</u>: Call me. X

I hope he's okay.

Sasha arrives a few minutes later, looking rough and still wearing the same dress from the night before, but with a shirt over the top. Tommy follows close behind, a bag of food in his hand.
He leans forward and kisses my cheek. I trade my son for the food and I lay it out on the table as they both make Dillan smile and giggle.
"Last night was fun," Tommy announces as we fill our plates. Dillan sits beside me in his bouncer.
"I barely remember it," I lie. I definitely wish I'd forgotten how drunk I was, how many times I fell over and how many times I vomited.
Sasha giggles and decides to give me the play by play. Great. Now I'm definitely never going to forget. "Shall we go to the park after breakfast? I feel like going to the park."
I shake my head. "I can't, I've got plans with Nathan." Another lie, but one I so desperately need to be true. I really need to talk to him.
"That's a shame." Tommy murmurs. "Tomorrow?"
I nod in agreement. "Tomorrow sounds good. So, you have lots to tell me?"
"I did, but I can't…" She trails off, her cheeks turning pink.
Tommy gives me a wink. "It's because I'm here and she can't tell you because it's about me."

"Oh." I frown in confusion and then it clicks. "Oh my god! You're seeing each other?"

Sasha shrugs, trying for nonchalance, but she can't hide the smile on her face, no matter how hard she tries.

Tommy just leans back, looking proud and slightly smug. He also looks like he just got himself a little somethin' somethin', as he used to call it back in university.

"I'm happy for you guys." I put my little finger and thumb to my mouth and ear, mimicking a phone and mime the words "Call me later" to Sasha, who nods eagerly.

We eat breakfast in a happy atmosphere. Mum joins us, which is nice, and tells Sasha all about her new flame. During this time I text Nathan three times, begging him to call me, but I get no response. Why can't things be simple?

Oh yeah... because I made them that way.

I've really messed up everything.

At least last night put things into perspective for me.

Sasha and Tommy both leave after an hour and I make myself pretty and get Dillan ready to leave. Maybe Nathan is home by now. It's worth checking. I really need to tell him how sorry I am and pray that he gives me another chance. I can't lose him. It's time to put Caleb to rest.

With the stroller moving ahead of me, I make my way up Nathan's driveway and sigh with relief when I see his car there. He's leaving the house and locking the door as I make it to his car. Is he going somewhere?

"Hi," I say nervously, flicking the brakes on the pram so it doesn't roll down the sloped driveway.

Nathan startles and turns to face me. "I was going to come and see you."

"Oh." I smile and move towards him, my hands awkwardly shoved in the pockets of my jeans. "Are you okay?"

"Yes. Are you?" He eyes me with his blank expression, the one that says he doesn't care about anything. I'm so glad I know this to be nothing but a mask, or my confidence would be wavering right now.

"Fine."

"Hangover?"

"Fortunately no. Umm... I want to talk to you."

He chews on the inside of his cheek and nods. "Yes, me too."

"You need to talk to you?" I joke, but it does little to amuse him. "Okay, sorry. I'll be serious."

"I'm sorry for everything," I say at the same time that he says, "I'm trying my best but..."

Blink. "What?" I say at the same time that he says, "Why are you sorry?"

"Let me talk." He clears his throat and looks up at the sky for a moment. "Do you think this was a mistake?"

"A mistake?"

"Yes." He turns and closes the boot of his car, leaning on it momentarily. I take this second to admire his arse in those jeans. Fabulous. Last night I got to grab that.

"Us?"

"Yes, you and I."

"I think we've been doing okay."

"I make you miserable and it's obvious I can't give you what you need or want."

What the hell? "You give me you, and that's enough."

His eyes soften momentarily. "You'll only want more eventually and I don't think I can give you that. I thought..." He exhales a long, mournful breath. "I'm trying, honestly I am, but I see it in your eyes every time we get intimate, every time we get close." His hands drag over his face and one of them reaches out to me. I take it and let him pull me closer. "I'm making a mess of everything. You're only going to leave me when all is said and done. I know that now."

"Stop it, don't do this." I say firmly, taking another step towards him, putting only an inch of distance between us. "We haven't even tried, not really. I haven't been understanding enough."

"What if you never move on from Caleb? What if I never move on from my past?"

"I will move on from Caleb, I swear. If this is about what I said..."

"It's not." He shakes his head and leans back against his car. "It's not about what you said. We're both too..." He sighs again and finishes his sentence on a whisper. "Broken."

"What should I do?" I place my hands on his chest. "Just tell me what to do."

"I'll never be able to have sex with you the way you want, Gwen!" He shouts suddenly, his hands balled into fists by his hips. "I'll never be able to do it without a condom with you. I'll never be able to taste you. I'll never be able to..."

I cut him off, placing my hands on his cheeks "I know it'll take time, but we can get past that. You'll see. We'll do it together, literally and figuratively." Again my humour falls flat. "I want to try properly. Me, you and Dillan. I'll move in. We can start over; we can date. I know what he did to you, I know how badly he must have hurt you..."

"You think it's because of that?" He asks in disbelief. "That's not why I won't enter you, Gwen."

"Then tell me why. Help me understand."

"I..." He clamps his mouth shut. "It's messed up."

"Nathan," I sigh, leaning back so I can look into his eyes. "It can't work if you don't help me understand."

He stares at me, pain and determination in his features. "My great grandfather molested my grandfather. Almost as brutal, if not more so, than my grandfather did to me." I can tell how hard it is for him to say it out loud, almost like the words are anchored in his throat and refuse to rise. "My grandfather abused me... See a pattern? And then there's my dad. I don't know if he was abused, but I know that he abused my mum. She didn't used to be this way. She used to love us, but he turned her into what she is now. Uncaring, unfeeling. She was scared to show us love and I guess it just stuck."

'Sometimes the abused become the abuser' rings through my mind. Now I feel extremely bad for ever letting that thought enter my head, now that I know it's the thought that's in his head.

"I can't... I've never felt a woman around me without something separating us. I've never pushed my fingers into a woman and made her scream, until you." He rests his forehead against mine. "I can't lose control."

"Why?"

The shutters that locked his emotions behind his eyes slide away and the pain I see there breaks my heart. The insecurity, the vulnerability, the betrayal and anger. All of it shines through and all of it soaks into my very core. "Because I'm scared I'll become like them."

"So why have sex at all?"

He clears his throat, shifting uncomfortably on the spot. "I can't reach climax without some kind of stimulation from somebody else. I'm assuming it's a side effect from…" He doesn't need to finish for me to understand what he's saying.

Not even through masturbation? "Wow. That's messed up." I have no idea what to say to make it better. I don't think anything I can say will make it better. "It's also the biggest pile of S. H. I. T. I've ever heard."

"Gwen…"

"No, I'm serious! You're not them!" I throw my arm out, pointing down the drive to emphasise my point. "You'll never be them! You're amazing…"

"You don't know that. What if once I get a true feel for what it's like, what if I lose control and start exploring other options?" He pulls my hands away from his face. "I don't want to be a monster."

"Have you ever thought of… a child in that way?" Please say no…

He lurches back, clearly repulsed by the idea, "Of course not. But I did shove you in my sleep!"

I almost laugh. That's hardly a fair comparison. "Nathan…"

Shaking his head, he moves away and runs his hands through his hair. "I'm screwed up. I can't even touch an apple with my bare hand. And I know with one hundred percent certainty that I'll never allow myself to lose control."

This is way above my pay grade. I have no idea what to say or do. I can see why he'd think that, but I also know in the very depths of my soul that he'd never, ever hurt a child the way he was hurt. He'd never even entertain the sick idea of it.

"Nathan…" I place my hand on his shoulder. "I love you. We'll get help, see a professional or something."

"You don't think I haven't?" He laughs coldly, shrugging my hand off his shoulder. "I never should have… you can't fix me any more than I can fix myself."

"Please." I'm not entirely sure what I'm pleading for. I just know he needs to listen.

"Seeing you with Eric, it killed me. Knowing I could lose you. You deserve normal and he is normal. He can give you everything I can't, so why choose me?" He laughs coldly. "Out of guilt? Obligation?"

"Out of love and the fact that I need you."

Looking at me over his shoulder, he slowly turns back towards me, his lower lip glistening from where his tongue has teased it. "You should tell me to go."

"I don't want to."

"I love you, Gwen. Truly I do, with all of my heart and soul, but you deserve better. You deserve everything. I finally understand why Caleb took you from me that day on the beach."

"Caleb did that because he was an arsehole! That had nothing to do with this." I shout, but he completely blanks me and climbs in the car. "You're not unfixable." He doesn't respond, even though I know he's heard me by the way his lips pinch and his shoulders sag. "I'm not giving up on you, but if you give up on yourself, I'm not sure even I can bring you back. This is just... I'm not sure what this is. But it needs to stop." He opens his mouth to talk, but I quickly cut him off. "I love you. We're not breaking up. We're not leaving each other and we're going to do this properly. The past is the past. Let's just leave it there."

"Gwen..."

"You can't keep doing this to yourself, or to us. That will break us. Thinking about Caleb hurts me, but I don't bring him up every time I'm feeling down and I certainly don't blame our problems on him. You can't keep doing that either. Your problems and us don't relate. We're us, and that was then. Two separate things."

"It affects me every day. It affects you every day."

"We'll get past it. You'll get past it."

He nods once and bites his lower lip. I can see the wheels turning in his head.

Cupping his cheek with my hand, I look directly into his eyes. "You'll never be them. I'll never let you be them. You're too good a person to ever be them. Trust me."

"I've ruined the day now, haven't I?" He smiles, grabbing me by the waist and pulling me flush with his body.

"No, I'm glad we talked. It's nice to kind of get it out in the open, you know?"

He kisses my lips gently. "I know."

"So, shall we go inside?"

Walking over to the pram, he clicks off the brakes and begins pushing Dillan to the door. "It's probably a good idea." Once inside, he leans over the baby and carefully lifts him out. "Come on little man. Are these new jeans?"

Snort. "They're the ones you bought for him." I smile when Dillan stretches, flexing his long legs out while bringing his arms to his head. When he opens his mouth to yawn, Nathan kisses it, causing Dillan to startle, making his little arms and legs jerk.

I giggle and push the pram into the cupboard by the door.

When I enter the room, Nathan is lying on his back on the ground, raising Dillan above his head before bringing him down to his face and pretending to bite his neck.

Looking at him now, I can't help but wonder how he could think those things about himself.

This is stupid; this is ridiculous. Is this why he shuts himself off from the world? He truly believes if he allows himself to enjoy sex, eventually he'll get a taste for darker things? That's madness.

What the fuck did you do to him you sick bastard? I mentally scream at his grandfather as I make my way into the kitchen, needing privacy for my thoughts.

I don't know what to do! Genuinely I don't. I'm completely stuck.

That poor boy. I want to kill the old bastard and string his innards on Mr and Mrs Weston's Christmas tree! How could they let this happen to him?

I'm so angry I could kick a frog.

No... I'm so angry I could wrap my hands around his father's neck and squeeze until he took his last breath. And I'm not violent, so these new feelings are ten times worse than they would be on a more aggressive person. I want to act. I want to scream and shout.

After downing a glass of water in an attempt to soothe my nerves, I head to the fridge and start pulling things out. Nathan enters the room with Dillan in his arms as I'm chopping up vegetables to make a salad.

"What are you doing?" He asks, pulling angry and then happy faces at the frowning baby, who can't seem to focus on what it is Nathan's doing.

"Making you lunch." I respond, throwing the veg into a bowl.

"You don't have to," he says, placing a calming hand on my shoulder.

"I know." I wipe the cutting board down and place the chicken breast on the shiny surface. "But I want to, plus this chicken needs eating today or it'll go off."

"Isn't Mummy brilliant?" He asks Dillan, who continues frowning. Nathan then leans forward and kisses the curve of my neck, brushing my hair away with his fingers at the same time. "I'll take him into the living room, give you some space."

"Okay," I whisper, not allowing my emotions to get the better of me.

They leave the room, but not before kissing me again. This makes me smile as I work.

When we sit down to lunch, Nathan stares at me for a while. I pick at my food, not really hungry from this morning's hearty breakfast. "Is everything okay?"

I admit. "Not really, no."

"I never did apologise for what happened with Eric." He wipes his mouth on a napkin and cocks his head whilst looking at me. "I shouldn't have done that. Would you like me to speak with him?"

"No." Shaking my head, I give him a weak smile. "It's done with. There's no going back now. You talking to him will only make it worse."

He nods and goes back to eating. "I am sorry. I got jealous. I thought... I guess I was worried that if you spent any more time with him you'd choose him."

"Forget it; it's fine. I probably would have reacted the same way. It's my fault for stringing him along."

His grin lights up his face, making him look handsome and alluring, "You would have reacted the same way?"

"I have a jealous streak. It's actually quite severe." I shamefully admit. "Do you want to do something fun? I feel like we should go out or something."

He blinks, seemingly shocked by my question. "Cinema?"

"Dillan." I arch a brow.

"Right. No babies allowed." His eyes narrow in thought. "We could go to the arcades?"

I snort. "You hate the arcades, the noise, the fact that you have to hold money in your hand..."

"I used to love the racing games. We could do that?"

"Okay." I smile broadly. "To the pier?"

He nods. "I'll clean up; you change Dillan and get ready."

"Are you sure?"

"Absolutely." He taps his lips when I stand, clearly eager to get ready and get going. Feigning annoyance, I lean over and swiftly press a kiss to his cheek, laughing when he holds my head and kisses my mouth deeply. When I pull back I'm out of breath and tingling all over. It's not until he gives me a small nudge in the direction of the door that I remember I'm supposed to be getting ready.

I skip the entire time I'm getting ready. I skip with Dillan to the door and then I skip down the driveway when Nathan starts locking up.

He laughs at my enthusiasm, pushing the pram for me so I can skip beside him all the way to the seafront. He immediately stops laughing when I suggest that I get a navel piercing. At this point he releases the pram, grabs the top of my arm and pulls me away from the shiny belly bars.

So unfair.

"It's my body," I snap playfully, pulling my top up slightly and frowning at my bare naval.

"No, it is in fact *my* body. You gave it to me when you gave you to me. You're not marring your perfection with a tattoo or any kind of metal piercing that could get infected and kill you."

"Dramatic much?" I mutter, but my thoughts are swiftly broken by the sight of teddies in one of those grabbing machines. "I want one."

"Now that is something I can allow you to do."

Three quid later and a whole lot of wailing on my part, we still haven't won a Winnie the Pooh teddy and Nathan is dragging me away.

Scamming machine.

It's okay though, because the scent of doughnuts takes my mind off that and I'm quickly moving on.

When we finally make it into the pier, which has a huge arcade running through the entirety of it, we immediately take up a car game where we can race against each other. Nathan places Dillan on his lap, informing me you're never too young to learn how to drive efficiently, even though Dillan doesn't know what's going on, nor can he see above the dashboard. Plus he's entirely too interested in chewing on his own sock, which he pulled off about twenty seconds ago.

Nathan, seeing this, immediately removes the sock from his mouth and chastises the poor baby for trying to eat something that's no doubt full of germs and bacteria from his tiny baby feet. I laugh the entire time.

Nathan is so good to him, too good. I think what makes it so amazing is the fact that he doesn't have to be. It makes me wonder what Caleb would be like.

Would he have been as good as Nathan is, or would the novelty have worn off after a while?

I guess it makes no sense asking a question like that. I should just be grateful for what I have. Which I am, I definitely am.

Nathan, catching my eye as he playfully chastises my son, winks and gives me a secret smile. One that promises me things for later, hopefully good things. Good things without a stupid condom I double hope.

I return his smile and then we race.

He wins and because I'm such a sore loser and he's such a smug winner, I don't talk to him for three minutes until he promises to let me win next time but make it look legit. I can live with that.

By the time the sun sets and we finish eating at a local restaurant, we're exhausted and ready to go home.

This has probably been one of the best days of my life so far. And I have crappy photo booth pictures to remember it by.

After showering, I tightly wrap a towel around me and make my way into the bedroom. Nathan, who had his shower the minute we walked into the house, is sat in bed leaning against the headboard, a book in his hands.

He puts it down and stares at me as I make my way across the room to the closet. His mouth falls open slightly and I hear him suck in a sharp blast of air when I pull the towel from around my body and use it to dry my hair.

Giving him an innocent smile, I do something I've never even had the courage to think of doing before and bend over, using the towel to dry my legs and ankles.

The way his eyes remain on me, the pupils dilating and his usually glistening lips seeming to dry as he watches me, makes me feel like the sexiest woman on earth.

"W…" He clears his throat and tries again. "What are you doing?"

"Getting ready for bed."

"It doesn't look like that from over here," he mutters and I have to turn my head to stop him from seeing my gleeful smile. "Maybe you should put some clothes on."

"It's warm. I was just going to sleep like this. You don't mind, do you?"

His throat bobs when he gulps. "I suppose not."

"I'll just braid my hair." I do this quickly and place the towel in the laundry basket. When I turn back to him, I notice the book he was reading is now lying face down on his lap. Over his crotch. "Have you finished with this?" I take the book from his lap and try not to smirk when I see the thin bed sheet pop up into a tent like shape.

"I have now," he says, his eyes narrowing with lust.

I quickly slide onto his lap, my crotch against his, with only his boxers and the thin sheet separating us. His hands rest against my hips and his eyes close when I grind against him.

"Let's try," I say quietly, running my hands through his hair.

"Try?" His voice sounds relaxed and languid.

"Yeah, let's try." I press my mouth to his and with remarkable skill, I work the sheet from between us as he's distracted. His eyes fly open when he realises what he's done. "Just try, that's all I'm asking. It's not a big deal if you can't, but you need to get over it sooner or later and I think I can help you with that."

He shakes his head. "You know it's not about whether I can or can't, Gwen."

"I know. And I think you've been doing this for so long, you don't know how to do it any other way anymore."

"I don't feel comfortable with this."

"Doesn't it tempt you at all?" I ask, referring to my naked parts against him. "How do you control yourself when you're actually inside?"

He blinks and exhales a slow breath. "With extreme difficulty."

So if I push hard enough, eventually he'll give in?

"I can see what you're thinking. Please don't," he says, almost harshly. "Please Gwen. You said we'd take it slow."

I shrug. "We are. Like I said, if you don't want to try, then push me away right now and we'll have sex the way we usually do."

There's a long pause and neither of us seems to breathe. I take this as a 'please continue,' and do just that. My mouth finds his neck. Then his chest, then his navel.

Then I'm on my back and Nathan has my hands either side of my head. "Not tonight," he whispers, kissing my lips sweetly.

I can't hide my disappointment. I got quite excited then. As soon as it comes, I push it away and nod with a reassuring smile. It's too late though, he sees my disappointment and winces.

Crap.

Chapter Eighteen

*G**wen, I've fed, changed and bathed Dillan. He was sleeping when I left. Got a call at seven, had to rush to the store. I should be back later but don't worry if I'm not.*
I'll call you.
I love you.
N

P.S. You looked too peaceful to wake.

I sigh and place the note back on the pillow. Dillan is definitely no longer asleep. I, however, still want to sleep. We may not have had sex last night, but we did stay up until three in the morning play fighting and then talking.

It was a good night, but a tense one; that's why we started play fighting I think. He's rough. I wish he'd be a bit more like that while penetrating me.

Dillan smiles as soon as he sees me. It's beautiful and it warms me down to my toes.

"I love you too little man," I say as I lift him up and out of his cot. When I see his outfit, I stare for a few moments, blinking rapidly. Then I throw my head back and laugh. "Uncle is a git isn't he?"

Dillan is in a baby sized suit. He looks ready to go to a wedding or a christening. Where did Nathan get this? It's adorable and I refuse to change him out of it now.

"Let's go and see Tiffany." I carry him downstairs and place him in his pram.

Once I'm ready and the changing bag is full, I exit the house into the unusually warm sun and talk to Dillan about everything I see that I wish he could see and point at.

We've been walking for about ten minutes when something catches my eye. Looking to my right I see a new poster along the clock tower and frown. It's a mattress commercial I think. The words seem to penetrate something deep inside of me,

What would you do if you were to wake up tomorrow and see that this was all a dream? Would you do it all over again?

To which a unicorn responds:

I'd buy a new mattress.

That's not an answer... it also doesn't make sense. I feel cheated.

What would I do if I were to wake up tomorrow and see that this was all a dream and Caleb were alive and we were getting ready to be married? It seems like an unfair question to ask myself. Would I be able to let the love I have for Caleb go to be with his brother?

Wow... I just totally caved in my own mind. I have no idea who I'd choose.

There's no use thinking like this though. It's stupid and pointless. Caleb isn't coming back and I'm not going to wake up and realise this was a dream.

What's worse is the fact that if it is a dream, I don't think I want to wake up.

A new wave of guilt fills me, but I push it away. I'm human. I don't have anything to feel guilty about right now. It's time to move on. If Nathan is the man I move on with, then so be it.

Sorry Caleb, but my mind is made up.

I make it to Tiffany's in record time and smile when her three-year-old son answers the door.

"Where's Mummy?" I ask when the bright blue eyed boy stares at me expectantly.

"You got chocolate?"

"Umm… no. Sorry."

"No entry," he snaps and slams the door in my face.

Blink.

The door opens again. Tiffany stands before me looking annoyed, frazzled and on the verge of killing somebody. "Sorry about him, his sister put him up to it."

I see a bright, blue eyed girl peek around her mum's legs. She must be about six. She giggles and runs away. Tiffany rolls her eyes and moves to the side.

"You look like hell," I snort. "Your shoes are on the wrong feet."

"Crap, I knew they were hurting for a reason. Go on through to the living room." She laughs as her daughter dances around her saying, "Crap, crap, crap." Oh dear.

"Bethany Megan Hardy! You get your backside up those stairs and think about what you've done."

The little girl races to the stairs, picks up a shoe, throws it at her mum and runs up the stairs still giggling.

"She seems sweet," I say, because I don't know what else to say.

Tiffany gives me a look that asks me if I'm serious. "She's a brat. Gets it from her dad."

"Heard that!" A male voice shouts from what I assume is the kitchen.

"Gav! Keep the kids away for a while. We've got the baby here."

"Who wants the park?" Gav shouts. I'm assuming his name is short for Gavin.

I shake my head. "You don't have to do that. Now I feel bad."

Tiffany laughs loudly. "Trust me when I say you'll feel worse if they stay. I love my kids but… they're not for everybody."

Crikey. Please don't let Dillan be naughty.

"So, coffee, tea?" She offers when the front door closes behind the kids and their father.

"No thank you."

"Wicked," she grins and immediately starts undoing the straps around Dillan. Lifting him with the expertise of a mother of two, she cradles him to her chest and coos sweetly at him. We sit on the large couch in the living room and share a smile when Dillan grabs her long hair and attempts to chew on it. "I see him and immediately want another one, but then I see mine and the urge turns to dust…poof. Gone."

I giggle and relax back into the soft cushions. "I want another one, one day. Definitely."

She gives me a horrified look. "Honey, take it from me when I say wait until your first is in school and then decide. If he's good, do it. If he's not, you'll never want another one anyway."

"I'm not wanting another one right away. Not for a long time. Being pregnant wasn't exactly a fun time."

"I hear you." She starts babbling to Dillan again, who smiles as if she's the funniest person on earth. "How is everything?"

"I was just about to ask you the same thing. You seemed pretty stressed when I came round."

She smiles softly. "Yeah, but it's definitely worth it. They aren't always naughty and even when they are, they're still really effing funny."

"He said that I couldn't come in because I didn't have chocolate."

"Bethany is the brains behind these operations. They've scared off a few visitors in their time. Poor Gavin, my son not my husband, is always getting stick for his sister's plans. He's too young to understand there are times he should say no to her."

"I always wanted siblings. It sounds like it could have been fun, although I would rather be Bethany."

"Ah," she sighs, shaking her head like she knows a secret. "You're an only child. You're going to be one of those crazy women who have six kids and love every moment of it, aren't you?" I open my mouth to respond, but she keeps talking. "I have three brothers and one sister. My mum was also an only child. Us with brothers and sisters understand the limits and usually end up with none, one, or, at most, two."

I burst out laughing. "That's not true."

"It should be. Growing up with my siblings. You'd see why. They're worse than my two, and my nieces and nephews… Christ, don't get me started."

"I bet it's nice having a big family," I say wistfully, picturing it in my head. Nathan and I will never have cousins, siblings or huge family barbecues. It's sad to think about. I wonder if we'll ever have a baby. I've never even thought about it before. Dillan is too young to be thinking about having another, but... it'd be nice one day. If Nathan has been like this with Dillan, I wonder what he'll be like with our future child.

"Yeah," she agrees. "It's ace. Can I ask one thing?"

"Sure."

"Are you both going to a wedding? What's with the suit?"

Snort. "It's an inside joke."

When night time falls and I'm tucked into bed at Nathan's house, I check my phone for the millionth time and frown when I see I've not received a text since two this afternoon. That text stated that Nathan would be staying in a hotel for the night and that he'd be back tomorrow.

I hope he's okay. It's odd that he hasn't called.

When morning comes, I feel my unease rise when I see that yet again he hasn't called. When I try and call him, I get no response. I'm worried. As I have every right to be.

It's not until eleven that I receive a call from Jeanine. It's a welcome surprise. I detach Dillan from my bosom and place him in his bouncer while I take the call, so as not to disturb his sleeping form.

"Hello?"

"Hi Guinevere, just a quick call."

"No problem, I'm not busy." I smile, genuinely happy to hear from my old friend. "How are things?"

"Great, really great in fact. I'm actually calling because I've just left Nathan's and well... he's there. I wasn't sure if you two fought or anything. He looks..." She seems to think for the right word. "Miserable seems a bit overstated, sad is understated."

"Oh." Why the hell is he there? "Was he alone?"

"Yes, as far as I could tell. I hope you don't think I'm causing trouble. I was just concerned that something had happened."

"No, everything is fine. As far as I'm aware, he's sorting out the store."

She hums and I hear a door close as she moves around her house I assume. "My husband says he saw Nathan's car in the driveway around noon yesterday. When I arrived this morning, it didn't look like he's left since he arrived."

What? "Oh... okay." My heart aches with worry. "Could you tell him to call me? You don't have to give anything away, just tell him... Dillan's sick or something. I don't know."

"Sure. I have to go. I've got a piano lesson in five minutes. Take care Gwen."

"You take piano lessons?"

"No sweetie, I teach them," she chuckles and the line goes dead. Oh my god. Was I that self-absorbed when I lived with Nathan?

No, I immediately defend myself. I was buried under too much grief to pay attention to anything else. Besides, it might be something she's only recently started doing.

When my phone lights up with Nathan's name, I don't delay in answering it. My relief is apparent when I say, "Hey."

"What's wrong with Dillan?"

"Nothing. It was a sly tactic I used to get you to call me." I frown, wishing I could see his face. "I miss you. What's going on?"

He lets out a long sigh and I hear his office chair creak as he sits. "I just needed some time away." Oh... that hurts. "No, don't, I can practically see your expression in my mind. It's not about you. It's me. Let's just say I need to battle a few demons."

"Why didn't you tell me?"

He laughs a little. "Would you have let me go?"

Meh... he has a point. "I want to help you; is that so bad?"

"No, but you were right when you said that if I give up on myself I can't be helped. I want to be better for you. It killed me seeing you disappointed when I said no the night before last."

I really wish I'd hidden my emotions better. It was just the first reaction, I didn't mean it. "I'm sorry."

"Don't be. It's not your fault."

I frown again, really wishing I could see his face. "It's not yours either."

"I know. For once I actually believe that."

My frown vanishes and a smile takes its place. My heart feels warm at his words. Could it be that we're breaking through? If so... finally. "I love you. If it gets too much, call me. I'll come straight there."

"I'll be fine. It's better I do this alone; you'll distract me."

"Okay then. Make sure you eat!"

He chuckles, the sound traveling straight through me and pooling in my stomach. "I will. I'll call you tomorrow."

Unfortunately he doesn't call me tomorrow. He doesn't call me the next day either. By the third day I've had enough. I no longer want to leave him to do this alone. I'm scared that the longer he stays away, the more he'll want to stay away. The easier it'll be for him to stay away and become the recluse he once was and the harder it will be for him to come back and be the man I know he can be.

Gwen: I need to borrow your car please.

Sasha: Why?

Gwen: I have to go to London.

Sasha: Why?????

Gwen: Nathan left. Can you have Dillan? Just until tomorrow. I need to do this.

Sasha: I'll pick you up in ten. Have him ready.

I barely speak to Sasha as I pack a bag and leave her with Dillan. I drive like a crazy person to the village. The sooner I get there, the better. My mind is plagued. I need to resolve this and so does he.

My phone rings as I'm heading down the motorway, keeping with the speed limit as it's been a while since I've driven. I don't want to cause an accident. Dillan needs his mother.

But his mother needs his uncle.

That would make an amazing novel. To read about it would be heart breaking and moving, but to actually experience it, it's terrifying, dreadful, shameful and so darn beautiful it hurts.

I don't regret anything, well... apart from stringing Eric along. Nothing good could have come from that and that's my mistake. No doubt karma will bite me in the arse for that one, although I hope it goes easy on me. I've suffered enough already. I'm not sure how much more I can take.

I'm not even sure what I'm doing.

Do I really want this?

I can't back out now.

It's when I reach his house in the middle of nowhere that my body begins to betray me by trembling like a leaf. I hate this place... but if it's where he is, I'll deal.

Here goes nothing. I knock on the door and wait.

"What are you doing here?" Nathan grips the doorframe, looking as frightened as I feel inside.

But there's no time for fright. I need courage for what I'm about to do.

I step up to him so my body is flush with his, my eyes level with his throat, and I see the strong corded neck bob in the centre when he swallows before tilting his head down. His eyes widen when I hook my arm around his neck and bring his lips down to mine. At first he's unresponsive, but I keep insisting he kiss me back by moving my lips over his. Forcing him to take a few steps back, I use my free hand to grip the lapel of his jacket and slide one side over one arm. His mouth parts and I instantly push forward, my tongue entering his mouth, and he tastes divine. Coffee and Nathan.

Like all of our other kisses, my body instantly responds as a scorching heat spreads from my lips to my limbs and to my core, causing it to clench in need. Not want, need. Pure lust and desperation for this man who I shouldn't want, but Christ do I want him.

His hands come up to grip my arms. For a moment he's about to push me away. I can tell by the way his body tenses. But at the last second I hold him tighter, not so much that it makes him uncomfortable, but enough to tell him I'm not going down without a fight. Nathan pulls me tighter to him. I feel his abnormally large shaft between us, no doubt pressing uncomfortably against the non-giving fabric of his suit pants. It only makes me needier. Overcome with greed, greed for this man, I push him backwards until his back hits the wall between the living room door and the stairs. His shoulder connects with the light switch, plunging us into darkness.

This is good. Now he can't see what I'm doing before I do it.

Releasing his neck, I grip the other side of his jacket, relieved when he shifts his arms in a way that helps me tug it from his body completely. My hand searches for the top button of his shirt. I'm grateful he chose not to wear a tie today. It makes my 'naked Nathan mission' that much easier to achieve.

"Gwen," he pants when I finally release his mouth.

I grip the top of his shirt, fuelled by a sexual desire I've been denying myself since the first moment he touched me so long ago.

"Don't talk," I order on a whisper. "Don't think."

Even in the dark I can see the magnificent brown of his eyes as they connect with mine and widen with lust, a hint of fear still lingering on the surface, fear that I'm determined to destroy.

The sound of buttons hitting the ground startles Nathan, or maybe it's the fact I've just ripped his shirt apart. I could have unbuttoned it, but I daren't give him time to back out. He needs this. I need this.

There's no hair on his chest save for a light sprinkle of it over his sternum. I make a note of this every time I get the pleasure of seeing it, which isn't often. Only a dark line of soft hair leads from his navel to the depths below. I love this too.

His chest is smooth and silky, velvet over steel. His solid muscles twitch and quiver as my fingers scrape over them.

Once more my mouth connects with his, but only for a second. My body jolts as I'm thrown over his shoulder. He takes the stairs two at a time before entering my old bedroom.

I've not even hit the mattress before his body is covering mine and his lips are assaulting my own. Squeezing his hips with my thighs, I wind my fingers through his hair and my body bucks against him. The dampness that was already between my legs only increases; it's uncomfortable. My jeans need to go.

Tearing sounds into the darkness and I feel the room's air lift the tiny invisible hairs across my chest and navel. He just ripped my top in half. I guess I deserve that.

We don't say anything as he lifts me slightly, enabling him to pull my top off the rest of the way without disconnecting our mouths. As soon as my back hits the soft quilt, I use all of my strength to push him onto his. He gasps slightly, clearly shocked at my abrupt movement.

I slide to my knees on the floor and grasp his belt with my fingertips. The buckle clangs and clatters as I pull the leather free of its tight hold. "Gwen," he warns, leaning up on his elbows, his eyes hooded yet nervous. "Don't."

"If you say stop and I know you mean it, then I'll stop," I assure him, which isn't necessary because he could easily overpower me. The fact he's letting me get this far with him shows his trust.

The belt finally pulls free, but his hand grips mine when I pop the button through the tiny slit and quickly slide the zipper down. "Condom."

If this were any other man I'd agree, but it's not. It's Nathan and he uses condoms for more than just protection against STIs and pregnancy. He uses them so he can't actually feel a woman's wetness. He uses them as a barrier between him and intimacy. I've learned this the hard way. I never want to be in that awkward situation again.

Pushing his hand away, I tug on his trousers until they slide over his tight navy blue boxers and pool at his ankles. He allows me to lift his feet and pull them off the rest of the way. His breathing is ragged and I'm not sure it has anything to do with being horny anymore.

This assumption is proven to be correct when my fingers hook gently over the waistband of his boxers. A sob like noise tears up from his chest and I suddenly notice his body trembling.

What the fuck?

Guilt encompasses me in a grip that steals all of the air from my lungs. My chest aches in a way it hasn't before. So much pain in such a seemingly strong man... I can't let him have it anymore. He needs to share it with me.

No.

He needs to give it to me, all of it.

I climb up his body and settle on him so my breasts squish against his bare chest, my ankles up in the air behind me. I wonder if he'll remove my bra. I really hope he will, but this is about him, not me, so I'm not going to remove it myself.

"Nathan?" I remove his hands from his face and scan his cheeks for any sign of tears. No tears, just fear and anger.

His accusing eyes come to me. I know he's about to say something bad to get me to leave him alone. There's no way I'm giving him that chance. I gently press my lips to his for a few seconds while my eyes close slowly and my body relaxes onto his.

CHAPTER EIGHTEEN

When I feel his shaking subside, I lean up, my hair cascading over one side of our faces. I rub my nose along his, up and down the side. He lets out a sigh and grips my arms, clearly intending to push me away.

So I say the words I've longed to say but had no courage to before, due to my fears of betraying a certain somebody, somebody I'm not going to think about in this moment. This moment is for us; Nathan and I. Nobody else. Not even you know who.

"I'm in love with you." Shutting my eyes once more to shield myself from the shock that plagues his, I press my lips gently to his again. In those five words I know something significant has changed in him. Something has changed in this moment between us. My lips move to his jaw as his hands relax on my arms and come around my back, trailing a gentle pattern over my spine.

I don't focus on the burning it causes in my stomach; instead I focus on what needs to be done. Sliding down his body, inch by glorious inch, my lips taste his flesh. Finally I reach the waistband of his boxers and I wait a while, kissing along the edge, before finally pulling them down and over his impressive shaft, which points to ceiling for a moment before lolling backwards towards his stomach.

"Gwen," he says and I see his hands go back to his face. "I can't do this."

"Trust me," I say and pull his hands from his face. "Don't look; just feel."

I trail the tips of my nails over the sack that hangs beneath his solid rod. How the hell I'm going to fit that in my mouth I have no idea.

It twitches when I trail my nails along the underside ever so gently. He lets out a guttural grunt that makes his entire body spasm.

"I'm going to hold you now," I warn him, giving him a chance to get used to the idea.

My hand wraps around him slowly, carefully, but with the right amount of pressure that I know he'll like. He shudders, the toned ridges of his abdomen clenching as he inhales a sharp breath.

Poking my tongue out, I gently touch the swollen, red tip of him. His hands come to my shoulders and his torso knifes upwards until I feel his smooth skin touching the top of my hair.

I don't give it another second. I instantly envelope him in my warm, wet mouth, salivating at the thrill of finally tasting him. He moans loudly, his hands coming to my head almost as if unsure where to hold and unsure whether or not he should push me away or push me down on him further.

"Gwen," he pants, as I slide him from between my lips, caressing the underside of his throbbing cock with my tongue. "Do that again." I try not to smile and fortunately succeed, even though I'm doing cartwheels inside. Back down I go, this time deeper, my cheeks hollowing as I suck and move back up with excruciating slowness.

My free hand strokes the inside of his thigh before settling on the delicate sack between his legs. I roll the balls gently between my fingers, my mouth picking up speed now that I know he's comfortable.

"Gwen," he repeats and I have to admit I love the way he says my name when he's clearly absorbed by the pleasure that I'm giving him.

My head is tugged away after a few more seconds, his hand fisted in my hair. He looks at me, his breath heavy, his chest heaving and his pupils fully dilated.

Gulp.

I'm lifted as he stands and pushed roughly onto the soft bed, my body bouncing once. My jeans are being tugged down my legs and I don't have time to lift my hips to help him as his strength does that for me.

Next my thong is gone and his eyes take me in for a very brief moment before he pushes my legs apart with his hands on my knees and lies between them. Instantly I feel his steel length pressing against my stomach as he presses his mouth to mine and grinds against me.

I've never felt so deliriously and deliciously aroused in my entire life, especially when he unclips my bra at the front with one hand and manoeuvres me until it's away from my body.

He shifts slightly to the side, giving himself space to guide the head of his cock to my entrance. He rests it there, the tip barely tapping at my tight core that wants to be filled by him so badly.

I tilt my head and catch his eyes. He grabs my wrists and brings my hands to either side of my face. I inhale a shuddering breath when he laces our fingers together and rests his forehead on mine.

"Nathan," I murmur softly, trying to give him the encouragement he clearly needs. His eyes are no longer on me; they're looking down, at nothing in particular. Tortured is the only emotion he's giving me right now.

"I need to put on a condom," he states and goes to pull away. I hook my legs around his thighs and hold him tight. He glares at me. "I'm serious, Gwen."

Freeing one hand, I place it against his cheek and kiss the corner of his mouth. My fingertips stroke the edge of his hair and the shell of his ear. I want to state the fact that he's still rock solid, so he can't be hating this that much. I don't. Instead I give him a moment to find his calm. I won't force him into this, but I won't let him back away out of fear and habit.

"Damn it, Guinevere," he snaps when my leg tightens reflexively and pushes his hips down a fraction, causing the head to rest directly on the entrance.

"What's so bad?" I ask calmly, working my fingers through the side of his hair. "Really... it's just me. You know me. I'm clean, I'm healthy and... I care about you."

"You know that's not the point," he mumbles, turning his face into my hand. The movement forces him to sink in a fraction of a centimetre. I wince at the tightness of the skin trying to give to let him enter. We both moan; it feels good, even if it is uncomfortable. "Damn it." I watch as his eyes close and he pushes forward. My slick channel slowly swallows the head. I feel it pop inside and shudder at the size of him. "Oh god, Gwen, you feel..." He pulls out slowly and my eyes close much like his have.

Slowly he glides back in. "Nathan," I whimper, when he manages to push his way in a few inches. It aches, oh how it aches in the best way. "More."

My legs tremble as he pulls out again, leaving only the head inside. If I thought the burning was bad before, I was wrong. This is overwhelming. His pelvis finally joins mine, my smooth skin against his trimmed, dark hair. Honestly I can't believe I've managed to fit him to the hilt; it feels glorious, especially when he starts to grind against me, his pubic bone rubbing against my swollen clit.

Whatever fears he seemed to have only moments ago have definitely gone. His hand leaves mine and pulls my thigh further up his hip, unhooking it from around his leg. This lets him in even deeper. I feel him hit the wall at the back of my core and hear him grunt at the obstruction, but not in annoyance or pain.

Almost chocolate brown eyes come to mine, nothing but lust and wonder in their depths.

I almost feel like I'm taking his virginity and I guess, in a way, I am. There's something really satisfying about that, knowing that out of everyone, it's me he's chosen to share this with.

"You feel so good," he tells me and slowly begins pumping in and out. I smile for a moment, but it's interrupted by a loud cry escaping me. The loud cry is because he pulls out sharply and slams inside. For some reason this sets off a chain reaction in my body that starts in my womb and works its way down my legs, clenching every muscle within its grasp. Yes I was tingly, but this… this orgasm had no warning. I wrap my arms around his neck as he gets more enthusiastic with each plunge, most likely due to my reaction.

The lingering vibration that my orgasm left behind doesn't subside, it only goes on for what seems an age before it builds again and explodes outwards. Down below I clench and release, over and over again. His breath becomes harder and faster, as do his thrusts.

Our foreheads touch once more, our eyes squeezed shut. I want to look at him but I just can't; my body is no longer my own. I'm floating on a wave of orgasmic bliss, the feeling constant.

It's not long before I feel his body tense and I know he's going to come. This was exactly the time he pulled away the last time we had intercourse. This time it can't be classed as intercourse; this passion, this feeling that we're creating together doesn't have a title. It's too good to be so clinically named.

He starts to lift and I know with one hundred percent certainty he's going to pull out and deny himself the orgasm his body so clearly wants and needs. I'm not a psychiatrist and I don't know how to deal with abuse victims, but in this case I'm choosing to not let him run. Maybe it's the wrong choice but right now, in my heart and mind, it feels like the right choice.

"Gwen." His tone is panicked. He stills completely. "Let go." I force my legs around him tighter and use my heels to push him back in. "Gwen!" He shoves up, his torso leaving mine to catch the chill in the air. "Let go now!"

He's going to pull out. Should I let him? I don't know what to do.

No. I'm not letting go. Placing my hands on his neck as he goes to break free, I begin grinding my hips up towards him.

He doesn't say stop; he's too close to the edge. Instead, his arms buckle but he catches himself before he drops on me and his torso jerks as his length swells even larger and begins to pulse inside of me. His hips begin hammering into mine. A loud, guttural cry leaves him as he presses his face into the pillow by my head.

It's brutal, his size, his strength, the way his hips piston up and down, forcing him in and out of me quite a few times. As his orgasm reaches its peak, he slams into me three times, still moaning loudly, and it's his moans that bring me over with the force of his delivery.

We stop at the same time. I can feel and hear our heartbeats intermingling. It's a strange sound, but a soothing one.

When my body finally becomes my own, I roll Nathan off me. He stares up at the ceiling, his face a blank mask. I don't talk; he clearly needs a moment. Crossing my leg over his, I pull his arm out and rest my body into the side of him, my nose against his neck.

He doesn't hold me, not like he did the last few times. He just lies here beneath me, breathing heavily and staring at the ceiling.

My gut gnaws at my insides. Did I push him too soon?

I guess I'll find out soon enough. For now I just want to rest here with him, enjoying the silence; or enjoying the calm before the storm, as it were.

Chapter Nineteen

I'M NOT SURE WHEN he left the bed. I passed out at some point after we shared that amazing experience together. It's still dark out, though, so I can't have been asleep for too long.

Wrapping the sheet around me, I climb to my feet and set out in search of Nathan. He's probably upstairs in his room.

He isn't.

Sigh.

The study!

I follow the dark hallway, my mind not on the possibility of ghosts but on how Nathan is feeling.

I tap lightly on the door but get no response, so, doing something I've never done before, I push the door open and peek inside.

Sure enough, he's sat in his comfy looking leather chair facing the window with a small glass of amber liquid in his hand. He looks tired and worn, which isn't surprising given the kind of activity we participated in. I'm shocked that he hasn't heard me take a few steps into the room, although he does seem very lost in his thoughts.

Instead of speaking, I step in front of him and move between his parted knees. He still doesn't look up.

"One of my favourite things about you is how kind you are, even when you don't want to be."

He doesn't respond, only brings his drink to his lips and takes a healthy swig.

"And how good you are with Dillan." He continues staring straight ahead, my covered navel the only thing in view. "And how intelligent you are, and how little you ask for, yet you give so much in return."

A shallow breath leaves him as he places the drink on the desk by his laptop. He reaches for me and presses his face against my navel. The top of his forehead just reaches where my ribs join. I place my hand in his hair and keep hold of the bed sheet with the other.

The way he nuzzles into my stomach and holds me tight with his hands on my arse feels almost desperate.

He lets out a choked sob and holds me tighter still. "I can't lose you. I don't remember how to live without you."

"You're not going to lose me."

"I will, if you find out the truth."

"Trust me."

"Trust *me*," he whispers and I gently massage his scalp. "I can't... Gwen... I can't let you go... but you'll make me."

"Then don't tell me," I breathe, my decision set in my mind. "I don't want to know."

He looks up at me with red eyes and dishevelled hair. "What?"

I nod. "I don't want to know."

"You promise? You'll never ask?"

And again I nod. "I swear it. I will never ask."

He stands, his arm lifting me as he rises. I immediately wrap my arms around his neck and my legs around his waist. The sheet falls from my body, remaining trapped between his arm and my back.

"Tell me you love me." He looks up at me, his eyes set and determined.

"I love you."

His arm that isn't holding me swipes everything from his desk. I hear the glass smash and the laptop thud against the floor, but I don't care because in seconds he's laying me on the long desk, which is cold against my back.

The sheet bunches up beneath me, forming an uncomfortable lump that digs into the base of my spine, yet I don't care.

I care even less when Nathan kicks off his boxers, pulls off his vest and climbs on top of me. Seconds later he's in me and is pounding me so mercilessly I slide up the table with each thrust until my head is hanging over the edge. It feels so good, too good.

Does this mean I've fixed him?

Or does this mean he's fixed me?

Maybe it means neither; maybe we're both just finally on the right course to healing.

As my orgasm rips through me and Nathan yells my name with his, I smile. For once in the past twelve months, I finally feel like everything is going to be alright.

"I know this is a little bit late to ask," Nathan says, both of us lying in his bed, with me draped across his chest as he plays with my hair. Shifting, I tilt my head back and wait for him to continue whilst staring at his handsome face. "But you did start taking the pill again, right?"

"Definitely too late to ask," I giggle, thinking back to our time in his office, then again in the hallway when we were supposed to be going to bed. Then again on the stairs, which isn't as easy or as comfortable as it looks, so we moved it to his bed. I'm deliciously sore and achy and the bed sheet that covered the mattress is now in a heap at the foot of the bed. Somehow we pushed it off during our love making and I'm not embarrassed in the slightest. "But yes, I did."

He lets out a breath and presses his lips to my hair. "I never knew it could feel like this."

"Me neither," I agree, running my tongue around his nipple, which causes him to gasp.

"You didn't?"

I shake my head and close my eyes. "It's different with you. More... intense. It's instinct or something. You seem to know exactly what I want and I seem to know exactly what you want."

He chuckles. "We're used to not talking that's why. We must have learned to read each other's body language during the time you lived here."

That actually makes sense. I fall silent for a moment, wondering whether or not to say what's on my mind. "I wasn't just trying to get you into bed when I told you I was in love with you. You know that right?"

His body gets tight and he rolls me onto my back, his face hovering an inch above mine. "I just thought you were saying it to make me feel better."

"How could you think that?"

"Because you're adamant about never loving anyone more than you love..." He trails off and, fortunately, that familiar pain I usually get when Caleb is mentioned doesn't come.

"You were right; I was wrong." I admit reluctantly. "It is possible to love two people at the same time, it's just a different kind of love."

He smiles broadly. "Did you just admit you were wrong?"

"Yes," I respond indignantly. "When have I ever not admitted I was wrong when I was in fact wrong?"

He chuckles and kisses my chin. "Well during the last twelve months, you've never been wrong. According to you at least."

"I just gave you the best sex of your life. If you don't want that privilege revoked, I suggest you don't poke fun."

Laughing loudly, he rests his head on my breasts and trails his fingers up and down my side. "Duly noted." His brow arches playfully. "Am I in the doghouse?"

Sigh.

"Are we having another tiff?"

Double sigh.

His eyes soften, his smile dimming to a gentle one, one full of love and a small amount of amusement. "When did you figure out how you feel?"

Good question. "When you tried to walk away from me the other day."

"Why didn't you say anything?"

"Because I didn't figure out what those feelings meant until you didn't come home and didn't call for two nights."

He lifts his head and sucks my nipple into his mouth.

"Careful," I warn, not wanting him to suddenly get a mouthful of Dillan's dinner. "It's different, so different. With you it's deeper, more intense. I feel it in my very soul. The thought of living without you hurts to the point of scarring every inch of me."

"And with Caleb?"

"It was fun, light and airy. I felt like I was floating. Every second with him was like walking on a cloud." I giggle a little. "I loved him very much." I can see that my words have affected him. "But with you, every second I spend with you it feels like I can do anything. You have the ability to crush me, the ability to shatter me, the ability to consume me. With Caleb it was never like that. People say you never get over your first love and maybe they're right, but I know in my heart that if anything were to happen to you, to us, I would *never* be able to move on from that."

"I'm not going anywhere, not this time. I swear it. I'm just sorry I didn't give you all of me sooner."

"Same." My arms wrap around his neck as my eyes drift shut. "Same."

I wake up to the bright sun pouring over my face, but that's not what woke me up. At first I panic when something slips inside me, but then I remember where I am and who I'm with and, without worrying about my bad morning breath or the state of my body, I raise my hips to meet the gorgeous man who gave me all of him last night.

"Does this mean you'll move in with me?" Nathan asks as we shower. "You and Dillan of course."

Oh darn. I did say that, didn't I? "I suppose."

A smile of pure joy lights up his face. He pulls me to him, our wet bodies clashing under the spray. "Yay!"

"You just said yay."

"I did."

"You don't like that word. You think it's immature."

He shrugs. "When one spends time with the common folk, one learns to adapt."

Bastard! I slap his arm.

Laughing, he spins me in his arms and runs his bare fingers over my back and shoulders. "Today?"

"What?" I'm too busy feeling what his fingers are doing to remember anything we were talking about.

"You'll move in today?"

"Let me tell my mum first and pack. I have to work tomorrow and Thursday."

"Yay."

"Yay!" I repeat, with a bright smile of my own. We climb out of the shower after another few minutes and get ready to leave.

"I don't like the thought of you driving back on your own."

"I did it last night," I point out.

"Yes and I'm very glad you did."

"Can I ask you something? It's about something you said." I chew on my lip, worried he'll close up on me again. His eyes turn wary as he nods for me to continue. "You said your mum wasn't always the way she was..."

He seems relieved and I guess it's because I'm not asking about what it is he knows that I don't; that piece of knowledge he thinks has the potential to destroy us. Of course it's eating at me, but do I really want to know, especially if it'll turn my world upside down? "I remember her being kind and thoughtful. She loved me. I remember that. But then my dad suddenly changed. We had a lot going on with..." He gulps and looks away. "I'm not sure why he started beating her, but it happened around the same time my grandfather started abusing me. We had a lot of stresses."

"You were only six. You shouldn't have had any stresses, other than whether or not you could sneak the biscuits out of the cupboard." I did that often, but I mostly got caught.

"Yeah." He takes my hand and leads me to Sasha's car. "I know. She became very withdrawn. She stopped hugging me, kissing me and eventually became the snotty cow she is today. I think she just forgot how to love."

"Nobody forgets how to love; they just forget how to share it," I mutter, thinking back to my own upbringing. It was very mild in comparison to his, but it still hurt when my mum treated me like I was a burden more than anything.

He changes the subject, his eyes staring through the trees ahead. "Have you ever wanted to find your dad?"

"Yes."

"Maybe you should try?"

"My mum doesn't remember him."

Nathan scrunches up his nose. He looks adorable. "That just seems like an excuse to me. Maybe he was married and she was ashamed. Maybe she was attacked... but I doubt she'd forget the face of the man who gave her you."

"I've thought this myself, but she's adamant that she doesn't remember him. A drunken one night stand apparently. I'm not that interested anyway. I used to be, but now I'm happy with what I've got. Sometimes the grass isn't always greener."

A wicked grin spreads his lips. "The grass will always be greener on our side of the fence, Gwen. You'll see."

"I don't have to see. I already know."

"Go on, Dillan awaits. I'll follow you shortly."

"Hey Nath?"

He brushes his fingers over my arm. "Yes Gwen?"

"Tell me to tell you that I love you."

The browns in his eyes twinkle with warmth. "Tell me you love me."

"I love you."

"Good."

Chapter Twenty

"Are you sure you're ready for this?" I can see the uncertainty and sorrow in my mum's eyes. I nod in response. "You know you can come back whenever you like." Her eyes darken. "Whenever you like."

I tense in response and give her a wide eyed stare. I can't believe she just said that.

"I know." I wrap my arms around her and kiss her cheek. "I love you; thank you for being my rock."

Her breath catches in her throat. "Thank you for being mine."

When I go to pull away, she doesn't let me go. We stand in the driveway holding each other. To an outsider we probably look silly, or like lesbians, seeing as my mum really doesn't look old enough to be my mum. To us, this is a huge breakthrough in our relationship.

When we finally release each other, Nathan tucks me under his arm and leads me to the car.

Ten minutes later, if that, we're carrying Dillan into his new home, one that I can't wait to decorate. Although when I start suggesting things, Nathan looks less and less enthusiastic about the idea of me choosing and suggests we wait a while until we can afford a professional.

I reluctantly agree and claim the amazing kitchen. This is my second time cooking in here and I have to admit, it is fantastic.

"Have you thought any more about going back to university?" Nathan pulls himself up onto the breakfast bar and plucks a grape from the fruit basket before popping it into his mouth.

"I won't be able to go back until September. We have plenty of time to talk about it and decide." I flip the wrap and drop it on top of the others. "Can you put these on the table for me?"

He drops to his feet and does as I've asked, whistling the entire time, which is weird because Nathan doesn't whistle... ever.

"I got a call from Lorna earlier," he announces and I'm shocked by the spark of jealousy that flies through me.

"Go on."

"She just called to say hi and to meet up. I told her that I'm seeing you now."

"Oh." The jealousy slowly slinks away and hides under a metaphorical rock, ready to pounce at the next woman who gets too close to Nathan. "So you're telling me because...?"

"I want to be open and honest, as promised, minus a few secrets which are better left unsaid. If I didn't tell you and you found out, you'd wonder why I didn't tell you and probably get paranoid."

He's got that right. "Well, thank you. Eric texted me, apologising for his friends' behaviour in the club the other night. I told him I was sorry and he hasn't contacted me since."

"Yes, I know."

Umm... how does he know?

He sees the question in my eyes and shrugs, completely nonchalant. "I checked your phone."

My mouth drops open. I don't know whether to laugh or to be mad. I have nothing to hide, but still... that's a huge lack of trust right there. "You can't check my phone!"

"What's the big deal? You can check mine."

"I don't want to check yours."

"Suit yourself," he chuckles, popping another grape into his mouth. "I took the liberty of deleting his number from your phone too."

"Of course you did," I say, but now I'm laughing. "You're such a geek. You do trust me don't you?"

"Yes."

"So why the checking of phones and the deleting of numbers?"

He shrugs again. His calm façade really grates me sometimes. "I'm getting rid of all temptation and competition."

Snort. "Of course you are."

"Not including me of course, I plan to tempt you constantly. Like right now."

I turn away from the chicken I'm placing into a dish and let out a bark of startled laughter when I see him sitting in the chair at the dinner table, his foot crossed over his knee, a newspaper spread between his hands. He's stark naked.

"Get dressed," I hiss, still laughing uncontrollably.

"Only if you sit right here." His hooded eyes scan me up and down as he points to the ground between his legs. "And do that thing you did the other night with your mouth."

Well, how's a girl supposed to refuse that?

The chicken hissing in the pan behind me snaps me from my sudden lust filled daze. I turn back to it and neatly place it all in the dish, before covering it with the sauce.

"You do realize you're going to have to grab the salad bowl from the fridge while completely naked and we have no blinds over the patio doors yet."

He blanches. "You do it."

"Nope. I've just made dinner. You promised you'd help."

He stands proudly, his naked body glorious in the bright sun that's spilling into the huge kitchen. My lips pinch together in an attempt to stifle my amusement when he uses the newspaper to cover his front, which is remarkably stiff right now. He struts to the fridge, grabs the bowl of salad and brings it back.

His body is just... gah. There are no words, only drool.

"Anything else?"

"Yeah." I rest back in the chair and place my finger on my chin. "Give us a very slow twirl."

The newspaper hits me in the face and when I finally peek around it, I'm disappointed to see him pulling his clothes back on.

"If you'd stayed naked for another thirty seconds, I so would have done what I did the other night."

"Food first, fornication later."

Unfortunately we don't get to that part until much later, due to Dillan suddenly not wanting to be put down for three hours straight. I'm pretty sure he's teething and, from what I've heard, this isn't going to be a fun parenting experience at all.

Nathan and I fall into a comfortable routine, one that seems to work perfectly for us. I go to work as he stays home and looks after Dillan. I cook most nights, but he cleans while I play with Dillan and put him to bed. Then we lose ourselves in our own bed, or wherever we are at the time of Nathan's arousal.

The man has become insatiable. He's become a monster, but not the kind of monster you fear.

I have zero complaints at all, not including my sore thighs and most likely bruised mound.

He seems a lot more at ease with himself, which is great. He doesn't seem convinced that he's going to become like the last three generations of men in his family.

We're happy, exceedingly so, and coming home from work has never been such a joy. I used to love work so much that I'd wake up excited to be there, but now that Nathan and I have come to a happy point in our relationship, I find myself waking up in the morning and not wanting to leave his side.

The comfier we get with each other, the happier and more relaxed we get.

Sure, Nathan still has his moody moments where he'll shut himself in his office and I won't see him for hours. It's irritating, but he needs his space so I don't complain. He still gets annoyed with me and he freaked out something awful when I forgot to hide the eggs.

I had to listen to him rant for days about his rule of no eggs in the house. He's so weird. It didn't help that all I did was laugh at him whenever he brought it up or asked me if I was taking him seriously or not. I definitely was not taking him seriously, not even a little, but then he threatened to bring a rat inside... I now hide the eggs on top of the cupboard.

Unfortunately he still wears his gloves whenever he touches anything, no matter how thoroughly we sterilise it first. This doesn't include when he's holding me or Dillan, though. Exploring my naked body with his naked hands seems to be his favourite pastime at present, not that I'm complaining.

Our last venture, only a week or so ago, took us to his new store and I have to admit, even though I didn't get a chance to help him plan the look of the new place due to the fact we were arguing that weekend, it looks amazing now that it's finished. It's just the outside that needs decorating now, and the inside obviously needs filling with sparkly, pretty things.

Now I'm wondering how he's going to run his store and live three hours away at the same time. Maybe he expects us to move to London, although he's made no mention of it. Perhaps he's...

Nope. I'm not doing it to myself anymore. I need to stop questioning things in my mind when I never bother to learn the actual answers to them.

"Oh my god!" I squeal, practically dancing my way over to a stand that seems to sell mostly beach toys and sticks of rock.

"What?" Nathan looks at where I'm pointing and smirks. "Really?"

"How often do you get a sugar dummy shaped as a penis?" The two women standing to the side, picking out flavoured rock, stare at me like I'm a loon. "Can I have it?"

He blinks. "No."

"But it looks so tasty."

"Get the one that isn't shaped like a penis." He waves his hand, pointing to the red, sugar dummies hanging from the ceiling by different coloured ribbons.

I pout, wishing I hadn't left my bag in the car. He turns to look at Dillan, who is sat in his pram playing with his feet. I take this second to shove my hand into his pocket and snatch his wallet.

"Hey," he moans, reaching for his property. I turn and bend over it and quickly pull out a five pound note. "Give me back my wallet."

"Fine." I throw it at him, trying not to laugh when it bounces off his forehead, and quickly run to the lady behind the till with the penis sweet in my hand.

"Are you old enough?" She quips, her grey brow rising with amusement.

"You really want to walk around with a penis hanging from your neck?" Nathan looks at me in disbelief.

"No." I shake my head, take my change and pull the clear plastic wrapper from the goody. "I want to walk around with a penis in my mouth."

The two ladies who were staring at me before burst out laughing, especially when Nathan's cheeks turn pink with embarrassment.

"Hmmm," I moan, sucking happily as I link my arm through his. "Want some?"

He stares at me in disgust. "No, I do not."

I shrug, release his arm and skip ahead. "Aww, booby shaped jelly sweets."

He places his hand beneath my shoulders and shoves me forward. I race to the stand next door and buy doughnuts.

Memories of the night when Nathan took me to the fair out of town makes me smile, especially when I had to feed him doughnuts. I wonder if he'll let me do that again.

It's not until I've received my doughnuts that I realise that Nathan is missing. Looking behind me and peering over people, I try to find him and Dillan.

"Nath?" I shout, using the shortening of his name, which he only lets me use. Sasha tried yesterday and he scowled.

Scratching my hair with one hand and holding the donuts with the other, I stand randomly in the middle of the street, ignoring the disgruntled people who have to walk around me. Déjà vu. This happened when we went to the fair together. He was buying pictures of our ride on the Ferris wheel, but I didn't know that until a while later when I found them in a drawer in his room.

"Nath?"

"Here." His voice comes from behind me. I'm wondering why it's slightly muffled until I see what he has in his mouth.

"They do booby shaped sugar dummies too?"

He nods, smiling around his treat. "Best tasting breasts I've ever had."

"Funny," I snap, scowling at him playfully. "I was going to say the same about my penis."

He laughs and throws his arm around my shoulders. "I think you need something to compare it to."

"You're right." I sigh dramatically.

His face lights up. "Are we going home?"

"I should have bought two."

His face falls. "Tease."

"Please, up until eight days ago you wouldn't let me touch you; now you're in my mouth all of the time."

He purses his lips and pinches my side. "Up until eight days ago I was almost a virgin. You stole my virtue."

A giggle bursts forth and doesn't stop once it starts. "Oh my god. Seriously?"

"Yes." And then he does something extremely out of character and wags his brows at me before saying, "Care to steal it again?"

CHAPTER TWENTY

We walk down the street tucked tightly to each other as I manoeuvre the pram around pedestrians. It doesn't take long to get home, fortunately. My feet are killing me. The entire way we talk about nothing and everything; it's nice. For once I actually feel like I'm able to be normal around Nathan. Well… as normal as one can be with a penis shaped sweet in her mouth.

"Christ!" Nathan exclaims as we reach the top of the driveway.

"What?" I ask, worried about his suddenly pale face. "What is it?"

He steps forward and immediately takes an envelope from the windscreen of his car. Oh dear.

"Why can't he just leave me be?" He shouts, pushing the door open with such force it smashes against the wall before bouncing back. I follow him inside and leave Dillan in his pram. He's sleeping, I shouldn't disturb him.

Nathan storms straight into his office and immediately shoves the thick envelope into the shredder. A startled gasp escapes me and my hand flies to my mouth. When the shredder doesn't chew it up as it should, he begins kicking it over and over again until the hollow base is in pieces and the electronic top seems to have lost its life.

I'm contemplating whether or not I should leave the room and leave him to his anger when he suddenly turns, his face set in an expression of pure fury, one I've never seen from him before. Never have I seen anyone look so blindingly mad.

"Na…" I'm cut off by his hand tangling in my hair and his lips slamming on mine.

He rips the penis lolly from my neck and picks me up, holding me against the wall with his chest against my ribs. I hiss when his teeth sink into my neck and his hands immediately flip my skirt up and tear my knickers in two, leaving one side still wrapped around my leg.

I'm terrified, petrified, exhilarated, and I've never been so turned on in my entire life.

His teeth bite harder and I'm sure if he puts just any more pressure on the skin, it'll break and I'll bleed.

That thought leaves me as he slides me down the wall until my hips are against his and pushes into me almost brutally. The pain is intense, but the pleasure that I feel shadows it almost completely.

I scream, a hoarse cry that erupts from my throat without warning or consent. He doesn't stop thrusting or pounding in and out, his own moans more like growls.

His right hand begins grabbing at my body, causing my left leg to fall until my toes are touching the floor.

My other leg is wrapped around his elbow and that hand is flat against the wall. Picking up speed, he releases my neck and takes my mouth instead. It's amazing, it's bruising, it's so not like Nathan I'm almost scared. I'm also grateful, because I feel something building deep within every time his pubic bone hits my clit.

Skin slapping against skin and moans and grunts are all that can be heard, up until I tighten around him with an orgasm that makes me momentarily dizzy. He follows, throwing his head back and hissing my name through clenched teeth.

There's no stopping him. Even after he fully spends himself inside me, I'm over the desk, my torso against the flat surface, and he continues pushing in and out of me.

It's almost like he's punishing me, or... trying to forget.

My mind isn't my own. Every cell, every hair, every single part of my body burns. I never want it to stop, yet it's so painfully good, I know that soon I'm going to need it to stop.

He climaxes again, with such a loud yell that I'll be shocked if the neighbours don't call the police. Their house is twenty feet away from ours and separated by twenty foot high fern trees.

Then he lands on my back, his chest heaving and his face covered in a thin layer of sweat that dampens the back of my neck.

"I don't want to see it," I reassure him and his fingers find mine and thread through them. "I swear, if I ever receive another, I don't want to see it." No matter how much it kills me.

He inhales a shuddering breath and for a moment I think he's crying, but he doesn't let me turn around, so I'll never be sure. As he softens inside me, he kisses the back of my neck and nuzzles me with his nose.

"Who's it from and why?" He should be able to tell me that much at least.

"My dad," he whispers, lifting off me.

Quickly pulling my skirt down, I turn to face him, ignoring the mess between my legs. "Why?"

"Because he doesn't want me to open the store and he wants money. He's going bankrupt," he bites out, tucking himself back into his trousers. I'm shocked when he runs his gloved hands through his hair without a thought for what they've just touched. Mostly, though, I feel anger towards his father. Hasn't the man taken enough?

I hide my anger and need to kill. Nathan doesn't need that right now. "If he's using it as blackmail, then why would he send it to me? It makes no sense."

He closes his eyes and when they open I see hate shining from them. "He knows I'm with you and knows I won't let you see. It's a threat, that's all. He doesn't want you to see or he loses his leverage, but he also needs me to realise that he's serious and he could ruin my life in a heartbeat."

"Is that just a theory?"

"Yes. It's the only thing I can think of, otherwise you would know already."

"What... what are you going to do? You can't give into him!"

His hate filled eyes soften as they come to mine. "I won't. But... I don't know how I'm going to stop him. When he goes bankrupt, and he will," his jaw clenches, "he's going to tell you, just to spite me."

I clear my throat and place a gentle kiss to his jaw. "Then maybe I should hear it from you."

His eyes close again and his arms come around me. "It seems to be the only option, but then I'll have a jewellery store and not you. I need you."

"I need you too." I admit, holding him even tighter.

"I hate him, Gwen," he says and my heart breaks at the sorrow in his voice. "I hate him so damn much."

Stepping into him, I wrap my arms around his waist and kiss his collarbone. It takes him a few very long seconds, but he finally encloses his arms around me. "I hate him too."

"I'm sorry." He says this with his lips against my hair. "Did I hurt you?"

"No," I lie. He did, but not in a bad way. He needed me. I'll never blame him for that. "Not in the slightest."

"I'm sorry I ruined our day."

"You didn't. I'd say that that was a pretty amazing ending." Then I look at the ground and frown. "You broke my penis."

He looks at the lolly on the ground, throws his head back and laughs louder than I've ever heard from him. Then he kisses me, still laughing and still shaking with it. "Christ I love you Gwen, so damn much."

"Does that mean I can have your boobs?"

He smiles down at me and shakes his head. "Not a chance."

Nathan vanished into his office the past three nights. I was concerned for him. He'd help me get Dillan to bed and then go straight to his office, without eating or saying more than a few words to me. Considering what happened the other day, I thought maybe he was ashamed of his actions.

Ever since the first night that I stole his virtue, as he calls it, he hasn't been able to keep his hands off me. Suddenly, after that almost violent session in his office, he's barely touched me and has only come to bed once he knows I'm sleeping.

So naturally, I got concerned and walked in on him. So many thoughts flashed through my mind: porn, a woman via Skype, Facebook sluts, anything, but what I discovered was none of these things and was actually something so shocking and funny I can't stop giggling about it whenever it flashes through my mind.

Nathan likes SpongeBob. He's been watching it on his laptop in his office. He apparently finds it relaxing.

Although he has been avoiding me because he's ashamed of how he reacted in his office the other day, the fact that he's been ditching me for SpongeBob makes me quick to forgive him.

Let's face it, how can anyone be mad at that? It's SpongeBob. And it's so not Nathan. Or maybe it's always been Nathan and I've just never realised it.

The look on his face when I walked into his office frightened me to the very core. It was shock and fear. I never disturb him in his office, so he didn't think to lock the door. When I saw his face, all of my fears were confirmed and I stomped over to his desk, pulled the laptop screen down towards me and stared at the screen.

"It's not what it looks like!" He blurted as I watched the yellow sponge blow a bubble shaped like a flower. "It helps me relax." I continued staring at the screen, trying to figure out what it was I was seeing. "Don't you dare laugh!" Of course I laughed; I laughed so hard my hand that held my weight on the desk, slipped over the edge and I fell to the ground.

We made love on the floor that night.

The entire time I was still laughing.

CHAPTER TWENTY

Right now we're on our way out, much to Nathan's annoyance. My mum has come over and is babysitting. Nathan, Tommy, Sasha and I are heading out for drinks at our old local. Sasha seems to think it will help me heal. I disagree.

Mostly I'm just hoping the people who used to work there and frequent it, the ones who knew us and knew Caleb and I, no longer do. The last thing I want on a relaxing night is to be judged and questioned.

"Stacey is a bitch," Sasha says to Tommy as we enter the taxi that has pulled up in our driveway.

"She's not a…" Tommy, seeing the scowl, quickly changes his tune. "Yeah, she's a total bitch."

"You don't even mean that!" Sasha slaps him upside the head.

"I do babe, honestly, she's always a bitch. Especially when she served me dinner with such a polite smile on her face."

"She wants you."

Oh dear.

"Really?" He feigns enthusiasm, earning himself a slap on the arm.

Nathan sniggers in the front seat and I glare at his profile. He sees me out of the corner of his eye and immediately puts a stopper on his amusement.

"So, bitches, how's it hanging?" Sasha asks, clearly bored of whatever the hell she was arguing about moments ago.

"Nathan's cheating on me with SpongeBob."

Nathan turns in the front seat and begins projecting the different ways he wants to murder me through his eyes. "Thanks Gwen." I only smile cheekily in response.

"What?" Sasha and Tommy both ask at the same time.

"Gwen thought that to move from Swindon to here you'd require a Passport and a visa." Nathan retorts.

My mouth drops open. "I thought you said Sweden!"

Nathan shakes his head, smiling at the memory. "No you didn't. You even said… 'Swindon? You lived in Swindon for six months? Don't you need a visa for that?'"

"Where the fuck is Swindon?" Sasha whispers to me. Tommy blinks and then he laughs, Nathan joining him.

"I have no idea," I whisper back.

It's weird being out with Nathan. I can see he's not comfortable, but I can also see he's trying for me. I begged him to come with me and, when he finally relented, he also let me know that he wouldn't be happy doing it. So I gave him the puppy dog eyes, to which he relented again and said "Fine, I'll pretend, just for you."

Good enough.

By the time we get to the pub, I notice that he's relaxed a lot more than he was when we left.

"This is going to be fun," Sasha says, bouncing on the spot after climbing out of the taxi.

I disagree; something is bound to go wrong.

Nathan, after paying for the taxi, immediately pulls me into his side. At first I think it's because of his discomfort, but then I realise it's actually his possessiveness getting the better of him. I'm wondering what is making him so on edge and I'm about to ask, but Sasha interrupts me by yanking me towards our old corner booth.

Tugging myself free, I stop and stare at the worn, red, padded bench seat that curves around a large circular table. I can see him sat there, smiling with a pint of beer in one hand. My heart stops and my lungs constrict.

His soft brown eyes come to mine and he tips his beer at me.

I'm pinned on the spot, staring at him and the love that shines from him.

"Gwen?" Nathan asks as Sasha waves a hand in front of my face and says, "Maybe this was a bad idea."

"No." I look at the now empty booth and smile slightly. "It's okay, it was just..."

Sasha places her hand in mine and gives it a squeeze. "It's okay; you don't have to explain."

Blowing out a long breath, I look to Nathan, whose sad eyes are on me. Stepping on my tiptoes, I press my lips to his and leave them there until my heart calms. When I pull back, his eyes are smiling and the back of his knuckles smooth over my cheek. We smile at each other, only slightly, but it's enough.

"Sit, I'll get you a drink," Nathan whispers into my ear, sending shivers down my spine.

"I've got these, mate," Tommy announces. "You paid for the taxi."

Nathan looks like he doesn't know what to do and looks to me for help.

"Go and help him carry them back."

He nods and follows Tommy to the bar.

Sasha leans into me and presses her temple against my shoulder. "It doesn't look like anyone comes here anymore."

"Life goes on apparently." I press my temple to the top of her head and stare out across the almost empty room. So much has changed in the past year. Did I really expect any different?

"So," she grins, our emotional moment gone, "what's he like in bed?"

"Sasha!"

"I'm serious! I've always wanted to know. It's the whole mysterious and broody thing." She fans her face with her hand and swoons dramatically. "Makes you want to tame him... you know?"

I unfortunately do know, but I don't say as much. "He's good."

"Just good?"

"I don't want to talk about my sex life," I hiss, turning away from her slightly.

She only laughs in response, a high pitched cackle that pierces my ears. "So you finally did it? I knew it!"

"Did what?" Tommy hands Sasha her drink as Nathan hands me mine and sits beside me.

"Nothing." I slap my hand over Sasha's mouth and turn to Nathan. "You're not drinking?" I whisper in his ear when I notice his gloved hands are empty.

He shakes his head, glancing around. "I'm not much of a drinker."

I already knew this, but everybody buys a drink when they go to a pub, be it a coke or an alcoholic beverage. "Do you want to share mine?"

"No thank you." He folds his arms over his chest and leans back, his narrowed eyes on nothing in particular.

"Shall we play on the bandits?"

He glances at the flashing machine and gives me a look that says 'Really?'

"Okay, okay," I sigh, turning back to my friends.

It doesn't take him long to pull me back to his side, but he still looks bored and annoyed. I think it's mostly discomfort, though. He's not a fan of crowds and never frequents the local pubs. I just need to get him out of his shell.

Tommy notices Nathan's lack of participation and quickly engages him in a not so thrilling conversation about money, business and politics. Fortunately they agree on most things and when Tommy winks at me, I know Nathan has won his stamp of approval. Not that it's needed. My friends vanished from my life for who knows how long. They don't get to judge me or pick and choose my partners with me.

"Shots!" Sasha squeals.

I look to Nathan. He shakes his head and gives me a different look this time. It's one that says 'No.'

Bugger.

"But..."

"You almost killed yourself last time," he complains, a beautiful frown on his face. "Take it steady tonight."

Sigh. "Fine. But you're doing the dishes tomorrow as apology."

He snorts and mutters, "Yeah right."

"Aww." Sasha smiles, leaning into Tommy as she wipes an invisible tear from under her eye. "It's like you're married already."

Chapter Twenty-One

Overall the night went pretty well. It's nice being able to see ourselves in a normal setting. We're so used to being cooped up together in one house with no visitors other than the housekeeper. It's going to be tough suddenly trying to be together in the real world.

I know that if I gave Nathan the chance, he'd whisk me back to the village in a heartbeat and keep me there for as long as he wants me. But that's not me. As much as I loved being there with him, even through the bad times, I need to be in the real world. I need to be around real people, with a real job of my own.

We get home just after eleven and I'm feeling a light buzz. I'm actually kind of glad that I didn't drink more. I'm not a huge fan of drinking. It always seems like a good idea at the time, until it no longer is.

"Did you have fun?" My mum yawns and stretches on the couch. Dillan is across her chest, his fist tucked against his pudgy cheek.

"It was actually really boring." I shrug. "Until Sasha fell over the bar stool and accidentally threw her drinks at some poor bloke sitting with his friends."

Nathan shudders. "It was horrendous. Why anybody goes to a pub for fun is beyond me."

"Nathan," I laugh, arching a brow. "You don't do anything for fun. Your idea of fun is SpongeBob in a dark..." His hand covers my mouth, but this only makes me laugh harder.

Shaking her head, she sits up, being careful not to wake the baby.

"I'll take him; don't trust her sobriety," Nathan states, pointing at me with his thumb. He steps over to my mum and reaches his hands out as she manoeuvres Dillan into a safe position to transfer him in. "Come to Daddy."

The room stills; none of us breathe. Nathan takes Dillan, but his eyes close as if he can't believe what he just let slip. When they open, he keeps them down and moves past me without uttering a word.

"Close your mouth, Gwen, or are you catching flies?" Mum stands and stretches again. She must see the look of total horror on my face as she tells me, "He is raising him and he has always been there. In my opinion, he's earned that title."

"But it's not something we've spoken about."

She shrugs. "It's up to you." Kissing my cheek, she smiles and pulls me to the door. "Lock up the house."

I nod, still totally dazed from what was just said.

Holy crap!

Suddenly bed seems so daunting. Or bed with Nathan seems so daunting.

Tamping down my nerves, I begin to ascend the stairs, switching off the light as I go.

As expected, I find Nathan in the nursery and stand in the doorway watching him for a moment. His defined arm muscles bulge as he grips the side of Dillan's cot. His shoulders tense and flex as his head hangs low and his back expands with each deep breath.

I open my mouth, but then close it again along with my eyes. I have no idea what to say. It's not even something I've thought about.

Mum is right; he does deserve the title, but he has already taken Caleb's place in a sense. It almost doesn't seem fair that he gets Dillan as well. Or am I being stupid?

"Come to bed," I say softly and begin moving towards him. "Come on, we've got a busy day tomorrow."

He sighs and turns to face me. "Is it really that terrible that I want to be his father?"

"No," I admit. "But it's a complicated situation. I think that until things are set in stone, we shouldn't do labels."

"Set in stone?" A nervous smile shines at me. "What's that supposed to mean?"

I move around him, lean over the bars of the cot and press my lips to Dillan's forehead. "Can we talk about it tomorrow?"

He wraps his arms around me. "You do know I'm not going anywhere right? I'd be a fool to leave now, not when I finally have everything I've wanted, including things I didn't even realise I wanted." He looks over to the cot while speaking the last words.

"Me too." I smile, letting his words soak into my skin and warm me from my very core.

"I've been neglecting you as of late," he whispers. "And for that I apologise. I was worried... after the last time, I thought I'd hurt you."

He didn't. He definitely didn't. "If you'd hurt me, I would've said."

We walk arm in arm to the bedroom, where I collapse on the bed face first. Nathan chuckles and I feel his hands at the waistband of my jeans. He slowly peels them over my arse and down my legs, before folding them and placing them inside of the laundry basket. Yes, he folds them first. I still have to clarify this with myself, yet I never fully understand it.

I fold my arms beneath my cheek and wait as he kisses the small of my back, making me shiver involuntarily, followed by a giggle.

"I don't know why, but this just brought back a memory of when I used to play Lego as a small child."

Blink. "Lego?"

"Yes. I used build little houses and then have my Godzilla doll knock them down."

"That's typical boy behaviour. I'm sure we'll see a lot of that from Dillan. I'm not sure how I feel about my arse reminding you of Lego." I smile into my arms and squeal when his hand connects with my soft globes. "What was that for?"

"I felt like it," he chuckles and does it again, making me flip over and glare at him. The slaps weren't hard, but they've left an after sting I don't much care for. "Anyway, I remember building this castle out of six thousand pieces. It was brilliant. It took me days, possibly weeks; at the age of eight you don't have much regard for time."

At eight I was playing with Barbies and dancing around my room in a fairy costume.

"What happened to it?"

He grins and smoothes his hands back over my soft globes once more, before giving them a gentle squeeze. "I took it apart."

"Why?"

"And then I built an even better one."

"I feel like there's a moral to this story." I hear something drop on the ground and, when I feel his bare hands on my skin, I realize it's his gloves.

"There's not a moral, more like a realisation." He slides up my back until his face is an inch from my ear and his body is completely covering mine. It's hard to breathe, but in the most amazing way. "You're my Lego castle."

Umm... "I'm not sure I understand."

"I'd work hard building it, placing the pieces perfectly until they formed rooms, and then I put them together and added a few towers and a roof. Next I'd sit back and admire my work, break it, and then do it all over again. It was the only time I was happy, the only time I felt like I was a normal boy." Chest pain. "The result never got boring; it always amazed me." More chest pains at the thought of a young brown haired boy, so sad and alone and in pain, finding joy in a Lego castle that he'd spent days building. "It helped me be young; it helped make me forget that I was in the house that brought me so much pain and misery. It's strange that when you're young, you don't associate pain and sadness with the person inflicting it. You tend to blame it on the area, or a nearby object."

"Like me with rats. I doubt I'll ever go camping again."

"Exactly. Anyway..." He gives the shell of my ear a gentle bite and rolls to the side, keeping his leg tangled between mine as he props himself up on his elbow. "Whenever I get the chance to undress you..."

"Which is quite often as of late, not including the past few nights."

He continues talking as if I hadn't have spoken. "The result is better each time. You amaze me." I let out a soft sigh when his fingers begin tickling my back with a barely there touch. "And every moment I spend with you, I forget all of the bad things. You're my Lego castle."

"The Eighteen rated version," I snigger, earning me another slap on my arse.

"And the sex... I feel like I've been dead for twenty five years."

"Twenty five?" I ask, confused. "You had a birthday?"

He winces. "No."

"Liar!"

"It was a while ago. Don't worry about it."

The guilt shining from his eyes tells me different. "When exactly is a while ago?"

"Look... I don't do birthdays. My birthdays have never been what you would call joyous occasions. Just forget about it."

Narrowing my eyes, I push myself up onto my knees and place my hands against his shoulders. "When was your birthday, Nathan?"

"I don't remember."

Growl. "When was your birthday?"

"I don't have birthdays."

My scowl deepens. "When was your birthday?"

"Can't we just make love and forget about this?"

Sigh. "We don't make love Nathan, or have you forgotten that you don't do oral? You need oral to make love in my opinion."

He barely hides his grimace. "I'll give you oral for your birthday."

Eye roll. "And how will you manage that?"

His face falls. "Is it really that important to you?"

"No! Of course not. I'm only joking."

"I'll work on it... maybe I can..."

I slap my hand over his mouth and stare into his eyes, hopefully projecting my irritation at his avoidance. "When was your birthday?"

"Last Monday," he blurts and grips my arms before I can start beating him. "It's not a big deal."

I beg to differ.

I move away from him and stand, forgetting about my lack of clothing as I move towards the door. "Where are you going?" He asks, following close behind. I ignore him and make my way towards the stairs.

I can't believe he didn't tell me it was his birthday! What is wrong with him?

"Are you going to respond?"

I almost say no, but then I realise that would be a response and quickly clamp my mouth shut.

He continues following me silently, all the way down the stairs and into the kitchen. It's not until I collect one of the cupcakes I made earlier today from the fridge and place it on the side that he asks me what I'm doing.

What can I use as a... ah ha!

"Really?" He snorts as I place the small round tea candle on top of the brown frosting, which I always store under the sink just in case of a power cut. "Oh come on, Gwen."

I light the small wick held firmly by the white wax and hold the cupcake to his face.

"Aren't you going to sing happy birthday?" He jokes, tapping his chin in thought. "I wish my girlfriend would speak."

He blows it out and smiles fondly at me. That is until I take the candle from the top and smash the cake against his mouth. "Happy birthday," I say sarcastically and leave him to his silent freak out, sniggering as I go.

That was very mean.

He deserved it.

When he finally makes it back to bed, I'm expecting him to scold me and pin me on the bed with those amazing arms as his eyes burn with anger. He doesn't.

Instead, he climbs into his side and flips onto his stomach so he's facing away from me.

I think I may have messed up. "Did I upset you? That wasn't my intention." Or maybe it was. I don't know.

"No."

I kiss the back of his shoulder and rest my cheek between his shoulder blades. "Please stop keeping things from me."

"Sure."

Sigh.

"Goodnight."

"Night," he mutters.

I sigh again and close my eyes.

It's not until I'm sleeping that he finally rolls into me. I'm not completely convinced that he did it because he wanted to and not because he thought he had to. This is because the moment I awoke, he rolled away.

The entire situation seems to be forgotten as soon as I go for the mail after breakfast and I spot another of those envelopes lying on the mat. It's been folded length ways to allow it to fit through the letterbox. My fingers burn as I scoop it from the ground, my mind desperately screaming at me to read it.

I have to close my eyes for a moment to convince myself that whatever is in this envelope could destroy us and I don't want that at all. I'm happy, for the first time since Caleb, as much as it pains me to say it.

The guilt still bites at me, but my happiness and eagerness to live seem to overshadow it.

Nathan seems to overshadow it.

When I open my eyes, I pad into the kitchen and dump the envelope in the bin. Then I skim through the pile of bills we seem to have been sent and discard the ones I daren't read.

Bill shock is a fatal condition. It's where there are too many zeroes after a certain number and you can no longer breathe.

Nathan picks these up and reads through them while eating half a grapefruit. Gross.

"What you doing baby boy?" I coo to my smiling little man and double check the harness of his reclining high chair is fastened properly. It is. A sure sign I worry too much.

"What did you put in the bin?" Nathan asks, not looking at me.

"Are you still mad about last night?" I frown. "I said I was sorry when I woke up this morning."

"What did you put in the bin?" His face remains expressionless.

"I'm not answering until you do."

He sighs, rubs his face with his hands and gives me a look that screams, 'do we have to do this now?'

I return a look that screams, 'Yes we bloody well do.'

"What you did was cruel," he says, placing the bills in a neat pile by his plate. I take them and shove them into a nearby drawer.

"What *you* did was cruel." I glare at him. "You hid your birthday from me."

He quirks a brow. "You've never asked when my birthday is."

I open my mouth to argue, but realise he's right. Scratching my head, I try to slide myself onto his lap but he stands and moves away. "I have to be at the store by noon. I have a delivery coming."

"I'm sorry for smashing cake in your face; you're right, it was cruel." And funny, but I don't say this because he's obviously not happy with me and I doubt my saying that will help the situation in any way at all. "Forgive me?"

"It took me half an hour to get it off my skin. I'm surprised I have any left."

What? "Cake?"

He looks at me with exasperation swimming in his beautiful browns. "Skin!"

"Oh." The floor is very interesting right now. I need to sweep and mop. "When will you be home?"

"I'll call." He pinches Dillan's cheek and kisses his head. "Oh," he stops suddenly, his empty eyes landing on mine. "Next time you upset me, I'll throw a rat at you and see how you react. I'll also laugh as I'm walking away, leaving you to deal with it alone."

Well, when he puts it like that. "God, Nathan... I'm sorry."

"Are you?" He checks his watch. "I really have to go."

"Nathan..." I reach for him, but he moves away. I deserve that. "I am sorry, you know that right?"

He says nothing, leaving me to feel small and severely sorry. I'll leave him alone for a while. He'll calm down, although he doesn't seem angry, only disappointed, which is even worse.

"Tell me to tell you that I love you," I practically beg.

His body seems to slump as if releasing all of his pent up anger, frustration and disappointment in one breath. He turns towards me and cups my cheek with his hand. "I love you and I know you love me. Right now I'm annoyed. That doesn't mean I don't know that we love each other."

"You should still say it."

"In case the worst should happen and we didn't say it before, I'm telling you now that until I say otherwise, or you say otherwise, this belongs to you." He taps the left side of his chest with his free hand, before placing my hand over it. I nod, lowering my eyes once more. He leans forward and places a gentle kiss on my cheek. "I'll see you tonight."

"Okay."

When I look up, I see the small smile teasing the corner of his lips, making his eyes narrow slightly. "I forgive you."

"I am sorry." I wait for him to kiss me. He doesn't delay and I instantly melt into him. After a few moments, he pulls away slowly and reluctantly then kisses my forehead and turns to leave.

Dillan shouts out a babble, almost as if telling Nathan not to forget about him.

I smile and watch him kiss Dillan's open mouth and chubby fists before giving me a wink and leaving for London.

I am such a bitch.

CHAPTER TWENTY-ONE

I spend another half an hour with Dillan, playing with him on the floor of the living room. He's still too young to crawl, but he's getting so good at lifting himself with his hands now. Although, after thirty seconds of dropping and lifting, he starts to get irritable.

After dropping him off with my mum, I make my way to work feeling happy and light. I remember when people told me that time will heal my wounds, and sure enough, even though my heart still has a gaping hole that Caleb left behind, I feel like I'm healing.

It's still hard, but I now know that it'll get better.

Besides, I have Nathan and he's amazing. He makes everything so much easier.

"Morning." Elle beams, giving me a wave. Tiffany slides a coffee my way and I snatch it from the counter as I make my way to the kitchen.

"Hey guys," I say, shrugging off my jacket. "What have we got on the menu today?"

Elle hands me a list as I sip my amazing coffee. I can detect the taste of gingerbread.

"Valentine has just gone to the supermarket. Those idiots with the van forgot the chocolate chips." Tiffany sighs, pinching the bridge of her nose. "And last week it was the caster sugar. I swear, we should go with a different company."

"And the week before it was the cinnamon," I point out, shaking my head with annoyance. "They're the best quality though. It's just unfortunate their staff are morons. I'll get started on these."

Tiffany nods and hands me my clean apron. I pull it on and get to work. I no longer get absolutely covered in ingredients, which is fortunate. I'm so sick of washing flour from my hair and jam from my skin.

By the time Valentine returns, we have a shop full of orders for the next day.

She returns with something I'm not sure was on her shopping list and immediately hands it to me.

I stare at the large brown envelope with fury boiling the blood in my veins. In the calmest voice I can muster, I ask Valentine where she got it.

"It was in with the post." She must see the anger I'm trying to hide. "What's wrong?"

"Nothing. If you get anymore, let me know." I shove it in the bin when her back is turned and bury it under the cakes from the day before yesterday that are nowhere near fresh enough to sell anymore.

"Okay. Can you stay until five today?"

It's only an extra hour I suppose. "Sure, no problem. Can I just make a quick call?"

She waves me away and I quickly race out of the bakery. The phone rings three times before he answers. I hear the sound of his car engine and the hum of wheels on the road as he drives. "Nathan... he's not trying to threaten you anymore."

"What?" Nathan asks, sounding worried and slightly perplexed.

"Your father sent one of those envelopes to my workplace today."

He goes silent for a moment. I hear his breathing come to a stop and immediately panic.

"Don't freak out. I didn't read it. I buried it in the bin under a lot of two day old cakes."

A long hiss sounds into the speaker. "I have to go."

"Nath..."

"I have to go." The line goes dead and I curse loudly. Looking up at the clear sky, I pray that Nathan doesn't do anything stupid. He's already a third of the way to London by now.

His dad lives in London!

Crap.

I try to call him back, but it goes through to voicemail. There's not much I can do from here, other than finish work and pray a million more times. I should go after him, but not only can I not let Valentine down, I also don't have any way to get there.

Please, please, don't do something stupid. He's not worth it.

Gah, I wish he'd just tell me.

Racing back inside, I try to keep myself as busy as possible so the day goes faster. I wait and wait for his call, text, email... anything would be nice at this point. I'm practically shaking with nervousness and worry. What's going on?

I call him during every break. I usually take five minutes at the end of every hour. Instead of sitting, I pace while listening to the ring tone going unanswered. This is driving me crazy.

CHAPTER TWENTY-ONE

"What's wrong?" Tiffany asks as I check the clock for the umpteenth time.

"Nathan's not answering." I check the clock again.

"Is he okay?"

"That's the million dollar question."

We listen to Valentine humming as she works in her part of the kitchen. Tiffany's eyes linger on the doorway. "Why don't you ask her if you can leave now?"

I want to; I'm tempted... "I promised I'd stay an extra hour."

"It's worth asking."

She's right. If you don't ask, you don't get. But I know Valentine won't go for it and it's not fair on her if I ditch work on such short notice. Sigh.

"It's fine; he'll be okay. Besides, I wouldn't even know where to begin looking for him."

"True." She rests her hand on my shoulder. "You can talk to me. You know that right?"

I nod, giving her a small smile. "The same can be said to you too."

"We should do something fun this weekend, take the kids on a playdate," she suggests.

"That actually sounds like a really good idea, although Dillan can't exactly play yet." My phone rings, causing me to drop the rolling pin with a loud clatter. I quickly press it to my ear. "Hello?"

"Hey, are you busy?" I almost groan with frustration when I hear Sasha's voice.

"Kind of, I'm at work."

"Okay." She seems sad. Has something happened between her and Tommy?

"What is it? I have five minutes."

"It's nothing important. I just need some new shoes and didn't want to go into town alone."

"Oh, sorry Sash. I'd come if I could."

"Yeah." I hear the smile in her voice. "Have a good day at work."

"I'll try." I hang up and check my voicemail, just in case. Nothing. Zero. Zilch.

Fan-freaking-tastic.

Sigh.

"He'll call," Tasha reassures me and, on all that is dear to me, I sincerely hope she's right.

Chapter Twenty-Two

By the time I'm home with Dillan, I'm in full blown panic mode. His phone is off, I've not received one response and I swear I just found a grey hair from all of this stress.

Good, because for this she's going to need a backbone.

Dillan babbles happily as he sits up between my legs, smacking at his toy drum. My phone never leaves my hand. Why hasn't he called?

I need to stop this. Dillan needs me right now.

"Are you hungry?" I ask him, but he completely ignores me and continues hitting the drum. Not that I expected him to turn around and tell me he fancies Spaghetti Bolognese with a healthy amount of parmesan. He's not even on solids yet.

After bathing Dillan and settling him in for bed, I pace in the hallway for a while. This is so irritating. Why can't he just call me? I know he has his charger with him. He has one in his car at all times, so his phone dying is no excuse.

What if his dad has hurt him? I have no doubts in my mind that he has confronted his father. What if it went completely wrong and they ended up fighting?

What if he was in a car accident on the way? They say don't drive angry, or did I make that up?

To take my mind off it, I decide to make dinner; nothing fancy, just a pasta bake and some garlic bread. It takes me a while to prepare, but does little to calm my mind.

I hate this!

I hate feeling so useless!

When dinner is ready, I can't even attempt to eat; food is the last thing on my mind, so I pop it back in the oven to keep warm and head up to bed. Maybe he'll come home soon. It is getting late after all. Maybe he's on his way home.

This is ridiculous. How difficult is it to call somebody?

You pick up a phone, dial their number and press ring. It's especially important to do this when you leave the previous conversation on such a dramatic note.

I wish Mr Weston, aka Stephen, would just burn in hell already. Why can't he just leave us alone?

"This is all your fault," I snarl at Caleb, even though I know he probably can't hear me. I instantly regret it and rub my tired eyes. "No," I correct on a whisper. "This is all my fault."

I'm not sure how, but I finally managed to fall asleep, I don't remember closing my eyes, but I know that they did because when my ringtone sounds I feel like someone has smacked me in the brain. My eyes only just peel open as I place the phone to my ear. Then I remember who it could be and in the blink of an eye, I'm wide awake.

"Hello?"

"Gwen," Nathan says, sounding solemn. "I…"

"Oh my god! Do you have any idea how worried I've been?"

"Gwen…"

"I thought you were injured, or in an accident… What the hell is going on?"

"I was…"

"How could you be so stupid? Do you have any idea how badly I've been panicking?"

"Will you shut up?" He snaps and I can tell by the tone in his voice that his hands are probably balled into fists. "I've been arrested."

Wait… what? "Come again?"

"It's a long story. My solicitor has only just managed to make it here and get me my phone call." He sounds exhausted.

CHAPTER TWENTY-TWO

I don't know what to say. "What happened?"

"I... I can't say right now. This isn't a private call."

"Who's pressing charges?"

"Who do you think?" He bites out, angry at the situation.

If I were a cat I'd be hissing.

"What can I do?" I ask softly, hating the thought of him having to spend the night in a cell. Unclean, cold and small.

"Nothing. Just stay at home, lock the doors and don't open the door to anyone. Do you hear me?"

Gulp. "I hear you."

"I love you, Gwen. I'll be okay."

I don't believe that. I can only imagine how he's feeling. "Okay." Then I choke out. "I love you too."

Well... this is a situation I've never been in before. I definitely do not like it.

But what else can I do?

My thoughts go to the boxes I have yet to unpack that I've placed at the back of my closet. My thoughts then start rifling through the contents. When my thoughts remind me of the one thing I need in order to do something I'd never consider under any other circumstances, I feel physically sick.

Blackmail is wrong. So wrong.

But this is Nathan... if I can get Mr Weston to drop the charges...

This isn't me! I don't do stuff like this!

Besides, I wouldn't even know where to start. How would I even get in touch with him?

Nathan's office springs to mind. He's bound to have some kind of contact number for his dad in there. He'd hate it if I were to go through his things though. Maybe I can find a contact number for his solicitor. Then I'll hopefully find out what's going on. That seems like more of a rational thing to do.

As I push open the door I wince at the scent of bleach, the same scent that assaulted me when we lived in the village and the same scent that assaulted me when I caught him watching SpongeBob on his laptop.

"Put it down," I demanded, glaring at the bottle in his hand before tugging it away.

"But..."

"I already cleaned yesterday. I used plenty of bleach. It doesn't need more."

"You didn't clean it enough," he snapped, pointing to the skirting boards which, in my opinion, were sparkling.

"You're demented. The fumes aren't good for Dillan. If you want to bleach something, bleach your office."

We stood staring at each other, neither of us relenting, neither of us giving in. "I'll just do it while you're gone. He'll be crawling soon. He needs clean floors."

"A layer of bleach and a layer of sterilising fluid is plenty clean, Nathan. He needs to be exposed to dirt and germs or he'll never have an immune system."

"But..."

"Fine, let's compromise." I smirked and flicked my hair over my shoulder. "If you bleach after I've already done it, I get to keep eggs where I can reach them and see them."

He chewed on his lower lip for a moment before snatching back the bottle and heading towards his office. After a fist pump and a victory jig, I called after him, "You should really see somebody about that Nathan!"

To which he responded by slamming his office door, which only made me laugh... a lot.

The place is sparkling, as I expected it would be. I remember the first time I wandered into Nathan's territory when he was ill. I was pregnant at the time. I feel a lot like I did then. Like an intruder.

This is his space; it's the only place he doesn't like being disturbed.

But he's not here, so I'm going to take my chances. I'm sure he'll understand.

Without another thought, I head straight to his leather chair and take a seat. I begin to check through the drawers for a phonebook, anything, but come up with nothing but files and boring paperwork.

In the bottom drawer I find a sketch book and have a quick flick through it. It's full of jewellery designs. Nathan's drawing skills are basic, but the shape of the jewellery speaks for itself. He's got so much talent.

I finger the faint pencil lines fondly before carefully putting it back and sitting back in the chair.

What am I doing? I rub my face with both hands and sigh deeply.

"I'm never going to find anything in here," I mutter to nobody and stare at the empty space where his laptop should be. I know he keeps most things on there, but he usually takes it with him wherever he goes, so that is a dead end.

I walk over to the filing cabinets in the corner and start thumbing through the almost empty drawers. Dead end... yet again.

I'm about to give up, when I remember the medium sized lockbox he carried from the car and straight into his office not too long ago. It was after his last trip to his house in the village.

Maybe that has something I can use... or maybe I'm just curious. But where would he keep it?

The room is basically empty, save for a few pictures on his desk, which sits in the centre of the room. There's a large filing cabinet in the corner and a small, dark leather couch in the far corner.

If I were a lockbox, where would I hide?

I almost laugh at myself. Sometimes I can be really weird.

I check under the drawers of the desk, behind the couch, behind the filing cabinet... nothing. Where the hell is it?

As I'm rechecking the drawers, I almost slap myself. The middle drawer has a hidey space. I pull everything out and place it neatly on the desk before tugging up the thin base of the drawer. Jackpot!

There's no key to said lockbox... sigh. He probably carries it with him. What's this?

I pick up the small leather bound book and notice the journal I bought for him a while ago hiding beneath it. Smiling, I unwrap the leather strap from around the small book in my hand and flick to the first page. My hands immediately snap it shut when I realise it's a diary of sorts. As much as I want to read it and see into Nathan's mind, I'd never betray him like that.

Something flutters to the ground, a single, folded sheet of paper. Shit. I'll never find what page it was placed on!

I carefully pick it up from the ground and I'm about to guess a page to slide it under when the large title shines through the thin paper.

<u>Last Will and Testament</u>

My fingers tremble as I peel it open and stare at the opening line, written in familiar scruffy handwriting.

Dated... two days before he died.

Signed by Nathan Weston and... Sasha Rutter.

My heart shatters and my hand flies to my mouth. My entire body begins to shake and the pain I feel in my chest is unbearable.

Why would Caleb write a Will and Testament?

He didn't know he was dying... he didn't know.

He didn't.

And Sasha didn't know either. She wouldn't betray me like that.

My mouth trembles as a lump forms in my throat. I read through the scruffy handwriting that states everything Caleb owned was to go to me upon his death, including his trust fund, car, life insurance...

Powerful tears beat at my eyes, making them sting and automatically close, pushing the salty fluid of sorrow from my eyes.

The hole in my heart, that was slowly filling, is now tearing open and gaping even bigger than before. It's as if it no longer exists for anything other than to hold pain.

I shouldn't jump to conclusions, I know I shouldn't.

But why would Nathan keep this from me? Why would Sasha keep this from me?

Does this have something to do with what Mr Weston has been sending me? Something in my mind tells me that this has everything to do with what Mr Weston has been sending me.

A flood of thoughts enter my mind, the first being Sasha. When we went to the park she hinted that it felt strange the way Caleb died, almost as if telling me to look into it, but I refused.

Her being okay with me and Nathan way before there ever was a Nathan and I. She was almost pushy with it. I remember because Tommy snapped at her to leave it.

It's almost as if she knew Caleb wasn't what he said he was and she wanted me to stop grieving and move on. Why didn't I find it weird? Am I really that dense? It's like a screaming, flashing alarm now.

Nathan... when he said his brother wasn't who I thought he was... I thought he was referring to the whole him taking me first.

But... how did Caleb know he was dying and I didn't? He was only ill for a few days before he left the earth.

I clumsily wipe away my tears and carefully place the will on the top of Nathan's desk. I stare at it for a long moment, willing it to vanish from the desk and my memory.

A cold wave of numbness washes through me, attacking every cell in my body until, finally, my tears dry and I feel nothing.

"Sasha," I say to her sleepy voice when she answers the phone.

"Yeah? It's midnight. What's wrong? Is Dillan okay?"

"I need you to come round; it's an emergency." I state. "Dillan is fine."

"Oh... okay, sure. I'll be there in fifteen." She hangs up and I fight the urge to slam my phone down on the desk.

A broken phone is not needed right now.

What do I do? What do I say?

The minute she walks in, I place the will in her hands. Her eyes go wide and her body starts trembling. "Where's Nathan?"

"Arrested. I'm not sure why. He was in London when it happened." I take the will back and make my way towards the living room, where I place it on the coffee table. "I'd like an explanation from you, seeing as it's impossible for me to get one from him right now."

"Gwen, it's... complicated. I didn't want anything to do with it," she whispers solemnly. "Please believe me. I mean... the will isn't even legal. Technically."

"It's not about the will. It's not about the money I haven't received!" I snap, glaring at her. "Did he know he was dying?"

She gulps and very slowly nods her head. "It's complicated."

"How did you find out?" I hiss, feeling the pieces of my heart that shattered upon Caleb's death slowly shrivel to dust. An ache I can't describe begins in my stomach. It feels like something is crawling inside me. I want to heave; I want to vomit. Instead I stare at her blankly, needing answers.

Her eyes fill with unshed tears and her voice is hoarse when she speaks. "I... I caught him doing something and he had to tell me. I didn't want any part of it, but... he was... he wasn't right towards the end. He was desperate to leave something behind. Anything behind."

My spine stiffens as her words penetrate my anger. "What are you talking about, Sasha? What did you catch him doing?"

"Babe... please..."

"What did you catch him doing?" I screech almost hysterically, my lower lip trembling.

"He was swapping out your birth control pills," she says, so quietly I can barely hear her.

My breath leaves me in a whoosh, my eyes widen in horror.

Her hands go up defensively. "It was already too late! I was going to tell you. He begged me not to, but it was already too late! You found out you were pregnant the next day. I... panicked. I didn't want to ruin that for you. Caleb said there was no use telling you now. God... I'm so sorry." Her tears fall, but I feel no sympathy.

"Did Tommy know?"

"No!" She shakes her head frantically. "No of course he didn't. Please Gwen... forgive me. I swear I didn't want to hurt you. I wanted nothing to do with it but... you were already so down about the pregnancy. I thought that if I told you... it would just tip you over the edge."

"You should have told me!" I shout.

"I know... but you only had months left with Caleb and then that turned into weeks. He deteriorated fast. He was worried he wouldn't be able to marry you before..." She sniffs and wipes her nose on a tissue from her pocket. "It was awful. I wanted to tell you so many times. I wanted you to figure it out."

"How... what was wrong with him? He always seemed fine to me."

"Brain tumour. I've forgotten the name of it. He'd been in remission for years. They said they couldn't remove it, but it should remain benign. It didn't. It was at the very top of the back of his neck. You'll have to ask Nathan; he knows more about it than I do."

"What else do you know?" I need to know as much as possible. I need to know everything.

"He was sick with it when he was little. He didn't get the all clear until he was about thirteen. Nathan... he was going to tell you. He was so angry."

I nod, sorting out my thoughts as everything clicks into place.

I remember asking Nathan not long ago....

"Was... umm... was Caleb..."

"No."

"I don't understand why it was just you that..."

"Caleb rarely went to our grandfather's. Maybe he didn't have the opportunity."

I remember not believing him. Something didn't seem right.

"Don't get me wrong. I'm glad that he wasn't... I wish you hadn't had to... but..."

"Spit it out."

"It makes no sense that he'd only target you."

Caleb was too sick to stay at his grandfather's, too sick to be a subject of his abuse. Nathan was probably pushed out so his parents could take better care of Caleb.

I want to be angry. I want to be sad. I want to be... anything! But... I can't muster any kind of emotion. I don't know how to deal with this.

"Gwen," Sasha says softly, her hand resting on my shoulder.

I look at her, my eyes as hollow as I feel inside. "I need your help with something."

"Anything," she promises.

Chapter Twenty-Three

I HAVEN'T SLEPT ALL night. I'm not sure why. I don't feel anything, so I'd probably be able to sleep easily. Exhaustion is definitely one of the more prominent feelings in my body right now.

Sasha is curled up in the chair by the window, her eyes puffy from crying. I haven't spoken to her in a couple of hours. I don't have anything to say.

She hasn't said anything either; she doesn't have anything to say.

It's light out when I hear a car in the driveway. I don't move from my spot on the couch.

When the door opens, Sasha sits bolt upright in her seat and stares at me. I remain numb, my head resting on my hand on the arm of the couch.

Nathan walks in looking dishevelled and worried. I try to muster up an ounce of sympathy at his time inside. I fail.

"Hey," he says warily and his eyes go to Sasha. "What's going on? You look like you haven't slept a wink." His tone is warm, soothing. I hate him for trying to be nice right now.

He cautiously walks this way and takes the seat closest to me. His hand goes to my thigh and I can't be bothered to hold back the wince.

His eyes go to Sasha, who nods towards the table. He glances at it, looks back to me and then whips his head around to stare at the table once more. When he fully reads the bold words on the sheet of paper, he lets out a choked gasp and grips my thigh with an almost bruising force.

"Gwen?" He whispers, his shaking hand moving from my thigh to my face. "Look at me. Please." I do. He winces at the look he sees there. "I love you."

Does he? I can't even remember what love is anymore.

"Don't you want to know how I found out?" I ask, my voice hoarse from lack of use and lack of water.

He shakes his head. "No, but I'd really like to tell you my side."

"Your side?" I ask incredulously. "You mean your part in it?"

"No... I mean yes. Please, let me explain," he whispers and kneels in front of me.

"You knew all along he was going to die."

His eyes fill with shame. "I did, but..."

"Then there's nothing you can say that will change anything. You didn't tell me. You let him be with me and get me pregnant!"

His eyes snap to Sasha, who instantly says, "I had to tell her, Nathan."

He almost chocolate browns close for a few seconds. When they come back to me, they're soft and sad. "Caleb wasn't in the right frame of mind towards the end, but he loved you."

Yeah right.

"He loved you a lot. You asked me why I hit him..." I look away, but his hand comes to my face and gently moves it so I'm looking into his eyes once more. "After I found out he'd taken you in the back of his car - or at least I thought he had; I now know he was telling the truth when he said he didn't - I confronted him. He told me he was falling for you, that he wouldn't do anything to hurt you."

I almost snort at this. Caleb was lying, obviously.

"He had this obsession with leaving something behind before he died. A legacy of sorts. But he convinced me it wasn't about that anymore. I tried to get him away from you, but he wouldn't budge. I genuinely believe he loved you. And then... the doctor told him he had months left, if that."

"The tumour," I say, and nod to Sasha. "She told me about that."

"Yes." He nods, lowering his head for a moment. "He thought he'd have years; we all did. We were wrong, obviously. I think he panicked. When I realised he'd gone back on his word, it was already too late. I confronted him. You were there, but you were already pregnant. I couldn't tell you; I didn't have the heart to."

"The night you punched him."

"Yes." His eyes glitter with wetness and his hands grip mine. "It was messed up, the entire situation."

I stare at him for a while, willing some sort of emotion to surface. "Why were you in town that day? Why did you take me in?"

"He came back to deliver the will, but like I said, it's probably not even legal." Sasha responds for him.

"I've got this Sasha," Nathan snaps. Dillan's wail pierces the silence that follows.

Sasha stands. "I'll sort him. You two talk."

Nathan nods his appreciation and turns back to me. "I came back to give you the will."

"But you didn't," I point out, thinking back to that day. "You didn't even mention it. And how does Sasha know you were there for that reason?"

"Because I promised Caleb when we signed it that I'd give it immediately to you and sort out a solicitor. When I didn't and you moved in with me, Sasha confronted me that night she and Tommy stayed over. She couldn't say anything because it would implicate her too. She knew once you saw the will you'd probably never speak to either of us again. She..." He clears his throat, his eyes imploring me to pay attention. "She saw that you were healing. She saw that you were well looked after. I promised her I was getting the money my father stole and would give it to you, but..."

"You never did. You got the money, but you didn't give it to me."

"No Gwen... I didn't, but..."

"Why didn't you give me the will? Why did you take me to live with you?"

He gulps, his hands sliding up and down the sides of my thighs. "I knew that if I gave you it, I'd probably never see you again."

Oh my god. "You sick bastard!" I throw his hands away from me, my mouth open in horror. "What the hell were you thinking?"

"I know... It was a selfish choice, but I always looked after you both. You can't deny that it was the right choice."

Is he hearing himself? Am I hearing him right? "Your brother died and you moved in on his girl not two weeks later!"

"It wasn't like that!" He shouts desperately. "It was never like that."

"No?" I laugh coldly. "What was it like?" I push myself to my feet and walk towards the window. "Did you get what you wanted?"

He follows me, his hand resting on my shoulder. "I stayed away from you. I didn't try anything with you at all."

"That's a lie!" I yell, turning to face him, my body trembling with fury and embarrassment. "You tried to kiss me only a month after he died."

He looks puzzled for a moment and then his eyes widen with realisation. His mouth opens, but he realises he can't say anything because it's true. I was sleeping at the time, but I woke up and felt him hovering over me.

"You're just as sick as he is." I whisper, ignoring the hurt in his eyes. "I don't want to talk anymore."

"Please, let me explain. When you've calmed down, let me explain." No, I don't care how sad you sound. I don't want to listen.

"I don't want an explanation. You can't explain this… it's sick. It's fucking twisted." I shout, my vision blurring as tears pool before spilling over. I dash them away angrily, glaring at Nathan who looks as devastated as I feel. "It's my life he ruined! For what?"

"You got Dillan…"

"You knew! All along you knew what he was planning to do. You knew… and you didn't say anything, you didn't stop it. Why?" I sob this last word, my knees shaking, wanting to give in and fall to the ground. "Why wouldn't you stop him?"

He takes a step towards me, his eyes wet. "He was my brother; he was happy. I wanted him to have that. He'd been sick most of his life and finally he was happy. He promised me he wouldn't do it. He said he loved you."

"Don't start lying now. I'm not stupid. You knew when he died I'd have nobody. If I was pregnant with nothing and no one, you'd have the perfect chance to swoop in and save the day."

"That's not what it was like!" His voice is desperate. He drops down onto his knees in front of me. "I didn't make that decision until I saw you…"

"You need to leave," I mutter, sitting on the chair Sasha vacated. My legs just can't hold me up anymore.

We're at eye level, but I feel nothing. That hole that Nathan filled, it's a hole again. "Please, Gwen, we can get through this… All I'm guilty of is not telling the truth, that's it. I had nothing to do with any of it."

"This isn't like you've walked into a shop, seen somebody steal and haven't said anything, Nathan. This is a man, purposely getting a woman pregnant, purposely ruining her life for the sole reason that he didn't want to die without leaving something behind." I laugh angrily. "What kind of twisted thought is that?"

"He wasn't right in the head, I know this... He'd been sick all of his life. I didn't know what to do, Gwen."

"So instead of stopping it and warning me, you take me in and help me raise his child?"

"It wasn't like that."

"So you keep saying."

"I swear it. I love you. I love you so damn much. You and Dillan are all I have. I can't lose you." He drops his head into my lap. "I can't bear it."

"Then you'll know how I felt when he died and left me with nothing."

"Gwen."

I stand and make my way to the hallway, needing as much distance between us as possible.

"Please. Don't leave me. I'm sorry, okay? I'm so sorry. I know I should have... could have done something. I didn't. But I will, from here on, I promise you I will never stop making you happy. I'll never stop trying to give you the life you deserve. We're perfect together; don't you see that?"

I should feel something when I see a tear fall from his eye. I don't.

Numbness is the only thing that's inside me right now.

"Gwen, I'll leave. I'll give you space to... to calm down. We'll talk tomorrow." He looks hopeful, even when his voice breaks, showing the sadness he feels.

"I don't want to talk," I say calmly, my voice almost robotic. "I never want to talk to you again."

He inhales a sharp breath, his body heaving slightly as his hands cup my cheeks. No more tears spill down them. Only a dry layer of the liquid sorrow remains and I swear to myself that these drying tears will be the last I ever shed for Caleb. "Don't say that. You'll change your mind. We can work this out."

"We can't."

"We can," he implores, pressing his forehead against mine.

"We can't."

"Yes." He nods, closing his eyes for another brief moment. "We can."

"Stop!" I scream, shoving him away from me. "I forgave you... for everything you did to me. I did nothing wrong! Nothing! And you threw me away like I was nothing. But I forgave you."

"I know and I'm grateful for that, truly I am."

"I wasn't going to keep him." I whisper, tears stinging my cheeks.

"What?"

I shake my head, trying to empty my mind, trying to relieve the ache that is torturing my body. "Dillan. I wasn't going to keep him!"

"You love Dillan," he says warily.

"But if you'd have told me, I wouldn't have kept him. I would have finished university. I'd have a life, a proper career. I wouldn't feel like this now!

He grips me by my shoulders and shakes me. "Gwen, you love Dillan. This isn't his fault. Blame me, blame my brother, don't resent him."

"I..." A sob tears through me. "I can't be here anymore. I need to go."

"Gwen, please," he begs, following me up the stairs.

I enter the bedroom, startling Sasha who is playing with Dillan on our bed... no, not *our* bed, but Nathan's bed. I head to the closet and grab a small suitcase. I just need the bare essentials. I can get the rest another day.

"Pack some things for him in the nursery please Sasha, just the essentials." I say coldly. "You owe me that much."

She nods and leaves the room quietly, with Dillan in her arms.

"Don't go," he begs, watching helplessly as I grab as many items as I think I'll need.

"I'm leaving." I say, throwing clothes into the case. "I never should have come back. I should never have forgiven you."

He stares at me from the middle of the room, his eyes flicking between me and the case.

"You're being irrational," he snaps. "You don't need to leave. We can work through this. This isn't fair on Dillan."

I freeze, my numbness vanishing and my anger reaching the red zone. My temper takes a hold of me, squeezing at me until I pop. Before I realise what I've done, I see Nathan duck and hear a smash when Caleb's photo from the nightstand hits the wall behind Nathan.

I don't stop to take note of what I've done. I don't stop when I place my hands on Nathan's chest and shove him. Then I shove him again, my chest burning with overexertion and emotion.

"Do you know what's not fair on Dillan?" I shout, shoving him again. "Growing up without a father! You and Caleb did that to him!" My hands push against his chest again. He goes back a step. "He'll never know what an amazing man his father was... but then again... he was never an amazing man anyway! He was a fucking liar. Just like you!"

His back hits the wall, but I don't stop shoving. My arms keep moving until I'm pounding on his chest.

"Gwen," he says, wrapping his arms around me and pinning me to him. "Christ Gwen, I'm so sorry."

"Let go of me!" I shout, finally pulling free and taking a few steps away from him, my chest heaving and my lungs burning. "Don't touch me." He withdraws the hand he was about to place on my shoulder.

"Dillan has you; he has me. You know I love him like he's my own. I'll never let him go without."

I stare at him incredulously and turn back to my bag, muttering, "You'll be lucky."

"Gwen, you can't take him away from me."

I don't respond. I keep piling things into my suitcase. Just before I grab the zip, it goes sailing across the room. Déjà vu. My clothes scatter on the ground as I stand staring at the now empty spot on the bed.

Nathan grabs me by the shoulder and pushes me against the wall, effectively caging me in with both arms. "You're not taking him away from me. I will fight for him."

"He's not yours Nathan. You have zero rights to him and you know it." I snap, trying to duck under his arm, but his quick reflexes catch what I'm doing almost before I know I'm doing it. His hand presses against my shoulder, holding me in place.

"Please," he says softly. "If I lose you, he's all I have. He's still my son. I've still been there for him. I'm the one who's raised him with you."

"Right... because you're so stable? What kind of mother would I be if I let my son be raised by a freak like you?"

He gasps and takes an involuntary step back. "You're just saying that to hurt me."

"It's true, isn't it?" I kick the suitcase across the floor.

"No... I'm good to Dillan. I'm good to you! What does it matter how we began? It's what we are now that matters!"

"If this were a fairy tale I'd believe you." I laugh humourlessly. "This... this is just a nightmare."

"I don't want you to go. I've made the mistake of letting you go before."

I stare at him, my mouth hanging open. "You didn't *let* me go! You *forced* me!"

"And it was the biggest mistake of my life," he shouts and stalks towards me, forcing me to move backwards like a mouse away from a cat. "I made a mistake. I should have told you the truth. I know that and there isn't a second that goes by that I don't wish I had. Haven't you ever made a mistake Gwen? One you wished you could take back?"

I inhale a shuddering breath. "Yes. You. You're the biggest mistake of my life. I should never have let you in."

He nods, his bottom lip vanishing behind his teeth. "You don't really mean that."

"You don't know what I mean, or how I feel," I spit, grabbing the front of his shirt. "You've never loved anyone or anything in your entire life. And the two people you claim to love you let someone fuck them over."

His jaw clenches. "Before Dillan was born and before I fell in love with you."

"Why do you look mad at me?" I scoff. "How can you be mad at me?"

"I'm not mad at you!" He groans, gripping his hair with both hands. "I'm mad at me, at... at this stupid situation."

"Stupid? You think this is stupid?" What the hell?

"Yes," he snaps, his eyes narrowing. "I think it's extremely stupid."

"I don't want to talk anymore," I state tiredly and move over to the bed. I sit immediately and rub my eyes. I feel nothing. Doesn't he even care?

"I know you're upset," he begins, making me snort. Upset? I think I'm far worse than just upset. "But none of it matters anymore. We can't change it. I can't; you can't; Dillan can't. It's happened. It's in the past." He's kidding... right? "It's not worth this."

I don't even know what to say to that, so I say nothing. I just stare at him with blank eyes and parted lips.

"I should have told you. It was wrong that I didn't." He drops down to his knees and tilts his head so he can look in my eyes. "But we love each other. And we have Dillan. You chose me. You forgave me once. Things have turned out okay; look around you." He motions to the room with his hands. "We have a nice house, a gorgeous son, good jobs and we love each other. We can get through this." His gloved hands cover mine on my lap. I resist the urge to pull them free. Another tear falls from my eye. He quickly wipes it away with his thumb and keeps his palm against my cheek. "I will never let you down again. Ever. You have my word."

"You've already promised that," I whisper, wanting to hear his words and absorb them. God, I want them to take away the pain so badly. "You've promised that twice, and this is the second time you've broken it. This is the second time you've broken me."

"Not intentionally. All of the hurt you're feeling now is because of my inaction over a year ago." His finger gently presses against the underside of my chin, effectively raising my face to see his. "I'd rather die than let anything hurt you now."

There's a knock at the bedroom door a few seconds before Sasha walks in. She glances at us both, but speaks to Nathan instead of me. "Dillan fell asleep. I put him back to bed. He's been fed and changed."

"Thank you," Nathan responds, his eyes never leaving me. "Sasha, you may leave."

She stands in the doorway for a long moment, seeming unsure about which option to take. Finally she nods. "I'll call you… or you call me when you want to talk, okay Gwen?"

"She will," Nathan tells her and lets out a breath when she closes the door. He loosens his tie and pulls it from around his neck. On any other day I'd be shocked at him throwing it across the room. "You must be exhausted. You haven't slept all night." His voice is soft, soothing. I hate it. "You need to sleep; both of us do."

Sleep? How can he think of that right now? I've just had my entire world torn apart, stamped on and thrown into a raging fire!

But I just don't have the energy to argue, even though my brain refuses to compute the fact that my body is exhausted.

"And then in the morning we'll talk." He shrugs off his jacket and throws that in the direction of his tie.

His hands go to my shoes. He tugs on the laces and takes them off, one foot at a time. My shoes soon follow the path of his jacket. When he reaches for the button of my jeans, I stop him and shake my head.

"You can't sleep in your clothes Guinevere," he admonishes, trying for the button again. I push his hands away. He sighs deeply but doesn't push me again. "We'll get through this." His voice is a whisper as his hands grip my hips and pull me to the edge of the bed.

His arm goes under my knees as the other goes around my back and he moves around the bed, placing me on the cool mattress. As soon as my head touches the pillow, the exhaustion I feel really settles in. It's disorienting being this tired while it's light outside.

Nathan soon joins me, wearing nothing but his boxers and gloves.

He immediately turns towards me, his arm trying to take its usual place beneath my neck. Shrugging him away, I move to the edge of the bed, needing my space right now. Clearly not taking the hint, he moves closer and slides his other arm over me.

When I feel his lips travel up the curve of my neck, I stiffen and stop breathing. At first I think he's just trying to comfort me, but when his hand wraps around my breast and his teeth nip at the lobe of my ear, I realise my original thought was wrong, very wrong.

"What are you doing?" I hiss, rolling onto my back.

"I don't know," he admits, shaking his head. "I don't know what you want me to do."

"I want you to leave me alone," I bite out, rolling back onto my side.

His voice is quiet when he responds. "I don't know how to leave you alone."

"Then learn, and do it quickly."

He moves away and I can tell by the pull of the blanket that he's lying on his back. "I love you, Gwen."

Squeezing my eyes tight, I will sleep to claim me. It does, but not before I felt his hand touch my hair, and not before I heard him let out a sound that can only be described as a choked whimper.

Still, I felt nothing.

Chapter Twenty-Four

My eyes are stinging when I wake up. I must look a mess, but I can't muster up the energy to care. I climb from the empty bed and make my way towards the bathroom. A shower is needed desperately right now.

I shake my head. "It'll always feel like this. Always." The water hasn't even turned warm before I'm standing under the heavy spray. My eyes squeeze shut and my mouth parts so I can breathe. Every move I make seems to cause my body unimaginable strain. I've only felt like this once before; that was after Caleb died and I stayed in bed for three days.

When out of the shower I quickly get dressed, not even bothering to match my clothes. Who cares about matched clothes at this time? It's pointless. I don't even bother to dry my hair; I just run a towel over it and pull it up into a bun.

"I think Mummy is awake," I hear Nathan say from the kitchen as I make my way downstairs. I follow the sounds of Dillan's babbles and smile at his chubby face smiling at the sight of me. He's always happy to see me, always. Nathan looks at me over his shoulder. "I made breakfast." He looks at the clock on the wall above the table and winces. "Well, lunch."

I peer around him and try to find some kind of emotion, maybe shock, when I note that he's in the process of making scrambled eggs and bacon.

"Sit," he orders softly. I do and he starts shifting food from pans onto a plate, before bringing it over to me with a glass of juice.

"You found the eggs," I state, picking up my fork and moving the scrambled mess around the plate.

"They're your favourite." He bends and touches his lips to my temple. "I thought you'd be hungry. And I thought we could do something fun today?"

Seriously? "Thanks, but I'm not in the mood." His face falls and his tongue snakes out to tease his lower lip.

He grabs his own egg free plate from the side and takes the seat next to me. I bow my head, scooping up a small bite of egg before placing it on my tongue. It smells like it should taste good, but I might as well be chewing on paper for all I can taste.

"Your mum offered to have Dillan for a few hours. I know there's a movie you want to see at the cinema." He reaches over and tucks an errant lock of hair behind my ear. I don't mean to tense, but I do and it doesn't go unnoticed. "We could do that?"

"Hmm," I mumble, and take a small bite of my toast. I'm not even sure why I'm eating. I'm definitely not hungry. Maybe because it's the first time he's ever touched an egg for as long as I've known him and he's done that specifically to make my breakfast.

He lied to you, a voice keeps screaming in my head. *He's broken you. Practically destroyed you with his lies.*

"Would you like to go?" He asks calmly, his eyes scanning my face for any sign of a reaction. He won't find one. "Or would you like to do something else?"

They knew he was dying and nobody told you; nobody prepared you for it. You were the one who woke up and found him dead. You've been blaming yourself for months, thinking over and over in your mind how you could have done things differently.

"Gwen?"

"I..." I push my plate away and stand. "I'm not hungry." I move around to Dillan and take him from his highchair. He smiles and gurgles as I pull him up to my chest.

Nathan moves to my back. "We'll get through this," he whispers, placing his hands on my hips. "I'll take him to your mum's and then we'll go out and have fun."

Fun? What's that?

"Just me, you and a huge tub of popcorn." He smiles and carefully removes Dillan from my arms.

"You don't like popcorn," I point out, taking the plates from the table.

"I'll do them when I get back. You go and sit," he says, frowning slightly. I ignore him and move over to the sink. "Gwen..."

"I can do dishes, Nathan. I'm not a child," I snap, scraping the food into the bin.

His brows shoot to his hairline and he runs the hand that isn't holding Dillan through his hair. "I don't want you to do it today. It's my job."

"Right." I roll my eyes and drop the plates into the sink. "Well, by all means, go ahead."

"Gwen," he sighs and steps towards me.

For months you've grieved for a man that didn't exist. For months you've blamed yourself. If somebody had told you, you could have prepared. But they didn't. They watched you deteriorate and even though you didn't say it out loud, it was obvious that you blamed yourself for his death. You blamed yourself for the fact that Dillan would grow up without his father.

"Hello?" Fingers click in front of my face. I turn towards the source and stare at him expectantly. "Did you hear what I just said?"

I shake my head. "No."

"I said that if you want, we could try and go to the beach. You haven't been in a really long time and..." His voice trails off and he chews on the inside of his cheek for a moment. "I'd really like to try... for you."

Just the mere thought of going to the one place that used to bring me so much joy but now brings me nothing but anger makes me balk at the thought. "No thanks."

"Okay... then why don't you choose?" I can see he's getting frustrated.

I don't care. "I don't want to do anything." Especially not with you. Does he honestly think that everything is suddenly going to be okay?

"It'll be good for us to get out for the day," he comments, bouncing Dillan on his side. "You look like you need some fresh air."

"Then I'll go for a walk," I huff, reaching for Dillan. "Just go to work or something."

"I'm trying here, Gwen," he says quietly, his tone solemn and soft.

It pierces through the bubble of numbness that is tightening its hold on my body and at his words, I feel a slight twang of pain in my chest. I just can't find the strength or energy to fully care.

"I know," I respond and move towards the hallway.

"I'm sorry," he states, but he doesn't sound like he means it. "I'm sorry for failing to protect you."

What about destroying my trust and breaking my heart?

"Damn it," I curse as I place Dillan in his bouncer in the room. I head back into the kitchen where Nathan is waiting for me, watching me cautiously as I pad towards the cupboard where we store the medicine on the top shelf. "I forgot to take my..." My hand stops as it clasps the cupboard door handle. The cold metal bites into my skin as a torrent of thoughts rush through my head. Oh my god. Oh my god! "You absolute bastard." My voice is a low whisper.

Nathan, seemingly shocked, takes a step back. "Gwen, it's not what you..."

He ducks when the half full bag of sugar flies at his head.

"Gwen," he warns, staring in horror at the sugar that's exploded on the wall and all over the floor and table.

"Don't you dare!" My trembling hands ball into fists and my eyes close in an attempt to calm myself. I want to wrap my hands around his neck. "You... god... Nathan, how could you?"

"I warned you," he rushes, his eyes widening with panic. "I warned you, remember?"

My mouth falls open and my eyes burn as I hiss, "Warned me?"

"Yes, I told you to change them..."

"No!" I laugh incredulously, even though there is nothing funny about this. "You didn't fucking warn me, Nathan! You said that they could be out of date! My doctor said they'd be fine, but she doesn't know they've been swapped with sugar pills!" My voice gets higher and higher with each word until I'm practically screeching the last two.

My heart pounds against my ribcage and all I can see is red. I've never wanted to cause somebody pain so badly before.

"I..." He starts to say, but quickly clamps his mouth shut.

"Get out." I order, needing him to leave, needing to be alone.

"Gwen..."

"GET OUT!" I shout, my breathing coming out in pants. I feel dizzy. Oh my god. What if I'm pregnant?

I can't breathe.

How could he do this?

"I couldn't tell you, I..." He moves towards me cautiously. "I'd have had to tell you the whole story."

"Please," I snarl. "You could have dropped the box in the sink, or put it in the bin and made me think I'd lost it. There were so many sneaky ways you could have made it so that I'd need a new pack."

"I didn't think..."

"Stop lying to me!" I cry, my hands going to my head as panic sinks in. "Just please..." I face him, my eyes streaming with tears, my hands now slack by my sides. "Go away. I don't want to see you anymore."

"Gwen... It wasn't like that. I never even thought..."

I storm past him, my exhausted body telling me I've had enough. There's just too much to handle. I'm surprised my brain hasn't shut down.

"Please, Gwen, I swear..."

I stop at the bottom of the stairs with my back to him. "We're leaving." I wipe away my tears angrily.

"No you're not," he says, grabbing the back loop of my jeans. "You're not listening... you're not..."

"I'm done listening to you Nathan!" I sob, turning to face him. "I'm done. I can't physically or emotionally take anymore."

"Then let me take care of you. Go lie down; I'll bring you a drink and you can relax."

Is he listening? Can he not see the damage he's done? "We're going."

"I won't lose you, Gwen, please! It's not what you think, I..."

"Take your hands off me, or I swear to God I'll scream. I'm trying, really trying to be mature about this. I'm trying to be calm about this, but if you don't release me this second, you will regret it."

He lets go and I ascend the stairs, taking two at a time in an effort to get to the room and get packed before he can stop me.

I feel sick. I can't believe he's done this!

"I didn't do this on purpose, not consciously," Nathan whispers from the doorway. "Please don't go."

"Whatever we had, whatever we were," I pile the clothes, which Nathan must have put away after throwing them all over my bedroom, back into the same suitcase as last night, or this morning, whichever way you look at it. "It's gone."

"No it hasn't." He denies, taking a small step into the room. "We love each other. We've been through a lot together. We can get through this."

"I don't want us to get through it," I sniff, zipping up the case before pushing past him and making my way into the nursery. "Honestly Nathan, at this point, I never want to see another Weston male for as long as I live, and even then it'll be too soon."

"You're upset; you don't mean that."

I grab the bag Sasha packed for Dillan the night before and sling it over my shoulder. Nathan blocks the exit, his hands gripping the doorframe.

"Move," I breathe. "Please, just move."

"Don't leave. Please... don't leave."

"I can't stay." I take a step closer to him. "I can't be with you. I can't trust you and I can't forgive you."

He grabs my shoulders and his desperate eyes come to me. "That'll come with time. I know I've been stupid. I've made so many bad choices, but it's not a lie when I say that I love you. You have no idea what you've saved me from. Before you I was nothing... my life was meaningless."

"Move," I beg, trying to duck under his arm. "Let me go."

"No. I promised you I'd never let you go again. I'm not letting you, not this time. We can get through this."

"We can't," I mutter, shoving against his chest.

"We can."

"We can't."

"It might seem like that right now, but it'll get better. Just like after Caleb, you healed..."

God, why won't he just listen? "I don't want to get better with you."

"I'll give you space," he says hopefully. "I'll stay out of your way until you're ready to talk, ready to accept me back into your life."

"It won't work."

"It will," he insists. "You'll see, it will work. Don't do this..."

"I don't love you anymore," I shout, feeling my body deflate with defeat at the same time as his does.

"You're upset," he grits out through clenched teeth. "You don't just stop loving somebody..."

"I thought so too." I look into his almost chocolate browns and try to feel something, anything, but get nothing. "But I don't. I don't even hate you. I feel nothing."

"You've had a shock. You're grieving," he tries again, gripping my face between his hands.

CHAPTER TWENTY-FOUR

"No. I'm sorry Nathan, but it's gone. Everything has gone. This isn't grief or shock or anything else. You've done this." I exhale a shuddering breath. "I don't want to see you anymore."

He bites on his lower lip to stop it from quivering. "Please... Gwen. I need you."

"And I needed you," I whisper, grabbing my suitcase and carrying it down the stairs. "Can I use your car? I don't want to have to call my mum."

"I'll drive you."

I snatch the keys from the desk in the hall and pull the front door open. Clicking the button on the key, I watch as the car flashes twice and make my way to the boot.

"What about Dillan?" Nathan asks after I close the boot and make my way back to the house. "Can I still see him?"

"I'll call you," I respond and step into the living room. "Hey little man!" I try to give him my biggest smile. Dillan seems to like it, even though it's forced and definitely fake.

I carry him out to the car, with Nathan trailing behind me. "I really wish you'd stay. We can work through this." I pull open the back door and strap Dillan into his car seat.

"I'll send mum for my stuff. You can pick your car up later. If you could pack everything, that would be a big help."

He lets out a choked breath and looks away for a moment, as if trying to compose himself. When he turns back, he leans into the car and kisses Dillan's forehead. Then he turns to me, his eyes moist and round with sorrow. "What if you're pregnant?"

"I'll worry about that if it comes to it." I refuse to address this part as of yet.

"Will you..." He clears his throat, his hands balling into fists by his sides. "Will you tell me?"

I stop in my tracks, my hand resting on the car door. I don't know what to say. We both know what my choice will be. "It's probably better if you don't know."

His hand wipes across his mouth, his fingertips pinching his lips for a moment. "You won't keep it... will you?"

I close my eyes, pushing more tears that I didn't know were building down my cheeks. Shaking my head, I slide into the driver's seat and place the key in the ignition.

"Gwen, god, I..." He chokes on his words, his eyes glistening. "I don't know what to say to make you stay."

"I don't think there's anything you can say," I murmur, swallowing the lump in my throat and taking a deep breath to calm myself. "It's done. I'll never get past this."

He looks up to the sky and inhales a large staggering breath. His eyes close for a long moment and I see wetness seep from between his lids and leave a shiny trail along the side of his nose. He wipes it away quickly and nods, taking a step back. "I'm lost without you, Gwen."

"You'll be okay," I reassure him, my chest tingling at the sight of his tears.

He moves away from the door and I quickly close it. Using two of his fingers, he kisses the tips and places them against the glass.

I put the car in reverse and drive away.

I don't look back.

It just hurts so much.

My chest feels empty. All I can feel is pain. So much pain.

When I pull into my mum's, I sit parked in the driveway for what seems like a lifetime. I should have listened to her. I should never have gotten with Caleb.

I smack my hands against the steering wheel, my eyes blurring with tears. Then I smack them again and again until finally my body gives out and I slump forward onto my arms. The tears come in streams, never stopping, never relenting, just like the pain I feel inside.

My sobs are loud and make it hard for me to breathe.

I feel like I'm dying. I feel like I'm drowning.

"Why me? Why couldn't you have found somebody else to ruin? I gave up everything for you!" The car door opens and I'm pulled out.

"Gwen, come on, let's go inside," my mum says softly and helps me towards the door.

As soon as we step inside, my legs buckle and we both fall to the floor. She holds me tight, her arms wrapped around me as I cling to her and cry into her chest.

"Everything's a lie," I sob. "Everything! Dillan, Caleb, Nathan. It's all a lie."

CHAPTER TWENTY-FOUR

What would you do if you were to wake up tomorrow and see that this was all a dream? Would you do it all over again?

I'd go back to sleep and never wake up.

It *has* all been a dream, one sick twisted dream where an innocent, naïve, immature girl has been sucked into a life that should never have been hers.

"How could he do this?"

"Baby," my mum says hoarsely, running her hand through her hair. "You need to tell me what's happened. I can't help you if I don't know."

"I trusted him. I loved him!"

"Are we talking about Nathan?"

I can't answer. My throat hurts; the lump in it won't shift and my eyes won't open, they're that swollen. "I hate them both. Where's Dillan?"

"He's in the living room; he's okay."

"I couldn't... I'm a bad mum. I don't... It hurts too much."

"Okay," she whispers, still stroking my hair.

"Nothing will ever be the same again."

"It might feel like that now..."

Chapter Twenty-Five

"*She doesn't want to see you.*"

"*She needs to hear me out.*"

"*She's not in the right frame of mind to hear you out, Nathan.*"

"*Please Dawn, please just let me see her.*"

She sighs, long and deep. "Just go. I think you and your brother have done enough damage."

I bring my knees to my chest and bury my toes in the sand.

"*Dawn...*"

"*No, Nathan. I knew there wasn't something right about you but you were good to them, so I ignored it. I should have followed my gut.*"

"*Please. I love her.*"

"*You've destroyed her!*" *She bellows and I cover my face with the blanket.*

A tear falls and then another.

"*I know,*" *he says, inhaling a shuddering breath.* "*I didn't want her to find out.*"

"*Well she did.*"

There was a pause and I heard my boy's protests, no doubt at being moved around. "*Please don't take him from me. If I lose her, he's all I have.*"

"*That's Gwen's decision.*"

"I made a mistake."

"Yes. You did." The front door creaks as it opens. "Now go. Don't come back until she says so."

"Dawn, please..."

"I trust you'll be giving her everything Caleb promised her?"

"Yes, of course."

"Good. Now get out."

The door slams.

The sun is setting. It's getting cold, but I can't feel it on my skin. All I can feel is my hair whipping across my face with the strong breeze.

This is where we met, Caleb and I. It's the first time I've been here since before he died. It's shocking how easy it is to sit here, to remember the good times we had. It feels like a dream; it doesn't feel real.

The only thing that feels real is my hate for him, my hate for Nathan.

My hate for the fact that I'm the one who got pulled into these sick and twisted games they've played.

And Dillan... poor Dillan. He'll grow up without a father because his father was a selfish bastard, and then the person who took on the role of his father let us both down.

"Please don't take him from me. If I lose her, he's all I have."

Get out of my head! Everybody just get out of my head!

My phone rings. It's mum. I answer. "I'll be home soon."

"Where are you? You've been gone a while. Dillan's getting hungry."

"Just ten more minutes," I breathe, my hands trembling from the cold I don't feel.

She exhales a long breath. "Okay, but be quick. I'm not sure how much longer I can distract him and we're out of milk."

Damn it. "Okay, I'm on my way."

"I love you," she says and I hang up.

Love?

It's nothing but a weakness. A plague.

I walk home slowly, taking the long way. I'm hoping for some kind of revelation, something that will make me suddenly feel better, like the punch line to a joke. Maybe Caleb will pop out from behind a car and go, "Just kidding!" Although right now I think that would make everything so much worse.

That's what this is right? Just one big joke.

I close the door and rush to my fussy little boy. He goes to me eagerly and accepts his dinner without bother. Mum watches me, her eyes sad and weary.

"Do you feel better after your walk?"

"Not really," I reply honestly. She can see from my face that nothing has changed.

"He was sitting up all by himself, though he fell a few times and got quite frustrated with himself." She smiles and follows me into the room.

"Did you?" I grin, using my baby voice to Dillan, who's still suckling away. His eyes come to me and I almost gasp at how much he looks like Nathan when he's frowning. Shudder. That's strange. "Don't frown. You'll get wrinkles."

"The same can be said to you," my mum says with a quirked brow.

I shrug and settle into the corner of the couch. My phone, which has been switched off since I left the other day, is sat on the desk beside the sofa and more than anything I want to pick it up and switch it on. It's weird not using it. I use it for so much, but I just can't handle anything right now.

"Is that Sasha coming up the driveway?" My Mum asks, peeking between the blinds over the window. "She's carrying something. You stay there, I'll get it."

"Okay." I wait and listen as the front door opens.

I wait and listen to hushed whispers. Then the door closes and mum returns to the room with a small box in her hands.

"What's that?" I nod at the box as she places it on the coffee table. She shrugs. "No idea. Sasha said that Nathan asked her to bring it round. She said that he insisted you read them before you make any final decisions."

I stare at the box, my mind completely blank. I'm not sure what to do with it. Should I read whatever is in there?

"She said he's a mess," she continues, her voice soft and cautious. "I told her it serves him right."

Again I don't respond.

"I'm surprised he didn't follow you." I know she's referring to Nathan. That much is obvious. Honestly, I was surprised too. It's one of the reasons I went to the beach. I knew he would never follow me onto the sand.

"He's giving me space."

"Well, that's good." She taps her fingers on her knee after taking the seat by the window. "Do you…"

"No." I cut her off before she asks me for the hundredth time if I want to talk about it. "I'm fine…"

"I might be able to help." Can she? She doesn't know the half of it. I haven't told her. I don't want to tell her that her daughter fell for two arseholes from the same family and might be knocked up again.

"I just need to deal with things myself first before I let other people give me their input." I stand with Dillan cradled to my chest. "Can you pass me the box please?"

She places it on my free arm, where I grip it tightly to the side of my ribs. "If you need me, I'm here until ten, then I have work."

"We'll be fine." I ascend the stairs, the box digging into my side.

I shouldn't want to look inside it. I shouldn't want to think of him anymore. I've made my decision.

Stupid curiosity.

When Dillan has finished eating, I sit him between my legs and pass him his favourite lady bug shaped teddy with shiny eyes that crackle when slapped or crushed by his tiny fists. He babbles happily to himself and his bug, squealing when he tries to chew on it but his own hands move it out of the way.

Mum was right; he is sitting up almost all by himself.

"Mum!" I call, making Dillan jolt. His chubby arms spasm mid-air and his legs kick out, causing him to fall backwards against my knee. I laugh and help him back up while waiting for her to respond. "Can you bring me my phone?" It's the only camera I have.

I hear her grumbling as she comes up the stairs. She throws my phone at me and grumbles all the way back down.

"Granny's mardy," I say to Dillan as my phone loads. "I think she's unhappy because Mummy is unhappy and Granny doesn't like it when Mummy is unhappy. Just like Mummy doesn't like it when Dillan is unhappy." He tilts his head and gives me a wide mouthed smile. "Are you following me?"

CHAPTER TWENTY-FIVE

Ignoring the numerous texts that begin assaulting my phone, I quickly start snapping pictures of Dillan sitting up all by himself. This is the first time I've felt something all week. I feel warmer, like I've been sitting in a fridge for a really long time and the door has finally opened.

As much as I want to, I don't read my messages. I'm too emotionally exhausted. I do, however, answer my phone when it rings and only because I know immediately who the number belongs to.

"Is it done?" I ask, chewing on my lip and praying that I sound confident.

"Yes. We sign everything Wednesday morning." I almost shudder at the sound of his voice. It makes me feel physically sick. "I'll collect on Wednesday, at five as agreed."

"And then you disappear and you never bother any of us again." I repeat what I said the last time we had this conversation.

"How do I know it'll all be there? How do I know you don't have more copies?"

"I have nothing I want from you." I laugh incredulously. "Nathan has everything he wants; you're still getting money. I haven't been unfair. If anything, I've saved the family business by forcing you to make a smart choice."

He harrumphs and clips, "Five. Wednesday."

"It'll be on the table in the dining room as promised. All of it. Or all of what I've found, anyway." My heart thrums a heavy beat and excitement floods my veins. "Bye Mr Weston."

He hangs up and I fall back onto the bed, wanting to cheer at my own brilliance at the same time as wanting to vomit from the immense fear and guilt I feel. I've never been reckless. I've never been mean, yet here I am blackmailing my son's grandfather.

I couldn't not do anything though. As much as I despise Nathan right now, he didn't deserve to go to prison or sully his reputation after everything he's been through. According to Mr Weston, Nathan accosted him in his office and beat him rather badly, breaking two of his ribs and his nose. I don't condone violence, but I can hardly deny that, if this is the truth, Mr Weston definitely deserved it.

"Come on," I say to Dillan after sliding the mystery box under the bed. "Let's go and book Granny for Wednesday. Mummy has things to do."

"Mum," I say, my voice sickly sweet. "You know you love me?"

"The question is, do I love you enough to say yes to whatever it is you're about to ask?"

"I have to go out on Wednesday. I'll be leaving at ten, but I won't be back until late. Can you watch Dillan? Please?"

"Where are you going?"

"I just have some things to sort out."

She frowns, wanting to press me further but not knowing how to. "What about work?"

"I'm on the rota: Tuesday, Thursday and the weekend." Thanks to Valentine and her sympathetic ways.

"You need to express then." She grabs the breast pump from the cupboard and places it and four sterilised bottles on the counter beside me. "Think you can manage it?"

I hope so. "Yeah."

"Please smile again Gwen," she whispers. "I miss it. You're so beautiful when you smile."

My bottom lip trembles at her words. I daren't speak, so I nod instead.

I roll the dough out, my usual joy in baking non apparent. Normally it would relax me, but with everything that's happening tomorrow, my nerves are on edge. I have this awful feeling that something is going to go horribly wrong. I'm probably just being paranoid.

"You have a visitor in the front," Elle calls and Valentine doesn't even bother turning around. She does however grumble about her friends never coming to see her.

I stiffen as I wipe my hands on my apron. It's Nathan. I just know it. Or Sasha, somebody else I refuse to talk to right now.

When I glance beyond the counter, I'm shocked to see my visitor isn't Nathan; nor is it Sasha.

I stare at the handsome blonde with a dimple in each cheek, smiling nervously at me with his hands tucked into his pockets.

"Eric?" I know it's him, so I don't know why I'm saying his name in such a questioning tone.

"Hey," he says, still smiling nervously. "How are you?"

I move towards the counter at the corner where we're mostly out of earshot and give him a smile as nervous as his is. "I'm okay. How are you?"

"Good... so... I am here for a reason," he states, scratching at the light stubble along his jaw. "Actually I came to ask a favour."

"Go on..."

"Well, it's the kid's birthday tomorrow." He chews on the inside of his cheek. "And she really, and by really I mean *really*, wants a cake shaped like a castle with these Disney characters or something." He holds up his phone and shows me the movie.

"By tomorrow?" I blink, staring at the snowman on the screen of his phone.

"I understand if you can't; it's just Mum ordered one two weeks ago and, well... they called us this morning and said they couldn't do it. I figured I'd cash in that something special."

I can do it... I'm sure I can. "It's no problem, but I'm not at work tomorrow. Can you come by later? At around sixish? Or I'll..." Crap, I don't have his number. "Call me at about four and I'll be able to give you a time to pick it up."

His shoulders sag with relief. "Are you sure? I mean, after everything my friends said. They were dickheads."

"I deserved it."

"No, you actually didn't. We never promised each other anything." He smiles again, this time it's less nervous and friendlier. "So I'm sorry."

"Me too." I clear my throat and nod towards the customers. "I should go. Do you have the character figures? That would help. We might have some in stock, but with how new it is..."

His eyes light up. "No, but I could go and get some?"

"I won't need them until the cake is done anyway, but you should be able to get them from the supermarket. Also, what flavour were you after?"

"Any, surprise us. Whatever you have going."

"Right."

"Brilliant, thank you." He beams, rubbing his hands together. "I'll call."

I give him a wave as he exits the store and then get back to work. This is going to be a very long day, but I do owe him one and I'm not one to renege on a promise.

"Who was it?" Valentine asks, watching as I grab the ingredients I need.

"Eric. He needs a cake by tomorrow." I draw a quick picture of the cake I'm going to make and she winces along with me. "Yep... this is definitely going to be a long day."

"We can get it done if we work together. I'm not letting you outshine me just yet." She winks playfully and goes back to her scones.

Shaking my head, I go back to mine. Well, mine are croissants not scones.

As promised I got a call at four from a happy sounding Eric, who managed to get hold of the figures we need to make the cake perfect. He dropped them off and has now returned to pick up the final product.

"It's a little bigger than we were planning on making it, but with the turrets and icing... it was hard to estimate," I say apologetically when we place the large white box on the counter.

I duck under and stand beside him as Valentine lifts the top off and shows him the cake. His gratitude comes in no small amount, if his smiling and praise is anything to go by.

"I'll help you put it in the car." I make my way to the door and hold it open as he carefully carries the box through.

"It's unlocked," he says and I quickly pull the front door open. After placing the box on the front seat and strapping it in with the seatbelt, which he seems to think is funny for whatever reason, he turns back to me with his easy smile. "Thanks Gwen."

I shake my head and pick at the drying mess on my shirt. "It was nice to see you again."

"Yeah, I'm glad things haven't been left the way they were." He admits, pulling a tiny marshmallow from the ends of my ponytail. I wear a hairnet whilst working, so lord knows how I get stuff in my hair. "It was nice to see you again. We should get coffee or something."

Yeah right. "Sure. Don't be a stranger."

He leans forward and brushes his lips against the corner of my mouth. I remain perfectly still, unsure of how to respond.

"For someone who works in a bakery, you're getting way too skinny," he comments playfully as he walks backwards towards his car. "You're losing my favourite assets."

I cross my arms over my chest, making him laugh, and roll my eyes. "Bye Eric."

"See you later." He taps the top of his car, waves and moments later he's driving away.

"That didn't take you long."

Holy crap! I jump at the sound of his voice so close to the back of my head and turn to see a seething Nathan, his fists clenched around a large, elegant and beautiful bouquet of flowers. He looks terrible. I'm certain his shirt is buttoned up wrong and the fact he has the shadow of a bear across his jaw and lips isn't a good sign. He's lost weight and his eyes have dark rings beneath them. He looks how I look. Depressed. "Don't do that!"

"Do what?" He holds the flowers out to me. "Here."

I stare at them. Why is he giving them to me? I check his shoes, wondering if maybe he needs to tie his laces and can't do it whilst holding a large bunch of flowers.

Staring at me expectantly, he shakes them slightly. "They're for you."

"No thank you," I respond blankly and try to step around him, but he immediately blocks my path. "Can I help you with something?"

His eyes narrow and the flower wielding arm drops back to his side. "You and Eric?"

"He ordered a cake." I don't even know why I'm defending myself. "Excuse me. I'm trying to get back to work." So I can finish and go home.

"He kissed you."

"Yes, he did, good observation." I sigh, rubbing my eyes. Christ I'm tired. "Look, I need to get back to work so I can finish and go home to Dillan."

"I said if you kissed him again I wouldn't forgive you." Is he not listening to a word I'm saying? "Are you dating him?"

"He ordered a cake," I snap. "Is there something you need?"

He holds the flowers out. "I've known you for just over a year and I don't even know what your favourite flower is."

"It's called move out of my way and it smells like bugger off." I go to step around him and again he cuts me off. "Nathan!" I come very close to stomping my foot on the ground.

"So I got one of everything." He shrugs, rubbing the back of his neck. "And now I feel stupid."

"Because I'm dating Eric?" I ask sarcastically and his face falls.

"You're dating Eric?"

"No, Nathan, like I said... he was ordering a bloody cake."

He smiles slightly. "Okay. Good. I was thinking we could go to dinner this Friday."

Blink. "You're joking. Right?"

"No." He definitely doesn't look like he's joking. What's he playing at? "What time do you finish work?"

"I'm not going to dinner with you." I laugh slightly at the hilarity of this situation. "I've made it clear where I stand on this..." My hand moves back and forth between us. "...situation. I want nothing more to do with you."

His face remains impassive as he answers. "We need to be civilised for Dillan's sake."

"You need to leave... for my sake."

"I want to see him. I miss him."

"And we need to go to dinner to solve this because...?"

"That's just because I miss you. And I'm not letting you ignore me anymore."

Wait... what? "You're not *letting* me ignore you anymore?"

"No." Why does he look and sound so calm and collected when all I feel is agitation?

"And how'd you figure that one out?"

"I love you. That's how. I miss you and I want you home."

"I'm not dealing with this." I sigh, this time managing to push past him. "Go away."

He clears his throat and announces. "I'm going to London tomorrow."

I freeze, only two feet from the safety of the bakery. "And?"

"My father is signing everything over."

"That's nice." Gulp. Don't ask. Please don't ask.

"I'd like to know why." He cocks his head, a curious look on his face.

"Do you remember when you said to me that you'd protect me from certain things, no matter what?" He nods, his eyes narrowing with suspicion. "Do you remember when I said I'd do the same?" He nods again, waiting for me to continue. "This is one of those times. You don't need to know."

"That's unfair."

"Is it?" I snarl. "Is it really unfair?"

"If this is a way to punish me..."

"It's not." I step into the hallway and turn back towards him. "Trust me when I say you don't want to know."

He blinks, a look of relief on his face. "You still care about me."

"Or maybe I'm just being spiteful."

"Which means you care."

"Honestly Nathan." I shake my head slowly, willing my tears away. "I don't care about anything right now, especially not you or your stupid brother."

"Okay." He bites down on his lip as his fingers wrap around my bicep. He gives it a squeeze and frowns, a pained look on his face. "You've lost weight."

"I've been under a lot of stress. What do you want?"

"I'll make you a deal," he says quietly, his thumb stroking the top side of my arm. I wish he'd let me go. I cross my arms and wait for him to continue. "Let me take you to dinner on Friday. We'll talk. Properly. About my brother, my parents, everything."

"Go on." I prompt, pushing his hand away.

"And I'd like to take you to the doctor to get a pregnancy test."

My eyes bug out of my head at his words. He's serious. "You've got to be kidding me?"

"No, Guinevere, I'm not." His almost chocolate brown eyes bore into me, determination in their depths. "I have a right to know."

"You mean like I had a right to know that you were trying to get me pregnant?" I snap, my hands going to my hips.

His eyes darken and his body tenses. "It wasn't like that."

"Well, whatever it was like," I wave my hand flippantly, not wanting to go over that argument right now, "I got my period two days ago."

The disappointment that comes over him is powerful; he doesn't try to hide it. "Right."

"Sorry," I find myself saying, though I'm not entirely sure why. "What's this deal you wanted to make?"

He shakes his head. "Nothing. It doesn't matter. It's over right?"

What? "Isn't that the conclusion we already drew?"

He nods, his tongue tasting his lower lip. "It's pointless trying." He holds out the flowers once more. "Take them."

"I don't want them."

"Fine," he bites out, turning sharply and throwing them onto the road. His hands go to his hair before lacing behind the back of his head. "Nothing I say or do is going to change your mind, is it?"

My face probably says it all. I know he gets his answer because his eyes glass over and he shakes his head in defeat. "I'm not going to give up, Gwen. Living without you, it's..." His hands drop to his sides before he takes a step towards me. "I don't know what to do, Gwen. I've never felt this way before." His hands grip my shoulders and pull me towards him. "I don't know how to cope; I can't eat; I can't sleep." When his forehead presses against mine, my hands automatically go to his chest to push him away, but his hold on my arms stops that. "Tell me what to do to make this better."

"Time's a great healer," I breathe, trying to push him away again.

"Time... you need time?"

That's not what I meant! "No. I meant..."

"Gwen, I know you're in the middle of a crisis, but we'd really like to lock up now," Elle calls from the doorway.

"I have to go." I finally manage to peel his hands off me. He takes a step back and stares as I walk backwards towards the door. "Just go home, Nathan."

"I am home," he mutters, looking up to the sky as my dying heart lets out a few thuds of pain.

"Elle can you give me a ride home?" I ask as soon as she closes the door behind me.

"Sure." She smiles kindly, glancing at Nathan out of the window. "He's gone."

Fingers crossed he stays gone.

Chapter Twenty-Six

The train journey was hell. Three hours and three changes. That's just madness. And I got stuck beside a person who reeked of ageing body odour and urine. I took my chances and stood beside the exit for the rest of the journey.

By the time I make it to London, I almost cry with relief when I see Jeanine standing with a hot coffee, waiting to drop me off at Nathan's.

"What's in the box?" She asks, patting the lid with her hand as she guides me out of the station and to her car.

"Just some things for Nathan," I tell her and decide a change of subject would probably be safer. "Thanks for picking me up. I would have driven, but nobody had a car they could lend me."

"And Nathan?"

"He's in London signing off on a new contract. I really wanted to surprise him." I lie, praying she doesn't see straight through it.

"That sounds nice." She grins, sharing my excitement, except my excitement is fake and hers is real.

We make small talk and catch up with each other as she drives. Even though the last thing I need right now is small talk, I've missed her, so it's nice hearing from her.

When we finally make it to Nathan's, she asks me if I need any help. Ten minutes later I manage to persuade her that it's all good, with the promise that I'll call her tomorrow.

I race up the stairs and straight into Nathan's room. I'm relieved when I find the DVDs in the cubby hole in the closet. Gathering them in my arms, I carry them back down and place them on the dining table.

I pull the rest out of my bag, the DVD and the memory stick with the clip of Stephen talking to his father, not long after Nathan suffered his first taste of abuse. Just the memory of it sets my stomach tumbling.

How could a father not protect his son from that?

I wonder how Nathan would feel, knowing his father beat his mother to protect the grandfather who molested him. I wonder if I'm doing the right thing by not telling him that his father knew and the only reason he was sent to live with his grandfather was so nobody would find out. He beat Mrs Weston so she wouldn't try to get Nathan back and it was all too easy when Caleb fell ill, because that became their new excuse for Nathan to be pushed away. And he protected their grandfather for money, because the business was failing.

Mr Weston effectively sold his son for money and beat his wife for the same thing.

That's what it all comes down to.

Money.

They're sick, all of them, and I hope they all rot in hell.

But it's over now. Nathan has the family businesses and I know he'll turn them around, I just know it. He deserves this. Even though it's not much and he deserves so much more, at least it's a start and at least his father will be out of his life forever.

It's sad.

It's tragic.

Once it's all on the dining table, I grab the box that Nathan had Sasha deliver to me and, with a bottle of water tucked under my arm, I head up the stairs and into his room.

I said to myself I was going to leave it behind, but... I can't. Whatever is in here has my curiosity and, even though it won't change anything, I need to see what it is.

Placing the box on the bed, I place the pillows up the headboard and lean back against them. As soon as I'm comfortable, I flip the box open and blink when I see what the contents are.

CHAPTER TWENTY-SIX

Journals... four of them, including the one I bought for him during my stay here.

I can't read these. They're his private thoughts.

I lay them on the bed, side by side. Each one has a sticky note on the front with Nathan's handwriting on them.

My hands grasp the one that says:

Read this one first.

I do, and the instant I do I become enthralled. This isn't like a teenage girl's diary where she starts it with a name. Mostly there are dates, times, events, random thoughts. There are paragraphs where he writes down something that happened during the day that made him feel angry.

I realise that this is probably what a professional told him to do to work out his frustrations.

I skim read the first fifty pages or so, but I stop skimming when I see the words...

I can't do this anymore. The dreams, the nightmares, the pain... it won't leave. I can't let go. I have nothing.

How dare he ask for my forgiveness? After everything he did to me. After everything they did to me!

Tomorrow is the day, I want to say goodbye to Caleb and that's it.

There's nothing holding me back anymore, there's nothing holding me here. It's better this way.

My hand flies to my mouth.

He was going to kill himself. I turn the page and keep reading.

I've thought of ways I can do this quickly, painlessly. But I don't want it to be quick and painless. I want them to know that I suffered, in life and before death.

I purchased rope this morning. The woman behind the counter asked me for my number. Is that how shallow people have become? I'd like to think I'd notice a man or woman, their face set, their determination set, whilst buying a length of rope. It's obvious isn't it?

Tomorrow this will all be over.

Tomorrow there will be no more nightmares, no more dreams, no more pain. No more writing in this ridiculous journal that does nothing but help me remember why I hate waking up in the morning.
It'll be all over.

I gasp, my fingers trembling as I turn the page again. I know he doesn't kill himself, I know, but reading about it... it's unnerving. It's scary.

I was going to do it. I stood on the balcony overlooking the beach, trying out the knot of the rope after tying it around the railing. The noose was already tied. That was the first thing I did.
But I paused, I wish I hadn't.
No I don't.
I'm not sure what happened. There was this girl on the beach. She had her arms spread wide and was walking backwards. I couldn't see her face because the wind carried her hair over it. I wanted to, badly.
I couldn't look away.
I grabbed the pair of binoculars from the next room, the ones my mum uses to look at the boats on the horizon.
She was still on the beach when I returned but this time she was walking normally, her face uncovered. Her smile in place. She's beautiful.
I'm not sure what this feeling is. I feel it now.
She looked so innocent, so carefree, so happy. It made me want to feel that way.

He's talking about me. My heart slams against my ribs, almost as if waking itself up after a long sleep. I rub my chest, my breath shallow and my eyes wide as I read on.

She was on the beach again today. I watched her for a really long time. Then I watched her walk back. I wonder what her name is. I wonder why she's so happy.

The next few days are written with similar things, all about me. All of them. Nothing else.

I have to meet her. I went down there today but the sand... I couldn't do it. I hate it.

I waited like a stalker at the pavement near the kids play area. It's as close to the beach as I'd allow myself to be.

She doesn't leave the beach, I watched her stop about forty yards from the pavement where I stood, turn and walk back. I tried to follow her path but the route she goes takes her behind a row of houses and no matter where I looked, I couldn't find the place where she exited and went home.

I felt disappointment.
I felt determination.

Oh my god. He wasn't lying... about any of it.

I saw them kiss. I saw them as I waited. I trusted him.
I never trust anybody but I trusted him.
He led her right by me yesterday, yet I still trusted him.
I confronted him about it, asked him why. He just shrugged... SHRUGGED!
You snooze you lose. You snooze you lose. You snooze you lose. You snooze you lose.

Caleb... how could you?

He's moving here. It should be me.

The next twenty or so pages are all about us. I daren't read on. It's painful to see this side of Caleb and to see Nathan's hurt.

I pick up the next book, once I make it through the first, and the first page grips my heart in a steel hand of hurt and squeezes.

She's pregnant. He did what he promised he wouldn't do. He didn't get bored.
I hit him.
I saw the way she looked at me. I thought she'd be horrified that I hit Caleb. She only seemed shocked and curious.

I know I shouldn't think this, but she's still beautiful. Even more so than she was two years ago. I should be disgusted that she's been with Caleb. I should be revolted.
Yet I only want to take her away.
I felt lost.
I felt alone.
I felt defeated.

Pages turn and my eyes blur. There's a picture of me taken with a Polaroid. I'm curled up into a ball on the couch, my eyes closed and my hair fanning out above my head.

I came home and she was asleep on the couch. I should have woken her.
I couldn't. She looked too peaceful. It's the first time since his death that she's looked peaceful.
I carried her to bed, she smelled divine. Like honey and almonds. The way she wrapped her arms around me and pressed her forehead to my neck.
It's wrong, but I've never walked so slow in my life. I didn't want it to end.
Why does she make me feel like this?
I felt confused.
I felt happy.
I felt protective.
I felt aroused?!?!

Day after day, after day, after day... I read and read and read. My eyes burn, my nose tingles, my chest aches...there's just so much. Too much. I don't know how much more I can take.

I threw her suitcase today. I wouldn't let her go.
I'm in love with her.

I remember that day well. I can't believe he was in love with me already.

She'll never accept me. I don't care about her reservations. I understood why she wouldn't marry me but I know she loves me. I just know it.
I should leave her alone but I can't.

....

She knows. She knows everything about me. I can't handle the pity in her eyes. What if she thinks I'll become a monster too? What if she takes Dillan from me?
Dillan... he should be mine.
I pushed her away and now she's gone.
I never want to see her again.
I can't handle never seeing her again.
Why couldn't she stay out of my room?
Why did she have to see?
What if she tells someone?
I feel scared.

I feel scared... his words echo through my mind like I'm hearing him read this to me, like I'm hearing him tell me his story.
All of the others he ended with 'I felt...' never 'I feel....' It breaks my heart.

I place the journal down on the bed and rub my eyes.
Only one more to go and then I have to leave. It's almost four.
My eyes start drifting as I read. My head is hurting, but I can't stop.

I had Dillan today. Does he see me as his father?
I hope he does.
I was going to talk to Gwen about it. I thought about telling her through the bathroom door a while ago. Mostly so I couldn't see her reaction and then take the rejection with pride.
I remember worrying constantly that I'd resent him because of my brother.
I've never felt love so unconditionally for another person before. Not including Gwen. But this is different.

I remember that. I remember him calling to me when I was in the bathroom. I never did find out what he wanted to say. I guess now I know.

We had sex without a condom.
It was.
Words can't describe it. Amazing, powerful, intense.

Love.
Freedom.
I should tell her about the pills. I should tell her they're fakes.
But I see Dillan and I see everything I didn't know I wanted.
Would it be so bad if she got pregnant?
I imagine her swollen with my child. Perhaps a girl.
I feel happy.
I feel carefree.
I feel fixed.

That's something we decide together!

She knows everything. Everything.
I wouldn't let her leave, I couldn't.
She could be pregnant.
I want her to be, because then I might not lose her. Maybe she'll marry me.
I need to show her that I care.
I need to show her that I'm sorry. I'll make her breakfast. I have to do something. She wouldn't let me touch her through the night. Even whilst she was sleeping.
I can't lose her.
I feel fear.

Only one more page left. I daren't read it. But I do.

She's gone.
I haven't cried since I was nine and now I can't stop.
She knows about the pills. She knows.
She'll terminate it. If she is.
And she won't tell me.
How do I live with that?
I feel empty.

Tears spring to my eyes and fall down my cheeks. Guilt hits me in the chest and cramps every single muscle in my body until I'm curled into a ball.

I should have told him. I could still tell him.

He really does love me...

My chest is burning; I think I'm getting sick. I try to inhale a large breath, but all I can taste is ash and it feels like my throat is closing.

What's that noise? It sounds like an alarm.

I blink open my eyes, but all I can see is a crowd of grey that seems to be coming in from under the door. What the hell?

Am I dreaming?

My lungs choke up again and I scramble off the bed, my body weak from lack of oxygen.

Oh my god.

Fire!

I race to the door and pull it open, wincing when the metal handle burns the palm of my hand.

My feet carry me to the stairs as I cover my mouth with my shirt.

Orange... all I see is orange and red. The walls are glowing.

The bottom of the stairs are completely engulfed in flames.

Fear grips me as I slam the door and think back to the lessons I took in school.

What to do during a fire. Why didn't I pay attention? I can picture it now, next to the school board. There were pictures... step by step guides on what to do. But I was ten! Why didn't they teach me again?

Think Gwen, think!

Fire brigade. Block the edges of the door with blankets to keep the smoke out. Open the window.

The window is probably the first thing I should do.

No. The fire brigade!

It's so hot, my hands are clammy and the burn on my palm is stinging.

I pick up my phone and dial 999. "I need the fire brigade now!" I bark out the address, tell her I'm at the top, that there's no way out, and quickly pad the area around the door.

"Where are you in the house?"

"Third floor. There's no way out." The reality of the situation sinks in and it takes everything I have not to panic.

"Is there a bathroom?" She asks and I look towards the en-suite.

"Yes."

"Wet your clothes, block the edges around the door and open the windows. Stay on the line. Keep low to the ground."

Wet clothes.

Block the edges around the door and open the windows.

The window in here is too small... shit!

I race back into the bedroom wrapped in a soaking towel. The heat... god... it's too much to bear.

I can't see anything. My eyes are burning.

The window won't open. I try to lift the handle, but it's locked. I'm going to have to break it. But with what?

It's too hot. I can't think. There's nothing in here I can use except the chair and I can't lift it.

I pound on the glass, the heat drying my tears before they can leave my eyes.

Somebody's out there. Maybe he's called for help too!

Who is that?

I slam my hands against the glass over and over. I scream as loud as my lungs will allow. Why's he just sitting there? Do something!

I check my phone, ready to tell the woman there's somebody outside, but the line must have failed. There's no one talking to me now.

The air is too thick with smoke, it burns.

I drop down to my belly, praying that the smoke has risen enough for me to get two short breaths of oxygen at least. It's in vain.

My phone rings. I pull it out of my pocket and place it to my ear. "Nathan?"

"Gwen?" He sounds panicked. "Where are you?" Is it him outside?

"I... I'm trapped. Your house, it's on fire." I cough, my lungs filling with burning ash. There's no more air in here.

"I'm on my way; I'm two minutes away," he shouts and I hear the gear stick jam as he tries to shift it too quickly. "Where are you baby? Talk to me?"

"I..." I try to inhale; I try to release another breath.

"Baby, I need you to tell me where you are."

"Y... your room. Window, won't open."

"Okay, go into the bathroom," he orders softly. "Close the door."

"Kay." I look at the door leading to the hall and watch as it begins to glow. "Fire."

"Gwen, can you open the window in my bedroom?"

I hear him talking, I hear him shouting. I hear my name echo through my mind as delirium kicks in. My head is swimming. The heat is unbearable. "Nathan?" I rasp and he instantly quietens.

I'm so grateful I didn't bring Dillan. My perfect little Dillan. His smile. His baby giggle. His tiny toes.

I'm never going to see him again.

"I'm here baby, I'm coming. I swear it."

No! He can't, he'll die! "Stay out Nathan, please."

I can't tell whether I said it out loud or not. There's a ringing sound in my ears and my lungs are slowly dying. I can feel it.

There's so much heat, but I feel numb.

I roll onto my back and close my eyes. I can feel the smoke on my skin, it's that thick.

There's nothing but darkness waiting for me.

What would you do if you were to wake up tomorrow and see that this was all a dream? Would you do it all over again?

No. But I'd do the last week over in a heartbeat and I'd spend one last night with Nathan and my little boy.

I feel something cool and wet placed over my body and I'm sure I'm moving. My eyes won't open and my lungs are wheezing.

"I'm here," Nathan says and I feel his lap beneath me as I'm pulled into his chest. "The fire extinguisher ran out and the stairs collapsed behind me. I can't get us out, Gwen. I'm so sorry."

I want to be angry that he didn't stay outside. Somebody has to be there for Dillan, but I can't be, because part of me is glad that I'm not going alone, as selfish as that is.

"I lied," I say, gripping his hand with weak fingers. Coughing wracks my body. I can't stop and when I do stop, all I can do is wheeze.

"I forgive you."

"No," I shake my head against his neck, feeling the wet towel that covers me begin to warm. With the last bit of energy I have, I place his hand against my stomach and hold it there. "I lied."

He leans forward and presses his trembling lips to mine. I feel a tear fall from his eye and land on my cheek. If I could cry, I would.

"She would have been as beautiful as you." He chokes on the air and presses his forehead to mine. "I love you, Gwen," he whispers, his entire body shaking with emotion. "I'm so sorry."

"I can't breathe, Nath," I mutter, feeling the weight of silence settle on my chest.

He holds me tighter, tucking me as close to his body as possible. "Go to sleep, baby. You won't feel a thing, I promise." He kisses me one last time and I feel another tear land on my cheek.

Seconds later I drift away but, before I do, something strokes my cheek and I hear a name whispered in my ear, a name I haven't heard in a really long time. "Gwenny."

Chapter Twenty-Seven

What's with the light? Christ my head hurts and my chest burns.

Oh my god. I've gone to hell haven't I?

"She's awake." Is that my mum? Why's she in hell? "Sweet girl, can you see me?"

Everything hurts. I try to talk, but there's something lodged in my throat. I can feel myself blinking, but all I can see is a really bright light.

My eyes roll around... I get nothing.

"Gwen." It's Jeanine, not my mum.

I start choking. My hands fly to my mouth, wanting to rid my throat of the intruder. My eyes stream with tears. I still can't see anything.

"Keep still, Gwen, they're clearing your lungs." Jeanine tells me and the tube is finally removed from my throat. I almost vomit but manage not to.

The effort of this forces me to close my eyes once more.

"You're okay." Her fingers brush through my hair. "She's okay, right?"

"She seems to be." Somebody whose voice I don't recognise responds. "We'll still have to take her in."

"What about Nathan?"

Nathan?

I open my eyes again and try to sit up. I feel like I have very bad sunburn. "Where's Nathan? Where is he?"

"He's in the other ambulance." Jeanine tells me.

My vision finally starts coming back, but my eyes sting badly. I don't care.

My lungs wheeze and I turn onto my side when painful coughing tears through my chest and throat.

"I'm not dead," I say suddenly, as everything falls into place. "Which means Nathan's not dead." My voice sounds hoarse and I cough in between every single word.

"Thanks to Nathan," Jeanine responds, her fingers teasing my hair.

"Where is he?"

The ambulance doors close and I hear the sirens turn on. A mask is placed over my face and held there when my breathing gets worse.

"Where is he?" I try to choke out, my eyes boring into Jeanine's.

"He's going to be okay," is all she says and my panic increases tenfold. I can't lose him too.

"What's going on?" I demand, pushing the mask away, wincing when the cool air assaults my charred lungs. The paramedic pushes the mask back over my face. "He's alive… right? Please tell me he's alive."

Jeanine looks to the paramedic, who looks down at me with sad eyes. "They had trouble resuscitating him." My heart stops and my hand wraps around Jeanine's wrist. "But I've seen worse cases survive. He was badly burnt on his back. His body went into shock."

"But… how did I…?" If he got burnt, then surely I did too? I don't feel burned.

"You need to rest," the woman says, her soothing tone irritating me. "I promise when we get to the hospital I'll get somebody to update you on his condition."

"I need to…" I start coughing again, this time more painful than the last. It won't stop and with each splutter I feel it pound against my brain like a hammer. My lungs are going to explode.

Nathan… he's more important right now. He tried to save me.

How did he get into the house?

No… he didn't just try to save me. He chose to die with me.

Please let him be okay.

I doze in and out of consciousness, my body still fighting to pump blood around my body after being asphyxiated for so long. Not to mention the fact I still can't breathe due to my charred lungs, so I'm barely getting enough oxygen as it is.

But none of that matters.

Nothing matters. This is all my fault.

I never should have gone into that house. I never should have blackmailed Mr Weston. He's done this, but I caused it.

"It's okay Guinevere," Jeanine tells me, her hands holding mine. "Everything will be okay. You'll see."

"No." I shake my head, looking at the curtain surrounding the bed I'm on. "I need to see him. I just need to know he's alive."

"Your throat sounds like it's been through a blender," Mum says as she steps through the curtain. "I'm so sorry. I got here as fast as I could."

Tears fill my eyes at the sight of her. She rushes over and hugs me gently. "Dillan?"

"He's okay; he's with Tommy and Sasha."

"Mum," I sob, grabbing hold of her top with one hand. "Please go and find Nathan. Please. Tell him I'm okay."

She nods, wiping tears from under her eyes. "Okay baby."

"Quickly. He tried to save me..."

"I'll go," Jeanine says and my mum gives her a grateful smile. "I'll see if I can get you some water too."

Mum winces when she looks at me and her hand goes to my hair. She runs her fingers through part of it and I'm shocked when I feel them leave my hair a lot quicker than they normally would. My fingers follow the same path hers did and I let out a gasp. "It's okay, baby, it can be salvaged. You'll just have to cut it into a bob or something. You'll still look beautiful."

I know it's stupid, almost dying and then getting upset about my hair, but I can't help it. I've had long hair for so long. I'm grateful I'm alive, truly I am.

My main priority right now is Nathan and the baby.

"Mum," I whisper, removing my hand from my burnt hair. "Please don't get angry."

"Oh no," she says, rubbing her hands with her face and sitting back. "It's okay Gwen, we'll get through this."

I nod, placing my hand on my flat stomach, imagining the life growing in there. "I didn't tell the paramedic. I didn't think."

"I'll deal with it; now please stop talking. You're going to damage your throat." She leans over and kisses my cheek before exiting the cubicle.

The severity of the situation hits me hard and my body starts shaking. I've never been so scared in my life. What's worse is the fact that during the situation, during the heat and the choking on the thick smoke and ash, I didn't feel scared. I felt detached, like my brain couldn't process the reality of the events.

The curtain pulls back and Jeanine walks in. She looks stricken and my shaking gets worse. My teeth start chattering and my eyes blur. "He's in intensive care. He's…" She shakes her head, choking on her words as sorrow overwhelms her. "He's badly burned on his back and… they've had trouble waking him up."

"What? But I'm okay!" I try to shout, but it comes out as nothing more than a rasp. "How am I okay and he isn't?" I pull the blankets off the bed, cringing at the hospital gown that's wrapped around my body. How long have I been out? How long has he been out?

"Gwen, you need…"

"To see him," I snap. "I'm fine. I need to see him!"

"Gwen…"

I stand, my legs shaking so badly I almost tumble. My chest constricts, but the pain is nothing right now. Pushing back the curtain, I grab my IV stand and wheel it beside me. "Where is he?"

"You won't be able to get in," she tells me, taking hold of my arm. "Nathan wouldn't want you putting yourself at risk. Just get back in bed." She's right, but… "Please Gwen. Before your mum comes back and tells me off."

Frowning, I do as I'm told, albeit angrily.

Mum finally comes back with a doctor, who immediately takes me for a scan of my womb to check the foetus. I don't look. I don't want to look if Nathan isn't here to see it with me.

"Everything looks fine; the heart beat is strong. I put you at six weeks." She clicks something on the monitor. "I'd like to keep an eye on things though, just to be sure, and we'll have to be careful with your pain relief. We don't want your body going through any more stress."

"Then tell them to let me see Nathan," I choke and rub my eyes with my hands. "I just need to see him."

She nods and places her hand on my wrist. "I'll see what I can do."

Mum grips the scan picture to her chest. "Are you sure you don't want to see?"

I nod, rolling onto my side. "Not without him."

"Okay baby." She strokes what's left of my hair and somehow... I fall asleep.

"Mr Weston!" I hear somebody shout, startling from my sleep.

He's come to finish the job, hasn't he? He's come to finish me! Mum grabs my hand when she sees my panic and the curtain flies open.

Oh my god.

"Nathan," I sob and he moves towards me before gathering me into his arms. He looks terrible, maybe even more so than me. "Careful, don't hurt yourself."

"I'm okay," he grunts, his voice sounding nearly as rough as mine. He holds my face in his hands and kisses me deeply. His arms come around me once more. I wince at the blisters along his left arm and move away from them. The hospital gown he's wearing isn't tied at the back and I see white tape and cling film type material stretching over his shoulder and around the side of his neck. My heart shatters and it takes everything I have not to cry or freak out. "We're okay."

"You stupid man," I try to shout, but end up coughing up a lung. "You shouldn't have come in after me." He ignores me, his hands moving my arms and gown, searching for any burns. "I'm fine. I swear."

"The baby?" His wide eyes come to mine. "Is the baby okay?" I nod and my mum holds out the scan picture for him to take. He sits on the bed, his back to my knees and stares at the tiny black and grey square in his hands. I avoid looking at his back. I daren't look at it right now. I'm too scared of how I'll react when I see it. "I'm so sorry, Gwen." He turns back towards me, wincing when he stretches his back. "I'm so sorry for doing this to you."

"It doesn't matter." I shake my head and this time take his face in my hands. "It doesn't matter anymore. I love you."

His lips slant over mine and his arms hold me tighter than ever before. "I thought you were dead... the staircase collapsed. I couldn't get you out.

I tried, but the back of my jacket caught flame and I couldn't risk that happening to you."

My eyes widen and my heart accelerates. "I don't... I don't know what to say. I just... your back."

"It's just skin," he whispers, his nose running along mine. "It doesn't matter. We're alive." His eyes water and he swallows, his long, perfect neck bobbing with the motion. "You're pregnant." He smiles and lets out a laugh. "You're pregnant."

"I wasn't... I'm so sorry. I should have told you."

He shakes his head, wincing slightly when the material on his back crinkles. "No, it's my fault. What I did was unspeakable." He runs his fingers through the short parts of my hair. I must look horrendous. "You look beautiful." He can clearly read my mind. "I think it'll suit you short." I don't care. Hair grows; skin, when burnt, doesn't. I deserve to suffer more than just a loss of hair. "When Jeanine called me and told me she could see smoke, I don't know why but I just knew, I knew you were there and..." He shuts his eyes for a minute. "When I heard your voice... god, Gwen, I've never been so scared..."

"It's okay, we're okay, we're safe."

"Christ Gwen." He presses his lips to mine once more, his kisses wet and desperate.

"You look stupid in a hospital gown" I joke, making him laugh, which causes him to go into a coughing fit.

He grins, his eyes tired and shining with love.

"Okay, time to go," the doctor says, taking Nathan by his arm.

Giving me one last kiss, he stands and follows the doctor to a waiting wheelchair. He looks at it, glares at the doctor and walks around it. It's not until now that I see just how large the burn is. The white gauze covers half of his back from the top of his shoulder to the bottom of his ribs. Then there's part of his neck that's also covered.

I place my hand to my mouth and stifle a cry. My mum instantly holds me and tries to soothe me. "He's fine, Gwen. He's fine."

"It's my fault," I whimper watching him until he vanishes from my sight. "It's all my fault."

Chapter Twenty-Eight

"Will you stop fussing?" Nathan snaps, his eyes narrowing on me. "I'm fine. I don't need help."

I sigh and run my fingers through his hair. "I didn't say you did need it. It's just what I want to do."

He smiles up at me, but it's squished due to the fact he's lying on his stomach and his cheek is pressed against the mattress. "Okay, fine, fuss away."

I flick his nose and stroke my fingers along his good arm. "Thank you."

"You know that this isn't your fault, right Gwen?" He says softly, entwining his fingers with mine. I kiss his hand and press my forehead against it. He hasn't worn his gloves since the tragedy that almost took our lives. It's only been ten days and he didn't get released until yesterday. I don't want to draw attention to the fact that he's touching everything with his hands because he doesn't seem to have noticed yet.

Fortunately the burn, which they thought was all third degree, was only third degree in the lower ten percent and the top twelve percent. The rest will heal nicely, but the third degree will require skin grafting to fix it.

"Did I tell you yet that I love your hair? You look older, sexier." He walks his fingers up my arm until they reach the ends of my jaw length bob, which gets higher at the back. I have to admit, I like it too. It's so much easier to manage.

I smile and kiss the palm of his hand.

"What are you going to do about the house?" I ask, not wanting to bring it up. We have to address it sooner or later.

"I'm tearing it down and selling the land, or maybe I'll build another." It sounds like a good idea. "Sasha called this morning. She wishes to speak with you."

"I know." I'm not angry at her for what she did anymore. How can I be? If I can forgive Nathan, she deserves my forgiveness too. Everything is just so raw and difficult right now. "I'll call her tomorrow."

He smiles and presses his lips to mine.

"Could you do me a favour?" His fingers dance along my collar bone and over the curve of my breast.

"Anything."

"If I roll onto my side, could you..." He nods towards the bottom of the bed.

I look there, but can't figure out what it is he's referring to. "Huh?"

"You know..." He rolls onto his side and nods to the end of the bed again.

"Still not following." I lean forward and kiss the good side of his neck.

He moans and threads his fingers through my short hair and presses me closer. "That feels good."

I hum in response and tease his flesh with my tongue. He tastes so good. He always tastes good.

"Lower," he whispers and I press a kiss to his left peck, before nibbling it with my teeth. His body shudders and his hand starts pushing gently at my head. "Lower." Smiling against his skin, I move to his nipple and run my tongue around the hard nub. "Christ," he bites out through clenched teeth. "Lower."

I move down to his perfect abs, tracing each line with my tongue like Pac-Man around a maze. He moans again, his breath coming out in shallow pants.

"Lower."

I circle his belly button, tracing the thin, dark line of hair that leads down to his boxers, which I slide down with both hands, freeing his hardened length.

"Lower," he breathes, putting more pressure on my head.

I kiss over his hip bone, leaving a shiny trail with my tongue as I go. He jerks when I suck on the sensitive skin in the dip of his groin. I feel his length throb against my cheekbone and smile. He's never let me take complete control like this.

It's fun, definitely fun.

CHAPTER TWENTY-EIGHT

I want to make him feel good.

"Do that thing you do with your tongue," he whispers on a choked breath as I tease the sack beneath his length with my lips. "Gwen... stop teasing."

"Nuh-uh." I continue torturing his skin, using the pads of my fingers to massage his thigh.

"Open."

I giggle, eliciting a growl from him. It soon stops when he moves my head away from him and pushes his cock against my lips. "Open."

My womb quivers and I clench down below, instantly becoming wet when his heated length slides over my tongue and straight to the back of my throat. He hisses out a long breath, his thumb stroking my cheekbone almost soothingly.

My fingers tickle the inside of his thigh as my cheeks hollow with each long pull.

"Christ," he groans, his body giving a jerk that ripples through his muscles and makes his legs tense. "Faster."

It's hard going faster when you're lying on your side with your legs hanging off the end of the bed so I slide onto the floor, my knees holding me up. Nathan, being careful of the wound on his back, shuffles his hips forward desperately.

I almost regret taking this position, because the width of his cock is almost too large to fit in my mouth. I tilt my head and swallow him whole, making him grasp my head desperately and pump his hips back and forth.

"Gwen," he mumbles, his hand holding my head still as he vanishes into his own world. "Gwen." He says, louder this time, his voice a choked cry. "Don't stop," he adds almost desperately, thrusting hard into my mouth, but fortunately not deep enough to make me gag.

I wrap my hand around him and peek up at his face. His eyes, which were clenched shut, open the second my eyes peer at him. His pupils, almost fully dilated, stare into mine. They close again and his entire body shudders and shakes.

Thrusting two more times, he spends himself into my mouth. It shocks me at first. I've never done this part before and it also shocks me because he's allowing me to do this for him. Whenever we got this close before, he'd push me away and take my body instead.

But then again, he was trying to get me pregnant. Now that he's succeeded, I suppose it doesn't matter where it goes.

I shouldn't think like that though. Nathan has always been weird when it comes to climaxing and I've forgiven him for his deception. Well... almost. It still hurts that he'd do that, but almost dying, almost losing him, almost losing us, I guess it forces other things to the surface that are so much more important.

It's done; it's too late to change and I'm not getting angry with a man who chose to die with me rather than leave me to die alone. Maybe I'm over dramatizing it all, but that's how it felt.

I love him.

I'll do anything for him and now I know that he'll do anything for me.

When his body stops trembling from his climax, I swallow, waiting for him to soften in my mouth, not really thinking about it as I do. He taps me on the head and then pats the bed beside him.

Climbing up, I settle myself against his chest, kissing his throat while feeling his heart beating beneath my palm.

"Tell me you love me," he mutters and places a gentle kiss on the end of my nose.

I smile and nuzzle his chest. "Always."

"Tell me you forgive me."

My breath catches in my throat and the sharp pain I feel in my chest at my sudden inhale reminds me that I'm still healing. It reminds me that we almost died because of me. "It's my fault."

"What is?"

"The fire... the house..."

He tilts my head up to his, our mouths only inches apart. His confusion is clear. "It was my dad, Gwen. He's been arrested. He confessed..."

"No." I take a steady breath and calm myself. He deserves to know. "It's my fault he was there."

He shifts his body slightly, wincing with the pain that the movement causes. Another bout of guilt slashes through me. "What are you talking about?"

"You asked me what happened between me and your father."

"I remember."

"Well... it's kind of a long story but... it..."

"Spit it out Gwen," he demands irritably, his eyes narrowing on my face.

"When you got arrested for assaulting your father, I blackmailed him so he'd drop the charges."

The sudden silence is disturbing. His mouth falls open, but I swear both of our hearts stop together. He shifts further away from me, a frown on his face. "You blackmailed him?"

"Yes. Well, Sasha told me what to say. She's better at stuff like that than I am. Not that she's ever blackmailed anyone, I just mean I feel guilty really easily and…"

"Gwen." He stops my rambling, giving me a moment to clear my thought process and explain properly. "Explain."

I chew anxiously on my lip before continuing. "Okay, so, that night I found the DVDs, I don't know how but the first one got stuck in my jacket and I took it home by mistake." He tenses but says nothing. "The title was weird. I didn't understand it, so… well, I watched it again." His eyes widen and he slowly sits up. I follow suit and sit beside him on the end of the bed after he shuffles himself down. "I skipped the parts where you were… you know… and well, your Grandfather had sent you to your room but he hadn't turned the camera off and your dad had come to pick you up."

"I remember that day. He walked in, took one look at me and walked out. I remember him and my grandfather arguing. I couldn't hear what they were saying." He closes his eyes and his jaw clenches as he continues. "I couldn't move off the ground."

My poor Nathan. "He knew." I place my hand on his, but he knocks it away. "Your grandfather told him he'd donate every penny he had to charity if he told anyone and your dad seemed to need his money to get his business started, or back afloat, or something. Anyway… he knew and there was the proof. So I… well, I copied it and Sasha found his office number, which led us to getting his personal number. I told him if he didn't drop the charges against you, sign over everything to you and leave you alone, I'd go public." I rush the last bit, not wanting to upset him anymore. "He agreed and we made the deal that I'd leave every single piece of evidence that you were abused on the dining room table and he'd pick it up at five, after you'd signed the papers."

"Go on." He snaps, his hands fisting on his lap.

"I was supposed to leave before he got there, but I fell asleep reading your journals. I read them all…" He says nothing, shows nothing and doesn't move an inch. I wish I could see what he was feeling. "When I woke up, well... you know the rest."

He doesn't look at me and this worries me. Then he stands and this worries me even more.

"Nathan..."

"Can I have a minute?" He says calmly.

I want to say no. I want to scream at him that I'm sorry, but instead I nod and leave the room, trying to hide the fact that I'm terrified I'm going to lose him.

Before I close the door I call to him; he doesn't look at me, so I speak anyway. "I'm so sorry for not telling you, Nathan, but I didn't want you to hurt any more than you already had."

"Go Guinevere," he hisses and I quickly close the door. When Nathan gets like this, sometimes it's just best to leave him to it. I don't want to upset him while he's in such bad shape. I wish I didn't have to tell him at all, but he deserves to know that he's in the shape he is because of me.

I didn't start the fire, but I played a big part in it. If I hadn't set off this stupid chain of events with my stupid need to get him out of that cell, none of this would have happened.

I forgave him for his deception. I hope this garners me enough points towards his forgiveness of me.

I check in on Dillan, who's having his afternoon nap, and sit in the rocking chair by his cot. He's sleeping soundly on his front, his pudgy fist against his lips. He's the only peace I find at the moment; he's the only silence that I enjoy.

After half an hour, I pick up my little boy and make my way into the hall. I'm wondering whether or not to go to Nathan. He might need something.

I knock on the door to the bedroom and wait a while for his response.

It doesn't come.

It's not until I push open the door to an empty room that panic sets in. Damn him. Where is he?

He shouldn't be out of bed!

I pull my phone from my pocket and call him, but his phone vibrates on the desk beside the bed.

That idiot!

What's he playing at?

CHAPTER TWENTY-EIGHT

The car is still here. I notice this immediately, after searching the house from top to bottom. The only odd thing is the fact the back door is wide open and I know for a fact I closed it.

Wrapping a blanket around Dillan, I step out into the wind and make my way down the long garden that turns at the end.

Seeing him standing only four feet from where the grass ends and the sand begins, one hand in his hair as the other rests limply at his side, makes me stop in my tracks. He looks so beautiful, his back so broad. Even with the covering that protects the burn, he's stunning. Every perfect male inch of him.

Taking slow steps, I stop beside him, Dillan babbling in my arms.

"I made a huge mistake three years ago," Nathan says softly, his eyes scanning the horizon.

"Mistake?"

He nods and takes my hand in his. "I couldn't walk on sand for you."

"Nathan," I look up at him, trying to find the anger he should feel towards me. "You ran through fire for me."

"So walking on sand should be easy," he bites out and kicks off his shoes.

I do the same, my heart thrumming in my chest as my body prickles with excitement.

He takes a step and breathes in deep. "You blackmailed my father."

I wince. "I know, it was stupid..."

"Yes, it was. You should have told me." He still doesn't sound angry, nor does he look it. I'm waiting for the explosion. "But I understand why you didn't. I think we've both hidden enough secrets from each other to last a lifetime." I nod my agreement and we take another step. "You forgave me." We take another step. The sand is so close to our bare feet. "You did something so incredibly out of character for me, to protect me." We take another step and my breathing stops completely. He's going to do it.

"I love you. I'll always protect you. You've been let down your entire life." I whisper and we take another step. "Somebody has to."

He shakes his head, a smile on his face. "I want to walk on the sand."

"Have you ever?"

He scrunches up his nose, trying to hide his disgust. "No. I used to think it looked fun, but then Caleb threw a spade full at me when I was nine. It got everywhere. It took me hours before I felt clean. I never went near it again."

"Caleb sounds mean," I mutter, hating the fact that the man I knew and the man he was are two completely different people.

"He wasn't; he just didn't understand me. He was always sick and I was always kept away. The only time we ever really got to know each other was when he'd come to my grandfather's every two months or so. At least now I know why my father never left when Caleb stayed. He knew there was no way they'd be able to hide it if Caleb were ever abused." He takes another step and squeezes my hand until it goes numb and my fingers start to turn purple. I keep Dillan close to me with my other arm and wait for Nathan to find the courage to take the final step. "We didn't get on very well. I just wanted to be left alone and because Caleb rarely had days that he felt good, he just wanted to play. By the time we were in our teens and his illness was in remission, we hated each other. He was everything I wanted to be and I had everything he wanted. I didn't realise just how angry he was over our grandfather leaving everything to me until he took you from me."

"You don't look like you blame him."

He gives me a small smile, his eyes narrowing at the edges. He looks so handsome. "I don't. He didn't know why our grandfather left everything to me. He thought he was being cheated out of his inheritance because I was the apple of my grandfather's eye." A laugh escapes him. "What's worse is, I almost told him once. I came so close."

I can only imagine how Caleb is feeling now. I wonder if he can see us, see this and see the past and what happened to Nathan. The guilt he's probably feeling worries me. It's not his fault. Just like it's not Nathan's fault.

"Why didn't you?" I ask, wondering when we're going to take that last step.

"I knew he'd kill him. As troubled as our relationship was, we were still brothers. My brother had a temper." One which I only witnessed once, when he threw plates against the wall. I can't even remember what that argument was about, but I remember being scared and him instantly calming down. "He beat our father up pretty badly when he was only fourteen."

"What?"

"It was bad. My father had attacked my mum, but Caleb gave up after that because she still wouldn't leave him and she chose him over us. I knew then that if Caleb found out what our grandfather had done, he would

CHAPTER TWENTY-EIGHT

definitely kill him. So I never told him and our relationship got worse from there."

I rest my head against his shoulder and close my eyes. The fresh air blows across us both, bringing me a little comfort as we take that final step.

"I don't like this," Nathan whispers and I open my eyes to see him looking at the thin layer of sand and grass beneath our feet. "But I'll do it... for you."

"Don't do anything you're not ready to do," I tell him, taking another step forward.

His chest expands as he inhales a heavy breath and we take five more steps, stopping at the edge of the garden with our toes buried in the sand.

He grins, clearly proud of himself, and I grin right back at him. I'm proud of him too.

"I have something for you." He digs into the pocket of his jeans and turns towards me. I gasp at the sight of my old necklace, the one I threw away when we first separated. Something shiny winks at me as the sky begins to glow orange. I stare at the object beside the flat patterned disk with the single tiny red gem and tears spring to my eyes. "I remember a while ago I told you that you needed to let him go." His hands move around the back of my neck and he quickly fixes the clasp of the necklace. "I was wrong. He'll always be a part of you, of Dillan... of us. Because of him, no matter what happens, we'll always be connected. I'm grateful for that."

A sob escapes me as I touch the engagement ring that Caleb gave to me so long ago. It hangs beautifully by the flat disk that Nathan made just for me.

I close my eyes, trying to calm myself as his thumbs brush the tears from my cheeks. "Thank you Nathan."

"I want to marry you Gwen," he adds softly and quietly and my eyes spring open.

He pulls my hand away from the necklace, smiling when Dillan tries to grab at it. Seconds later I feel something cool and slightly heavy slipping onto my ring finger.

"I want to die with you when we're old and grey and have more grandchildren than we can count." He runs his finger over the single diamond that's surrounded by a cluster of smaller, more colourful stones. "You don't have to say yes now, what with everything that has happened."

His eyes come back to me and his forehead rests against mine. My body shakes with emotion so I press it to his. "I understand if you're not ready."

"I am," I breathe, pressing my lips to his. "I am ready."

His tongue pushes into my mouth and his arms wrap around the three of us, Dillan, myself and the foetus in my womb.

He smiles, his eyes glistening, and he kisses Dillan's open mouth before kissing my trembling one. "Tell me you love me."

I laugh once and nod. "Always. I love you. You know I do."

"Always," he repeats, smiling even wider. Then he drops to one knee and places his lips against the skin of my navel.

I thread my fingers through his hair, softly stroking his scalp before he stands once more and claims my lips again. "Don't give up on me. I don't think I'll ever be normal... but without you I'm broken."

"Never," I promise, lacing our fingers together as Dillan manages to grab my necklace and shove it in his mouth, making us both laugh and battle to pull it away.

I settle in Nathan's arms, my cheek against his chest, and stare at the orange horizon. There may not be a setting sun, but it's still beautiful, and in this moment it's just perfect.

SNEAK PEAK INTO THE FUTURE

"DAD!" I WINCE AT the sound of Emily's screech as she comes in through the front door and quickly duck into the kitchen. There is no way in hell I'm getting involved with this one.

"I said no," Nathan snaps, following Emily up the stairs.

She's just like her father, just like him, in almost every single way; looks, stubbornness, sternness, playfulness and her determination is just crazy. When she wants something, she gets it. If she can't get it, she's sour about it for days and sits in her room brooding about it.

I face Dillan, who is currently leaning into the open fridge, spooning butter frosting into his mouth using his fingers. I grab the newspaper from the side and hit him on the back of the head with it.

"Mum," he laughs, turning and giving me that easy smile that reminds me so much of Caleb. "What's for tea? I'm hungry."

"Stay out of the frosting," I sigh, taking the tub from his hands and gasping at how much is missing. "I made this an hour ago!"

"I'm hungry! You never feed me," he whines, running his fingers through his hair. The ones that he just used in the frosting.

Gross.

"You cheeky git, I fed you an hour ago," I scoff, this time tapping him on the back with the newspaper.

"Yeah! She did! I remember," Ashlyn says smugly, crossing her chubby arms over her chest and staring at her older brother with a sly grin on her face.

Now Ashlyn is all me.

Even I can't deny the resemblance, from her dark hair and grey, green eyes to her pale complexion. She's also only six, putting her almost ten years behind Dillan and eight and a half behind Emily.

Dillan scoops his sister off the ground and tosses her over his shoulder.

Ashlyn, whose personality is like mine, just sighs and rolls her eyes. "I wish you'd stop doing that," she snaps, punching him between the shoulder blades.

He takes her into the hallway, deposits her in the cupboard, closes the door, comes back into the kitchen and retrieves the frosting, before racing up the stairs to his room.

Meanwhile Emily is shouting about some concert she can't go to and Nathan is trying to explain that she's too young. At only fifteen she needs to have parental supervision.

"But none of my friends have parental supervision!" She whinges, clearly expecting him to change his mind, which he never does. Give it ten minutes and she'll be asking me. I'm softer, even though I shouldn't be.

"Fine, I'll take you," Nathan states and I almost face palm.

"For a man who's so smart, you can be so moronic," Emily snaps and I hear a door slam. "Emily. Open this door!"

Banging can be heard, followed by more screaming from my teenage daughter.

Ashlyn pads into the kitchen, a bored look on her face. "Why does he put me in the cupboard? It's not like I can't get out. I'm six. I know how to open a door."

Chuckling, I lift her onto the side and hand her a large plastic bowl and a wooden spoon.

"Want to mix?" Her eyes light up and she nods eagerly. My little girl is going to be a chef just like Mummy. I just know it.

"Dillan didn't tidy his room this morning," she tells me, clucking her tongue like a mini adult. "And I told him. I said that it's a pig sty, but he doesn't care."

"He's a teenage boy; he doesn't care about anything other than food."

"And girls. Daddy said that he's on his third girlfriend this month."

Actually it's this week, not month. It's no secret that Dillan is a hit with the ladies. He's very handsome and, even though he seems to treat them well, they never last long.

"Am I allowed a boyfriend?"

"Ask your father," I laugh, cracking an egg into the plastic bowl.

She starts mixing like a pro, her little chubby wrist flicking back and forth and her tongue poking out of the corner of her mouth. "He told Emily that she's not allowed a boyfriend until she's married."

I throw my head back and laugh. I remember that conversation. Nathan's logic, where his Princess is concerned, is sometimes not very logical at all.

"But he also said she's not allowed to get married until she's forty," Dillan adds, walking into the kitchen with an empty frosting bowl. "Seriously Mum, I'm starved. Where are the crisps?"

"It's not fair! Dillan gets to go where he wants, when he wants!" Emily cries, storming into the kitchen, her face bright red and her anger evident.

Nathan follows, looking up at the ceiling with his hands clasped beneath his chin.

"Dillan has a curfew for ten at night and he sticks to it." Nathan says and he has a point; Emily did come home two hours late a few weeks ago. I thought Nathan was going to have a heart attack. I've never seen him as frightened as he was the day she was born and she got stuck. I had to have forceps to get her out. It wasn't a pleasant experience and it lasted almost two days.

Ashlyn was a lot easier and a lot quicker. Just like Dillan.

"Yes, but I do all of my chores, I keep my room tidy and I get the best grades in my entire year! Dillan only just passes, his bedroom is a sty and he pays his six-year-old sister to do his chores!"

She has a point.

Dillan tries to sneak by the both of them, but Nathan snags him by the back of his collar, effectively stopping him in his tracks.

"Have you been paying your baby sister to do your chores?" Nathan grumbles, his jaw clenched.

"Umm..." Dillan looks frantically around the room for a way to escape. He doesn't find it.

Nathan pulls him in further and stands him next to his sister, who he sticks his tongue out at before giving his dad that easy smile that we both know so well.

"I'm preparing her for the real world?" He tries to use, but Nathan's glare doesn't flicker at all. He is not amused. Unlike me. I'm finding this entire thing quite funny. So is Ashlyn, who is still mixing away but watching the scene with avid interest.

"Fine, I'll make you a deal," Nathan says to Emily and I'm shocked that he's relenting. Then again, it is Emily and she is his little girl through and through. "If I can drop you off and pick you up, then you can go into the concert to watch whatever boy band it is you're obsessed with this month."

"Thank you, Daddy!" She squeals, throwing her arms around his neck and hugging him tight. I see him sigh and melt. She gets him… every single time. "Go to your room. You're grounded until the concert and then you're grounded until you're eighteen."

"What?"

Why? Why must he torment her?

"For giving me a headache." She rolls her eyes, still smiling and kisses his cheek. "Love you." Dillan steps forward, his arms spread wide, and goes to embrace his father the same way Emily did.

Nathan, used to Dillan's jokester ways, flicks his nose and snaps, "Stop paying your sister to do your chores! She's six."

"And a half!" Ashlyn adds grumpily. "Stop forgetting the half!"

Nathan grabs Dillan in a headlock and scrubs his knuckles on his scalp, before practically throwing him into the hallway. "And tidy your bloody room!" He turns to me, his frown still in place. "Why do you never help me?"

"You had it handled," Ashlyn answers for me, her chin raised defiantly. Nathan takes the bowl from her and places it on the side, then he lifts her over his shoulder and vanishes into the hallway. I hear the cupboard door open and close along with a sigh that belongs to my daughter.

He comes back without Ashlyn.

"I'm pretty sure that's not legal." I scowl, slapping his arm playfully.

"She likes it." He's right; she definitely does. When she started crawling, we used to find her in there sleeping all of the time. It's where she'd go for a nap. So Nathan padded out the inside and gave it a clean. He even installed a butterfly light that comes on when you open the door.

It's probably not a good thing to show to other people; they wouldn't understand.

"Besides, everyone's gone. We can snog now," he chuckles, sucking my bottom lip into his mouth.

I cringe at the word snog but say nothing, because he's right; it's rare that we get to do this when the kids are home. They would probably think that it's gross and Nathan isn't a fan of public displays of affection. Not unless it's in front of a man who, he is convinced, wants me.

I think it's definitely not gross. I think it's the best thing in the world.

"I have to make these cakes. Sasha will kill me if they aren't ready in time." Sasha and Tommy's little boy turns nine tomorrow.

He's an amazing little man and just like his father, but he looks just like Sasha.

"We have a few minutes," he mutters, his bare hand squeezing my breast as my fingers travel up his arms. My lips travel from his mouth to his neck and settle over the burn scar that peeks out from above the collar of his shirt. "We're opening another G and N store in Seattle next week. The Forever Connected charms have really hit it off," Nathan whispers against my mouth, his hands gripping my arse and pulling me against him.

I beam, or try to because he takes my mouth again. "That is fantastic." I try to say. "You're a jewellery making genius."

He pulls back and we both look at the bracelet on my wrist. At least twenty-three tiny charms sit around the gold and silver entwined chain. Each charm tells a story, signifying a big event in our lives. The one that affects me the most is the tiny, dangling, orange crystal shaped as a single flame. It reminds me every day that the man by my side would run through fire to be with me, because that's exactly what he did. The love is requited. One hundred percent.

Smiling at the man of my dreams, I pull his head down to mine and let him lift me onto the counter whilst massaging my tongue with his own.

Is it bed time yet?

Sigh.

"I didn't see a thing," Ashlyn announces, walking into the kitchen. She covers her eyes and walks back out again, almost slamming into her brother on her way past.

"No, but we did and it is so going on Facebook!" Dillan roars with laughter, his phone aimed our way from the doorway. Emily is crouched down, filming us through the gap in his legs.

"That is so wrong," Emily adds, giggling hysterically.

I close my eyes, because I know what's coming. I also cover my ears and I do it just in time to protect my ear drums from the kids' screams of fear induced glee and their heavy footsteps carrying them away. When I open my eyes and uncover my ears, the kitchen is vacant save for the ginger cat that adopted us two years ago.

I scratch him behind the ears and touch the tiny yellow crystal on my bracelet shaped like a cat, which sits directly beside a blue dummy, a pink bottle and a lilac heart.

One for each of my kids.

Our entire lives on one bracelet.

Keeping us forever connected.

"Do you remember the time we were worried we'd never be normal?" I ask Nathan when he re-enters the kitchen looking dishevelled and out of breath.

He's so handsome, even more so than the first time I met him. Age suits him and the hair above his ears that's starting to grey only makes him more enticing. God, I love this man.

His smile is wide and full of love and his hands immediately pull me to him. "I don't think we have anything to worry about anymore."

Acknowledgments

Thank you to Rivka Spicer, an amazing person, friend and editor who has had so much patience with me and my terrible grammar. Who also worked on my book whilst ill just so I'd meet the deadline I'd set for myself. I'll be forever in your debt.

To Ramya, Nikita, Elizabeth, Heather, Innie, and Meleila (Erotica Book Nymphos blog) thank you so much for reading through this and giving me your complete honesty and support. You guys rock, seriously.

Helen, I'm sorry we've had little time for each other as of late, I miss you and appreciate all of your help. Please let Tiff get an Xbox.

Thank you Nora, you hold nothing back and call me on my mistakes without fear. I love this about you. Don't ever change.

To my kids, Alyssia-may and Aydin, the two most beautiful people in the world to me. Thank you for being such well-behaved and amazing children whilst Mummy works. I hope you never read this, because that would be awkward.

About The Author

A. E. Murphy is the queen of sarcasm and satire, she likes long walks in the park, as much as ice cubes like to chill in a roasting oven. She's efortlessly independent and so good at adulting it's unfair on the rest of the world. She only napped twice today and has only avoided the dishes for three days before making the child slaves do them this morning. Winning! (Kidding, she has a dishwasher now.)

Her favourite hobby is writing, her worst hobby is reading through that writing. Also, she has four cats that carry toys to the top of the stairs and drop them down so they can chase them. They do this repeatedly in the middle of the night. Who cares if she has work the next morning? Not the cats, that's for sure. And if it's not the cats doing the waking, it's the ridiculous amount of children and bonus children she has constantly asking for a snack, or the fiancé being a needy bear. This is likely why she is so happy all the freaking time, but not without coffee and chocolate.

P.S. Please leave feedback, if not on the book then on this ridiculous bio she wrote herself. It's the least you can do seeing as she'll forever talk in the third person now.

Alex loves her readers. Alex says thank you. Alex smiles.

CONTACT

Facebook
www.facebook.com/a.e.murphy.author
Email
a.e.murphy@hotmail.com
Instagram
aemurphyauthor
TikTok
@authorxelaknight
@authoraemurphy

ALSO BY THE AUTHOR

Standalone Novels
VICIOUS
Becoming His Mistress
NAKED OR DEAD
DANCE OR DIE
Masked Definitions
HIS FATHER
STEPDORK

Seas of Seduction
Seizing Rain
Freeing Calder

The Little Bits Series
A Little Bit of Crazy
A Little Bit of Us
A Little Bit of Trouble
A Little Bit of Truth
A Little Bit of Guilt

The Distraction Trilogy
Distraction, Destruction, Distinction
The Broken Trilogy
Broken, Connected, Forever

A Broken Trilogy Spin-off
Disconnected (Dillan)
Sweet Demands Trilogy
Lockhart, Lockdown, Unlocked

Colouring Books
NAKED OR DEAD colouring book edition
Laurie's Life Lessons a colouring book novella (Becoming His Mistress Spin-of)
VICIOUS colouring book edition
Audiobooks
NAKED OR DEAD
HIS FATHER
BECOMING HIS MISTRESS

XELA KNIGHT
(Paranormal Books)
Syphon 1A, Syphon 2A, Syphon 3A

Printed in Great Britain
by Amazon